PRESIDENT LINCOLN'S SPY

P9-DCH-182

STEVEN WILSON

KENSINGTON BOOKS
http://www.kensingtonbooks.com

KENSINGTON BOOKS are published by

Kensington Publishing Corp.
850 Third Avenue
New York, NY 10022

All Kensington titles, imprints and distributed lines are available at special quantity discounts for bulk purchases for sales promotion, premiums, fund raising, educational or institutional use.

Special book excerpts or customized printings can also be created to fit specific needs. For details, write or phone the office of the Kensington Special Sales Manager: Kensington Publishing Corp., 850 Third Avenue, New York, NY 10022. Attn. Special Sales Department. Phone: 1-800-221-2647.

Kensington and the K logo Reg. U.S. Pat. & TM Off.

ISBN-13: 978-0-7582-2514-6
ISBN-10: 0-7582-2514-8

First Kensington Trade Paperback Printing: May 2008
10 9 8 7 6 5 4 3 2 1

Printed in the United States of America

If it were done when 'tis done, then 'twere well
It were done quickly. If the assassination
Could trammel up the consequence, and catch,
With his surcease success, that but this blow
Might be the be-all and the end-all here . . .

—William Shakespeare, *Macbeth*, Act I, Scene VII

PRESIDENT LINCOLN'S SPY

Chapter 1

July 21, 1861
The 98th day of the war
Near Bull Run Creek, Virginia

Captain Fitz Dunaway studied the ragged line of Confederate infantry trotting across the field a half mile
away, the enemy formation obscured by a low cloud of dust
beaten out of the hard-baked ground by several hundred feet.
They marched into position, their officers—as new to war as
their men—laboring to form the column into line. The mid-
day sun, burning and pitiless, glinted off polished bayonets
and flashed from the officers' swords. They weren't regulars,
Fitz thought, damned short of that to be sure, but his men
were just as clumsy—just as new to soldiering as that ragged
band in the distance. It made no difference—they would set to
killing each other with enthusiasm shortly.

He blew a silent breath through his teeth, licked his dry
lips, and turned to his command. Company C stood with the
other nine companies of the 95th Ohio Volunteer Infantry,
waiting for their chance to face the enemy. He should have
had a hundred officers and men in his company; he had sev-
enty-six. Disease, the unseen enemy of any army, had thinned
the modest ranks of his command. Mumps, measles, the
bloody flux—the curse of soldiers too long in squalid camps
waiting for their generals to make sense out of the web of

grand strategy. A quarter of his men had been struck down before they faced the Rebels as surely as if they had been shot. And when the shooting started, Fitz calculated, maybe another twenty-five or thirty dead, wounded, or missing.

He sniffed at the irony of it. There was no glory in dysentery and not much on the battlefield when your body is torn open by hot metal.

Fitz's company—front rank kneeling and rear rank at ease, file-closers and officers behind the line—waited. He took a scarred pipe from his mouth and patted the bowl against his palm, knocking free the cold ashes. His mouth tasted of dust, the grit crunching in his teeth. He slipped the pipe into his pocket, decided against lighting it, and walked slowly down the line.

"Don't get anxious, boys," he said. "Be steady. Don't fire until I give the command. Mark your targets." He heard men praying and saw a few cross themselves. *Some of you will piss your pants,* he thought. *There's no shame in that. Fear makes you forget everything—even your bladder.* "Make sure to cap your pieces. Slow and easy. Three shots a minute. Remember the drill."

Lieutenant Griffin, a nervous youth with a large nose, ran up to him, his boots slapping the hard ground. Throwing a quick salute, he said, "Captain, the enemy is about to—"

"I know what the enemy is about, Griffin," Fitz said in a low voice, irritated that this child had left his position to point out something as obvious as the fact that the enemy was forming to attack. "I can see as well as you. Now get back to your men."

Griffin, looking like a puppy that had just been whipped, shook his head as if to say: *yes, yes, that's exactly right, I should have done that.* Fitz watched him trot back along the line—a boy in a blue suit. They were going to see the elephant today—be in battle—for the first time. Fitz glanced up and down his line and walked back to Sergeant Gillette, one of the file-closers.

"No one is to fall back unless I give the order," Fitz said.

That was what the file-closers were supposed to do, make sure that no man fled. "Officers and men, you understand," Fitz continued. "No one runs. Keep them in line with your bayonet or the butt of your musket." He began to walk away when he thought better of it. He turned on Gillette. "If that doesn't work, shoot them."

Gillette's eyes widened. "Shoot them, sir? Dead?"

"Dead or otherwise, it makes no difference to me. Just as long as they can't run."

Gillette, his mouth firm, nodded. Fitz returned to the line.

The enemy would advance across the rolling field in a matter of minutes—he could see that their lines were nearly dressed with the regimental flag hanging motionless in the humid air.

The 95th Ohio was on the extreme left of the Union line and they had done nothing all day but lick parched lips and stand in sweat-soaked woolen uniforms that clung to their bodies like a second skin, listening to the sounds of battle coming from the far right. Now the enemy was swinging to its right to find a way to breach the Union line. The Rebels were coming after them.

Fitz looked to the rear. Three companies of the 95th were held in reserve, nearly three hundred yards behind the line. They stood at parade rest, perfect targets for enemy artillery and musketry. Some damned idiot had set them there and wandered off and now they were a solid mass of dark blue on a golden field of parched grass. "Get down, you fools!" Fitz muttered.

The sharp rattling of drums brought him back to the line. The enemy was moving, stepping off nicely to the stark cadence. By this time another Confederate regiment had fallen into line and Fitz watched as a third took its place. The ground shimmered as the enemy advanced—waves of heat distorting the scene so that the enemy was a mirage. Thin clouds of dust floated just above the hot ground: veils ready to descend on dead soldiers.

Fitz worked to bring saliva to his mouth. He swallowed

and tried to growl the dryness out of his throat but nothing worked. His mouth demanded water. He fought the urge to take a drink. *Not yet, wait until you can't stand the thirst anymore and then take a short pull of the foul water from the wooden canteen.*

He checked the caps on his Colt .44, spinning the cylinder to make sure that each chamber, except one, bore a cartridge. He let the hammer down on the empty cylinder, took a deep breath, and waited.

Fitz heard his name being called. One of Colonel Pettibone's staff officers rode up on a thick roan, tossed a salute, and shouted with excitement, "Colonel Pettibone's respects, Captain, and you're to move your company out of line by the left and fall back."

"Fall back? What the devil does that—" Fitz caught himself, and wiped the sweat from his face. "What does Colonel Pettibone mean, fall back? The enemy is advancing. If we turn our backs to them they will be on us like a duck on a june bug."

"It is what the Colonel ordered," the officer said, trying to behave with soldierly aplomb.

Fitz walked up to the officer's horse and twisted his hand into the bridle, pinning the animal in place. "You go back and tell that storekeeper," Fitz said, "that I will not endanger my men by following some asinine order." He pointed across the field. "There is the enemy, sir, and that is where our muskets will be pointed. Just twenty miles to the rear is Washington, sir. And the capital is not prepared to receive visitors."

The young officer started to say something but, seeing the look on Fitz's face, changed his mind. He spurred his horse and rode off.

Captain Jacobs, a big-boned officer who looked like the farmer that he had been less than a month before, jogged up, trying to keep his scabbard from slapping his leg with one hand while pinning his plumed black hat to the back of his head with the other.

"Fitz," he gasped. "I just heard. What am I to do? I don't

know the order to turn my men endways and march them off."

"Keep your company where it is," Fitz said. "I think Pettibone has lost his nerve and wants to pull out. Just stay where you are for now. I was ordered to lead the regiment out and I refused the order. The fault lies with me if we don't move." He looked over Jacobs's shoulder to a clump of horsemen riding down on them at a gallop. Pettibone, elbows and knees flapping in the air, led them. The colonel reined up, his face beet red, streaks of sweat streaming down his dust-covered jowls.

"Goddamn you, sir!" he shouted at Fitz, his voice shrill with frustration. "Goddamn you to Hell. I've had enough of your insubordination, Dunaway." He jumped from his horse and drew his sword. He snatched a red bandana from around his neck and wiped his face. "Lead your company off now, sir!"

"Look there, Colonel," Fitz said. "Those boys are coming our way and coming quick. If they smell us falling back it'll be at the double-quick and there'll be hell to pay."

"I will not have my orders ignored!" Pettibone screamed. He turned to the group of aides. "Did I not give the order to fall back? Wasn't that my order? Cannot one of you do as I say?" He glared at Fitz. "This army is defeated, sir. I intend to save my regiment."

"I see no sign of a defeat, Colonel, but by God, if we disengage there will be one. That's for certain. Those boys in front of us are as new to this business as we are. Let us stand and fight."

Pettibone glanced from Fitz to his staff in wild desperation. This was not about tactics or maneuvers, Fitz knew, this was fear. It was in the colonel's eyes, the frantic, wild look of a trapped animal that can smell his own death. Or shame at his own cowardice.

"Goddamn you!" Pettibone shouted and rushed at Fitz.

Fitz jerked his cap from his head, threw it in Pettibone's face, and stepped to one side. As the thick blade of the saber passed inches from his ribs, Fitz brought the barrel of his pistol against the colonel's head. There was a sharp crack and Pettibone sagged with a gasp. He lay at Fitz's feet, a crumpled bundle in a dusty uniform.

"Now listen to me," Fitz shouted to Pettibone's staff before they could react. "This regiment stands its ground! You"—he pointed to an officer—"my compliments to General McDowell. Inform him that a brigade of infantry is attacking us. Tell him that I fully intend to repulse that attack."

The man hesitated.

Fitz aimed his pistol and cocked it. "Ride!" The officer sank his spurs into the horse's flanks and bolted off.

"You, go and tell those idiots to lie down," he motioned to the reserve. "You, and you." Two officers straightened. "I want the first five companies on the right of the line left oblique. Pass the order that we will fire, at my command only, volley by company from the left of the line. The enemy is going to try to roll us up by striking hard on the left and I want a hot fire kept up. One volley and then fire at will."

One of the young officers looked stunned. "Left oblique . . . ?"

"Have the men turn a bit to their left so that their fire is directed at the enemy," Fitz explained. Young officers get rattled if their blood is up. "My company will fire a volley first and then each succeeding company will fire in turn. Now go, we don't have much time." To Jacobs, who had remained frozen throughout the encounter, Fitz said, "Return to your company. Make sure they fire and keep on firing until I tell you otherwise. You men," he shouted to the remaining mounted officers, "take Colonel Pettibone someplace where he won't be in the way." He detailed one of the men, a sleepy-eyed first lieutenant he thought was competent enough to stay with Company C.

"I'll be with the colors at the center of the line," Fitz said.

He ran to the Color Company and drove his sword into the ground next to the regimental colors. "As long as that sword remains," he said to the regimental color sergeant, "so do you."

He watched the enemy line advance. Confederate officers tried to dress the line as it marched, but the ground was broken and the heat was taking its toll on the men. Gaps appeared in the line as soldiers fainted under the broiling sun or simply fell out, too tired to continue.

Sweat rolled down Fitz's forehead and into his eyes. He wiped his face again, rubbing his mustache and the little tuft of beard that hung below his lower lip. His dark eyes flashed with excitement as he unbuttoned the top buttons of his frock coat. This is where he belonged, on the battlefield.

The officer that he had sent off to see McDowell rode up and dismounted.

"The general's compliments, sir," he said, gasping for breath. "You are to hold this line."

Fitz figured the distance to the enemy line—seven hundred yards. "Tell the company commanders," he said to the man. "No one is to fire until I give the order. And then come back here." Fitz gave the line one last look, making sure that the file-closers were properly positioned and that the reserves were out of sight. His eyes narrowed in concentration.

Five hundred yards.

White puffs appeared along the Confederate line and then Fitz heard the flat report of muskets. *Too far away—they're wasting ammunition.* "No one fires!" he shouted to his men. "The first man to fire without orders gets my boot up his ass." Excitement and fear caused fire discipline to vanish, taking with it a good chance of winning. Control it, Fitz knew. *Control the excitement and your men and your own nerves.*

More musketry from the enemy, at four hundred yards. Then .577 caliber Minié balls buzzed overhead, the soft lead bullets the size of the last joint of the little finger. They tore into a man's flesh, making a hole about the size of a thumb, and ripped an ugly, black crater about the size of a fist when they exited—if they did. Sometimes they shattered in the bone and sometimes they remained buried deep within the meat, the lead, grime, sweat, and fabric. The flesh putrefied until you could smell your own decay, and with it your death.

Fitz heard a grunt and saw a soldier fall to the ground to his left. The line dressed to fill the gap. Wide eyes in white faces stared at the still form. Blood, bright red against the yellow grass, flowed from under the man's body.

"Eyes to the front," Fitz ordered. The stench of shit filled the air. Someone's bowels had failed him. The young officer Fitz had dispatched to warn the men not to fire until ordered rode up. He crouched low over his saddle, his eyes on the enemy line.

Fitz patted the horse's sleek neck. "Does everyone know what to do?"

"Yes, sir," the officer said, his voice shaking. "I said if they didn't do as you ordered you'd have them shot."

Fitz smiled. "Very good. Now ride back to C Company and tell Lieutenant Griffin that when he sees the national colors dip, he is to fire. Not until then. Understand?"

"Yes, sir."

Fitz slapped the horse's rump and sent the boy on his way.

Three hundred yards.

The enemy line stopped. Fitz heard the faint commands and saw the muskets leveled.

"Oh, God," someone gasped, and then the world exploded.

The volley tore into the 95th Ohio, bits of flesh and blood sprayed in all directions, men cried out in agony, and the air was filled with the high, piercing screams of the wounded.

"Dress the line!" Fitz shouted. "Dress up!"

Men shifted to their right, filling the gaps left by the enemy's fire. White smoke drifted off as Fitz fought to make out the enemy through the cloud that hung low over the battlefield. A sudden fear that Griffin would not be able to see the signal flashed through his mind but it was too late now. The music had started—the dance was on.

The enemy continued to advance but the Union line stood.

Fitz laid his hand on the color sergeant's shoulder. "The colors," he ordered.

The sergeant nodded and lowered the flag. The Union line erupted in fire.

A crash followed by another, and another, thundered down the blue line. Each perfectly timed volley discharged from the regiment spewed destruction into the enemy ranks. The sickening smell of black powder engulfed Fitz as he watched the Confederate line shatter. A massive storm of lead sliced into them from less than two hundred yards away, tearing great chunks out of the neat array.

The volley fire passed from company to company, washing over Fitz like a rolling wave. Now the men were on their own, firing at will—loading, cursing, and screaming—maddened with excitement and fear. The enemy was returning fire, the whine of Minié balls cutting through the air.

Fitz strode up and down the line shouting encouragement over the awful din, forcing men to take their time loading and firing—peering through the white smoke to glimpse the Confederate line. The enemy had to break, they had to. But they did not. They stood, two hundred yards away from the Union line, exchanging volley for volley. Farmers, students, teachers, clerks, merchants, tailors, laborers, blacksmiths, men and boys, not one in a hundred with any experience as soldiers, trying to kill one another under a blazing July sun.

He stopped at B Company and saw a half dozen soldiers clustered near the center of the company line. Fitz pushed his way into the crowd and forced them back into position.

"Damn you, boys! You've got to fight." Two boys looked at him in terror. They were mirror images of one another. "Brothers, aren't you?" Fitz asked. "Well, one brother can help the other. Listen to me, all of you," he shouted to the men. "We're going to load and fire by the nines. Do you hear me? Just like camp, except there is the enemy." He pointed across the smoke-laden field. "Attention to orders!" he shouted.

The men looked at him dumbly as the racket of gunfire increased.

"Attention to orders, Goddamn you!" he said. They drew to attention, looking straight ahead.

"Load!"

The soldiers dropped the butts of their muskets to the ground with a thud, trigger guard to their knees. Their hands reached for cartridge boxes located on their right hips.

"Handle," Fitz ordered, eyeing the line, "cartridge!"

The soldiers pulled paper cartridges from the boxes and placed them between their teeth. Some were trembling so much they could barely find their mouths.

"Tear, cartridge!"

Ripping the ends off the cartridges, they placed them against the musket muzzle. Fitz studied them, waiting for each man to be in position.

"Charge, cartridge!"

The soldiers poured the powder down the barrels and forced the Minié balls into the muzzles with the ball of their thumbs. Their hands fell to the ramrods, grasping them between the thumb and forefinger.

"Well done, boys. Well done!" Fitz shouted over the roar of musketry. "Draw, rammer!"

The men did as they were ordered.

"Ram, cartridge!"

Their arms worked like pistons, the long metal rods driving the paper cartridges, balls, and remaining powder deep into the musket barrels. The ball was properly seated when a soldier could feel the reassuring thud of lead ball against steel breach.

"Return, rammer!"

They did as they were told, Fitz noted. At least he wouldn't hear the loud whirl of a forgotten ramrod shot from its musket.

"Prime!" he shouted.

The soldiers raised their muskets, muzzles even with their eyes so that they rested against their bodies. They thumbed the hammers back to half cock—threw off the old caps and replaced them with fresh caps from the pouches on their hips.

"Shoulder, arms!"

One of the men was struck and fell face-forward without a sound.

"Steady," Fitz said. "Shoulder arms was the order, boys. Now!"

The soldiers brought the muskets against their right shoulders, trapping them in place with their right forearms. They dropped their left arms to their sides and waited, glancing at Fitz.

The face of one of the soldiers exploded in a red cloud. He stumbled back, dropping his musket, and collapsed.

"Close ranks," Fitz ordered. When the men had done so, he ordered, "Ready!"

The men swung the muskets from their right shoulders and brought the butts against their left sides.

"Aim!"

The weapons came into position; butts settled against their right shoulders, the men struggling to keep the muzzles of the ten-pound weapons from weaving in the air. The hammers were pulled to full cock. All was ready.

"Fire!" Fitz shouted.

The line exploded in a crash, smoke and fire belching from the muskets.

"That's how it's done, boys!" Fitz said as the smoke drifted away.

A soldier smiled at him in relief.

"I reckon we forgot, Captain."

"That won't happen again," Fitz said to the soldier. "You lead the others. If they forget, take them through the Manual of Arms."

Fitz felt a tug at his sleeve. He examined the fabric. A ball had passed through the cloth, leaving a jagged hole. Two inches to the left and it would have struck him. He made his way down the line.

The clatter of gunfire rendered all other sensations numb. He could not taste the dust or the powder. He could not smell the blood or the stink of gutted bodies. He could no longer hear the voices of men. All were superseded by the staccato bark of the muskets.

It went on for hours. It seemed there was nothing else except the noise and confusion of battle. One image bled into another, whole scenes melting away as ice under a summer sun. Sometimes plaintive voices escaped the din, calling through the madness. Cries to God for salvation; pleas for safety; the weird, high-pitched wailing of the wounded; the short, heated burst of profanity when a man battles an overwhelming fright with an unreasoned rage unleashed in all directions. It was good to surrender yourself to rage—it kept fear at bay.

Fitz went from man to man, soothing them, exhorting them, threatening them, but in the end none of it was needed. The men sank into the discipline of killing. But it had to be managed. Once lost they were of little use. Their blood was up and they forgot to soldier well. They would load and fire without capping the piece, or shoot their ramrods into space, or just lose track of what they were doing. Fitz had only to bring them back to being proper soldiers. *Aim carefully, boys. Take your time. Remember to cap your pieces.* But this was battle; descent into another world along twisted, shadowed trails that may—or may not—lead you back to the place where death is only an occasional visitor.

The crash of musketry diminished. The enemy was going, disappearing into the ground, consumed by the smoke and dust that covered the battlefield. Fitz watched them go and rewarded himself with a modest pull at his canteen. The hot water, thick with the foul taste of tin, refreshed him. He slid the cork back into the opening and tapped it into place.

"Cease fire," he shouted. "Cease fire!"

The Union fire slackened and the line fell silent. What followed was a ragged cheer, which, only momentarily, covered the screams of the wounded.

Clumps of bodies appeared as smoke drifted off the battlefield. Wounded soldiers crawled to their lines while others lay on their backs, their hands outstretched to the sky, calling for water. Many men did not move—torn, gutted, smoldering bundles of flesh scattered across the open field. They were past soldiering.

Fitz felt nothing. He would not until he was well away from it. He walked along the line calling for the men to fill in the gaps. Members of the regimental band, detailed the grisly task of picking up the wounded, rushed forward with stretchers. Soldiers along the line tended to their comrades. Some men sat slumped on the ground, heads in their hands, crying, unwounded except for their souls.

Fitz saw the sergeant's body, the chest torn open, the blood and organs a glistening mass under the harsh sun. A corporal stood next to him, grasping the regimental colors.

"We busted them up some, didn't we, Captain?" the corporal asked.

"Some," Fitz agreed. "I don't think they'll be back." He knew it to be a fact. The enemy line had been broken and officers would play hell trying to reform companies and regiments; and time and opportunity would pass like a fast cloud sailing over the sun. The enemy commander would try to find another place to pierce the Union line. It was a macabre chess match—move and countermove, all done by vainglorious men in splendid uniforms from a safe distance. The exercise came to a conclusion when common soldiers died.

"Dunaway!"

Fitz turned to see Colonel Pettibone, blood streaming from under the bandana that he had pressed to his head. Several officers and a corporal's guard accompanied him.

"Damn you, sir! I'll see you hanged!" Pettibone sputtered. "This is mutiny, sir."

"Sir," Fitz said, tired of words. "I have the honor to report that the 95th Ohio has turned the enemy."

"Damn you," Pettibone said, shaking his finger in Fitz's

face. Spittle flew from his mouth. "Don't you change the subject on me. I have witnesses, sir. They've seen it all. They'll testify to it. By God, victory or not, I'll have you arrested."

Fitz wiped his forehead with the back of his sleeve. "You're not the first man to threaten me with arrest," Fitz said, glancing up into the pale blue sky. He looked at Pettibone. "Or the best."

One of the officers stepped forward. "Captain Dunaway, your sidearm, sir."

Fitz smiled, pulled the pistol from its holster, and handed it to the officer butt first.

"Be careful," Fitz said. "It's loaded."

Chapter 2

September 14, 1861
The 153rd day of the war
U.S. Army Provost Guardhouse
Rock Creek, Maryland

Fitz Dunaway waited as the young provost captain read the orders releasing him from the guardhouse. One thing that the army was never short on was young officers who labored over official papers for fear of overlooking a comma or disregarding a period.

"Those orders release me to Colonel Moore," Fitz urged, trying to hurry the process along.

The food had been disgusting, riddled with more weevils than usual, but the boredom had been the worst of the punishment. There were few newspapers to read, and those were filled with outlandish claims that the Rebels would soon march down Pennsylvania Avenue, or that the British fleet had been spotted just entering Baltimore Harbor. It was defeatist talk but considering the debacle at Bull Run, there was nothing else to expect. The Confederates had mauled the Union army, with the only bright spot being Fitz's defense of the flank. And for that he was incarcerated in the guardhouse; for how long, he didn't know. Being jailed came as no surprise considering his handling of Colonel Pettibone. The surprise was

Will Moore's arrival with a sheaf of orders giving him his freedom.

The provost captain looked up and then, deciding that his career would not be jeopardized, said, "Go on, then." He handed the papers back to Will. "I guess it's all in order."

"Thank you." Will tossed a glance that told Fitz to follow him before the captain changed his mind.

Outside Fitz felt the warmth of a kind sun on the back of his neck. Nearby trees rustled a welcome and he heard the thunder of a battery of artillery galloping through camp. To his right was a forest of stacked muskets, the soldiers marched off to some duty or other. *How forlorn they look,* he thought, and realized the melancholy was his own, and had nothing to do with abandoned weapons. He had been deprived of these scenes since he was placed under arrest.

Will Moore, holding the door open, waited near the carriage. "Fitz, I rented this vehicle by the hour."

Fitz climbed into the carriage, joining his friend, and closed the door behind him.

"We're going to be late," Colonel Moore said, tapping the roof of the Rockaway with his knuckles. The carriage started out with a jolt. "The assistant secretary of war is a man that you don't keep waiting, Fitz." Will took up more than his share of the interior. He was taller than most men and inclined to a belly.

"My guards were reluctant to release me," Fitz said. "They take this arrest business seriously."

"Perhaps you should as well. This is an opportunity for you. Let me remind you to be careful."

"I'm always careful. What do you take me for, Will? A common idiot?"

"Oh, Fitz! There's nothing common about you."

"Sometimes," Fitz said, teasing Will Moore, "I have to remind myself that you are my friend."

Will refused to take the matter lightly. "Fitz, I have made

every effort to gain you an audience with a man who could get you released from arrest . . ."

"A politician! What good will that do me?"

"What difference would it make if he were the King of Siam?" Will pointed out.

"A politician got me into this mess, Will."

"With your able assistance," Will said. He took a deep breath. "Now, Fitz. Please help me to help you. Choose your words with care, keep your emotions firmly in check. Do not take offense at everything that the assistant secretary says."

"You think that a possibility, do you?" Fitz asked, growing irritated at his friend.

"I think it a certainty. Prescott is a cagey old rascal—"

Fitz began to speak when Will cut him off. "And must be treated carefully. God help me, Fitz, can I not make you understand your predicament? House arrest, striking your superior officer, conduct unbecoming. Could it be any worse?"

"I could have shot the bastard."

Will grimaced. "No levity, please. I don't have the heart for it."

Fitz had done it again, put Will squarely in the middle. "Oh, Will. I know. I'm more than a challenge. Blast it, I make mistakes."

"Fitz," Will said in a calm voice. "Everyone makes mistakes. It's your cracking people across the head that makes your life complicated. I can't stand to see you come to this. Prescott can help. He said that he wants to help. Will you just remember all that I have said and conduct yourself accordingly?"

Fitz offered an apologetic smile to his friend. "Of course, of course. I know that I've been a burden. I know that you've done everything that you can to help me. I appreciate that, Will."

They rode in silence before Will spoke again and his tone took on a new urgency. "Fitz, this is your last chance. You've made too many enemies in the army and now outside of it as well. For God's sake don't fail me. Don't fail yourself." After a few minutes Will said, "I hope that this will repay my debt to you."

The statement was unexpected and painful. "Blast, Will. Why did you bring that up? There's nothing to it."

"I know my accounts, Fitz," Will said.

"Don't be daft. That's all forgotten. That was years ago, another war. You would have done the same for me—"

"But I didn't," Will said, dismissing Fitz's argument. "I know my accounts, and I pay my debts."

"Well," Fitz said, pulling his kepi over his eyes and sliding down into the seat. "You mark whatever you please in your ledger book but I've forgotten all about it." He closed his eyes, listening to the steady rhythm of the hoofbeats on the hard-packed road, but he was troubled by Will's words. Fitz knew that his friend was ashamed of what had happened, and he tried not to think of it himself. A soft summer wind or the smell of sunbaked grass took him back to the Dakota Territory and the flat prairie near Fort Laramie.

> *The sun was high in the sky but hot, and the air tasted of dust and smelled of horse dung and fear, but the fear was not emanating from Fitz or the Cheyenne braves seated on their ponies just across a shallow creek bed. It clung to the young officer sitting on the big roan next to Fitz. It was then that Fitz knew that Captain Will Moore was about to make a bad decision.*

Assistant Secretary of War Thaddeus Prescott rubbed the end of the pen against his nose, as he did whenever he was troubled, and read the report. His green eyes devoured each word.

The few strands of brown hair that remained to him fell from an alabaster dome to curl over his shirt collar, ending in a field of white dandruff sprinkled over the shoulders of his black broadcloth coat. He hovered over his desk, burdened

by the indefinable weight that eventually crushes all bureaucrats.

To his left stood Lieutenant Colonel William Ferrell
Moore. He was clean-shaven, only because his blond hair offered nothing more than a hint of beard, making him seem
much younger than he was.

Next to him, slumped in a chair that appeared far too small
to hold this rough hulk of a man, was Ward Hill Lamon.
Broad-shouldered, coarse, with long black hair to match a
thick goatee, his size belied a surprisingly soft voice. He could
be blustery, Prescott knew, and damned impatient as well as
brutal if he thought his close friend from Illinois, Abraham
Lincoln, was the object of any sort of attack. Lamon was
known to go about well armed, a practice from his days on
the western prairies of Illinois riding the circuit with the man
who had just been made president.

Prescott turned a page and cleared his throat, tossing a
wary glance to the fourth man in the room.

Captain Thomas Fitzgerald Dunaway, United States Army,
stood in front of Prescott's large desk. He was of average
height—a thin man with sharp features. His kepi was trapped
against his side by his elbow and his eyes were fixed on a spot
on the wall three feet above Prescott's head. He'd had the
forethought to have his dark blue uniform coat brushed and
sky blue trousers cleaned. Fitz had taken the time to polish
his brass buttons to a high gleam himself. It took his mind
off his situation. He wore a sparkling white collar and had
managed to talk Will out of a pair of white cotton gloves in
respectable condition. He knew he looked like a soldier and
he felt like a soldier. Now he hoped that the others saw him
as a soldier.

Prescott read the last page, gathered the report, and laid it
to one side. He lined the edges of the pages with his fingertips.

"You've led an adventurous life, Captain Dunaway," he
said, folding his hands together on his desk. "How is it that
you've come to survive this long?"

"Good fortune on the battlefield, sir," Fitz said.

Prescott smiled. "No, Captain. You've missed my sarcasm. With all of the charges brought against you throughout your career, how is it that you haven't been hanged?"

"I don't know, sir."

Prescott thumbed through the report again, spoiling the perfect order. "Fort Laramie, Dakota Territory. Conduct unbecoming. How do you explain that one, Captain?"

"Which of the incidents, sir?" Fitz asked. He didn't care for this man. He was too polished by far. Prescott was a politician's politician, Fitz decided. But he remembered Will's words.

"Which?" Prescott exclaimed with a chuckle. "Well, bless my soul if you aren't right! Here is one with a wagon-train captain. Tell me about that."

"I had a disagreement with him, sir," Fitz said. Everything was clear enough to anyone who took the time to read the report, he thought. "He failed to follow my orders. I found it necessary to subdue him."

"Oh, well. Yes, of course," Prescott said, peering at the document. "With, according to your superiors—'the butt end of a Colt pistol rendering him stupid for the better part of one week.' "

Lamon belched and stuck a plug of tobacco in his mouth. His eyes never left Fitz but what was worse, they surveyed the captain with suspicion.

"He was difficult to convince, sir," Fitz explained.

Colonel Moore rolled his eyes.

"Was he now?" Prescott retorted. "How much worse for him had he been more so?" He closed the report and looked at Fitz. "What of Colonel Pettibone?"

Fitz froze. He could feel Will looking at him. "That was a different matter."

"Yes," Prescott said. "I was sure that it would be. Don't be modest—let me hear every bloodcurdling detail."

Fitz felt Will's cautioning glance.

Prescott produced a charming smile. "Indulge me, Captain," he said.

This was it. *Choose your words, don't lose your temper, and don't elaborate. Your last chance,* Will had said. "Very well, sir," Fitz said. He did not want to talk. He did not want to explain himself and he did not want to banter words with the assistant secretary of war. He wanted to be out of Washington and back on the battlefield. Let Will talk to him, let Will explain everything. He felt his last chance to escape court-martial slipping from his grasp. But he had no choice. He began his explanation. "The battle started out well enough. The regiment was not called into action until sometime in the early afternoon. We were immediately engaged. After about an hour of hot fighting to our right, we found the enemy attempting to turn our flank."

" 'We' being the 95th Ohio Volunteer Infantry," Prescott said, scratching his cheek with thick fingers, "Colonel Horace Pettibone, commanding."

"He commands the regiment. Yes, sir."

"You are aware of the Ohio Pettibones, are you not, Captain?"

"No, sir. Nor any other Pettibones that I know of."

"Ah," Prescott said. "Please continue."

"I was in command of C Company, on the extreme left in line. The enemy was pushing hard on my flank and front when I received instructions to withdraw. I sent word to Colonel Pettibone that it was impossible to disengage and that if we showed a little spirit, it might be possible to break the enemy's advance."

"Colonel Moore?"

"I read the reports, sir. It was a difficult situation," Colonel Moore explained. "General McDowell could not support some elements of the line, including Colonel Pettibone's."

"Do you agree, Captain Dunaway?"

"I don't know what sort of day General McDowell was having, sir. I was otherwise occupied with about two thousand Rebels in my front."

"Continue with your account, Captain."

"Colonel Pettibone rode up. He told me, 'By God you had

better get your men moved' or words to that effect. I said
that if we pulled back now the regiment would be routed."

"You saw this as a possibility, did you?"

"Yes, sir. As clearly as I see you."

"Go on."

"Colonel Pettibone came at me with his sword. So I
cracked him on the skull with my pistol."

Prescott arched his eyebrows. "The pistol again, Captain
Dunaway? Have you ever considered the fruitful art of nego-
tiation?"

"There wasn't time for talk, sir. I think Colonel Pettibone
intended to run me through."

Prescott nodded and waved for Fitz to continue.

"I assumed command of the regiment, strengthened the
line, and we held until the enemy disappeared."

"At this point Colonel Pettibone, of the Ohio Pettibones,
regained consciousness long enough to have you arrested?"

"Yes, sir."

Lamon straightened, drawing his long legs to either side of
the chair. "Where are you from, Captain?"

"From?" Fitz asked. "I don't—"

"State, man," Lamon snapped. "Where in the Union?"

"Tennessee, sir."

Lamon stood, his face flushing a deep red. "Tennessee. For
God's sake, Prescott, does he have to be from a Rebel state?"

"Indeed, sir," Prescott said. His manner was smooth and
patient. "This particular task requires that the officer be believed."

"Task?" Fitz asked. He felt the currents in the room swirl
around him.

"It is fortunate that our good friend here is from Tennessee.
This opens opportunities that might otherwise be denied us,"
Prescott explained.

"Tennessee," Lamon snorted and then extended his legs in
front of the chair, falling into a languid pose.

"Colonel Moore," Prescott said, returning to his inquiry.

"Is it common for junior officers to disobey orders from their superiors?"

"No, sir. It is not."

"And for junior officers to whip their superiors with a pistol?"

"No, sir, but I would like to add that Captain Dunaway's actions saved the regiment . . ."

"Yes," Prescott said without enthusiasm, "heroic indeed. Worthy of a medal or two, I'm sure." He gave Fitz an enigmatic smile. "You do know, Captain Dunaway, that Colonel Pettibone, with two uncles and a brother in Congress, is very well connected?"

"He may be very well connected in Congress, sir, but he flew all to pieces on the battlefield."

"For God's sake, Fitz," Moore said.

"No, no, Colonel. Our outspoken captain is entirely right. Unfortunately, being right has nothing to do with it. A fact, I am sure, which will be pointed out at Captain Dunaway's court-martial." He smoothed the back of his head, sending dandruff cascading to his shoulders. He continued, "I will tell you something, Captain Dunaway, that I urge you to consider. This is a politician's war. Oh, the army and the navy do all of the fighting. But it is far too big for the army and navy alone, which makes it a politician's war. That is why colonels like Colonel Pettibone, who I believe owns a freight company in Columbus and has contributed significantly to the Republican Party, can raise regiments and buy commissions. Talent and training have nothing to do with it. Do you agree that this is the way of it?"

"It ought not to be, sir."

"Spoken like a true innocent and more's the pity, Captain Dunaway. Apparently, you are unaccustomed to traveling the dark pathways of politics. Will assures me that you're a first-rate fighting officer. We shall need more men like you to make up for the Colonel Pettibones in the army. But when men like you run afoul of politicians . . . Well, I suppose there is little else to be said."

"I was only doing my duty, sir."

"The very words that will be emblazoned on your tombstone after you are shot or hanged, or whatever the army does, for this latest offense." The assistant secretary stood and stepped to the front of the desk. "Colonel Moore, would you excuse us, please?"

"Of course, sir," Moore replied. He shot Fitz a warning glance.

After he left, Prescott crossed his short arms over his ample belly and sighed, studying Fitz. "First in his class," he said. "You were his classmate."

Fitz realized that Prescott was speaking of Will. "Yes, sir."

It was mathematics that had brought them together. And horses. Fitz could outride anyone at the Academy and thought a course for soldiers should consist only of those lessons taught from horseback. His instructors disagreed. Will could barely ride, and Fitz complained that fractions were useless devices that should be left to others. Will and Fitz's friendship began as one of mutual need.

"You can teach me to ride," Will had said, "and I will teach you the finer principles of mathematics."

Fitz began to decline, unwilling to be seen wanting in another plebe's eyes, especially one who appeared to slide through every class unencumbered by doubt. He reconsidered Will's offer because he was accumulating more demerits than passing grades, and because Will's bargain came with an honest handshake and a broad smile.

"You were last in the class?" Prescott asked, returning him to the present.

"Yes, sir."

"The Alpha and the Omega, if you will."

"If you say so, sir. Latin was never one of my strengths."

"No," Prescott said. "I can see that. Tell me, Captain Dunaway, what exactly is your strength?"

"I don't quite . . . ?"

"Your skill, your ability. That at which you excel."

"Getting at the enemy, sir," Fitz replied.

"Indeed," Prescott said, considering the answer. He brushed his lips with his thick fingers. "As it happens, I am in need of a man who will 'get at the enemy.' Interested?"

A tiny voice warned Fitz to be careful. "I don't know, sir."

"With a blatantly unequivocal answer like that we shall certainly make a politician of you yet, Captain," Prescott said. Lamon offered a shrug in return.

"I never aspired to the profession, sir," Fitz said. He could see that Prescott was losing patience with him.

"You have few options left to you, sir," Prescott said. His manner turned cool. "I would at least give this one a careful hearing."

"Yes, sir," Fitz said. He was trapped. "What I meant to say, sir, is that you took me by surprise. I hadn't expected any course except dismissal from the service."

"From now on you must expect the unexpected, Captain Dunaway." Prescott warmed a bit. "I need a man of rare qualities. A man not only possessed of courage, but one whose mind is keen." He looked through the tall windows. "God help us, Captain, but Washington is stuffed with brave and loyal men whom some good fairy ought to knock in the head. They are good for nothing but posturing and pretension. They are of no use to me. Not for what I have in mind. Shall I continue?"

Fitz remained silent.

"Good," Prescott said, motioning to a chair. "Sit down and let us dispense with the formalities." The assistant secretary of war took his seat behind the desk, poured himself a tumbler of water from the pitcher at his elbow, and drank. He examined the contents of the glass. "One thing that we have managed to manufacture in this city besides incompetent army officers is dust." He ran a finger over his desktop and showed Fitz the result. "A fine layer covers everything. I taste the grit in my mouth each morning when I awake and feel it on everything I touch. If it is not fortifications being constructed, it is bomb-proofs. One in the basement of this very building. If the amount of dust generated in the capital is any indication of success, then we have surely won the war. You see how close the war is, Captain? Look out the window, if you can penetrate the grime. Endless columns of wagons bearing God knows what, going God knows where."

Fitz said nothing.

"You don't care about that, do you, Captain Dunaway?"

Fitz didn't know what else to say. "No, sir."

"No, I didn't suppose that you did," Prescott said. He pulled open a desk drawer and held up a document. He looked at Fitz. "I hold in my hand a warrant for a colonelcy in the Regular United States Army. This is not a brevet rank, Captain. It's a colonelcy in the Regular Army, something that, at your current rate, you will never see. It's yours, Captain, if you agree to help me."

"Help you, sir?"

"Help the nation, Captain."

"I took an oath to do so, sir. I would do it no matter what was offered."

Prescott dropped the warrant on his desk. "A great many men took an oath, which they seem to have forgotten. The exodus of army officers resigning their commissions and heading south is positively breathtaking. Let us speak plainly, Captain Dunaway. If Pettibone has his way, and the Pettibones nearly always get their way," Prescott said, "you will be dismissed from the army at the very least. The Pettibones stand by one another."

"I wish that they had stood in Ohio."

Prescott chuckled. "So do most members of Congress." He grew serious. "This is what I propose. I would like you to come to work for me, for this department. On the surface you will be a member of the president's guard, which in itself is a difficult proposition because our president feels that such is a waste of manpower. He is a most informal soul."

Garrison duty, Fitz thought. He couldn't think of anything worse unless it was rotting away under house arrest while the gods debated his fate. He saw himself dressed in his finest uniform, serving as little more than decoration for official functions.

"That is how you will be presented. However, we expect your position and your difficulties, not to mention your pedigree, to attract those who might have an interest in harming the president. They will try, we hope, to enlist your aid. You will, of course, alert us, and we will do the rest. Let us consider the shadow occupation as an agent. One of several in my employ. You will work secretly, reporting only to me, no one else. Reports of your activities will be sent to Mr. Lamon." He nodded toward the big man, who sat cleaning his fingernails with a penknife.

"Sir?"

"Mr. Lamon is a particular friend of President Lincoln. Mr. Lamon fears for Mr. Lincoln's life and his concern is fully justified."

"The president . . ." Fitz began, astounded at the idea that anyone would kill a president.

He had avoided the notion of politics, certain that most men that held or even desired public office were scoundrels. But even before Lincoln was elected, Fitz had a different feeling about the man, reading newspaper accounts of the tall candidate's desire to avoid war, occasionally thumbing through a pamphlet that carried some of Lincoln's speeches. He had liked what he read. The man's thoughts and ideas were logical, without the bombast of a politician. As he read the candidate's speeches, he came to understand that here was a different kind of politician; a man with ideas uncluttered by rhetoric; a man whose desire for office didn't reduce him to pandering to the lowest layer of the population. Lincoln's thinking was clear, and his powers of analysis rendered even the most complex problems to simple issues of right and wrong.

Fitz developed an admiration for Lincoln, not bothering to vote for him because he always held that a soldier should never vote, but tracking Lincoln's progress during the election and celebrating, quietly, when Abraham Lincoln became the sixteenth president. All celebration ceased when the first cannonball exploded over Fort Sumter.

"You must be the original innocent, Dunaway," Lamon said, standing. He closed the blade on his knife and stuffed it into his vest pocket. "There have already been two or three plots to kill Lincoln and God knows how many more in this scheming town. Goddamn it, sir, if conspiracy were an industry, this city would lead the world."

"Mr. Lamon is quite right, Captain," Prescott said. "Washington is a Southern city, a former slave capital. The government itself was once composed primarily of Southerners and still houses a few Northerners who agree with their friends from below the Mason-Dixon Line. There are a considerable number of men who would find cause to celebrate President Lincoln's death. Not every man in Washington agrees with Lincoln's notion of maintaining the Union at any cost. Some say let the South go. 'Wayward sisters, depart in Peace!' To them Lincoln is a tyrant. Some say that he will free the slaves."

"I had hoped, sir—"

"Hope is a charming but absolutely worthless word under the circumstances," Prescott said, cutting Fitz off. "Now you see the times, Captain Dunaway. Wars are not always fought on the battlefield."

Fitz thought over Prescott's words. There was something unsettling in his tone—something that told Fitz to stay away from this business. "Mr. Prescott," he said, "I'm a soldier. That's all that I've ever been. That's all that I know. You said that this is a politician's war. I've more than proved myself incapable of dealing with politicians. My best service is in the field, sir. Against the enemy. Not here. Return me to a regiment where I can serve my country."

"You don't have that option, Captain Dunaway," Prescott said, letting the weight of the situation rest squarely on Fitz's shoulders. "Not now, at least. I can safeguard you and provide you with an opportunity to advance, but you must give me a reason to do so. You have balanced precariously between condemnation and commendation from the moment that you entered West Point. Help me, Captain Dunaway, and I can help you." Prescott held the warrant for Fitz to see. "And you get this in the bargain."

The paper beckoned Fitz seductively. He was torn. An agent—he meant a *spy*. The word was distasteful. But to continue as he was, waiting for the wheels of military justice to grind him to dust was . . . He had been under arrest nearly a month, and each day that passed took him farther from the war. He had been forgotten; confined to quarters. Through the tiny window of his room he had seen troops drilling on vast parade grounds, endless tent cities, wagon parks and artillery parks; and every day, each day—new regiments marching into camp with flags flying and drums beating. He was afraid. The hollow beating of his heart matched that of the drums that led others off to war—away from him. And a colonelcy—that would lead to a regiment. His regiment. He asked, "What does an agent do?"

A tiny smile crossed Prescott's face. "Watch. Listen. Report. Your duties as a member of the president's guard will take little of your time. Find those men who plot to harm our president. Bring them to justice."

Fitz felt a chill travel up the back of his neck. He was considering it, as if one part of his mind had detached itself and set up shop on its own. The sound of his voice surprised him. "You want me to be a spy."

"Call it anything that you like, Captain," Lamon said. "Beggars can't be choosers. I ain't as sure about you as Prescott here but he knows the lay of the city and I will keep Lincoln safe."

Prescott's tone was more sympathetic. "I told you what would be required of you. If you find the duty distasteful, consider yourself President Lincoln's spy. There. An agent of the Executive Mansion."

"I can't do it."

"Don't be noble, Captain, you can't afford it," the assistant secretary said. "Keep your eyes and ears open and make reports. Is it so much to ask?"

"Mr. Prescott, I am not your man. The notion of being a spy is—" He sought to find the right word.

Prescott cocked an eyebrow. "Really?" he asked, pinning the warrant between his fingertips. Fitz watched in horror as the assistant secretary began to rip the document in half.

"Wait! Wait," Fitz said. "Give me a moment. Just one moment. Let me think." He glanced around the room, seeking an answer. But there was none, except what Prescott offered. He felt Will standing next to him. *Take it, you fool! If you don't it'll be the end of you.*

Prescott recognized victory. He dropped the warrant on his desk and smiled. "The worst part of the city is a section called the Island, a haven for criminals and traitors. Even the Metropolitans, our local police force, will not venture onto the Island at night. We've had constant reports of a conspiracy brewing. I'm sure that you will be led eventually to that locale. The taverns and saloons there are the most likely place to ferment sedition." He laughed at an unspoken joke. "Or the parlors of some of our finer homes." Prescott returned to his instructions. "You will frequent these establishments, in civilian clothes, of course, and report on what you find. You must, out of necessity, assume the role of a Southern sympathizer."

"How—?"

"Colonels are as common as gnats, while you remain a captain. I'm sure you can manufacture just cause to be angry with the government. Give that bitterness voice. If nothing else, lie. Besides," he smiled, "I will have the other agents weave stories about you among the malcontents. Will you accept my proposal?"

"Can I have time to think this through?" Fitz asked.

"Of course," Prescott said. "You can have until tomorrow

morning, at which time you will continue under house arrest or be well on your way to the rank of colonel. Doesn't seem like such a difficult choice, does it, Captain Dunaway? Let me caution you to speak to no one about this, not even Colonel Moore. Only you, Mr. Batterman, Mr. Lamon, and I will know about this conversation."

"Batterman?"

"My private secretary. He was in the outer office when you arrived. You will dictate the reports to him."

"Yes," Fitz said. He felt the decision crushing the breath from him. Prescott became sympathetic. "Come, Fitz. Let's not be this way. Here is a new beginning for you. Your own regiment to do with as you please. And acquired without having to whip anyone with a pistol."

"It is difficult to become enthusiastic under the circumstances."

"On the contrary, you should muster nothing but enthusiasm. Get a good night's sleep. See me at seven o'clock tomorrow morning."

"I'll need a pass to return, Mr. Prescott. I'm still confined to barracks."

"We'll take care of that," Prescott said, striking the call bell with his palm. "We can't have you making such a momentous decision in your barracks." The tiny ring brought Batterman, a thin young man with a thick mustache and large eyes, to the door.

"Yes, sir?"

"Have Captain Dunaway's things sent to the Royal Boarding House. Sign whatever papers our friend here needs to walk the streets of Washington." Turning to Fitz, Prescott said, "Mr. Batterman will give you directions to the Royal. I know the proprietress, Asia Lossing. It is convenient to every location in the city and reasonably priced." Prescott, troubled, poised over another thought. "Captain Dunaway, there have been some rumors of suspicious activity at the Royal. I find such tales disturbing. Asia's father was a close friend of mine; that poor soul has been dead for some time. Asia Lossing is at the mercy of a rogue. She is a charming woman, married to a worthless creature. The whole affair, I speak of the war, has turned out the scoundrel in a number of men. It's best to keep your eyes and ears open."

Prescott's attitude changed to that of a man pleased with circumstances. "Well, Captain, I think Colonel Moore's recommendation is an excellent one. The man and the hour have met, as it were. Remember to keep this matter confidential. Trust no one. Sleep on it, Captain Dunaway, and don't disappoint me. Would you be so kind as to wait in the outer office?"

Fitz understood that he was dismissed. He rose, snapped to attention, saluted, turned, and left.

After the door was closed, Batterman turned to Prescott and Lamon.

"Is he the sort of man that you're looking for, Mr. Prescott?"

Prescott's eyes narrowed in thought and he said, "For the sake of the country, Mr. Batterman, I pray that he is exactly the man that we are seeking."

"I ain't convinced," Lamon said, spitting a stream of brown tobacco juice into the fireplace. "I think he's the clumsy sort. He doesn't know politics from polecats and by God, the man's from the South."

"You are from Virginia, are you not, sir?" Prescott offered.

"That ain't got a damn thing to do with it," Lamon bellowed and then, catching himself, said, "This city is a nest of Rebel intrigue and I don't like the idea of using that man. I'll bet you a twenty-dollar gold piece that he turns on us."

Prescott dismissed the notion with a sliver of a smile. "Mr. Lamon, you must really learn to have faith in human nature. Colonel Moore has the utmost confidence in Captain Dunaway and I have the utmost confidence in Colonel Moore. He comes from a good family and his reputation is sound. I'm sure that our only difficulties will be in making certain that the good captain does not fall into his old habit of bludgeoning people." He returned to his desk. "You are quite right about one thing, Mr. Lamon. This city is ripe with intrigue. I fear that having uncovered one scheme, we may leave a dozen more hidden."

Chapter 3

Barlow's Tavern, The Island
Washington, DC

Whaley let his fingertips slide down to the end of the pencil. He turned the pencil over and repeated the action. He listened carefully as the man opposite him—a man dressed in a fine linen coat and an expensive silk waistcoat—told Whaley how much money it would take to smuggle the pair in. Whaley's eyes, dark and brooding, shaded by thick eyebrows below a gentle forehead, followed his fingers down the length of the pencil.

Whaley let Henry Lossing talk because he wanted the man to become nervous and frustrated, and because they had all the time in the world to reach an agreement. They would not be disturbed in the back room of the tavern. Whaley had seen to that. He was very careful about such things. Very careful about his safety. Careful not to be taken off guard. He gave the man across from him a smile that said, *I'm listening, and I'm not to be taken for a fool.*

Lossing, a man known to smuggle medicine out of the city to Confederate agents, cleared his throat as he continued his reasoning. He was rich, and Whaley, born near the docks in Baltimore, hated the rich. Lossing was a lawyer and his speech was precise, peppered with words that Whaley had never heard before, and he suspected the lawyer used them just to make him feel small. Well, maybe. But the reason that he disgusted Whaley was that he was greedy, eaten alive with greed, his eyes darting back and forth as he looked for opportunities to make money. Whaley was all for money; not having had much of it growing up, he saw it only as another tool to be drawn upon when necessary. The lawyer practically trembled at the thought of making money.

"We had a deal. I just don't see," Whaley said, his eyes following his fingers as they slid down the pencil, "how it costs more to smuggle someone in, than someone out."

"It's the size," the lawyer said with a chuckle, as if it should be obvious to Whaley. "And the army is patrolling up and down the river. We have to be very careful to avoid the patrols."

The fingers stopped and Whaley raised his eyes. "I don't see it," he said in a low, cool voice, watching the man's smile disappear.

"Well," Lossing said, struggling to recover his calm, "getting medicine out is not difficult. I mean it's difficult but it can be moved in small containers."

Whaley went back to the pencil. The lawyer preferred to use the word "moved" instead of "smuggled." As if it were somehow less offensive. Less illegal. Or less traitorous.

"Small amounts, you see. I can move medicine out of the city in small amounts. But since the army has tightened the travel restrictions coming into the city, by river, or road—the railroad, too, of course—someone coming into the city without a legitimate reason—"

"How *much* did you say?" Whaley asked, as if he had just realized the price the lawyer had put on his role.

"Two men," Lossing said, trying to sound confident. "One thousand dollars each. Two thousand dollars total." He nodded to himself, his argument justified. "Two thousand."

Whaley laid the pencil on the table. "That is a lot of money. I don't know if I can get that much money."

The lawyer felt his argument being undermined. "Well. It's

fair. I mean to say it's fair considering the effort involved. I have to pay people—"

"How much do you pay them?" Whaley asked.

The lawyer argued his case. He was very good at that. He *used* to be good before he gave up practicing the law for the call of gaming tables. He still had the skills, however. He could pile conditions and pleas around himself so that they formed a fortification that could withstand any assault. But this man, Whaley—at times the danger that surrounded the tough seemed to pierce Lossing's fortress. "It varies. Sometimes more. Sometimes less. Things are never exact, you know. This is a dangerous business."

"It is that," Whaley confirmed. He wanted the lawyer to remember just how deadly the whole episode could be. "I'll get the money."

"When—"

"Tonight," Whaley snapped. He would not be pressured, and he would never let a fop get the better of him. The man dressed well, and spoke well, and rode about in a fancy carriage, and his purse bulged with gold coins, but he had no insides. He was hollow, Whaley knew. "I'll get the money."

"Well," the lawyer said, relieved that this difficult business was over. "They're on the Virginia side of the Potomac. I'll get them crossed and down to the city." He eased back in his chair and managed a smile. Money would be coming his way—a substantial amount. Such occurrences, even under circumstances such as this, pleased him, refreshed him. "Well, these men must possess valuable traits—" He saw that he had gone too far. Whaley's cold eyes pinned him in his chair, and he knew that he had made a horrible mistake.

"Who these men are," Whaley said, the words piercing the lawyer's soul like a dagger, "what they do, is none of your concern. If I hear a single word of what was spoken here, I will slice you from crown to crotch."

"Now, see here," the lawyer said, standing. He had to defend himself. It was an old lawyer's trick—build a case when you have none. He would shame this ruffian back to his own place. There would be no more colorful talk about threats.

Whaley jumped to his feet, throwing his chair against the wall. "See! What are you going to show me? What are you going to tell *me?* Go on. What do you have to say?" His hand brushed the tail of his coat and wrapped itself around the bone handle of a bowie knife. Whaley was a head taller than the lawyer and his bulk filled the room. He jerked the bowie knife from his waistband and drove the tip of the blade deep into the tabletop. The light from a candle traced the knife's edge. "This here is what you have to see." His huge fist was still wrapped around the handle, ready to use it.

The lawyer swallowed. "Of course," he said. "Of course. Lawyer's confidentiality. Nothing will be said. I promise you that. You have my word." He held out his hand, knowing that if Whaley took it the danger was past.

"Good night, then," Whaley said, unmoving.

The lawyer said, "Yes." He moved the chair back, the legs scraping against the rough floorboards. He offered Whaley a strained smile. "Good night. I'll wait to hear from you."

Lossing walked out through the tavern, ignoring the questioning glances of the vermin that occupied the rough tables scattered around the dank interior, and into the street. He forced himself to breathe and began to tremble. He decided to head north. He should be able to find a cab several blocks up, and from there he could go to Madame Spence's and relax.

His feet were surprisingly light on the cobblestones and he knew that his nerves would calm and every sense return to normal. Dealing with men like Whaley was like playing cards. There was the anticipation, and the plan, and then action, and your heart raced as your mind sought to grasp the direction of the game, and then you bet to build the pot or bluff your opponent or lull your opponent into believing that your cards were worthless and that you were a mindless twit waiting to be taken.

Lossing did not go to Madame Spence's for her ladies—although they were certainly the most beautiful in the city—unlike the high-ranking officers and well-placed government officials who conversed in her parlor, drinks in one hand and fine cigars in the other, waiting for smiling women to come lead them to a discreet rendezvous. He had no interest in women. He found the abandonment to base passion disgusting and besides, sex intruded on his gaming.

No. He went there because Lola Spence, besides having a need for the best hair dye from France, enjoyed gambling as well as any man and had devoted two rooms in the back of her stately house to that pursuit. It was there that men serious about the cards, and amateurs, anxious to prove their skills, faced each other across felt-covered tables. The games would last two or three days, until the plebeians were stripped of their money and their dignity and sent on their way.

Lossing hailed a cab. The driver demanded a portion of the fare up front because this was the Island and he stood either to be robbed or fleeced.

When Lossing climbed in he began to calculate the money he would make from Whaley and wondered if there was another way to turn this endeavor so that he made even more. He converted the prospective coin into hours at the tables and then planned the next few days. He would return home to suffer the cold silence of his dear wife, bathe and change clothes, and then go to Madame Spence's.

A plump figure entered his thoughts, and he remembered a boarder's name. Hogan, or Logan, or some such. The man was always sniffing around, looking for a way to make money. There might be an opportunity. A contractor, Lossing thought, but contractors in Washington during war do more than contract goods. They fabricate opportunities. He thought of Logan again and decided; there might be an opportunity.

Whaley sent for a beer and sat back, waiting. Too many people, he thought. Too many people knew his business or part of his business or *thought* they knew. That was how it was to be, and when he protested he had been told that there was good money to be had if the job was done right but none if it was botched. More than enough good money, he was reminded, but only if the thing was done when and where it was planned.

"A good marksman," Whaley scoffed. "Hell. A fair marksman could kill him in less time than it takes me to strike a match."

"That's not how it's to be," he was told by the man who paid him. "Anyone can kill a president, we're out to topple a government."

It was the word "topple" that convinced Whaley. He saw the image in his mind, like the huge marble blocks scattered around the Capitol grounds. They had been plucked from the grassy knoll, one after another, by a steam crane and set on the building. He'd even taken some time to watch the process, drawn, like many of the people who stopped to watch, by the ponderous, boring practice of dismantling one dome in preparation for another. "Topple" explained it all. After agreeing with the man whose money he was taking, that it made more sense that way, Whaley became more damn dangerous than anyone had thought. He demanded more money. His demand was refused with a smile that was both regretful and final, and, surprisingly, a pat on the hand like a father would give a son. The matter, he was informed with no hard feelings, was concluded.

But the complexity of the thing burrowed under Whaley's skin and erupted like a pus-filled sore when the matter came up again. Men being smuggled and tunnels being dug—a goodly distance, mind you, and no variance to it, because if the tunnel wandered even a few feet, all the powder in the world wouldn't amount to a puff of hot air. The tunnel. Two men were coming. Trained men who knew mines and could survey, and they had instruments that said how far and in what direction to dig. It was time for them because the tunnel was well on its way to its destination. Lossing was to bring them but Whaley didn't trust Lossing.

"Forget it," Whaley ordered himself, draining the last of the hot beer from the pewter mug and slamming the vessel on the table. And he was told that a soldier would likely appear to ask questions and Whaley had better make ready to receive him. A stalking goat, he was told, and the man with the manicured hand patted his shoulder and reassured him that all would be well. The cultured voice said, "Don't trouble yourself about this. Remember: It's not to kill a man. It's to topple a government."

Chapter 4

"**B**last!" Fitz spat as he left the War Department, sliding into the torrent of people that streamed down the broad wooden sidewalk. He shouldered his way into the mass of soldiers and civilians, all trying to get somewhere in a hurry. He was bumped and jostled until he found the flow of the throng and hoped to hell that he didn't have to stop—he would be trampled to death. It was a foul bunch of humanity that squeezed around him, stinking of sweat and filth, faceless bodies that passed in a blur. Early autumn or not, the city still reeked of heat and sweat.

A squad of cavalry thundered by, shrouding the sidewalk in a boiling cloud of dust. They were gone in an instant, accompanied by a wild creak of leather, the jingle of brass buckles, and the sharp clang of metal on metal, phantom warriors in the dun-colored mist. Fitz remembered that old expression—whoever saw a dead cavalryman? They were fine enough for couriers or parades but damn useless when the infantry reached out with their long muskets and emptied saddles. Then he remembered that he had once been a cavalryman years ago.

Fitz made his way to the curb, trying to find a safe haven to collect his thoughts. He watched the horsemen disappear, their backs to him as if he were invisible—not worthy of their attention. He hated them for how they made him feel; he was an outsider, a soldier without an army. When the last of them was lost to the heavy traffic he joined the crowd again. He seethed at the stupidity of it all. He had done right, he had fought and defeated the enemy. He had acted as he should have; as a soldier in command. And for this he was being punished. No, far worse, for this he was being condemned to hell on the Potomac. He was numb to the noise and the crush of people—trying to draw a single breath that did not reek of humanity.

Fitz continued walking under the indifferent gaze of the three- and four-story buildings that towered over the sidewalk. Their narrow, soulless windows watched him fight his way through the crowd, staring at him, as did the other travelers on the creaking board sidewalks. The streets were lined with trees, planted to soften cold brick façades and the barren avenue, and to add dignity to the frantic scene. Now the trees were pitiful, dust-covered sentinels; their dry leaves and spindly limbs long ago dulled to match the surroundings.

Signs suspended over building fronts advertised tailors, haberdashers, doll makers, lawyers, dry goods, firearms, and now, in response to the massive need, uniforms made in short order. But the signs were cheap and garishly painted, like the banners of a battered traveling carnival. They looked as temporary as the stores' occupants—as if they would one day join the trees that lined the avenue.

Gomorrah on the Potomac, Fitz thought as the solid shoulder of a passing workman stunned him. How could anyone live in a city where fresh piles of coarse green horse dung littered the street like nature's cobblestones? It was an affront to a man's sensibilities, to his sense of right and wrong—his sense of smell.

Fitz glanced at Batterman's map. Give me house arrest, he prayed. At least the air is fit to breathe.

He felt a rough tap on his shoulder and turned to see a young lieutenant backed by two large corporals. Provost guard, Fitz knew right off. The crowd flowed around the motionless trio.

"Pardon me, Captain. Your pass, please," the lieutenant said.

"Why me?" Fitz asked, looking around. "There must be a hundred other officers and men within sight."

"Orders, sir. I'm told to check everyone."

"Well, check someone else," Fitz said. "I don't want to be trampled."

"Your pass, Captain," the lieutenant said again.

"All right," Fitz said, pulling the pass from his tunic pocket. "While you're confirming my pass, perhaps you can tell me how to get to the Royal Boarding House. I have a map." He gave the map to the lieutenant. "Now, tell me where I am."

"One moment, sir," the lieutenant said, checking the pass. The young man returned it and took the map from Fitz. After studying the map he said, "The Royal Boarding House is on 20th Street, near Pennsylvania Avenue. This is New York Avenue, sir. You're headed in the wrong direction."

"Trust a civilian to draw a map upside down," Fitz said.

"The map is correct, sir. It looks as if you went left when you left the War Department instead of turning right."

"I know my left from my right, blast you," Fitz said, jerking the map from the young officer's grasp. "Where is Pennsylvania Avenue?"

"That is 18th Street," the lieutenant said, pointing. "Turn right and walk to the second cross street. Turn left and walk two blocks. The boarding house will be on your left." He gave Fitz a perfunctory salute. "Good day, sir."

Fitz followed the young man's directions, sidestepping people as he walked along the board sidewalk. He came to a cross street and darted between lumbering freight wagons stuffed with barrels and boxes, heaped precariously on the sideboards. A courier dashed by, his horse's hooves beating a mad tattoo on the dusty street. Come and gone, Fitz thought, as the horseman wove his way through the traffic and disappeared into the distance. Come and gone like a soldier. *You're not a soldier now,* he told himself; *you're a spy.*

Not yet, blast it! I haven't taken that on yet. I'm a soldier.

Come and gone, like a soldier, he thought. Come and gone like a war. Like this war; over in six months or a year and then it's . . . what? Dishonorably discharged? Prison? Reduced in rank? Perhaps asked to resign. Maybe sent back to the West. *If I'm lucky it will be the plains of the Dakota Territory,* Fitz told himself, *but luck has been as elusive to me as rank.*

He continued walking, careful that he kept track of landmarks so that he wouldn't get lost again. Behind him was the unfinished dome of the Capitol; to his left was the stub of the Washington Monument, shimmering in the distance. He tugged at his uniform collar, trying to force a bit of fresh air in to dry out the sweat. He'd forgotten how much he had hated the steamy heat of the South and wondered if the rank odor that accompanied it came from a nearby open sewer.

What's left to you, Fitz, he asked himself, *if not this proposition?*

I'm not a spy—I'm a soldier, he replied, but the words were weak.

Not now, a voice reminded him. Denied the good graces of Mr. Prescott you're a soldier without an army.

A man shouted behind him and when he turned he heard another. He saw the reason. Several blocks to the southeast, a thick column of smoke curled over the tops of the buildings. Fitz watched it, trying to make sense of the scene. He started toward it, increasing his pace until he ran, keeping his eyes on the billowing mass.

It was white smoke mixed with a dirty brown and it was thick. That meant that it had a good source of fuel at its base. But what? Not the Executive Mansion, it was some distance from that. Something in the canal—a ship of some sort? Supplies piled on the dock?

As he got closer he found himself part of a mob that was both curious and concerned. People were shouting opinions or raising cries of alarm and one man tried to press Fitz for his opinion of what was burning.

Fitz ignored him and raced on. It was close to the President's

Park but west of it, and then Fitz knew: the White Lot. In a large open field within shot of the Executive Mansion was a cavalry remount depot, holding thousands of horses. Surrounded by a white fence to keep thieves out, it had been given the name White Lot. Along the eastern edge of the enclosure was a vast array of stables, smithies' sheds, saddlers, and tack rooms. Throughout the lot were huge stacks of hay for the horses and mules. If one of those had been on fire it would simply be a matter of letting the mass burn itself out. But what Fitz saw as he arrived at the north gate to the lot was much worse. The stables were on fire. Straw burned instantly in thick white columns of smoke but as the flames consumed the buildings they pumped dirty brown smoke into the mix.

Fire jetted a hundred feet into the air, the heat reaching out to strip the breath from Fitz's lungs, but that was not the worst of it. The ultimate horror was the screams of the horses being roasted alive.

Fitz jumped over a low gate and ran to a stable. Its roof was smoldering, on the verge of bursting into flames, when he reached the stalls. A red-haired soldier, hatless and frantic, fumbled with the picket line that tied down a dozen frightened animals in the large open stalls.

Fitz pushed him aside. "Get a knife. You can't untie this with the horses thrashing about."

"I don't have a knife," the soldier said.

"Find one!" As he ran off Fitz dodged a string of frantic kicking horses and found the end of the picket line. It was firmly knotted, twisted through a cast-iron ring. He kicked aside mounds of hay, trying to find something he could use to free the horses. He heard the soldier shouting and tried to find him in the thick smoke.

"Here! Here."

Fitz saw the soldier approach through the thick smoke. He had an axe in his hands. Fitz snatched it from him. "Stand back." He raised it above his head and brought the blunt end down on the ring. The impact stunned him and a sharp pain ran through his hands. No good; he would have to cut the rope, but the horses were racing about so much that they kept the rope taut.

"Go to the other end," he ordered the soldier. "Shoo them in this direction. I've got to have some slack in the rope."

The soldier ran off, and Fitz again swung the axe. The horses screamed in fright but moved toward him as they fought to get away from the new threat.

Fitz watched the rope loosen and fall against the timber holding the hoop. He swung and buried the axe head in the timber, severing the rope. The horses bolted out of the stable, colliding with one another as they twisted to free themselves of the picket rope.

Fitz saw the soldier running toward him. "Come on," he waved. "Let's get the others."

They ran along the line of stables, dodging panic-stricken horses and flaming debris. Other soldiers ran from building to building, trying to save some of the thousands of horses at the remount depot.

Fitz passed a blackened building that still blazed but had to turn his eyes away. Dozens of steaming mounds were scattered about the stalls. He forced the sight from his mind. It was too much to ask an old cavalryman to see something so hideous.

"Up there," Fitz's companion shouted. "There's another."

"Same as before," Fitz called. "Scare them my way." This building was going to be worse. Half the roof was afire and Fitz saw the telltale whips of white smoke snake out of piles of straw. It would burst into flames any moment. He positioned himself next to the pillar and shouted, "Hurry!" He doubted that he could be heard. The agonizing cry of the terrified horses and the hideous crackle of flames filled the air.

He raised the axe, heard the horses stumbling in his direction, and the rope went slack. He drove the axe into the timber, snapping the rope. This time, the horses, frightened by the fire and the men among them, charged at Fitz.

He dove out of the way as the animals thundered past.

Pulling himself to his feet, he searched for the axe. It was gone, either knocked aside as the horses ran by or embedded in some animal's body.

They were gone, though, safe. He trotted away from the burning building, putting as much distance between himself and the blaze as he could. He looked around. The fire was under control in most of the other buildings and all that remained was for the cavalry to collect its frightened mounts.

Fitz retraced his steps to find the red-haired soldier and thank him for his help. He found him, sitting against one of the stable beams. His head was smashed in. Some poor, dumb creature, driven insane with fear, had lashed out at the only target in sight.

He called to some stretcher-bearers, and watched as they swung the body onto the stretcher. They disappeared in the drifting smoke.

As he collected himself, he noticed two men standing near the shattered White Lot fence. They were apart from the crowd, drawn to the disaster, Fitz thought, and—this made no sense—they were watching him. They were an odd duo, one man large and imposing, the other one dwarfed by his companion's size. Bystanders, Fitz thought, but why was he of so much interest? Seemingly satisfied with what they saw, both walked away, with the little one dragging his leg. A cripple. The big man was an ominous character, Fitz decided. Why would this strange pair be watching him? Had they followed him to the White Lot? There would have been no other way to locate him in the smoke and mayhem. *Don't be ridiculous. Why would I be the object of anyone's pursuit?* A cloud of smoke floated over the ground, covering the men's disappearance.

Fitz brushed himself off, found a watering trough, and washed his face and hands as best he could. He thought about the boy who'd helped him, killed by accident. A sad end for a soldier.

As Fitz struck out for the boarding house, he wondered if

the fire was an accident. Southern agents? There were several buildings on fire at one time. But embers floating in the hot wind could just as easily have caused that. Or several men with matches. Conspiracies, Prescott told him. A whole city filled with traitors. Had he seen some of their handiwork?

Chapter 5

The Royal Boarding House
Washington, DC

The tall white columns of the Royal Boarding House glowed with a soft golden color in the dying light of the sun. A modest lawn—obscured by trees, flower-bound trellises, and hedges—separated the house from the mayhem on Pennsylvania Avenue. A rusting wrought iron fence along the edge of the sidewalk provided an additional line of defense. It was a magnificent house and Fitz doubted that he could afford a room here, despite Prescott's comment about reasonable prices.

He twisted the door ringer and waited. The door opened and a small Negro woman of middle years appeared.

"Yes, sir?"

"I'm Captain Dunaway. Mr. Prescott recommended this place."

The woman stepped back. "Yes, sir. He sent word on ahead. I'm Clara. Please come in."

Fitz removed his kepi and entered. He found himself in a broad hallway with a checkerboard marble floor and a gas chandelier suspended over him. To his right was a set of thick wooden doors, heavy with opulence. They were closed. A wide staircase with an elaborately carved newel post stood in front of him. To his left was another set of double doors, open. He could hear male voices and caught a glimpse of several men, obscured by a thin cloud of smoke, lounging on settees and wasp-backed chairs in the day parlor.

"May I take your hat, sir?" Clara asked, holding out her hand.

Caution made Fitz grip his kepi. "Just how much are these rooms?" he asked.

"I don't know, sir. That is a matter for the missus. May I have your hat?"

Fitz hesitated but relinquished his cap. "Have my belongings arrived?"

"No, sir. A boy just brought word that they should be arriving soon. Would you like to meet the other gentlemen?"

"I don't know that I care to meet anyone. I'm not so sure that I'll be staying." He scanned the hallway. "I don't know that I can afford this luxury."

"Yes, sir. Right this way," Clara said, as if she had not heard him.

Fitz followed her into the parlor. The three men in the room looked up. A short, round man with spectacles spoke first.

"Well, well. Another inmate and a boy in blue at that. Hello, Colonel!"

"Captain," Clara replied before Fitz had a chance to. "This is Captain Delaney."

"Dunaway," Fitz corrected her. "Captain Dunaway."

"Excuse me, Captain," Clara said. "I'll be back in a moment to show you to your room."

Fitz was about to stop her when the short man slapped his chest. "Ira Hogan, leather goods. You need anything in leather, I can get it for you. Army and navy contracts. Civilian contracts, too. No need to worry about that captain-colonel business around here, we're all friends. All fellow inmates. We've all come to Washington to help out. Help ourselves while we're at it, too, but you get my meaning."

Hogan's manner irritated Fitz. His thick lower jaw bit upward and he sucked in breath with each word, like a bulldog biting off a hunk of meat.

"Say, you smell a bit smoky. Hanging around the campfires, no doubt. Let's meet everyone, what do you say? That fellow there," Hogan said, "is James Pennbrook. He's a recording clerk at the War Department." Pennbrook, a balding man with a thick beard, smiled.

"Your typical clerk," Hogan continued. "Every government needs them. This government has legions of them, don't you think, Captain? Can't run a good war without an army of clerks. By God, but the city's full of them. That's George Hastings." Hogan pointed to a portly man with a soft red beard. "Claims and Disbursement clerk for the United States Congress. Another clerk, but a congressional one. He could be worth knowing—the army fights the war but Congress controls the purse strings."

"Gentlemen," Fitz said in greeting.

"Our hostess is pursuing her husband again," Hogan continued. "Am I correct, gentlemen? He's quite the gambler and she must care for the man the way that she chases after him. Shame you've missed her—handsome woman. Handsome. Constantly after the man. Can't fathom why. Can you, gentlemen?" He didn't wait for them to answer. "Mysterious, I say, but there you have it. Just because there's a war on needn't mean that business stops." He leaned forward and said confidentially, "Hasn't even slowed business. Matter of fact—it's booming." He stood back. "What's your business in Washington, Captain?"

"My own, Mr. Hogan," Fitz said. "I find it best to keep it that way."

"Now, Captain," Hogan said with a laugh. "Don't take offense. There is more than enough business in Washington to command any man's attention." He winked at Fitz. "More than enough to make a man wealthy. Gold and silver rain from Heaven. Heaven being Capitol Hill, of course. Congress can't stand to have a penny put aside. Can't say that I think the war is a good thing, you understand. Still, it ain't all bad. Mrs. Hogan and the five little Hogans find it so."

"Wealth does not concern me, Mr. Hogan," Fitz said. "If it did, I would have chosen a different profession."

"Hear, hear," Pennbrook said. "Well spoken, Captain."

"Mr. Hogan's world turns on profit," Hastings said.

"Every man profits from something," Hogan said. "There's no use denying that and there's no use for you two to get up on your high horses. You've just not learned how to make your positions pay, that's all. You need to be creative—show enterprise. Seek out opportunity. Am I right, Captain?"

"No."

Hogan was surprised at Fitz's response. "No! Well, bless me. The man's serious. You mean a man can't mix patriotism and gold, Captain? It's done all the time. Every war runs on gold, sir. It's the grease that lubricates the wheels of the government. Nothing wrong with that, is there, sir?"

Clara returned before Fitz was forced to reply. "My room?" he asked her, seeking any excuse to get away from Hogan.

"Follow me, please."

Hogan called as he left the room, "Pleasure, Captain. We'll talk again soon. Get to know one another."

"Is Mr. Hogan always that way?" Fitz asked.

"It's his nature, I reckon," Clara said.

She led the way up the broad stairs to the third floor. The corridor was narrow and dark, and the walls were painted rather than wallpapered. This was the servants' level.

"Here, Captain," Clara said. She unlocked a door on her right and handed the key to Fitz. She stood to one side as he entered.

The still air was laden with heat and stank of cedar. A small bed was pushed against one wall, under a window. A wardrobe stood to the right of the door with a chest of drawers on the far wall. A flowered bowl and pitcher stood on the chest with a blue towel folded next to the bowl. A pan for night soil peeked out from under one leg of the bed. Still, it was better than his quarters at the provost camp. There he'd had a straw mattress suspended on a wooden bed frame by a latticework of poorly tied rope, inhabited by a whole regiment of bugs. His business was taken care of nearly a quarter of a mile away at a bank of latrines. Although the guards were good enough to give him a washbasin, a thick layer of dust from the drill field covered the water at all times.

"This is a small room," Fitz commented. "I trust the rate will reflect the accommodations?"

"It's all we have," Clara said. "Your things should be here directly. I'll have them sent up."

She left, and Fitz forced open the window, hoping to cool the room. The evening brought nothing but a hot, clinging breeze. Faint yellow lights blossomed in windows throughout the city as darkness seeped over the horizon. The noise of the traffic had died down. He pulled his tobacco pouch from his tunic pocket and filled his pipe. Lighting a match and holding it close to his body so that the current of air would not snuff it out, he passed it over the bowl. The harsh, hot taste and the acrid scent of the tobacco were somehow reassuring. They reminded him of the closeness of soldiers' camps: soft music of harmonicas and guitars, the clatter of tin plates being scrubbed with dirt and put away, the wind sighing through the picket ropes, the occasional snap of a tent flap. He drew deeply, looking out the window.

Fitz could have used Will's advice. Which do you think, Will, dishonorably discharged or undertake Prescott's offer? No, he could not ask his friend that—Prescott forbade it. He remembered Lamon's dark eyes questioning everything that he said. *He has no use for me,* Fitz thought. He thought it best to keep that from Will as well.

Good old Will came from one of those families that everyone knew. An ancestor had been one of Washington's staff, and an uncle was at Fort McHenry. The women in the Moore family were all beautiful and the men married well. Mention of the Moore name was enough to gain entry to the finest homes in the East. Solid, dependable, as clear and honest as the western sky. He had a keen mind, too.

Will had helped Fitz at the Academy and now he was helping him again. Captains, especially those under a cloud, do not have appointments with the assistant secretary of war. Unless someone smooths the way for them. Good old Will.

The idea of Will's debt intruded into his thoughts and Fitz shook it out of existence. *He has no cause to think that way,* Fitz told himself. *What's past is past. Will's made good. He's made colonel now and it's I who need his help.*

What happens, Fitz thought, *if Will can no longer help?*

A toy soldier on display. An investigator, like some damn detective, some dark-hearted soul that snoops about other people's business. *I'm a soldier, not an investigator. I belong on the battlefield, not in a barroom. But I'll never get that opportunity unless I do as Prescott suggests.* Fitz rubbed the edge of his lips with the stem of his pipe. When does a suggestion become an order?

Chapter 6

September 15, 1861
The 154th day of the war
The War Department Building
Washington, DC

Fitz left the Royal Boarding House in plenty of time to arrive at the War Department at seven o'clock the next morning. He was careful to search for the landmarks that he had identified on the way to the boarding house. The thought of getting lost again irritated him.

Batterman rose as Fitz entered the assistant secretary's outer office.

"Good morning, Captain," he said. "How did you pass the night?"

"Well enough, thank you."

"Will you have a seat? Mr. Prescott is not in. I'll see if he left your orders on his desk. We had a bit of excitement yesterday, just after you left. There was a horrible fire at the White Lot."

"So I heard." Fitz walked to the tall window instead, too anxious to sit. He didn't want to talk about his experience with the horses, especially with a man he barely knew. He heard the door to Prescott's office close behind him.

Below him 17th Street was strangely quiet and nearly barren of traffic. Then he heard a soft, rhythmic tramp—the sound of hundreds of shoes on the hard-packed dirt street. He recognized it at once, infantry, parade step. He leaned out the open window, straining to see between the interlacing branches of trees. He saw heads and shoulders swaying in unison, the flashes of the newborn sun on musket barrels, the perfect pattern of rank and file. Red fezzes, yellow trim on short blue jackets, and those ridiculous red baggy trousers, Zouaves. Leading the way was the national flag and next to it the regimental flag. A colonel mounted on a splendid-looking charger led the regiment. He was trim with a sharp beard and a calm manner. Well, he looked the soldier all right, Fitz mused, but could he fight? Behind the colonel marched his men by companies.

It made Fitz remember something Will had once quoted from the Bible. "Terrible as an army with banners." Fitz shifted, straining for a better look.

Their feet beat the dust from the street; their legs pumped evenly, one vast, long animal, so complete in purpose and intent that it could not be mistaken for anything else; it was born for battle. A regiment on the march just a stone's throw from him.

He saw himself at the head of his regiment, sitting erect in the saddle, felt the power of the men marching behind him, heard the steady, unyielding cadence, knew that it had to be his.

A soldier or a spy, Fitz? Or first one and then the other?

"Captain Dunaway?"

Batterman had returned.

"Captain Dunaway, I have just a few things to clear up. Would you mind waiting in the hall? The army, you know. Things move slowly even during wartime."

"Mr. Batterman?" Fitz asked before the private secretary disappeared. "How long am I to serve"—he could barely make himself say it—"as an agent?"

Batterman mused over Fitz's question. "How long, eh? I see your dilemma."

Fitz remained silent, watching Batterman consider the issue.

"I'm sure that Mr. Prescott will be satisfied if you serve for six months. I can't foresee the whole adventure taking much longer than that. After that you will be released, with the colonelcy's warrant in hand, to join your comrades."

"Six months?" Fitz asked. Only six months? He couldn't believe it.

"Yes," Batterman said. "Would you be so kind as to wait in the hall?"

Fitz did as he was asked, finding a bench just down from Prescott's office. War Department employees, faceless and nearly formless, brushed past him. They disappeared with a clatter of doors into offices.

He had time to think, waiting on Batterman, and he was surprised to discover that he had made his decision to accept Prescott's proposal, as much as the idea sickened him, on faith. Not that he had faith in Prescott or the government or even in his own ability to get himself out of the mess that he had gotten himself into. Fitz's faith was based on his limited knowledge of but certain conviction in the rightness of Abraham Lincoln. The man's words had found a place in Fitz's soul, not in any religious sense, but because they spoke of a good man in a time when good men were at a premium. It was like, Fitz reasoned with his soldier's mind, riding next to a comrade on campaign and being sure that that man would come to your aid no matter what. It was a feeling that couldn't be identified, it just *was*.

If the country was to have a chance, Fitz was sure, then the man who led it had to be one of confidence and vision. No grand reviews or marching bands, or long-winded speeches. The man who led the country had to be sure of himself and the objective. And what's more, he had to be given a chance. Fair is fair, Fitz thought, and as painful as the notion was that he was to be a spy, some of the sting was taken out of it by the realization that he had an opportunity to help a comrade in arms. Even if that comrade was a politician.

Lincoln deserved a chance, Fitz concluded, and that single notion sustained him while he sat waiting on one of the Four Horsemen to make its appearance.

He saw Will approach.

"Fitz," Will said. "How are you?"

"I haven't decided."

"What?"

"I'm waiting for orders."

"Let's go into my office," Will said, unlocking the door. "I never supposed that there would be this much paperwork and this many meetings. I tell you, Fitz, when I received orders to the War Department, my blood ran cold. Thank God that you don't have to endure this. I've long since given up the notion of getting into the field." Will led Fitz into his office and hung his kepi on a hat rack. "Well?"

"Well?"

"For God's sake, man, don't keep me on tenterhooks. Are you still under arrest?"

"No."

"Thank God. What are you to do?"

Fitz remembered Prescott's admonition—tell no one. "War Department. The White House guard."

"Fine, Fitz," Will said, appearing relieved. "You'll have a chance. Not your regiment, I know, but Prescott has given you an opportunity to prove yourself."

"Yes," Fitz said, feeling that despite Will's happiness, he had made a bargain with the Devil.

"You'll be close to Lamon," Will said. "He is a black-hearted snapping turtle, Fitz. Watch yourself around him. He does not care for anyone who is not a Republican appointee. He will not take well to you being seconded to him by an old public functionary like Mr. Prescott."

"Everyone in Washington seems to be irritated about something. It must be the water. I trust Mr. Prescott is not irritated with you for any particular reason?"

"What?" Will asked. "No. No. But I must tell you, when I went to Mr. Prescott, I was not sure that I could get you out of trouble."

"Perhaps you shouldn't have taken the risk."

Will opened his hands in exasperation. "The men of that

regiment were lucky to have you on the battlefield. You prevented a rout. I want to see you where you belong, at the head of a regiment." His face fell. "It appears, because of the lofty position of my family, that I shall ever remain a staff officer, far from the sound of battle."

Fitz's anger faded away. He felt guilty and humiliated, betrayed by his own temperament. He should never have argued with Will. It was a chance, maybe his last chance, and Will had given it to him. His old friend could have walked away but he had not. *Do what has to be done for six months and then get out. Don't blame Will.* "I'm sorry, Will. Blast it, but I'm hardheaded. You're right. You're right as usual. Blast!"

"Very hardheaded."

"I know that I have a bad temper."

"Are you angry because you lost your temper or because I'm right?"

Fitz grinned, his anger tempered by the truth of the situation—he was still in the army and he still had a chance for his regiment. "Some of both." He held out his hand. "Thank you, Will. I won't disappoint you, you have my word on that."

Will wrapped his hand around Fitz's. "You can thank me, Fitz, by staying out of trouble for the duration of the war."

"I'll go back in the hall to wait for my orders. You look as if you have plenty to do."

"This army runs on papers, Fitz. I'd give my eyeteeth to get out in the field but it would take a miracle. Perhaps I should approach Prescott for a command. You seem to have done well by him."

"Yes," Fitz said, not as certain as his friend.

"Let us try to get together," Will called after Fitz. "We ought to be able to manage a free moment to talk about old times."

Fitz returned to his bench and waited. He consulted his watch impatiently over the next several hours, wondering how long it took Mr. Batterman to act. He kept his mind clear of his situation, concentrating on the bleak hallway and the arrivals and departures of clerks. He was nervous, and he wished for a good night's sleep—but it had been denied him over the past weeks. Every time he lay down to sleep his thoughts raced over his dilemma—first the arrest and now this.

Fitz leaned forward in thought, resting his elbows on his knees, staring at the dark veins that were sewn randomly throughout the gray marble floor. He made designs out of them, his eyes following one until it butted up against another, or splintered into several thin scars. He soon forgot the sound of clerks tramping up and down the hall and the brutal slams of thick wooden doors.

He found one vein, wide and meandering, making its way the length of one of the broad slabs that made up the floor. He decided it was a river. The Platte River.

They were within sight of Fort Laramie, just upstream of the somnambulant Platte, a river that could reach a mile across from bank to bank, but so shallow the running waters barely grazed a horse's belly. Other times it was brash and erratic, narrowing between chasms with its speed charging what had once been a lazy river with all the powers of a torrent.

It was like the West, Fitz had decided when he and Will were both posted to Fort Laramie, three years out of the Point—deceptive and dangerous all at one time.

The river had grown lazy in the heat of a dry August, and Fitz could barely hear the water's murmur over the clatter of the approaching horses. He counted eighteen Cheyenne warriors, and facing them, with Will and himself, were just eight soldiers on horseback.

"Come along with me, Fitz," Will had insisted. "We've been ordered to chastise those savages."

Some cattle had been run off from a passing wagon train, and a lesson was to be taught. Fitz was still a lieutenant, Will a captain beginning his inevitable rapid climb up the ladder while Fitz stumbled from rung to rung. It was the nature of a peacetime army. Except peace was often an elusive commodity on the Platte.

Now they sat, waiting—Will, Fitz, and an ancient corporal named Pennick who favored his bottle more than his stripes—as the Cheyenne, led by a young chief with a cruel face, reined in.

"You're late," Will snapped, his voice booming into the Indians.

Fitz watched them. They were skittish, their eyes darting from soldier to soldier. They knew that they were considered guilty by agreeing to parley.

There was something else that he saw, something that startled him: Will was frightened. As he talked, too loudly, Fitz thought, and with too much disdain, his voice cracked and he stumbled over his words. His attitude increased the Cheyenne's alarm and Fitz watched as they looked at one another. He was about to ask Will if they understood English, when the young captain drove his spurs into his horse's side and bolted forward, next to the chief.

The chief pulled back in surprise and his horse pitched to one side.

"Will," Fitz cautioned, his eyes never leaving the dangerous scene unfolding before him. Will was taking too many liberties with these warriors. He was insulting them—pushing them too far when he should have been treating them as equals. Fitz did not have a chance to say anything more.

It all began slowly, the scene dipped in molasses. Will tried to jerk a carbine out of the chief's hands and as the surprised Indian fought back, it went off.

Fitz heard a flat bang, and saw the blue smoke engulf both Will and his adversary. Everything stopped for a fraction of a second, as if God had commanded that all present gather his senses about him. No one listened to God.

The scene, just a few feet from the listless Platte River, exploded.

One of the Cheyenne pulled a pistol as the chief spun his pony around to put some distance between him and the soldiers. He got off three wild shots, but Fitz saw Will's horse stiffen and collapse.

Fitz pulled his own pistol as Pennick appeared at his side, took aim with his Burnside carbine, and shot an Indian out of the saddle. The other five soldiers came up just as some of the Cheyenne unleashed a volley of arrows. Fitz was on the ground and just handing his reins to Pennick so that he could help Will when he heard a loud grunt.

He looked up to see a quivering arrow jutting out of Pennick's broad forehead. The corporal's arms dropped to his side but his strong thighs instinctively locked around his mount. The horse galloped forward, taking the soldier straight into the enemy.

"Dismount and form around the captain," Fitz shouted, letting go two shots. He knew one of the soldiers would act as horse-holder, so that would give him four men. They each dropped to one knee around the unconscious Will, took aim with their carbines, and fired.

The Cheyenne fell back, using the dust kicked up by their ponies as cover. Fitz slid his pistol into his holster, dug his arms under Will's shoulders, and tugged.

A dozen arrows whipped through the air followed by the crack of firearms.

"Aim," Fitz ordered his tiny command as he strained to pull Will out from under his dead horse. "Keep them back. Take your time." He wrapped his fingers in a handful of uniform fabric and leaned back against Will's weight.

A bullet struck near his foot and he turned to see several braves galloping to the left. "They're flanking us," Fitz warned. He pulled his pistol and fired three shots at the enemy. He knew that he had no chance with a pistol at that distance. "You and you," he ordered the two soldiers on the outside of the shallow arc around Will. "Go out three paces and keep them off our flanks." To the other two, sliding metallic cartridges into their carbines, he said, "Keep them off our front."

*   *   *

Fitz sat up, fighting the battle over in his mind, his thoughts racing about so quickly that his heart beat frantically. He forgot the War Department, Washington, and the marble floor.

He leaned as far back on his heels as he could, struggling with Will, and just barely felt the man's body move. He tightened his grip, throwing his body back so that his weight would counteract that of the downed horse and rider. Will slid a few inches and at the same time he groaned, and suddenly Fitz was flat on his back. He scrambled to his feet to find Will out from under the animal and trying to roll on his side.

An arrow struck the saddle with a hollow thud and Fitz turned to a brave riding at him. He pulled Will's carbine from its boot, pulled back the hammer, and fired.

The horse collapsed, throwing the brave into the dust.

Fitz threw the carbine to the ground, slipped his arm under Will's shoulder, and helped him to his feet.

"Will? Will! For God's sake, pay attention. We're in a tight spot. You've got to walk. Do you hear me?" Fitz wasn't sure if Will heard him or understood; he just dragged the larger man as best he could. "Troop," he ordered, "fall back."

The fort was only a short distance away, but they were separated from it by two hills and a stream that tumbled down to join the Platte near a copse of trees. The garrison should hear the gunfire as it echoed across the nearly flat terrain, but Fitz didn't have time to look for salvation. The Cheyenne were pressing forward, and as he gathered his men and started back he saw why.

The horse-holder lay crumpled on the ground near the bodies of three of the troopers' horses. The other animals were dim shapes in the heavy dust, galloping for the safety of the fort.

Fitz yanked Will's revolver from its holster, trying to keep Will upright. "Spread out," he ordered his men. "Fall back. Take your time." He had a plan. They would seek the cover of the creek bank, using it for protection. By that time help would arrive. Maybe the Cheyenne would grow weary of harassing them.

He saw them gallop back and forth, moving targets on spry ponies—darting in and out of the dust, shooting, pulling away, reloading. Superb horsemen, reins dangling, guiding their mounts with a gentle pressure of knees, drawing an arrow, aiming, firing. It wasn't their fault they hadn't hit the small party of soldiers struggling to reach safety—these men were veterans of the Indian wars, they knew what to do, how to fight, how to survive. And they knew not to be captured.

A trooper shouted in Fitz's ear. "If the lieutenant will take the private's carbine, the private will help the captain a bit."

Fitz released Will and shook the circulation back into his arm. The private handed him a fistful of cartridges and half-carried, half-led Will toward the creek.

Fitz glanced around as he loaded, making sure that they had not left anyone behind, making sure the men were well paced and firing with deliberation. He jammed a cartridge into the breech, closed the carbine, took aim at a distant shadow, and fired. He missed, but the shape pulled back. That's the most they could hope for, he decided; keep them out of range.

He heard the bugle call, distant and tinny, and then the low boom of the fort's gun. It was loaded and fired just three times a day—at reveille, at noon, and at retreat. This time, it was a signal: hold on—we're coming.

The sound of a scattered volley reached them just as he saw the Cheyenne turn and gallop away.

"Cease fire," Fitz ordered. The carbine was almost too heavy to hold.

Major Johansson led the troop that came to their rescue. His fractured English was the butt of jokes in the officers' mess, but Fitz decided then and there he would never say another word against the thick-bodied Swede with white hair.

"Lieutenant Dunaway," Johansson said, looking at the survivors of the action with a critical eye. "What goes here?"

"Cheyenne," Fitz forced from his parched mouth. And

then he spoke the lie that would hide Will's stupidity and ease the captain's rise to higher command. "Captain Moore tried to disarm the chief and all hell broke loose." There. It was said. Two soldiers were dead and a band of hostile Cheyenne would carry the story of the insult back to their tribe so that plodding wagon trains would be targeted for retribution. Will had let arrogance and fear rule his actions and had come close to getting them all killed. But that would never be said.

It was the debt that Will had spoken of and the shame that Fitz carried—because he kept the truth hidden.

The personal secretary appeared, spotted Fitz, and handed him the orders. He also advised him to buy a suit. "That uniform isn't welcome in some parts of the city."

By that time it was nearly eleven thirty. Fitz sat, reading the orders, wondering if this was really the way to regain a command.

Chapter 7

September 18, 1861
The 157th day of the war
Thirty miles North of Washington, DC,
on the Potomac River

Henry Lossing paced in the darkness behind Tom Carling's clapboard house. It was difficult for Lossing to see anything in the night; Carling was too cheap to invest in more than one oil lamp, and he kept it tied to a pole on one end of his ferry. The ferry itself defied description, although most people said it was best to ride it at night; that way you couldn't see that you were taking your life in your hands.

The vessel was as filthy as Carling, stained with manure and tobacco juice, a collection of timbers and planks held together with castoff rope and wooden pegs. But Carling never asked questions and never ventured opinions, so when a stranger wanted to cross in secret, or a parcel had to be delivered to the Virginia side, Tom Carling was your man—for a price.

The thought of money eased Lossing's anxiety. Whaley was tough and smart in his own way. A man who used his fists to negotiate. But Lossing had seen his kind before and was never impressed by their strength or homegrown intelligence. He had led Whaley into a maze and turned him round and round until the big man was too confused to realize that Lossing now had the upper hand.

He walked out from behind the building, spying a pinpoint of light in the darkness. He had convinced Whaley that it took more money to bring his friends up from the South, more than they had originally decided on, and Whaley had agreed. But more importantly, and this fact had surprised Lossing, Whaley had come up with the money. There was a real fortune to be made here. Smuggling medicine out of Washington and across the Potomac on Carling's wretched ferry was barely profitable. This single trip for Whaley was worth ten of the other.

The light grew larger and he could see the indistinct outlines of the ferry rope, the crude wooden barricade that kept cattle from tumbling into the river, and the hunched form of Carling grasping the line and pulling it from bow to stern. It was a tedious occupation. Pull a flat-bottomed scow attached to a thick rope from one side of the river to another. It was the only link to both banks, a wound bit of hemp as thick as a man's arm. Carling grasped the rope, walked back the length of the ferry, and continued the process until the boat's prow nestled into the opposite bank. The perfect pursuit for an unimaginative man.

Lossing didn't see the two men he was expecting. His mouth went dry and he hurried down to the ferry landing, his mind racing through the possibilities. The one he dreaded most was Whaley's reaction if the men had been delayed.

Lossing calmed himself by speculating about how much more money he could squeeze from Whaley. He could come up with a plausible explanation—delays in transport, bribes to be paid to federal officers. He had it all mapped out when he saw two figures emerge behind Carling. He was relieved, but he tried to convince himself he was disappointed; it might have meant more money if it was handled right. He ignored the tiny voice that reminded him that Whaley could be pushed only so far.

"Is that you, Lossing?" Carling shouted, his reedy voice

echoing across the water. He stooped, picked up a coil of rope and, hefting it in one hand to gauge the distance, threw it at Lossing. It unwound gracefully, one end striking near Lossing's feet. "Here, lend a hand and pull us in. My arms are played out."

Lossing was irritated at Carling using his name, and shouting it into the night for all to hear. He wondered what was wrong with the two men on the ferry—couldn't they help? Lossing grasped the rope and pulled. The rough hemp was picking his calfskin gloves, but it was too late for him to do anything about it.

The prow of the ferry struck the bank and while Carling was tying off the vessel, the two men sprang ashore.

There was nothing remarkable about them as far as Lossing could see. One was older than the other, with a neatly trimmed beard. They were both average height, but the younger man was clean-shaven. It looked as if the journey had worn on them both. Their clothes were filthy, frock coats hanging like bags off their shoulders, and their faces were smudged with dirt. He wondered if Whaley would think them worth two thousand dollars.

"I'm Sanderson," the young man said. "This is Dutton."

Dutton glanced at Lossing, too weary to do anything else.

"Do you have a wagon?" Sanderson asked. "We've got some equipment on the ferry. We need a wagon."

"I've got a buckboard," Lossing said. "Over there."

"Will you unload our belongings?" Sanderson asked Carling.

"Nope," Carling said. He pointed at the lantern hanging on the pole. "You got light and three strong backs among you. I got paid to pull the ferry. Turn out the lantern when you're done. Oil's a costly commodity. Good night, gentlemen."

Lossing and the others watched as Carling disappeared into his hovel.

"Let Dutton bring the buckboard up," Sanderson said, walking back to the ferry. "He's got a bad back."

Lossing, disgusted at Carling's abandonment, followed him. "How much do you have?"

"Not much," Sanderson said, handing Lossing several long boxes.

Dutton guided the buckboard down to the edge of the ferry landing. Lossing loaded the boxes in the back while Sanderson carried several small crates up the riverbank. He returned, carrying two carpetbags.

"What is in the crates?" Lossing asked.

Sanderson ignored him, and got into the back of the buckboard, making a seat of the boxes.

Lossing climbed onto the seat, sitting next to Dutton. "Turn around and follow this road out. Once we get to the main road, turn right." He was glad to let Dutton drive; he was tired and didn't feel like making conversation. He'd find out about them soon enough; he'd listen to everything they said and keep what he'd learned until he could use it.

They drove on, Lossing almost succumbing to the gentle pad of the horse's hooves on the hard-packed dirt road and the warm night air. A thought arose, prodding him as they rode, and its existence surprised Henry Lossing. It was about his wife.

It was apparent that she no longer needed him. It didn't matter that he offered her nothing, she had to *need* him. That was what wives did. But she had slipped from his control and was obviously happy in her own way.

Henry Lossing was troubled by the notion even though he seldom cared what his wife did. His only concern up to that point was that she never interfere with his cards. She did not, and he was satisfied. A joint apathy had been established and maintained. Now, things were different.

All thoughts of Asia ceased when the man on horseback appeared.

Lossing was first to see him and grabbed for his pistol. He felt the hammer hang on the lining of his jacket.

"Put it away," Whaley said. He walked his horse to the

wagon, a menacing dark shadow whose hat and shoulders were tainted by a quarter moon. He studied the other two men in the buckboard. "I could have been a regiment of cavalry riding down the road for all the care you took. Who are you?"

"Sanderson," the younger man said. He pointed to the driver. "Dutton."

"You're who I'm lookin' for," Whaley said.

"You scared me to death," Lossing said, trying to appear calm. "What are you doing out here?"

Whaley slid from the saddle and handed the reins to Lossing. "Why don't you ride out about thirty paces so I can have a word with these men?"

Lossing started to protest but changed his mind. Whaley had said nothing about meeting them. What was he doing here?

He climbed off the buckboard and swung into the saddle. Whaley was watching him but he couldn't bring himself to return the look. A voice whispered that Whaley was going to shoot him in the back as he rode ahead. Lossing assured himself that would never happen—he was too important to Whaley. Wasn't he?

He drove his heels into the horse's flank and galloped up the road. When he thought he had gone the prescribed distance, he eased the horse into a walk, congratulating himself on his management of the situation.

He rode on for an hour, never bothering to look back, assured they were following him by the distant creak of the buckboard. He heard a horse whinny and thought it strange that sounds were thrown about randomly in the forest. He was anxious to get back to the city, back to surroundings that made sense and among which he could find comfort.

Lossing heard a horse whinny again and this time the noise came from ahead. Another horse answered, confusing him.

"Hold there, mister."

Three soldiers rode out of the trees and down a shallow

bank to his right. One held a lantern, one had a carbine lying across the pommel of his saddle, and the third man, a corporal, did the talking.

"State your business," the corporal said while the other two took positions on either side of him.

Lossing had his answer ready. "I'm headed to Washington. I came across the river on Tom Carling's ferry not more than two hours ago. You must know Tom?"

"I know that he's not to be trusted," the corporal said. "People out this late are usually up to something. Who are you?"

"Henry Lossing. I'm an attorney. Here. I have a card—" He reached into his vest pocket for his calling card when the soldier with the carbine swung the muzzle of the weapon at Lossing.

"Stay that hand!" the corporal said. He leaned forward and jerked Lossing's pistol out of his pocket, ripping the coat lining.

"I wasn't reaching for the pistol," Lossing said. "I swear. I only carry that for self-defense against road agents."

The corporal turned in his saddle. "Road agents," he said to the soldier with the carbine. "Maybe—"

His face exploded in a spray of blood and tissue and before his lifeless body slid off the horse, the soldier with the carbine dropped the weapon. Lossing heard the flat report of the shot as the soldier clutched at his throat. Blood, black in the darkness, welled between his fingers as he fell back out of the saddle.

The last soldier dropped the lantern and grabbed for his pistol. It was a race with death, and Lossing saw by the look in the young soldier's eyes that he knew he was already dead.

Whaley stepped into the road behind the soldier and raised a carbine as if he had all the time in the world. Lossing watched, transfixed, as Whaley thumbed the hammer back, took aim, and fired.

The young soldier jerked upright as the bullet struck the back of his head and his face disintegrated. His horse, startled by the gunshot and the smell of blood, bolted, throwing the dead soldier into the road next to the corporal.

Whaley pulled the spent cartridge from the carbine and replaced it with a live round. He stepped from soldier to soldier, inspecting the results of his ambush. Ignoring Lossing, he whistled for the others. He motioned Lossing to dismount as the buckboard with Sanderson and Dutton approached.

"I ain't new to this business," Whaley said, sliding the carbine into its boot alongside the saddle. "I know the patrols up here and when they run. I know how much it costs to carry a tick across the river and what the going rate is for a man." He swung into the saddle. "You take those two on in to Washington. Don't ask them no questions. Don't tell them nothin'. And think twice before you try to cheat me again."

Lossing watched as Whaley galloped down the road. Then he vomited.

Chapter 8

Fitz walked to the Royal Boarding House, now feeling more comfortable with the layout of this section of the city, locating landmarks and streets. The scent of fried chicken overwhelmed him as he followed the path up to the front door. He entered to the sound of a spirited conversation and the clatter of serving dishes. He removed his kepi and placed it on a rack in the hallway. Clara greeted him.

"We're just serving supper now, Captain," she said, gesturing down the hallway. "The dining room is this way."

He could hear Hogan's voice dominating the conversation as he approached the dining room. When he entered he noticed two men, other boarders no doubt, whom he had not met last night.

Seated at the head of the table was a woman of striking beauty, her delicate face framed by russet-colored hair. She looked up as Fitz entered and smiled at him. Her exquisite features, and the ease with which her green eyes greeted him, startled him. He felt as awkward and embarrassed as a schoolboy.

"This must be Captain Dunaway," the lady said. Her voice was gentle—the words well formed and evenly delivered. Her mouth was gracious and welcoming, without a hint that she was aware of her impact on him. Her lips creased in a welcoming smile. "I am Asia Lossing."

Fitz bowed, not trusting himself to say more than, "Your servant."

"You've met everyone?" Asia inquired as Fitz took a seat. She indicated the others with a delicate hand.

"Not these two gentlemen," Fitz said.

"Mr. Canfield. Mr. Woodbridge," Asia replied. "Both employees of the government."

"Clerks," Hogan confirmed. "How are you, Captain? Where are you working?"

"The War Department. I start tomorrow," Fitz said as a dish of chicken and dumplings was passed to him.

"War Department?" Hogan asked. "I know some contractors who would like to talk with you. I'll have them stop by tomorrow. They can take you to lunch. Make them take you someplace fancy before you talk. Get to know each other. What do you say, Captain?"

"I say that it will prove unsatisfactory to them, Mr. Hogan. I am assigned to the president's guard."

"Old Abe? Why, by God, man, you can write your own ticket," Hogan said.

"Mr. Hogan," Asia said. "Your language, please."

"Oh, certainly, certainly," Hogan said, anxious to get back to Fitz. "Why, the man's a certified hero. Saved a whole company of soldiers at the White Lot fire just the other day. Heard all about it this morning."

Fitz winced at the distortion. "Your facts are incorrect."

"Are they, Captain Dunaway?" Asia asked. "A modest man in Washington. I'm impressed."

Hogan pursed his lips in appreciation. "Well, that's something. I don't recall her declaring that about any of us."

Asia smiled. "That recollection is correct."

Hogan fell back to a previous subject. "No. No. It was the Rebs all right. And Captain Dunaway there pitched in and did his duty. Ought to give you a medal. You ought to ask after it."

"I will keep that in mind, Mr. Hogan," Fitz said.

Hogan stuck a fork into a dumpling. "Old Abe," he said, his eyes bright with avarice. "Just let me know when. I'll have them right there. Say, Canfield? You're in the War Department, aren't you?"

"Navy Department," Canfield said, savoring a roll. "Steam engines and boilers."

"Well, you can't help me. Unless you can use leather drive belts," Hogan said.

"I have nothing to do with those," Canfield said. "I'm in Accounts."

Hogan leaned forward in interest. "You handle the money, eh?"

"No," Canfield said with no interest in pursuing the conversation. "I calculate numbers. I never see any money and I don't care to see any money."

"Perhaps you know of someone who needs drive belts then," Hogan pushed. "A friend of a friend?" He winked at Fitz. "That's how it's done around here, Captain—somebody who knows somebody. Get to know and be known, I always say. You'd be surprised what you learn. There's profit in knowledge."

"Do you search for profit in everything, Mr. Hogan?" Hastings asked.

"How else do you expect to prosper?" Hogan asked in surprise. He looked around the table. "Am I right, gentlemen?"

"Captain Dunaway," Asia broke in. "You are new to the city?"

"Quite new, Mrs. Lossing," Fitz said. He found her attention to him distracting.

"What do you think of Washington?"

His eyes were drawn to her as he blurted, "I think the man who laid out the streets was drunk."

Asia suppressed a laugh. "That is an interesting observation. My father contended the man was mad. Perhaps he was both. Some years ago it was much easier to get around. Of course, there were fewer people in Washington. Are you regular army or a volunteer?"

Fitz froze. He felt bile rise in his throat. "Mrs. Lossing, I am regular army."

Asia tilted her head like a tiny bird tracking an insect in the reeds. "Do you find the question insulting, Captain?"

"No, Mrs. Lossing. I simply don't want to be taken for a newly minted soldier who doesn't know his left foot from his right."

"I see," Asia said. "Then we can all be certain that you do?"

"Do what?" Fitz asked, wondering what he had missed.

"Know your left foot from your right foot."

Hogan quizzed Canfield. "Little Mac is regular army, isn't he? Just wait until Little Mac gets after the Rebels—then you'll hear some howling. I tell you, Scott was a feeble old man. What's your opinion of Little Mac, Captain?"

"I have no opinion about General McClellan, sir," Fitz said. He glanced at Asia. She was beautiful all right, but quick-tongued, and Fitz vowed to keep his ideas to himself.

"No opinion?" Hogan asked, slapping the table. "A man in Washington without an opinion? That's not natural."

"I find it refreshing, Mr. Hogan," Asia said. "So many of the men I have known took great stock in their opinions, but eventually their opinions proved to be of little consequence."

Hogan whistled. "That was some speech, Mrs. Lossing. If you weren't already spoken for, I'd court you. Beauty, brains, a fine big house, and the owner of a healthy set of darkies."

Fitz saw Asia tense as Clara set an additional basket of bread on the table.

After the servant left, Asia said, "Mr. Hogan. Do not ever again employ that word in this house. I own no one. You must be speaking of my husband's business."

Hogan looked up, wiping crumbs from his mouth. "What?" He glanced at the others. "Oh. The darkies. I didn't mean to excite you, Mrs. Lossing. No offense intended, you know. It's a common enough notion."

"Not in this house. Do you understand me, sir?"

"One hundred percent. No need to tell me something more than seven or eight times," Hogan said, running a piece of bread around his plate to pick up the last morsels of food.

"Did I not see you deep in conversation with Mr. Lossing just the other day?" Canfield asked.

Hogan examined a sliver of chicken. "What? Who, me?"

"Indeed," Canfield said.

"Not I," Hogan said, stuffing the piece into his mouth.

"An earnest conversation," Canfield pressed. "Yes. Yes, I'm sure of it."

"What's your point, man?" Hogan asked.

"Nothing," Canfield defended himself. "But knowing your penchant for dealing—"

"Well," Hogan growled. "It was nothing. You make much too much of it."

Fitz watched Hogan. Why did he reproach Canfield? Was there something more than bluster to this man? He glanced at Asia Lossing. Prescott had advised Fitz to beware of Mr. Lossing. She behaved as if the man did not exist. What was the distance between them? Or was it a feigned circumstance?

Hogan tried to pry a piece of food from between his teeth. He clearly coveted money and seemed to never cease searching for chances to make it. Did he find a companion in the mysterious Mr. Lossing?

Clara entered with a covered dish, set it on the table, and paused next to Asia, whispering in her ear.

Asia Lossing stood. "Excuse me, gentlemen. I shall return shortly."

"A man should always find a way to make money," Hogan said, prodding Fitz as Asia's silk dress brushed the back of his chair.

"There he goes again," Pennbrook said.

Hogan, unwilling to give up his knife and fork, jerked his elbow at Pennbrook.

"Clerks. Pay them no mind."

"You're constantly underestimating the importance of clerks, Mr. Hogan," Pennbrook said. "Do you realize the government would fall and the military cease to function were it not for clerks? Nothing happens that we do not play a role in. Who do you suppose prepares the documents for signature? Who copies and files orders? Who arranges for the transfer of government bonds?"

"Who at this very moment is boring me to death?" Hogan asked.

"Mr. Hogan, clerks are privy to the most intimate details. The knowledge that you value so much—that 'somebody who knows somebody'—is held in the hands of a clerk in some department of government," Pennbrook continued. "Yet we are the unseen and unnoticed. You should have more respect for clerks, Mr. Hogan."

Hogan bowed as grandly as his round belly would allow him. "Mr. Pennbrook, you have my deepest apologies and my assurances that I will never again malign clerks. If nothing else than to avoid another lecture from you."

"Mr. Smithson's collection should not be missed," Hastings spoke, as if he had just found his voice. "Near the canal. You must see the Capitol, although it is undergoing construction."

Fitz needed more information about the city, especially the Island. He knew generally where it was and about its reputation, but he wasn't sure how one made his way to the mysterious place. Or how one returned. "Is there easy transport to the Island?" Fitz asked. He winced at his clumsiness. He should have thought of a better way to inquire.

"Why do you ask about the Island, Captain Dunaway?" Woodbridge asked. It was the first time that he had spoken and his deep voice hung ominously over the table. "Have you acquaintances there?"

"No reason."

"Reason enough, I'm sure," Woodbridge said as an aside to Pennbrook.

"The worst lot of them all on the Island," Canfield offered. "Plug Uglies, murderers, thieves."

"Worse than Swamppoodle," Hastings allowed.

"Secesh run rampant down there, don't they, Mr. Hogan?" Woodbridge asked. "Isn't it rumored that Southern agents make their headquarters on the Island? It is a hotbed of secessionist activities, is it not?"

"Secesh on the Island? Yes, I suppose there are," Hogan said. He caught Woodbridge's point and looked at Fitz. "But they have the run of the entire city, don't they, sir?" he asked, trying to back out of the trap set by Woodbridge. "No harm in the Captain asking, is there, Mr. Woodbridge? Just a fine place to stay away from, Captain. Come with me one day and we'll take a tour of the city."

"What about those men murdered last week?" Pennbrook asked.

"Their throats were cut," Hastings added. "Dumped in the canal."

"Everything is dumped in the canal," Hogan said. "Common laborers, weren't they? Digging bomb-proofs, I heard. Killed for their pay. They should have known better."

"They had families," Hastings chided Hogan. "Be generous to the dead."

"I'm generous to everyone," Hogan chuckled. "Especially me."

Pennbrook and Canfield joined him in laughter.

Clara appeared beside Fitz. "Sir, a package has arrived for you from the tailor. Would you like me to put it in your room?"

"Yes," Fitz said. It was his suit—ready-made or not, it had required some alteration.

"Don't care for my jokes, huh, Captain?" Hogan asked.

"You don't like to spend much time with us, do you, Captain Dunaway?" Woodbridge asked. "Perhaps it's the conversation? Maybe it makes you uncomfortable, talking about Secesh? I, for one, would hang every traitor we were fortunate enough to trap in the city."

"Are you especially familiar with traitors?" Fitz asked. He suspected that Woodbridge wore a cloak of patriotism. But what lay beneath his jabs at Fitz? It was as easy for a scoundrel as for a saint to spout loyal words. But which was Woodbridge?

"I, for one, am interested in your opinion, about the war and General McClellan, Captain Dunaway," Woodbridge said, his voice smooth but insistent—as if he were due an answer to every question he asked. "If for no other reason than to be educated by a professional military man. How soon do you think that we will take Richmond?"

Fitz hesitated. Everyone waited for him to reply. He took a drink of water and brushed his mustache with a napkin. "We won't take Richmond," he said. Here it was, an opportunity. *From now on,* Prescott had said, *you are a bitter and disgruntled officer. Playacting,* Fitz thought. *I am now an actor on a stage*—but in this case a bad performance could be the death of him.

"I think," Fitz continued, "the government was hasty in calling for troops. We don't have the means to wage war against the South. I saw Rebel soldiers not twenty miles from here less than two months ago. They mean to keep on fighting until they win their freedom. Our men ran, sir. They closed the distance from Bull Run to the Capitol in record time." He resumed eating, but he felt the eyes of the others around the table on him. He was ashamed of his words; his men had stood as long as he asked them to.

Woodbridge, red-faced, leaned forward. "I don't quite understand you, sir," he said. "We will not take Richmond? Did I hear correctly? How is it that everyone else in the city is certain we will, and yet you state we will not? It's perplexing, wouldn't you say? I mean, your comment. Perhaps I misunderstood you. How was it intended, sir?"

"Just as it was stated, sir," Fitz said. Even without playacting he knew that he was right and he knew as well that there was no way to explain it to armchair generals and fireplace strategists.

"You imply that the Rebels have every right to fire upon the flag when you speak of their freedom. I see it differently, sir," Woodbridge said, surveying the table for support. "I trust that I am not alone in my feelings. They seized federal property. They fired on Sumter."

"Perhaps it was simply a matter of self-defense," Fitz said, tired of the conversation.

Woodbridge smiled. "Well, I expect as much from a man who was nearly court-martialed for cowardice on the battle-field."

Fitz fought back his rage. "What did you say?" he managed.

Woodbridge caught Canfield's attention, dismissing Fitz. "I heard that Captain Dunaway had to be taken to account by his superior officer for failing to do his duty."

Fitz stood, his lips white with anger, flashing eyes pinned on Woodbridge. "I ought to shoot you like a dog. You are a liar."

Woodbridge climbed to his feet to face Dunaway. "I heard it, sir, from a reliable source. How dare you call me a liar?"

Asia swept into the room. "Gentlemen. I will not allow such talk at my table. And I prefer that we refrain from discussing the war or politics." Hastings held her chair as she bade all be seated. "The former for its volatility, the latter simply because I find it boring."

There were hollow laughs from the others, except for Woodbridge and Fitz, who remained standing.

"There she is, gentlemen. There she is!" Hogan said. "My, but she has spirit, always willing to put a man in his place." He hovered over his plate, smiling at her. "Where, in your opinion, Mrs. Lossing, is the ideal place for a man?"

Asia returned the smile. "Why, under the wheels of a speeding carriage, Mr. Hogan." She kept a close eye on the two men facing one another. They appeared to relax a bit. "Captain Dunaway's opinions may be unusual for an army man but it is my opinion that he demonstrated his character at the White Lot."

Fitz flushed with embarrassment and was on the verge of protesting her unexpected defense of him when he caught sight of her eyes, coyly meeting his.

"I cannot stand the thought of dumb animals suffering," Asia continued, "the male of the species excepted." She threw a glance Hogan's way and was rewarded with good-natured laughter from everyone. "And Captain Dunaway's noble efforts to rescue those poor horses, are, to me"—her gaze never wavered from his direction—"most commendable."

"Well said," Hogan said with a loud laugh. "Anyway," he continued, cutting into his meal, "I don't know a thing about Little Mac. This war may go on for ten or fifteen years. Who am I to have an opinion? I was just talking off the top of my head. Don't know a thing about the army or fighting. Just wanted to throw a skunk on the table."

"What an indelicate comment," Pennbrook sniffed.

"You are not alone in that deficiency, Mr. Hogan," Fitz said. He sat down. This was not the place for a confrontation. "It seems that politicians overwhelm this city. I've seen that. Firsthand."

"You appear to see a great deal," Woodbridge said to Fitz, unwilling to give up the contest. He sat down, convinced that he was the victor. "Perhaps you could enlighten us who are uneducated in the art of warfare? Perhaps you have sufficient reason for such opinions? What is it, Captain? Unfit to command, so you've been left in Washington? Maybe your words were indiscreet and found disfavor among your superiors?" He looked around the table, letting silence bracket his next words. "Maybe you were just a bit reluctant on the battlefield."

Fitz gathered his napkin and laid it next to his plate. "I believe the lady of the house made her position clear on the discussion of politics," he said to Woodbridge. "That is sufficient for me."

"It is hardly sufficient for me, sir. I require an answer. You have little faith in the government, is that it? No faith in the righteousness of our cause, Captain?"

Fitz pushed his chair back. "Mrs. Lossing, I would like to speak with you at your convenience," he said as he stood.

"Now is convenient, Captain Dunaway. Before my boarders come to blows."

"I asked you a question, sir," Woodbridge said. "I would like an answer."

Fitz ignored him and followed Asia.

She led him to a small library across the hall and closed the double doors behind him. Books cluttered shelves that ran from floor to ceiling, except for one wall, which held a large marble fireplace framed by tall cabinets. He realized he was alone with her and awkwardness rushed over him. He stepped back so that he maintained a respectable distance. Still, her presence unnerved him. She was smaller than he had realized and very slender, but her manner was strong-willed.

"Yes, Captain?"

"I will take my meals in my room from now on," he said, his words delivered as an order instead of a request. He realized it was a mistake but he made no move to apologize.

"Indeed?" Asia asked, apparently unimpressed by his command.

"Yes. I was also not told the cost of my lodging."

"It is $7.50 a week."

"What—$7.50 a week!" Fitz said. "I did not intend to buy the house, Mrs. Lossing, merely to occupy one room."

"Captain Dunaway, full board in the better houses in the city runs from $5.00 to $25.00 a week. My charges are quite reasonable. There will also be an additional charge for your meals to be carried to your room."

"I beg your pardon?"

"Your hearing is not somehow damaged, is it, Captain Dunaway?"

"It is not."

"Nor your eyesight, I trust?"

"Both function perfectly," Fitz said.

"Your limbs as well. Which is to say it won't be necessary for us to have you carried to your room?"

"Mrs. Lossing, I—"

"Since I find that I am repeating myself, I was curious to compile an inventory of your infirmities before this transaction went any further. I require an additional $2.50 a week for your meals to be delivered."

"In that case," Fitz said, reluctant to concede defeat, "I will dine at the table."

"An excellent decision," Asia said. "One other thing, Captain Dunaway—I don't know what your circumstances are, but I recommend that you keep your somewhat unusual opinions to yourself. Washington is a city of talk. It is the coin of the realm. Words carry forward long after they are given birth and they become distorted beyond recognition—"

"Mrs. Lossing, I assure you —"

"Your assurances are unnecessary and unsolicited, Captain. I recommend that you carefully consider what you say and in whose company you say it. Your comments may be considered inappropriate by some."

She grasped the doorknob, but waited. Fitz knew she expected a response.

"I say what I think, Mrs. Lossing. I am prepared for the consequences."

Asia said, "I hope that you are, Captain Dunaway, but I fear that you do not realize the true nature of these most unsettling times."

Fitz thought of his situation. "I am more than aware of the times, Mrs. Lossing."

"That pleases me, Captain Dunaway, for I should hate to have to ask you to leave. Of course, I would have no trouble finding another boarder—they are as common around town as fleas on a dog—but I hate to be annoyed with it."

"Fleas on a dog, Mrs. Lossing? I hope that you were not implying that I am a pest?"

"I meant that only as an example, Captain. No offense intended to the dog or fleas."

"I suspect that I come someplace between the two," Fitz said.

"Do you, Captain?"

He felt challenged by her. "Mrs. Lossing, surely you are not one of those women who insist on having the last word?"

"Why, Captain Dunaway," Asia said as if speaking to a child, "how could you possibly imagine that?"

"It is more than my imagination."

"I have some difficulty imagining a more lively imagination."

"You misunderstand what I say!"

"Do I?" She fanned herself with her hand. "Dear me, it must be my poor female brain. I do sometimes fail to comprehend what men think that they are saying."

Fitz felt himself flush as he struggled to keep his irritation under control. What a contemptible woman! Her arrogance was astounding, even more so as she waited for him to speak. "Mrs. Lossing," Fitz said. "It is unbecoming of you to make a contest out of this conversation."

"Oh, Captain," she said. "You needn't worry. Bantering with you is no contest at all. Good evening."

Chapter 9

September 20, 1861
The 159th day of the war
The War Department Building

The next day, Colonel Cornell, a soft-bodied man with jowls, scanned the orders. He was a desk-bound officer, Fitz decided, overwhelmed with anything that fell outside of regulations.

Around him Fitz could hear the frantic scratching of pens and a hurricane of rustling papers accompanied by the low voices of clerks and soldiers. The room was crammed with desks and file cabinets, all arranged in some futile attempt to force order over the turmoil.

"You must be important, Captain," Cornell said.

"Orders, sir," Fitz returned.

Cornell did not try to hide his disgust. "From the assistant secretary of war? Come with me."

Fitz followed the colonel out of the large office, down the broad central hall, and up the iron staircase to the second floor. The hallway was dark and dingy, and smelled of mildew.

Cornell led him along a corridor. Paint feathered off the walls on either side, and the woodwork was stained black by coal smoke. Oil lamps hung overhead, their glass chimneys black with soot. The floor creaked with each footstep and the passing door panels were grimy with the press of a thousand hands.

"In here," Cornell ordered, leading Fitz through a tall doorway.

They entered a large room with an arched ceiling. Windows, equal to those on the first floor, lined one wall, but they were dulled with a layer of dust and smoke. In the center of the room were a dozen or so desks arranged in two equal rows. Along the opposite walls were bookshelves stuffed with ledgers, piles of papers, gun models, and books. At the far end of the large room sat a round, fleshy-faced officer with white hair and piercing eyes: General Winfield Scott.

Cornell stopped at a respectful distance. "Sir, here is Captain Dunaway."

The ancient officer looked up and brushed away a clerk who was at his elbow.

"Why should I care about Captain Dunaway, Colonel?"

"Orders, sir. From Assistant Secretary of War Prescott."

Scott's watery eyes swept over Fitz.

Cornell explained. "He's assigned to the president's guard, sir."

"Eh?" Scott snorted. "Put him to it, then. That should suit everyone." His unyielding stare bore into Fitz. "Let me be plain about this, Captain. If I find you lacking in any way, I'll send you back to that old fox. The president shall and will be protected."

Fitz straightened. "I'll do as ordered, sir."

"See that you do. Take him away, Colonel. I'll waste no more time on him."

Cornell turned Fitz over to a bored sergeant, who led Fitz back into the hallway, down an iron staircase, and onto the first floor. Halfway down the hall the sergeant turned to Fitz and announced, "This is your office, sir. I'll have duty sheets and daily schedules brought around to you."

"What am I to do with them?"

"Review them, sir," the sergeant replied, as if it should have been obvious. "They contain sentry duties at the White

House, patrol schedules of the President's Park, an account-
ing of the president's travels including his comings and goings—but I wouldn't count on that too much, Old Abe has a
mind of his own when he decides to light out."

The sergeant produced a key, unlocked the door, and forced
it open. A thin cloud of dust, jarred loose by the door's movement, surrounded them. He handed the key to Fitz. "Most of
the daily business is routine, sir. You shouldn't have any trouble."

Fitz watched the sergeant disappear down the empty hallway. "Routine," he said. He entered the small room. A thin
light filtered in through a small dirt-caked window near the
ceiling. In the center of the office was a desk on which sat an
ancient oil lamp. A tattered leather chair that tilted to one
side was the only other object in the room. Fitz held the lamp
up, and finding there was oil in it, removed the globe, adjusted
the wick, and lit it. A weak yellow glow filled the room. Fitz
looked at the tiny window above his head. Cobwebs flowed
from its corners, and two of the glass panes were separated
from the lead casing.

"If I drag the desk to the wall, I can climb up and throw
myself out of the window," he said.

"Sir?"

A corporal, bearing a large stack of papers, stood behind
him.

"Did you say something, sir?"

"No. What is it?"

The corporal set the papers on the desk. "These are the
day's reports, sir. Colonel Cornell says that you are to review
them. Each report is to have your signature. The signature
certifies that it has been reviewed and accepted by you. When
you have finished with them, they go to the colonel."

The stack was twelve inches high. "I'm to read all of that?"

"Yes, sir," the corporal said. "Today." He looked around
the room. "I'll talk with the quartermaster clerk about a cabinet, sir, although they're hard to come by. The war, you
know."

"Yes," Fitz mumbled. "God forbid that we run short of cabinets and feather dusters."

"I'll have an inkwell, pens, and nibs to you shortly, sir. You'll need a pounce box. We're running very low on bone so you might have to use sand."

"Yes," Fitz said. He was suddenly aware of the distant sound of hammering followed by a low rumbling. "What in the world is that ungodly clatter?"

"The bomb-proof, sir," the corporal said. "We've all gotten used to that noise. You'd think as long as they've been working on it they'd have one large enough to hold a regiment. But bomb-proofs ain't none of my business, sir."

The corporal went over a list of items that he would need, but Fitz did not hear him. He stared at the stack of papers and damned himself for believing Prescott. He could almost hear Will's voice: *patience, Fitz, patience.*

Fitz spent nearly two hours reviewing the reports before deciding he was wasting his time. The papers contained nothing of consequence—guards were replaced, President Lincoln visited Mr. Seward, Mr. Chase visited the president, an emissary from the King of the Belgiums accompanied the president to the Navy Yard. Fitz threw the papers on his desk and stood, kicking his chair into the corner in frustration.

What madness was this? An account of the comings and goings of men he had never heard of and cared nothing about. Was this how he was supposed to protect the president? Was this what a spy did? Fitz cursed himself for his stupidity and fled the office. He heard the sound of laughter and a curious clicking just down the hall. He was drawn to the sound, thinking that at least he would find companionship. He knew he was feeling sorry for himself, and the realization did not help his mood. He felt abandoned and betrayed, but he knew that he was responsible for his own condition. A sign above an open door identified the room as the Telegraph Office and a burst of laughter greeted Fitz as he entered. There were four or five young soldiers at desks cluttered with message pads and papers. Two clerks manned desks at the other wall, busy consulting what Fitz knew were codebooks. Three other men were seated around a small table, drinking coffee, sharing a communal ashtray, and listening intently to a long-legged man with a beard.

President Lincoln sat just a few feet from Fitz, leaning back in a chair, thumbs hooked in his vest. He was tall, as tall as everyone said, and when he wanted to emphasize a point in his story, he would detach his thumb from his vest and sweep the air with his big hand. Fitz thought it odd that his voice was high-pitched, not shrill or unpleasant, but clear and confident. Fitz smiled as the president spoke; he was from the West all right. He plucked the *g* off the end of any word with *ing* trailing it, and his speech was littered with easy homilies Fitz hadn't heard in years.

"It seems there was this old country church," Lincoln said, rubbing his nose. "And this preacher was givin' a hot sermon. All fire and brimstone. On and on he went. The subject of his sermon was the many faults of mankind and men. 'Now, in all history,' the preacher shouts, 'there ain't been but one perfect man.' " Lincoln slapped his hands together like a clap of thunder. " 'And that man was Jesus Christ himself.' The crowd hollers 'amen' and 'hallelujah,' and everybody feels the spirit of the Lord." Lincoln leaned forward and lowered his voice, drawing his audience in. "The preacher could have stopped there, you know, but like all good preachers, he just loved to hear good preachers preach and he figured that he was one of the best. 'And,' he says, 'cause the spirit of the Lord moved him, 'there ain't no account of no perfect womin anywhere in the Good Book or in history.' 'Amen, hallelujah,' everyone in the church house shouts, stampin' their feet and clappin' their hands. But in the back of the church house, in the way-back pews assigned to sinners and backsliders, this old country womin stands up."

He looked from soldier to soldier, enlisting their help. "You've seen the type before, ain't you? Broad as a river with a face like hickory and hands as hard as a persimmon?

'Preacher,' she says with a voice like a hard rain, 'yer wrong. I knowed of a perfect womin and I heared about her every day for the last six years.' "

Lincoln drew back, his face wreathed in surprise. " 'Who is she?' " he asked, becoming the preacher. " 'Who is this remarkable womin?' "

He let the question hang for a moment. "The old womin looks down at the fella sittin' next to her and says, 'My husband's first wife.' "

The group burst into raucous laughter, Lincoln loudest of all. Fitz found himself laughing as well.

"Well," Lincoln said, when he saw Fitz. "Who's this? Advance and be recognized."

Fitz snapped to attention and saluted. "Captain Thomas Fitzgerald Dunaway, sir."

"At ease, Dunaway," Lincoln said. "We don't stand on formalities around here, do we, boys?"

The men in the room laughed again.

"I'm Lincoln and I suppose you'll git to know these fellas after a while. What's your function here?"

"I'm a member of your guard, sir," Fitz replied, relaxing. Something about Lincoln made him feel comfortable in his presence, despite the fact the man seated before him was his commander in chief. Lincoln's gray eyes were warm and kind and they seemed to brighten when he smiled. They were deep with intelligence as well, filled with knowledge.

"Guard?" Lincoln laughed. "Now, I ask you, Dunaway, who'd want to harm an old boy such as me?"

"Many people, sir," Dunaway said, feeling protective of this unusual man.

"Well," Lincoln said, winking at one of the telegraph officers, "I don't see much danger in that. I've got Hill lookin' out for me and he's big enough to stop a cannonball and there's old Ginral Scott"—his hand swept the room—"and these fellas here. But, I never liked to interfere with a man's work so you carry on with guardin'. Just don't git crossways with Mrs. Lincoln. She can be a hard case." He slapped his broad hands together and stood, towering over the others. "Ginnalmin, duty calls." He approached Fitz and stuck out his hand. Fitz took it and winced at Lincoln's powerful grip. The president pumped his hand. "Dunaway, walk along to the house. We'll talk a bit."

"Yes, sir," Fitz said, stunned. He was about to mention he should inform his superiors he was leaving his post at the behest of his commander in chief, but the president's long legs were already carrying him to the door.

Fitz caught up with him and saw Lincoln pull a pocketknife and a piece of pine from his pocket. He ran the blade over the wood, carving tiny slivers. His head was down in thought and Fitz wondered if the president remembered that he accompanied him.

"Where are your people, Captain?" the president asked, turning the wood back and forth to inspect his work.

"Tennessee, sir," Fitz said.

Lincoln replied. "What do they think of all this?"

"Where I was born, in East Tennessee, they're nearly all Union men."

"That's what I've heard," Lincoln said, shaving a few more slivers from the pine. "When'd you join up?"

Fitz forgot to be cross at the assumption that he was a volunteer. "I'm regular army, sir."

"Is that why you remained in the army, then? Your people being Union men?"

"I took an oath, sir," Fitz said.

"Well, I did, too," Lincoln said and then fell back to whittling. "Say, Captain, you and I have something in common. I was a captain, too. In the Blackhawk War. It wasn't much of a war and I sure wasn't much of a captain. Couldn't handle my boys. Too good-natured, I suppose." He laughed at the memory. "My colonel, he got disgusted at me. Took away my saber and gave me a wooden sword. Said that was all I deserved. I was mortified. Especially since the company had elected me their captain."

"Sometimes, the task can be taxing, sir," Fitz admitted.

"Were you at this latest set-to?"

"I was," Fitz said, adding, "sir."

"Our boys got whooped. Pretty badly, they say. Old General Scott"—it was "Ginral" again—"he said I should have waited before we tangled with them. I guess I don't know much about soldierin', Captain. I figured we were about even, the Rebs and us."

"Yes, sir," Fitz said. "All we needed was some gumption."

Lincoln laughed, his high voice carrying over the dry lawns of the President's Park. "Gumption. That's just what we needed, I suppose. Well, we can issue ball and powder, Captain Dunaway, but a man's got to come equipped with his own gumption."

"Yes, sir. I think so as well."

Lincoln stopped and slid his knife in his vest pocket and tossed the pine to the ground. "You know, Captain. I'm mighty slow to set my foot down, but when I do I'm not likely to move it again. This is the biggest case I've ever pleaded and I mean to give it my all."

Fitz listened as he saw sadness slide its dark fingers around the tall man.

"I'm for the Union and keeping the Union and that's all there is. What I need are a few men to stick with me on this, no matter what. The end will see us out all right, if I can keep a few such men around me."

"Men with gumption," Fitz said.

"Gumption, yes. Determination. Resolution. The kind of men who look like they could drive their heads through a brick wall and mean to do it."

This time Fitz laughed. "I've a friend of mine who says my head is hard enough to do it." Will.

President Lincoln held out his hand, fingers extended, broad palm scarred and weathered. Fitz felt his hand swallowed by the president's.

"There we are, Captain Dunaway. We've made an agreement. You do what you have to, and I'll do my part." His gray eyes crinkled as he smiled. "Between the two of us, we might just lick the Rebs yet."

"Yes, sir."

"Well, sir," Lincoln said. "I'd best be getting up to the house. Mary has some shindig or other set up and she gits a bit sharp when I ain't on time. Come up and visit a spell when you git a chance, Dunaway. Meet my boys, Willie and Tad. They're a handful, all right, but I wouldn't take a dime for either one of them."

"Thank you, sir," Fitz said, as Lincoln turned and continued his journey. "I will."

Fitz was now struck by something that he had not noticed. The president's shoulders were slumped as if he bore the weight of the nation on his back. And then he realized that this plodding man with his long arms hanging at his sides did carry the responsibility of not only the North but the South as well. Fitz felt his eyes soften at the notion that a single soul would be so tested by circumstances, and vowed that he would stand by this strange man. It was then that Fitz knew his work as the president's spy, no matter how distasteful it was to him, was the most important thing he would ever do.

Chapter 10

October 4, 1861
The 173rd day of the war
The Royal Boarding House

Fitz swung open the gate to the boarding house and trudged up the narrow gravel walkway as he had each day for nearly three weeks. Somehow, entering the modest grounds isolated him from the noise and confusion on the street. He was convinced that it could be nothing more than an illusion, because the cacophony was too great and the grounds far too tiny to provide protection. He decided to sit for a while in the gazebo nestled between some hedges and a clump of small trees, to smoke his pipe and gather his thoughts. The tedium of the assignment was robbing him of enthusiasm. He wanted to protect the president; he wanted to do his duty, but all he had done for the past week was sign reports. *Is this how I am to serve out the war?* he asked himself. But there was no answer, only an accusing silence.

He filled his pipe, taking a moment to approve of the cool evening with the soft rays of the sun burnishing the shrubbery. The weather was between autumn and winter, between harmony and hardship. It was a period, like spring, when Fitz was most at ease with life. It was still too warm in the city for his taste, and the air was fat with humidity. But as the sun settled, the cool air, a teasing of the winter ahead, would descend. He looked down. The ground was covered by dry leaves that whispered as his boots brushed over them, "winter is coming."

Fitz saw Asia Lossing, a maroon shawl covering her shoulders, sitting in the gazebo. She smiled at him.

"Captain Dunaway. What a pleasant surprise. Won't you join me?"

"I didn't mean to intrude, Mrs. Lossing," Fitz said. "I only thought to have a pipe before dinner."

She indicated a bench next to hers. "Have it with me."

Fitz joined her, unable to find a logical excuse to decline. He wanted only to be alone with his misery. It might be self-pity, he thought, but if it was, so be it. As he sat down he was startled to see that she held a tumbler in her left hand and a cigar in her right. The material of her dress nearly obscured a bottle of whiskey sitting at her feet.

"My method of relaxing," she said, noting his glance. "Father and I used to share a glass and a cigar before supper. It clears the mind. And the palate."

Fitz lit his pipe and drew. He was nearly out of tobacco.

"You seem distressed, Captain."

"Not at all."

Asia took a sip of whiskey and smiled. "You're a poor liar. Our city doesn't agree with you. I was born here, and I find it taxing. Now, especially. In a matter of months Washington has gone from a village to a city."

Fitz studied his pipe. He wondered if he should question her, and then grew concerned his attempts to learn more about her and her boarders would be all too transparent. *"You don't have a devious bone in your body, Fitz,"* an uncle had once commented to him. *"And that makes you ill suited for life."*

Are you a Rebel? he thought to ask, taunting himself. *Is your house full of spies? Where do your sympathies lie?* He gave it up as a lost cause and decided instead to listen. Surely someone would say something that he could latch onto. *Oh,*

Mr. Prescott, Fitz chided, *you made yourself a bad bargain with this spy.*

"Not so long ago you had to be careful of geese or pigs in the streets," Asia said. "Now one runs the danger of being crushed by caissons. Where is your home, Captain?"

"The army is my home, madam."

His answer amused her. "Of course it is. I mean, where were you born?"

"Tennessee."

"Is your father a military man?"

"A farmer."

"Really? My father was a lawyer." She looked over her shoulder. "He left me this house. All it lacks is the sound of children." She traced the edge of the glass with her fingertips. "My husband and I were never that fortunate. He is an attorney as well. He and my father were once partners. Long ago." She spoke in fond remembrance. "Proud and influential my father was. A scoundrel at times but an honest one. There are so few like him. He loved to have a good time. He loved to laugh. I am fortunate to have the same qualities. In life one needs to cultivate a sense of humor."

"I suppose that is true," Fitz agreed.

"I noticed—" Asia said, sending a cloud of smoke into the air and watching it dissipate in the mild breeze, "you devouring the newspapers. It's the war news, isn't it?"

"Yes."

"I thought you to be a man who is not interested in the course of the war."

"I did not say that I wasn't interested in the news, Mrs. Lossing. It is just that my interests differ from those of others. Call it a professional interest," Fitz said, edging away from the despair that he felt. Devoured the newspaper, he had done that all right. Every scrap of news, every sly hint about where the army was going, who was commanding what regiment, what was happening in the war, every word taunted him. Every word reminded him that he was far from the battlefield and that the war was moving as inevitably as thunderclouds across a summer's sky.

"No offense intended, of course."

"Of course."

"How have you been getting on with Mr. Woodbridge?" Asia asked. She was serious but Fitz caught the playfulness in her voice.

"I keep my distance."

"A sensible approach to the situation."

Fitz was struck by the comment. "Mrs. Lossing, that is probably the first time in my life that anyone has called anything that I did 'sensible.' "

Asia poured herself another drink. "Were you, by any chance, given sour milk as a child?"

Fitz coughed as a burst of smoke forced itself down his throat.

"I'm sorry," she said, but she did not try to hide her smile.

"I would take more comfort in your words if they were sincerely delivered."

Asia never had a chance to answer. A man Fitz had never seen before appeared in the doorway.

"What's this?" Henry Lossing asked, leaning against the edge of the gazebo. "My wife keeping company with another man?"

Fitz stood. Lossing was drunk, or close to it, and his words, meant to sound playful, had an edge to them. He was hatless and the black hair that fell over his forehead needed a good washing. He looked ill, but it could have been the pallor of his skin—that of a man who got too little sunshine and just minutes of sleep. He had probably been handsome at one time, but he had traded his good looks for the freedom to pursue his interests. Interests, Fitz concluded, that were robbing him of his health.

"Captain Dunaway," Asia said, "my husband, Henry Lossing."

Lossing's smile hardened. "My dear," he greeted his wife. He nodded at Fitz. "Captain Dunaway."

"Sir," Fitz said.

"Are you home for supper?" Asia asked. Her manner was polite.

"Why else would I return?" Lossing asked. "Oh, sit down, Captain. I'm not going to challenge you to a duel for my wife's affection." He looked at Asia. "That won't be necessary, will it, dear?"

Her cheeks reddened with emotion. "Clara should have supper ready," Asia said.

"Then I will adjourn to the house," Lossing said. He was about to leave but stopped. "Is Mr. Hogan about?"

"This is his time to return," Asia said. "He is very punctual where his stomach is concerned. Why do you ask?"

"Business, my dear," Lossing said. "Always business."

Asia said, "Then I won't detain you."

Lossing bowed to Fitz. "Your servant, sir," he said in a mocking tone and then smiled at Asia. "A role that I am quite used to."

Henry Lossing followed the gravel pathway to the house, undid the buttons on his vest, and entered his room. Throwing his coat on the bed and pouring a generous amount of whiskey in a tumbler, he saw the soldier and his wife sitting side by side. He savored the whiskey, vest thrown open, hand gripping the glass so tightly that his knuckles turned white. Jealousy burned into his soul as he relived the scene.

The Union officer had an interest in Asia.

Men had approached Lossing's wife before, stout men with thick gray mustaches who sought the excitement of their youth. And Asia was well known in Washington; the best hostesses often invited her because she was charming and bright, and her father had been one of the leading attorneys in town. Men sought her company at parties and dinners, and Henry watched as these pathetic men yearned for some indication that Asia Lossing found them interesting. She was polite. She never offered more than that.

But this captain, Dunaway. Henry watched Asia's eyes sparkle as Dunaway spoke and knew that Asia Lossing was, for the first time, being more than polite.

After Lossing left, silence fell over Fitz and Asia.

"Perhaps I should go as well," Fitz said.

"Captain," Asia began, troubled. He could tell that she wanted to explain, perhaps apologize, but she was torn. "Sit down and finish your pipe."

He felt stupid, knowing that he could not comfort her. "My intention was not to trouble you."

"Captain Dunaway," she said, raising her hand to stop him. "My husband is not happy. I am the cause of his unhappiness, not because of what I have done, but because of what I did not do."

Fitz concentrated on his pipe.

Asia shook her head in resignation. Fitz could see that regrets plagued her, but he was unsure of what to say. He found it surprising that a woman as lovely as Asia Lossing should be troubled by anything and he wondered about the cryptic accusations issued by her husband.

"Henry," she said, committing herself to an explanation, "is weak. What I saw in him, when we first met, was a man as fun and charismatic as my father. As time passed, another man was revealed. I could have helped him, I suppose, but I did nothing but find fault. I was horrified to learn, after several years of marriage, that I had become a shrew. Confronting one's true nature is unpleasant."

Fitz knocked the ashes from his pipe and rose. "Mrs. Lossing, I know nothing of such matters. I do believe that courage comes in all shapes and sizes. It takes courage to address those qualities in ourselves that we despise. And it is cowardice to flee from them."

Asia stood, examining Fitz with appreciation. "Why, Captain Dunaway," she said with a smile. "I do believe the heart of a philosopher beats in your bosom."

Fitz declined the compliment. "Mrs. Lossing, nothing

could be further from the truth. I am a soldier, first and fore-most." He held up his pipe. "And I am also out of tobacco."

She glanced at the sky. "It should be time for supper. Let's go in."

They joined the others in the hallway, preparing for supper. Fitz could tell by their manner that the other boarders were growing wary of him. He had been cold and abrupt, prefer-ring to steer clear of friendships or acquaintances. He seldom discussed the war, cutting off any attempts to solicit his opin-ion on military operations. That did nothing but arouse an undefined suspicion of him by the others. The only one who found no fault in his position was Hogan. Fitz suspected that Hogan would embrace the Devil himself were it to his advan-tage.

"Is there a tobacconist nearby?" Fitz asked Asia as they entered the dining room.

"Yes, just two blocks down. Shall I send Frederick to fetch you some tobacco?"

"No," Fitz said. "Don't trouble yourself. I can use a walk. Is the store open this late?"

"The owner is a Scotsman, Captain," Asia said. "He does-n't close until the last penny has been squeezed from the last customer. Excuse me. I'll see to the meal. When you leave the front door, turn left and walk two blocks."

"Madam?"

"The tobacconist, Captain Dunaway. That is where you are bound for, is it not? Turn left, walk two blocks, and he is on the left. I don't mean to be curt, sir, but I have a great deal to attend to. Enjoy the evening, sir." She disappeared down the hall.

"Good night," Fitz said, opening the front door. As he drew it closed, he noticed Woodbridge watching him from the edge of the staircase. Fitz could read the loathing on the man's face. There was trouble there, no doubt about it.

"Going out, Captain?" Woodbridge asked, advancing. "You'll miss a delicious supper, I'm sure."

"Yes," Fitz said. "For tobacco. I've an indifferent appetite in any case."

"Well," Woodbridge said. "Have a pleasant walk but I would remember about the dangers of the city if I were you."

"There is danger everywhere, isn't there, Mr. Woodbridge?" Fitz asked. "By your leave."

Fitz rolled troubling questions over in his mind as he walked down the street. The sun was loath to give up the day, but darkness pooled around buildings and seeped into the street. Prescott had told him that the Island reeked of Secesh, but traitors could be anywhere in the city; surely Prescott knew that as well. Of course he did, Fitz reminded himself; Prescott had said, "Start with the boarding house." What about Prescott's other agents? Perhaps they were already doing their job, making it known that Fitz was disloyal. Woodbridge? Was he a true Unionist? He played the patriot readily enough, but that did not make it so.

What about Hogan? The man saw nothing but money in every opportunity. He was privy to secrets as a contractor and he wasn't an ethical man.

Fitz grew frustrated. Suppose none of this was true and nothing would come of his efforts? Suppose he was seen as nothing more than an embittered officer? Suppose Prescott's agents were a band of bumbling incompetents? Fitz had seen his share of that type in the city.

He decided nothing would come of it until he made his way to the Island, and he could not make himself go, just yet. Perhaps it was donning civilian clothing. *My own traitor's cloak,* Fitz decided, his new suit. Go to the Island in uniform and risk being torn to pieces. Go as a civilian—well, the danger was less, more so if the inhabitants of that hell on the Eastern Branch believed him to be harmless. That was the true gauntlet. *You have your suit,* he told himself, *now you can go to the Island. Yes,* he thought, *I have my lovely black suit. Just in time to be buried in it.*

* * *

He found the tobacconist shop and went in. A cloud of warm, exotic aromas greeted him. The proprietor, a small Scot with sharp, black eyes and a cautious nature, approached him.

"I'm Baird," he said, the words heavy with a thick brogue. "The importer of the finest tobacco in the world. What will you have?"

Fitz pulled his pipe from his pocket, tapped it free of ashes into an ashtray on a wooden counter, and studied the large glass jars filled with tobacco. Only two men were in the store—a tall man hovering near the cigar case and a man who looked to be eighty rubbing his chin in thought over a stack of snuff tins.

"Some of this if you don't mind," Fitz said, pointing to a jar.

Baird took the pipe from Fitz, removed the jar lid, and pushed a pinch of tobacco that barely covered the bottom of the bowl into the pipe.

Fitz looked at Baird. "It's difficult to judge the quality of a blend when there's so little to smoke."

"Ah, but you look like a discriminating man with a ready mind. You'll have no trouble choosing, I'm sure," Baird said. "Enjoy that while I go help the unfortunate Mr. Conover find a tin of snuff right beneath his nose."

Fitz struck a match and lit his pipe as Baird shuffled off. He waved the match out and looked around the small shop. A case of pipes drew his attention as the door opened and another man entered. He looked them over, his eyes, as always, drawn to the straight stems with large bowls. He found those best on the plains where even the faintest light, visible for miles over the great open distances, could betray you to the enemy. The trick was to partially fill the large bowl, light it by curling your arms and shoulders around the match, and smoke it with one hand cupped over the bowl so that the glow was trapped. The only evidence that remained was the scent of tobacco smoke, and the ever-active wind took care of that. He missed those nights. The sky was an endless black field, and the stars seemed as big as a man's fist.

"Lovely, aren't they?"

The words came from the man standing next to him, gazing at the pipes. His head was far too large for his small body, and even the fact that he was losing his hair did nothing to detract from his boyish face. An innocent, Fitz thought, as the man's large brown eyes pretended to study the case from behind thick glasses. He threaded the brim of a worn hat through his fingers, glancing up once to offer Fitz a hopeful smile. There was something familiar about him, Fitz thought. He must have followed Fitz into the shop.

"Yes," Fitz said.

"I've always wanted to smoke a pipe," the small man said. He shrugged in explanation. "But I have weak lungs."

He spoke in a soft Virginia tone. The accent was cultured with the broad *a*'s and *r*'s of refined living. It wasn't like Fitz's Tennessee accent—the rough edges rubbed smooth by time and distance from the mountains. He noticed that the man's right boot was oddly shaped.

"A clubfoot," the man said, catching Fitz's interest.

Fitz said nothing, ashamed at having been caught looking.

The small man's hand shot out. "My name's Bishop," he said.

"Dunaway," Fitz said, taking the man's hand. The handshake was firm, but Fitz felt that it took all of Bishop's effort to make it so.

"Captain," Bishop noted, nodding at the shoulder straps of Fitz's uniform.

"Yes," Fitz said. He read envy on the little man's face.

Baird appeared at the case. "Well, is that taste to your liking?" he asked Fitz.

Bishop limped away.

"Yes," Fitz said. "How much is it?"

"That is seven cents an ounce."

Fitz pulled out his tobacco pouch. "This is a two-ounce pouch. I'd like two full ounces, please."

Baird sniffed in response. "I run an honest house here. You get what you pay for."

"What do you smoke?"

"Nothing," the Scot returned. "It's a filthy habit, and I'll have nothing to do with it."

Fitz heard the door open and close. He turned but did not see Bishop. What a strange encounter, he thought, as he watched Baird fill the pouch—and what an odd little man Bishop was.

The White Lot! The small man who shuffled along the edge of the damaged fence with the big man. Someone surveying his handiwork? An arsonist or an observer? Where was the other—waiting to ambush him?

He paid Baird and left.

Outside of the shop he filled his pipe and lit it, drawing deeply. He exhaled and was rewarded by a cloud of smoke that bathed him in a comforting presence. Fitz headed toward the boarding house, determined to find out who Bishop really was. It was then that he felt someone's presence at his side.

"May I accompany you, Captain Dunaway?" Bishop asked.

The little man's appearance startled Fitz. "Yes." Was he wrong about the cripple? He couldn't be sure that he was the man at the White Lot. Or for that matter, that he wasn't.

"Thank you. That's most kind of you," Bishop said, falling into step, dragging his crippled foot. He closed his eyes and inhaled. "What a wonderful aroma. What is the blend?"

Fitz pulled the pipe from his mouth. "I don't know. The Scotsman recommended it. At seven cents an ounce, it ought to be gold."

"It's delightful. My father smoked a pipe. I remember sitting in the parlor as Mother played piano. Father read the newspaper and smoked one of his pipes. He owned quite a few."

"I have one, which does me well enough."

"Yes," Bishop said. "Of course."

The little man struggled but kept pace. The right boot was built up and the extra weight caused Bishop's foot to brush the ground. The noise was a whisper, but it pled the man's deformity.

"Have you been long in the city?" Bishop asked.

"Not long," Fitz said, and then, trying to find a way to be pleasant to the cripple, added, "How long have you lived here?"

"I was born here. I've lived here all of my life. My, but the city has changed since the war began."

"So I've heard."

"It's remarkable. Remarkable. There must be one hundred thousand people in Washington now. But it's sad to think it's all because of the war. So much destruction. So many young men dying." And then, after a split second of deliberation, Bishop added, "Over nothing."

The statement alarmed Fitz, not because it was spoken, but the clumsy way in which it was delivered, as if the little man had practiced saying it over and over until it had lost its meaning and retained only the husk of the words. The question was meant to draw Fitz out—that much was obvious.

"You believe that?" Fitz asked.

"Yes," Bishop said. "That is to say, you seem like the type who would agree."

"I've thought about it," Fitz answered, not sure of what else he should say. He sensed he was being tested and despite his earlier feelings about his situation, felt an unanticipated surge of excitement.

He could almost see a weight fly from the little man's shoulders. Now what, Fitz wondered? Do we rush to a secret meeting where I'm administered an oath of allegiance to the South? Am I to be enlisted in the Confederate army? He realized how flippant he was being. Do your duty, he told himself, no matter how hateful it is.

"Yes," Bishop said. He scratched his nose, dislodging his thick glasses. He settled them into place before continuing. "Forgive me, Captain, I am very nervous talking in this manner. Frightened, in fact. People think the war should never have begun. That Lincoln is a tyrant."

"Some people feel that way," Fitz agreed. Time to playact.

"Yes," Bishop said.

They continued on in silence before Bishop, in a voice filled with equal amounts of hope and fear, asked, "What is your opinion about President Lincoln, Captain Dunaway?"

Fitz tapped his pipe in the palm of his hand to dislodge a crop of ashes. He remembered the long figure relaxing in the chair at the Telegraph Office. "My opinion is my opinion, Mr. Bishop. I've been told it's not safe to speak your mind in Washington these days." He smiled, wondering what Asia Lossing would say if she were to hear him now.

"Of course, sir," Bishop said. "Forgive me. I meant no dis-respect."

"Don't trouble yourself, Mr. Bishop."

Fitz sensed Bishop mulling over an action as his own mind raced over what to do or say next. This was tricky business. One misstep and Bishop would be warned off, and then Fitz would have to start again. His heart beat with excitement, but he fought to keep it contained. He waited for the little man to speak.

Bishop smiled. "Captain Dunaway, I'm not cut out for this, you understand. I know some men, friends of mine, who I'm sure would soon become your friends. We share like opinions. Would you like to meet them?"

Fitz stopped Bishop. Here was the time that would tell all. He had to draw out Bishop, but in a way that did not make him appear too anxious. "How do I know that, Mr. Bishop? How do I know anything about you and your friends? How do I know this is not a trap? How do you know what my opinion is?"

"S-Sir," Bishop stammered. "Captain Dunaway, you must believe me. My intentions are—"

"Damn your intentions, Mr. Bishop. They won't stop me from being hanged. How did you come to choose me?"

"Captain Dunaway, I did not mean to offend you."

"I don't know your meaning at all, Mr. Bishop. Answer my question!"

"Yes, yes," Bishop said. "Please, sir. Don't take offense, I beg of you. I was told that you may—"

"That I may, what?"

"That you were dissatisfied. That is all. I promise, sir."

"Who told you this?"

"A friend of the cause," Bishop said, and then added, "It was passed to me by a companion. A man I trust. A friend. I thought that he might become yours as well."

The little man was a bundle of harmlessness. He was sincere; there was no doubt of that. And strangely, Fitz felt that he was a good man in his own way. He almost felt sorry for the cripple, but his own words came back to him. These are dangerous times and they could be deadly for the unwary.

"If I wanted to meet your friends?"

Bishop brightened and there was relief in his voice as he replied, "On Q Street, near the Eastern Branch. Rachael's Haven. Are you familiar with it?"

"No."

"It is a tavern. Near the Eastern Branch of the Potomac."

Fitz grew irritated. "I don't know Washington, Mr. Bishop."

"Of course, sir. Forgive me. Rachael's Haven. It's on the Island, Captain Dunaway. Are you familiar with the Island?"

"I've heard of it." Now things were happening.

Bishop edged closer to Fitz. "We can meet there. When you come, sir, take caution. The Island is a dangerous place, especially for one who doesn't know it. I have lived there for over a decade."

The look on Fitz's face said everything.

"I know what you think," the little man said. "How is it a cripple is able to survive such a place? I'm inconsequential, Captain Dunaway. And the people down there know me well. We're all alike, I suppose. They have little, and little enough to lose. Death could snap them up at any moment. I am deformed, a castoff. My father hated the sight of me, but he left me a small inheritance. My angel mother left me the soul of a poet. You don't know what it is like, do you, Captain Dunaway, to be on the outside? To be an object of contempt because you are not like others. I have poetry to comfort me, and a few friends, but the look of disgust from normal people when they see my deformity still cuts deeply. The Island is my home, my sanctuary. My bell tower."

"If I come," Fitz said, pacing his words so that Bishop knew that he had yet to make that decision, "there had better be no welcoming committee. Don't think that you know my opinion of the government or the war, because you don't."

"I understand, sir. Can I look for you tomorrow evening? At ten o'clock, shall we say?"

"Look all you want, Mr. Bishop. You'll see me when you see me. Good evening, Mr. Bishop. I can find my way home on my own."

He left Bishop and walked to the boarding house, studying the encounter.

My playacting is bringing results; here is a man who is going to lead me to a nest of traitors. Or a trap. No, not a trap. Just a handful of people know why I am here: Prescott, Batterman, Lamon—Lincoln called him "Hill." The only danger comes if I am unable to convince these Rebels that I want to throw in with them. More playacting. No, Fitz decided. *Not like before. Now it is the real thing. The deeper I get into this, the more the danger increases.* "I would not like to see your body pulled from the canal," *Prescott said. Nor would I,* Fitz thought.

Chapter 11

October 5, 1861
The 174th day of the war
The War Department

Prescott listened carefully to Fitz's account of his exchange with Bishop, while a bored Batterman, seated nearby, scribbled down everything said. The assistant secretary of war drummed the desk in deep thought before he spoke.

"Then there is an informer at the boarding house? Lossing himself?"

Batterman waited for an answer, the absence of scribbling an accusing silence. *Where was the answer, Fitz? Someone for certain? One of the clerks?* After all, Bishop had said "he."

But a thought that had troubled him during the night re-emerged and it sickened Fitz. Asia had sent him to the tobacconist.

"Well, young man," Prescott asked. "Does anyone of your newfound acquaintances strike you as being of interest?"

"No one that I can think of," Fitz said.

"No? No? Bless me, perhaps there is hope for the loyalty of this city's inhabitants."

They talked for a few minutes more, exchanging nothing of consequence. Prescott rambled on about the demise of a once-beautiful city, and then questioned Fitz, seeking details he could not supply. The assistant secretary commended Fitz on his loyalty.

"You shall not be forgotten, young man," Prescott assured Fitz. "Of that, I am absolutely certain."

But Prescott lost interest in pursuing disloyalty in the boarding house. The change of heart perplexed Fitz. The assistant secretary was determined to catch offenders but then was satisfied to slip into an homage about Washington.

Fitz left Prescott's office, wishing for once in his life that he had the stomach for drinking.

As he walked down the hall, he saw Will just ahead of him.

"Will?" Fitz called out, and then regretted it. He did not want to lie to his friend; he didn't want anyone's company. Better to leave and do what had to be done.

"Fitz. Where have you been? Doesn't Prescott ever let you out?"

Fitz caught up with his old friend. "How goes it?" he asked, appearing as if nothing troubled him. He knew that it was no good—he was a poor liar.

"I could work sixteen hours a day on arms contracts," Will said, "and never get it all done." He noticed Fitz's discomfort. "And you?"

"Everything is splendid," Fitz said.

"You've been to see Prescott," Will said. "Something is amiss. What's that old fox got you into?"

"What do you mean?"

Will made sure that they were alone before answering. "Fitz, I asked Prescott to find a position for you. When you told me about the president's guard, I thought nothing of it, but now I see that you're troubled. Is there something else?"

"Is there always something behind everything that's done? Do even the shadows have shadows?" Fitz asked.

"Well, is there?" Will pressed. "Listen, Fitz, Prescott is my superior but he is a cagey devil. It's best to keep an eye open if you're dealing with him."

"Oh, blast this business! If you feel that way then why did

you get me involved? Why didn't you let me alone? I should have taken my chances with a court-martial."

"What business, Fitz? What is it?"

"Nothing," he said, calming. "Nothing. I've got to be going, Will." He had to get away from his old friend's concern and his questions. He wanted to turn away from false-hoods and the darkness of his own self-loathing. "I can't talk to you now," he said and then hurried away.

I'm behaving like a fool, he thought as he walked to the boarding house. He was caught up in his own lies and could not even confide in his friend. What did Will mean about Prescott? *I am not to trust him? If not him, who am I to trust?* It seemed the only person whose motives were certain was Bishop.

Honest Abe. Fitz felt ashamed. He had seen the man and was moved by the compassion and intelligence that flowed from his soul. Fitz remembered thinking, after his conversation with the tall man, that what he was doing was the most important business he had ever been involved in. But the reality of his work as a spy—the double life that he was forced to live, strung together by a web of lies—ate into him. He remembered the president's kind gray eyes. *Lincoln must know he lives among scoundrels and liars.*

"God, what a city," Fitz said. "The only trustworthy man I've met is the object of danger." Trustworthy man. What about a trustworthy woman? Is Asia such a woman? Fitz pushed the question from his mind and raced home.

He went to his room without seeing anyone and dressed in his new suit. Before putting on his frock coat he slipped on a shoulder holster and pulled a little Colt revolver from beneath the mattress, pushing the pistol into the holster. He shifted the holster until it fit comfortably. He slipped into his coat, picked up his black hat, and once more gave thought to what he needed to do.

Come out of this in one piece, he answered his own thoughts.

He left his room and was just descending the stairs when he saw Asia Lossing at the bottom of the staircase.

"Why, Captain Dunaway," she said. "How handsome you look when you are not irritating someone."

"I take it that is your compliment?" he asked.

"You may, but don't let it go to your head. Will you have supper?"

"No."

"We're having roast beef," she said, and added, "apple crisp for dessert."

His stomach rumbled before he could reply.

Asia enjoyed his distress but asked, "Why don't you join us, Captain Dunaway? I promise to be on my best behavior."

"Indeed?" Fitz replied, but with no malice. The invitation was tempting. He could think of nothing but the lovely scent that surrounded Asia. Lilacs, he supposed, or perhaps some other flower. He found it enticing and the fragrance called to him—suggesting he steal a glance Asia's way. Perhaps to catch a glimpse of her moist lips, or the way her breasts rose gently with each breath.

"Well, well, well!" Hogan entered the front door. "All the children waiting on Papa to come home from work."

"Mr. Hogan, you're late," Asia said.

"Couldn't be helped, Mrs. Lossing," Hogan said. "What a city, I tell you! Murder and mayhem everywhere."

"Will you join us for supper, Mr. Hogan, or do you prefer to while away your time in the hall?" Asia asked.

"Supper, of course," Hogan said. "But I've been busy." He reached into his back pocket, pulled out a pistol, and pointed it at Fitz.

Fitz heard Asia cry out as he jerked it from Hogan's grasp.

"Mr. Hogan," Asia said. "I should eject you from this house immediately." She glanced down the hallway to the dining room. "What would my other guests think?"

"It's for protection," Hogan protested. "It's not loaded."

Fitz removed the cylinder and turned it over. "It's loaded."

He pulled the percussion caps off the nipples. "Every chamber."

"I didn't know," Hogan said.

"What possessed you to bring a gun into this house, Mr. Hogan?" Asia demanded.

"Preserving the life of Mother Hogan's child, Mrs. Lossing," Hogan returned. "They pulled two more bodies from the canal just this morning. I tell you, criminals have taken over the city. I saw the bodies myself, on the way to work," he continued. "Laborers from their dress. Their throats were slit and when they were fished out they were as white as chalk."

Asia put her head in her hands. "Mr. Hogan, I will forgive you the gun, but please keep your dime-novel descriptions to yourself."

"Certainly," Hogan said, patting his stomach. "I wonder if there's any corn left? Those fellas are worse than locusts." He walked toward the sound of conversation and dishes.

Fitz placed the pistol and cylinder on a bureau. Asia stepped close to him and he hoped that even for an instant, their bodies would touch.

"Captain Dunaway, thank you for disarming Mr. Hogan," she said.

He felt foolish, knowing he hoped for too much. Instead he looked away in embarrassment and said, "It was purely self-serving. The pistol was pointed at my head."

"I suppose he is right," she said. "The city can be a dangerous place."

Fitz glanced over his shoulder. "Even more so at the Royal Boarding House," he said. "I am more than prepared to take care of myself."

"I never doubted that, Captain Dunaway," Asia said. "I simply meant that I trust you will take every precaution when you travel about Washington."

Asia's hair gleamed in the light of the gas chandeliers as her eyes searched his for a reply. He was uncomfortable with her beauty and her proximity, wishing he could say what he thought—what he felt. *What was that, Fitz? That whenever she looks your way you feel as if butterflies have been released in your stomach? Or, when she is near, words stick in your throat? Or that she may be your enemy and you cannot entrust your life to her?* He had never had enough time or opportunity to share the company of a woman, although he had often felt desire prodding him in that direction. Twice in his life he had considered himself truly in love. Once he realized that he was only enchanted with an untrustworthy woman.

Sufficiently forewarned about the opposite sex, he had avoided entanglement until his last year at the Academy. She was a major's daughter who demanded Fitz resign his commission upon graduation.

"I cannot bear the army one day more," Norah had informed him. "And if you choose to make me your wife, you must divest yourself of that blue coat."

He was stunned and hurt, and the thought of being without her filled him with despair. "I cannot honor your wish," he had replied, his heart breaking. He hoped that he sounded worldly and urbane. Knowing that she would never understand, he added, "It took me too long to find it."

"Keep out of harm's way, Captain," Asia urged.

"I will keep that in mind," Fitz said.

Chapter 12

Washington, DC

Fitz swung aboard the half-filled omnibus as it slowed near the corner of 20th Street and Pennsylvania Avenue, an hour after taking his leave of Asia. He had seen the boxy yellow wagon weaving its way between the Capitol and the edge of town, its interior crammed with travelers. If you were lucky, you were in time to find a seat along one of the benches on either side. If not, you could slip your hand through one of the leather straps and stand until the patient vehicle reached your destination. The omnibus carried only a handful of passengers between dusk and dark, and again after dawn before the day's workers pushed aboard.

The driver appeared to doze on his stool as Fitz found a seat, the reins wound through his fingers leading to a pair of plodding horses who looked as if they would have no trouble joining him.

The avenue was a cloud of dust ground axle-high by passing vehicles. There were no more young gallant officers galloping the length of Pennsylvania Avenue, trying to impress young ladies—McClellan had put a stop to that. But the avenue was seething with military traffic. Fitz watched them pass, an anxious reminder of his situation. For the present at least, he was no longer a soldier.

Fitz sat back against the wooden bench, crossed his arms

over his chest, and took stock of Washington in the orange glow of an early dusk. It was the way he prepared himself for encounters—once the planning was done and the adventure begun, it was best to remain calm and let the thing unfold. When everything that can be done has been done, an old soldier once told him, get some sleep. What would happen, would happen, Fitz knew. Fate was a mysterious creature that revealed nothing until it pleased her to do so. Fitz would not rely solely on Fate—he carried a .32 caliber revolver to assist her.

The omnibus soon came to the President's Park. Fitz glanced at the Winder Building and saw the War Department Building across from it. He pictured stacks of reports and shivered at the endless hours he had spent reading them. They passed behind the west end of the Executive Mansion. Attached to it was a huge mountain of green glass and cast iron, just a stone's throw from the War Department. The graceful shapes of trees and tall plants in the conservatory were silhouetted against the glass panes. Fitz wondered at the extravagance of the wealthy; a building dedicated to the care of flowers.

As the vehicle moved on, the view of Lincoln's house was blocked by a dozen small outbuildings. Fitz heard the gentle low of a cow answered by a squawking chicken and wondered if the animals belonged to the president's boys. They were brats, Hogan told them at supper one evening, always getting into mischief. But it was well known they didn't hold a candle to Mrs. Lincoln; she was a hellcat all right, Hogan said.

They turned right at the State Department onto 15th Street and went a block and a half before turning left, back onto Pennsylvania Avenue. As they passed Grover's Theatre, Fitz noticed the north side of the street had a brick walk and substantial buildings. Fashionably attired couples promenaded in a practice that seemed ridiculous with men dying not fifty miles away. He watched as the gentlemen tipped their hats and the women gazed at shop windows. He shook his head in wonderment. How could men and women stroll the street oblivious to the war? Yet he longed for a chance to join them and be done with this filthy business. To forget for an instant who he was and what he had to do. Then anger washed over him at those ignorant fools wandering about as if nothing had changed. He recognized the feeling for what it was: envy. His world was turned upside down so that nothing was familiar and all of the old landmarks—duty, honor, and country—were gone. They lived normal, safe lives while his hung from the slender thread of his own misfortune. *No,* Fitz reminded himself bitterly, *mistakes of others.* There was one vital difference: failure for him meant either disgrace or death.

Across the 160-foot width of Pennsylvania Avenue stood the south side, a dismal row of low shacks and weathered sheds that might have been located in another town had they not been face-to-face with their richer brothers. Fitz caught the irony; here were the north and the south of it, he thought, separated by a common avenue.

An odor of decay enveloped the vehicle. Fitz covered his nose and mouth as others in the omnibus whipped out handkerchiefs and clamped them to their faces. The smell became worse, and tears welled up in Fitz's eyes. What was that ungodly stench? Fitz was familiar with the scent of death, but this was putrid beyond anything he had encountered before. It must surely be the canal, nothing more than a large, open sewer for the city's inhabitants.

He saw a sign that read City Market over a rank of ancient shacks of gray-mottled boards and random timbers. It was a haphazard collection of small structures with nothing in common except their dilapidated appearance. The avenue ran roughly parallel to the canal at this point until they nearly joined at 4th Street. Fitz considered removing his hat and covering his face with it as protection against the horrible smell, but instead he took as few breaths as possible and clamped his lips together.

The vehicle drove around the Capitol grounds and stopped.

Fitz got off and took a tentative breath. The stench had lessened considerably. The pale bulk of the Capitol building was just ahead.

The grounds were covered by debris, as if the building had exploded and showered the surrounding area with piles of white marble blocks and mounds of coal. Ramshackle sheds ringed the unfinished Capitol, adding to the shabbiness of the scene. Large stretches of the vast lawn were denuded of grass where hundreds of workmen had trampled the life out of it. A skeleton of rough-cut lumber scaffolding encircled the unfinished dome, looking oddly like a beacon of decay. A giant crane of huge beams bearing pulleys and blocks the size of a man's chest, linked by giant cables, jutted upward from the center of the Rotunda. It gave the dome the appearance of an animal whose skin had been stripped away. Black steam engines, resting on grids of thick timbers, puffed resolutely—complex organisms of drive belts, flywheels, and reduction gears. A steady gang of Negro laborers fed the engines, heaving coal into fiery maws.

Fitz found a cab—a boxy, mud-spattered carriage waiting at the foot of the Capitol building—whose driver was willing to take him to the Island. They drove down 1st Street East and over a small bridge that crossed the canal. Fitz fished in his pocket and pulled out his pipe and tobacco pouch. His hand brushed the pistol, its weight adding comfort to his journey.

The cab stopped.

"This is it," the cabby said.

Fitz stepped out and paid the driver. "How far to the Capitol?" he asked, trying to gain some idea of distance in this confusing city.

The cabby counted his money. "A little more than half a mile coming across the bridge. 'Course, it ain't that far if you go straight up South Capitol and swim the canal." He looked up at the sky. "Sun's going down. Mister, if I were you I'd be indoors and stay indoors when that happens."

The cab drove away, leaving Fitz standing in the narrow street. He was facing a dingy, nondescript two-story brick building, jammed in between others remarkably like it. There were no signs anywhere and the windows on either side of the wooden door were boarded up. Fitz thought the driver had duped him until he heard the sound of voices. Shadows from the setting sun were seeping into the street and across building fronts, lapping at the front door of Rachael's Haven. Fitz recalled the driver's words, and he wondered how much of a haven the tavern would be.

As he opened the door and entered, he was overwhelmed by a blast of noise and smoke. Indistinct forms waded through the sharp stench of unwashed bodies and the heavy odor of stale beer. It was dark except where lanterns and candles pierced the gloom, but the light added nothing to the scene, it only lessened the darkness. The place was filled with coarse men and loud talk, peppered with occasional bursts of raucous laughter. Cheap tobacco smoke swirled into Fitz's nose and helped mask the stink of the crowd. He felt a dozen pairs of eyes trailing him as he walked to the bar. He caught the attention of the bartender, a rough-looking brute with a jagged red wound across his cheek that looked fresh.

"Coffee," Fitz ordered, thinking that anything boiled would be the safest drink in the tavern. A large man standing next to him pivoted unsteadily.

"That ain't no man's drink."

Fitz ignored him as the bartender set a tin cup on the plank bar. The harsh smell and thickness of the steaming coffee caused Fitz to reconsider his order.

"Didn't you hear me?" the large man asked, poking a thick finger into Fitz's shoulder.

Fitz turned. The big man outweighed him by at least fifty pounds and he was a good head taller, with a laborer's broad chest and scarred hands to match. His battered face and drooping right eyelid told everything that Fitz needed to know. He was a brawler.

"Go away," Fitz said.

The men around them faded back.

The big man grinned. Half his teeth were missing or broken, and those that remained were nearly black with decay. Fitz saw the man's fist tensing and he knew what would happen. The man would try to drive his fist under Fitz's chin, stunning him until he stepped back and began swinging those big arms. Then he would batter Fitz senseless.

That is why Fitz threw the coffee in the man's eyes.

The big man clutched his face and staggered backward, screaming as he tried to wipe the coffee from his scalded face. Other patrons scrambled for safety, overturning tables and chairs as the man fumbled at his belt. Fitz saw the knife come up. By that time he had his pistol out of its holster. He swung it, catching the big man on the jawbone. The man stiffened with a grunt and collapsed to the floor. He groaned as a cloud of dust settled around him.

Fitz retrieved the knife from the man's side. He flipped the knife, catching it by the tip of its huge blade, examined it, and turned to the bartender.

"Coffee," Fitz said.

Fitz took stock of the tavern as the cup was set on the bar. Bishop was sitting at a small table, near a door in the rear of the room. He gave Fitz a subtle wave.

Fitz picked up his cup and the knife, and joined Bishop. He took one of the chairs at the table and turned it so that the back was toward the wall. He had a full view of the room.

"That was remarkable," Bishop said, his face radiating amazement. "The manner in which you handled that bully."

"He gave me no choice," Fitz said.

"Are you always this calm, Captain Dunaway?"

"No," Fitz said, sipping the coffee.

Bishop said, "I don't have that manner. Fighting, I mean. I was never very good at it. I'm a small man, you see."

"Napoleon was a small man," Fitz said.

"Oh, but he had an army behind him. And Josephine."

Fitz smiled.

"If I were a leader such as Napoleon with a woman such as Josephine on my arm I suppose I could conquer the world.

That is how I am, Captain—I'm a romantic and a dreamer. My world is books. Do you read?"

"Just Hardee's," Fitz said. The tactics manual had been his bible. "And newspapers."

The big man staggered to his feet, leaning against the bar to steady himself. Fitz watched him search the room until their eyes met. Fitz sipped his coffee and set the cup on the battered table. He waited, watching the ruffian. The big man wiped his mouth in thought and said something to the bartender. Fitz slipped his hand into his coat, wrapping his fingers around the butt of the pistol. The man made his decision, staggering to the door. Fitz relaxed.

"He was a big man," Bishop said in appreciation.

"Yes," Fitz said, blowing on his coffee. "I thought it best not to mollycoddle him. Where are your friends?"

"My—? Oh, the others. They should be along shortly. They are cautious, you understand. It's a dangerous business."

Fitz said, "I've heard that about treason," he said, remembering Prescott's admonitions.

"No, sir," Bishop said, anxious to correct Fitz. "It is not treason when one fights for one's country against tyranny. Lincoln and his Black Republicans want to destroy the South. They prefer to have the Negro on the same level as the white man. That must not be allowed. How can it be called treason?"

"Call it anything you like, Mr. Bishop. Each man has his own reasoning."

Bishop glanced around and leaned closer to Fitz. "Captain Dunaway, it may be best for you not to take that tact with my friends. I am an educated man. I understand the need to engage in philosophical discussion. It cleanses the intellectual palate. The others are less educated and might take offense. Your choice of words concerns me, Captain."

Fitz finished his coffee. "My landlady would agree with you. I will do my best to lessen your concerns, Mr. Bishop. How many friends do you have?"

"Oh, why there are five of us. Six counting you. We are small in number but mighty in resolve. The odds do not trouble you, do they?"

"Not when I'm competently armed."

"Six, then. We are a young group, newly formed, that is. Men from all stations. What we have in common is a love for our country, a love for the South, and a hatred of the abolitionists."

"You don't strike me as a man who hates, Mr. Bishop," Fitz said, trying to take the measure of the little man across from him.

"But I am a man of passion, Captain Dunaway. I do feel things deeply, and I understand the importance of a cause. Do you understand that as well, sir? Isn't there one thing in your life above all others? What moves you, sir, to take the actions you do?"

"My own interests, Mr. Bishop," Fitz said.

His answer caught Bishop off guard and the man tried to conceal his disappointment. "I'm not sure I can accept that answer from you, sir. I suggest there is more to you than meets the eye."

Fitz leaned back in his chair, sliding his hand to the edge of the table, closer to his pistol. He watched Bishop—he was not sure what the little man was getting at and, although he looked tame enough, his comment could mean trouble. "Explain yourself, sir," he said.

Bishop removed his glasses and, producing a handkerchief, cleaned them. He must be blind without them, Fitz thought. What is he doing in this business?

"I believe that you function on a higher plane than you realize, Captain Dunaway," Bishop said, replacing the glasses. He adjusted them, blinking. He reminded Fitz of a baby owl. "I believe that you have more than your self-interests involved. You may be a soldier of fortune but I don't think that this is the case. I believe you believe in a greater cause than you give yourself credit for."

"You're wrong, Mr. Bishop," Fitz said, relaxing. He swept

the room. Every man in the tavern appeared to be absorbed in drinking, playing cards, or talking. No one cared about his presence. "Where are your friends?"

Bishop pulled a watch from his vest pocket. Holding it close to his face to read it, he said, "We must be going."

"What?"

"It is a few minutes after ten." He held the watch out to Fitz. "Is it not?"

"I'm not going anywhere," Fitz said. "We were to meet your friends here."

"Yes, that is true," Bishop said. "But my instructions were to wait until ten o'clock and, if he did not arrive, to take you to my rooms."

"Who was to arrive?"

"Oh, I'm afraid I can't give you his name. That must remain a secret."

"I'm not going anywhere, Mr. Bishop," Fitz said.

Bishop's eyes widened. "Oh, dear. I hadn't considered this. Captain Dunaway, you must believe me when I tell you that there is no danger. I give you my word as a gentleman."

"Who is this man? His name?"

Bishop furrowed his brow in thought. "I will tell you, but you must give me your word never to reveal it."

"Done."

"It is Whaley. Mr. Jakob Whaley. Can we go now, please, Captain? My rooms are only a short distance."

"This way," Fitz said, pointing to the back door.

"But that leads to the alley. The alleys in this part of the city are unsafe."

"I'll wager no more so than the street. My new friend may be waiting in ambush for me. Or perhaps your friends."

Bishop looked hurt. "I gave you my word, sir."

"That'll be small comfort when I'm murdered," Fitz said.

Fitz led Bishop to the back door and stepped outside.

It was a clear night and a weak moon did its best to ease the blackness of the narrow alley. He pulled Bishop by the sleeve, placing him in the lead. "Walk on," he ordered, his revolver in his hand. He stopped to make sure that they weren't being followed. The noise of the tavern faded as they moved down the alley. There were no sounds except for the hissing sound of Bishop's clubfoot dragging across the hard-packed earth.

They reached a battered boarding house. The stairs creaked in protest as they made their way to the second floor. Bishop unlocked a door and led Fitz into his rooms. A match flared in the darkness as Bishop lit an oil lamp set on a tiny table. Adjusting the wick, he said, "I'm afraid that I have nothing to offer you. I usually don't receive guests."

Fitz nodded, surveying the room. Stacks of newspapers and books littered the floor. Two large bookcases on one wall were filled to overflowing and a small table in the corner was covered by notepaper. A few cheap pens and a half dozen nibs were scattered on the desk, next to an inkwell.

"My poetry," Bishop said. He picked up several sheets of paper, and handed them to Fitz. "It's not very good, of course. Well, perhaps it is. You know how an artist feels about his own work, don't you? There is always that struggle. The torment that an artist undergoes. Many times I've been tempted to toss every bit of it in the fireplace, but then I come to my senses. I do have some water. Would you like some?"

Fitz shook his head. "What's in there?" he asked, gesturing to the other room.

"More of the same, I'm afraid," Bishop said. "Books. My settee. I sleep in that room.

'*In visions of the dark night*
I have dreamed of joy departed —
But a waking dream of life and light
Hath left me broken-hearted.' "

Bishop smiled. "That is Mr. Poe's work."

"Is he another one of your friends?" Fitz asked, his interest in the other room.

"Edgar Allan Poe?" Bishop asked. "You've never heard of America's greatest poet?"

"I was out West."

"I have everything that he has ever written," Bishop said, pulling two books from the shelves. "Here. And here. Masterpieces. The man was a genius, Oh, how I long to be like him."

There was a sharp knock at the door. Fitz stepped away from the meager light and cocked the pistol.

"Please put your gun away, Captain," Bishop said.

Fitz waved the notion aside with his pistol. "Answer the door."

"Who is it?" Bishop called out.

Fitz heard a muffled reply.

Bishop opened the door and stepped back. A man entered, and Bishop closed and locked the door behind him. Fitz sized up the new arrival. He was just less than six feet with a large head and a head of thick, shaggy black hair. His clothes were common enough: a soft wool cap, baggy wool trousers, and a checkered coat with the cuffs rolled back. A workingman—there was no fat on his thick body and his hands were broad with misshapen knuckles. His face said most about him—it was roughly worked clay, the sculptor unable to bring out more than a hint of the man's features—full cheeks, heavy chin, and battered nose. His eyes drew Fitz's attention. Even in this light he could see that they were nearly black and lifeless.

The other one, Fitz realized. The man from the White Lot. Now the pair was complete.

"Put that gun away," the man ordered Fitz. His voice was gravelly and crude. "Shoot me and half a dozen of my men will be on you."

"They'll be your pallbearers, then, won't they? Open your coat and let me see what you're carrying."

The man pulled back his coat to reveal the handles of two bowie knives.

"Lift your coat and turn around," Fitz ordered.

The man did as he was told. He had no other weapons.

"You're Whaley," Fitz said.

Whaley shot Bishop a murderous look. "Why don't you learn to keep your mouth shut?" He focused on Fitz. "Yes, what of it? You've had your question answered. Now. I've got some of my own. Put that gun away and let's talk."

Fitz returned the gun to the holster but kept his coat pulled back. Whaley appeared to relax and become almost congenial, but something warned Fitz not to accept this sudden change in manner. The man's eyes were still cold.

"Bishop says that you want to throw in with us," Whaley said, finding a chair. Fitz remained standing. He said nothing.

"There's a lot of us feel the way that we do," Whaley said, rubbing his knee. "This ain't a country for darkies. It's for the white man. Lincoln and those other nigger lovers want this country overrun by those black bastards. I say kill every one of the sons of bitches. What do you say?"

This was the moment Fitz had prepared himself for. If he could not convince Whaley why he was here, he knew he was a dead man. No amount of lying would do it, he wasn't that good, and he was convinced that any man with half a brain would see that it was a lie. *So how do you tell a lie that isn't?* Fitz had asked himself in the quiet of his room, finishing the last pipe of the day, when his only companions were the darkness and his own thoughts. Bishop spoke of passion earlier and that was what Fitz knew that he had to draw upon.

"I don't care anything about the South or darkies."

Whaley jumped to his feet, his eyes accusing Bishop of betrayal. The little man stepped back in fear.

His eyes pleaded with Fitz. "Captain—"

"Mister," Whaley said to Fitz. "You had better make yourself real clear real fast."

"I've given my life to the army," Fitz said, heat building within him. "I've asked for no recognition or special treatment, only what was due me for all that I have done. Instead I am reprimanded and arrested and a fellow officer has to beg for me. Now I'm given a thankless job behind a desk. Idiots are promoted over me, and I answer to file clerks. Why do I want to join you? Because I did my duty, and I was betrayed. Because I only wanted to be a soldier but was denied that. Because I cannot stand the sight of pompous asses straight out of Congress strutting about the streets of Washington in the uniform that I have devoted my life to. Damn you and your niggers, Mr. Whaley; they mean nothing to me. But I want revenge, sir. I want to make someone pay for this inequity. If I can't join your band of cutthroats and murderers, I'll find my own way."

Fitz waited for Whaley to act. He prayed that he was convincing. He wondered if Whaley could throw a bowie knife faster than he himself could draw his pistol, and gauged how much room he had to fight it out.

When Whaley spoke, it was with the wary tone of a man who only half-believed what he heard. "We've got plans, mister. You don't like Lincoln. All right, we don't, either. There's work to be done. Enough for everyone. But only the right sort. Goddamn the man who isn't."

Whaley stopped talking. Fitz could tell nothing from Whaley's expression.

"I'll have to think you over," Whaley said. "That was a pretty speech you made. Pretty words. It don't tell me nothing about how much you can fight and if you've got the stomach to do what has to be done. Maybe you parade around in your fancy blue suit and impress other folks but that don't impress me." Whaley left, letting the door hang open behind him.

Chapter 13

October 24, 1861
The 193rd day of the war
Corner of 19th Street and Pennsylvania Avenue
Washington, DC

The air turned cool and the sky became a dull, gray wash of thin clouds. Fall had been fleeting—a casual statement that seasons change but never entirely as they should. The leaves left on the trees were shriveled reminders of brilliant fall colors that had come and gone. To Fitz the city was nothing more than a hideous patchwork of browns and grays, which each day came closer to crushing him. Soon it would be winter.

Long columns of cavalry and infantry marched down the streets in a sight that was so common that crowds were no longer moved to cheer. McClellan was building his army on the outskirts of Washington, and a mighty army it was reported to be. Each day new regiments of earnest young men burning with a desire to see the elephant paraded through the streets, regimental colors flying, arms and legs pumping, a steady tramp of invincibility.

Fitz stood on the sidewalk with the others, watching them pass.

His journey to the boarding house, letting the cool air bathe him, was accompanied by a vague notion of where he was and where he was going. He had told Prescott of the meeting in Bishop's rooms and three days after making his report it became apparent to Fitz that he had failed. Whaley had not contacted him. Prescott, sitting behind his desk like a potentate and pressing his fingertips together in deep thought, had counseled patience. Fitz fought to control his irritation. Batterman was there, of course, scribbling down all that was said, and then locking the report in the safe.

Fitz stopped and lit his pipe at the boarding-house gate.

He had begun making a habit of eating supper quickly and retiring to his room, minimizing exposure to the endless chatter of Hogan and the suspicious gazes of Woodbridge. Or Asia's questioning glances. More than once he had wanted to tell her everything, to lose himself in those liquid eyes. The idea was absurd, of course, and he berated himself for having had such a silly, romantic notion. It was the nature of women, he told himself, to be kind and nurturing—it was the nature of men to require such care at times.

He shook the match out, inhaling, letting the hot smoke fill his lungs, cleansing him of all thought. He had been out only twice—both times to the tobacconist's, seeking to be contacted by Bishop or Whaley. He was not.

Fitz heard the bright notes of a piano coming from the parlor. He walked in and saw Asia seated behind the instrument, intent on her music. She noticed him and smiled.

"One of my many talents," she said. "Shall I continue?"

"Please," Fitz said. "May I join you?"

"By all means. The rest of my audience is in the dining room, seeking other forms of sustenance."

She continued to play as Fitz settled into a chair near the fireplace. He was amazed as her fingers combined chords and individual notes in a melody, dashing from one end of the keyboard to the other. He glanced down to see her feet dancing over the brass pedals in a contrarhythm to the music. It was wonderful and mystifying, that a human being could coax such beauty from a wooden box. A low flame burned over the remnants of a few glowing logs, filling the room with charitable warmth.

"What is it?" Fitz asked.

"Stephen Foster. 'Jeannie With the Light Brown Hair.' Do you know it?"

"No."

" 'Vulgar' my mother called it. She preferred the classics." She held up a burning cigar. "She despised this." She drew on it and returned it to the ashtray.

"The music is lovely," Fitz said, feeling melancholy. The sight of Asia and the gentle strains of the song caused some unidentified ache to grow within him. He surrendered to the music and let his mind wander back several days.

Asia intruded on his thoughts. "How was the War Department today?"

"Boring beyond measure," Fitz said, glad that she took him away from his laments. "I made the unfortunate mistake of referring to the reports as 'paperwork.' I was instantly reminded that they were 'documentation.' "

"Shame on you. Such a declaration could cause the government to fail."

Fitz laughed.

"Why, Captain Dunaway, what's gotten into you? I believe that you laughed."

"It was unintentional," Fitz said. He felt like teasing her. "I'll try to be more careful in the future."

She turned a sheet of music and played on. "My father loved humor." She grew wistful and meant to say more but decided against it.

"A friend of mine has a hearty laugh," he said. "Good old Will. That's what everyone calls him. His temperament and spirit never change. He is as calm as I am volatile."

The music stopped. "Please note that I have the good manners not to comment on your volatility."

"So noted."

"Are you close to Will?"

"He is my best friend. Sometimes my only friend, I think."

"I think," she said, "that if you allowed yourself, you would have more than one friend."

"Oh, I have acquaintances, men whose company I enjoy. The army before the war was a small family. But it is different with Will. He doesn't judge me. I suppose that's it."

"That is a rare gift indeed," Asia said. "I thought my husband was like your friend Will. It is a wonder that one can be so mistaken about a person."

"Yes," Fitz said, glad that her husband's failings continued to accumulate. He was concerned this beautiful woman so regretted her role in making her husband the man that he had become. "I think that your husband's faults are his to claim. I have come, lately, to consider that life has many surprises to offer. Some not pleasant. But I think that we are who we become by our own hand."

"Still," she said, not convinced, "I might have driven him to it. I compared all of my suitors to my father. All were wanting. Perhaps it is this that drove Henry . . ."

"Henry rides his own horse, Mrs. Lossing," Fitz broke in. His tone was harsher than he intended but he did not regret his words. Henry. Fitz disliked hearing that the man had a name, he preferred the anonymous husband to the man with a name.

Her eyes sparkled. "I can be a very strong-willed woman."

"Please note that I have the good manners not to comment on your strong will," Fitz said.

Asia resumed playing before commenting, "The army is your life."

"Yes," Fitz said. "It is all that I know."

She lingered over a passage and then her delicate fingers plucked several notes from the keys. "What do you like about it?"

He'd never had to answer the question before and he had never given the subject any thought. He had followed his interests and they led him to the army as surely as the army led him to battle. He asked, "What do you like about your house?" He thought this the best way to explain himself.

"What it represents to me, Captain Dunaway. Growing up, parties in the parlor, the garden, conversations with my father in the library." Her eyes fell on the keys in memory. "Playing the piano for my father. Have you suddenly become wise?"

"No," he said. "It came to me just how much you care for this house. In my own poor way I was trying to explain my life in the army."

"Routine and pageantry? Uniforms and regulations?"

"Routine is poison to me. I am constantly ensnared by regulations. I did not join the army to fill out forms. Garrison duty is drudgery." He shook his head at the memory of it. "I enjoy campaigning. Life in the field. Leading men."

"A warrior," she said. "One great, glorious charge.

'Cannon to right of them,
Cannon to left of them
Cannon in front of them
Volleyed and thundered;
Stormed at with shot and shell,
Boldly they rode and well,
Into the jaws of Death,
Into the mouth of Hell
Rode the six hundred.' "

She responded to his blank look with, "It's a poem. 'The Charge of the Light Brigade?' "

"Edgar Allan Poe?"

"Alfred, Lord Tennyson."

"I never thought as myself as a warrior, just a soldier. Some would argue that I never thought much at all."

She closed a booklet of sheet music. "To cover yourself with glory."

"What?"

"A warrior's dream?"

Fitz cast about for an answer that explained everything. "Command of a regiment. Let me lead my men south to fight the enemy. That would suit me."

"You're a crusader."

Fitz said, "Nothing quite so grand, Mrs. Lossing. I'll leave crusading to my superiors and politicians."

Asia stabbed her cigar out in the ashtray sitting next to her. "We've missed you at the supper table, Captain Dunaway."

"Do you speak for Mr. Woodbridge as well?"

She revealed deeper feelings when she said, "I've missed you at the supper table."

She came to him. There was her scent again and her strong, deep eyes that seemed to beckon Fitz into a warm pool. There was the graceful fall of her neck and the gentle slope of her shoulders and the fragile curve of her jawline. He felt his heart race and his mind spin and every bit of the world ceased to exist as he fell into a ridiculous schoolboy's trance.

He managed, "I did not feel that I would be good company."

"Truly?" she asked and held out her hands. He took them in his and stood until her face was just inches from his. "Perhaps you misjudge your impact on others." She leaned forward and kissed him. Her lips were sweet and warm and when they parted Fitz's surprise gave way to a desire for more. This time he kissed her and his arms encircled her lithe body. He drew back to speak, but he could find no words to fill the silence.

Asia spoke as if an idea had suddenly come to her. "You've never been to a Canterbury?"

"What? No. I—"

"Go and put on that splendid suit of yours and meet me in front in forty-five minutes."

Fitz asked, "Why?"

"Because we're going out, Captain Dunaway. Out. I'll have the carriage brought around."

Where? Fitz wondered.

She hesitated and the caring soul that had just been in his arms threatened to disappear. "You don't fear me for some reason, do you, Captain?" she asked.

"On the contrary, Mrs. Lossing," he said. "You—"

"I intrigue you, Captain," she said. "I am my own woman, sir. Forty-five minutes, Captain Dunaway."

Fitz hurried to his room and washed, trying to remove some of the grime of the streets from his face. His mind raced through the possibilities of Asia's invitation. Is it, as it appeared on the surface, an innocent outing? Why would it be anything else? Her husband is an unreliable rogue—she admitted that herself and regrets her role in having made him so. But, were her feelings genuine? Fitz continued his own argument, buttoning his vest. Henry. What an idiotic name! He was a drunk and a gambler. No combination for any man and not for Asia's husband. But a traitor? Or the husband of a traitor?

He opened the top chest drawer, searching for a fresh collar. He saw the shoulder holster and pistol. He stood looking at them, his mind flashing through reasons to take the pistol, but rebutting each with a reason to leave it behind. Fitz realized that the reason he wanted to leave it was that he wanted to trust her. In this business of lies and half truths, he wanted Asia Lossing to be free of duplicity. Wanting was one thing, getting it was another thing.

He slipped the shoulder holster on. *"Trust no one,"* Prescott had said.

Chapter 14

Fitz met Pennbrook just as he was coming through the front door. Right behind the clerk was Woodbridge.

"Going out, Captain Dunaway?" Pennbrook asked.

"Yes," Fitz said.

Pennbrook glanced at Asia, seated in a low runabout at the curb. It was a small, delicate carriage meant to carry two, but it appeared to Fitz barely capable of transporting one. "I trust that you will have a pleasant enough time with our charming landlady."

"She has surrendered quite easily to you, hasn't she, Captain? Perhaps I would do well to storm the barricades?" Woodbridge asked.

"Tell me, Woodbridge, are you done trying to convince everyone what a patriot you are?" Fitz asked. "Or have you just resigned yourself to irritating us all to death?"

Woodbridge flushed. "You are an impertinent rascal, my friend."

Fitz smiled. "Neither impertinent, Mr. Woodbridge, or your friend. Pardon me, gentlemen." He started down the sidewalk when Pennbrook caught up with him.

"I beg your pardon, Captain, for intruding. Please forgive Mr. Woodbridge's unfortunate choice of words."

Fitz looked over Pennbrook's shoulder as Woodbridge disappeared inside. "That man tries my patience, Mr. Pennbrook." He turned to go again when the clerk stopped him.

"Captain, please, a word. Mr. Woodbridge is well placed on the Joint Committee on the Conduct of the War. They can destroy your career in an instant over nothing. I simply beseech you to use discretion, sir."

"Thank you, Mr. Pennbrook," Fitz said. "I will use whatever is required."

Asia was adjusting her skirt in the open carriage as Fitz reached her. The team, a handsome pair of black geldings, pawed the cobblestone street. She was dressed in a dark green dress and a matching pillbox hat with a slender white feather canted from the right side. A shawl covered her shoulders and a carriage robe was tucked over her lap, falling to the floorboard. She gripped the reins, looking as impatient as the team was to be off.

"Did you bid Mr. Pennbrook and Mr. Woodbridge good evening?" she asked.

"As well as I could without drawing blood." Fitz looked around. "You have no driver?"

She smiled. "I prefer to drive myself."

Fitz climbed into the carriage. He was not accustomed to riding with a woman unescorted, and he had never ridden with a woman who drove her own carriage.

"Captain Dunaway," Asia said, noticing his awkwardness. "Don't tell me that you're one of those men who are uncomfortable with women doing for themselves?"

"Not at all," Fitz said, as she snatched the buggy whip from its mount.

Grinning, she said, "You don't know how that pleases me." She drew the whip back over her head. "Hold on!"

The whip cracked like a gunshot, and the horses bolted forward, pitching Fitz back into the seat. They jetted to a gallop, the little buggy skidding back and forth on its thin wheels.

"Good Lord," Fitz cried out, gripping the seat rail with both hands.

The horses whinnied with pleasure as they lengthened their stride. Asia cracked the whip over their heads and yanked hard on the right rein. The carriage slid around the corner, its rear wheels bouncing into the air as the vehicle fishtailed into the center of the street. They headed for an omnibus.

Fitz had no time to cry out a warning before the carriage cleared the larger vehicle by inches. Fitz saw the omnibus passengers pass in a blur—wide eyes and open mouths.

"Hold on," Asia shouted again above the clatter of hooves and the thin rumble of the wheels on the street.

Fitz saw a shallow culvert approaching. The horses jumped in unison and the front wheels hit next, throwing Fitz in the air. He landed sideways on the seat when the rear wheels hit. He was jerked to one side. He threw an arm around Asia's shoulder to grab the rear seat brace.

She gave him a sidelong glance. "Why, Captain Dunaway, aren't you the forward one."

"Mrs. Lossing," Fitz said, fighting to keep his jarring teeth from biting off the end of his tongue. "I am only interested in my survival." He jammed his legs under the seat, using his calves to wedge himself in.

The carriage careened onto Pennsylvania Avenue in a cloud of dust.

"Can you not slow down, madam?" Fitz asked.

"Slow down? I want to go faster." She cracked the whip again and the carriage jerked forward as the team sped up.

The buildings on Pennsylvania Avenue raced past as the carriage bounced in and out of traffic. Pedestrians fled from the street to the safety of the sidewalk, and a provost guard scattered before them like a flock of geese. Fitz felt a flash of satisfaction, but terror snatched that small triumph from him.

The buggy skidded off the hard surface of the avenue, throwing Fitz clear of his seat. His fingers ached from gripping the seat brace as his legs burned from the strain.

"If you intend to kill me," Fitz said, the words broken up by the rough road, "why don't you just shoot me?"

"What," Asia returned in a joyous voice, "and lose a

boarder?" Something attracted her attention. "Do you like beer?"

"Beer? No!"

"Too bad, Captain, we're about to hit a beer wagon."

The broad side of a huge beer wagon lumbered into their path. Fitz snapped his eyes shut and waited for the collision. Instead, he felt the buggy slide to one side, the rear end twisting in a sickening arc. He opened his eyes to see the Capitol building in the distance.

"Will you slow down, Mrs. Lossing!"

"Speed up?"

"No, for God's sake! We almost hit that beer wagon!"

"How could you tell, Captain?" Asia asked above the rattle of the carriage and the steady drum of the horses' hooves. "Your eyes were closed."

"Hasn't anyone taught you to drive this contraption?" he shouted.

"My father, of course," Asia said. "But he ordered me never to drive unless I gave the horses their head."

Amazed, Fitz offered, "Moderation is always an option, Mrs. Lossing."

"Not for me," Asia said as the carriage cleared another vehicle.

They bounced around another corner and onto a side street. She slowed the team to a walk and adjusted her hat.

"I didn't lose my feather, did I?"

"How do I know? My eyes were closed."

"Oh, Captain, you must learn to relax."

"I will relax when this vehicle stops and my feet touch the ground. My heart feels as if it will burst from my chest."

Asia slid the buggy whip into its sleeve. "They say love will do that, Captain Dunaway," she said.

"Fear as well, Mrs. Lossing," Fitz replied.

She guided the carriage into a narrow alley. Fitz slid his hand into his coat, feeling for the pistol. He tensed, waiting, taking in the surrounding buildings. They loomed on either side of the carriage, the brick walls of a trap. Ahead was a livery stable and to the right of it another alley. That was the only escape except for the way they came in. *Don't take counsel of your fears,* Fitz told himself. *Be patient. Wait.*

She could not be involved, he thought. Fitz saw her at the piano. Her nose was upturned, a trait he had not noticed before, and the corners of her mouth curved up, as if she were amused. No, happy, and Fitz realized that for the first time he saw Asia unburdened by cares. She was lovely.

Come to, you damned fool! She could be the enemy.

"Where are we going?" he managed.

"Going? Why, no place, Captain Dunaway. We are here."

An elderly Negro appeared in front of them and took the horses by the bridles, stopping the carriage.

"Miss Jones," he said in a deep voice. "I haven't seen you in ages."

"Hello, James. How are you?"

"Well, thank you, miss. And you? Well, I hope?"

Asia tied the reins off to the iron frame of the dashboard and stepped from the carriage.

"It has been a very long time," she agreed. She cocked her head at Fitz. "Aren't you coming, Mr. Brown?"

Fitz swung out of the carriage. The Negro looked harmless enough, but he could not tell who was lurking in the shadows. What was this business about Jones and Brown? He took his time in moving to the front of the team, making sure that he kept the horses between the livery stable entrance and himself.

"James," Asia said. "This is my cousin Mr. Brown, newly arrived from the country. Mr. Brown, this is James Sill."

"A pleasure, sir," James said. "I'll just take the horses in now, miss. They'll be ready for you when you return."

"Thank you, James," Asia said, as the horses were led away. "Follow me, Mr. Brown."

Fitz still had his hand on the grip of his revolver when he fell in beside her. " 'Newly arrived from the country?' "

"I hoped it would explain your country-born look," Asia said. "And fashionably unfashionable suit."

He examined his clothing. "I just purchased this from a reputable tailor."

"How charitable," Asia said. "So few men have the courage to wear clothes produced by blind craftsmen."

"Why are you being so mysterious?"

"Am I?" she asked. "If I am, is there anything wrong with being mysterious?"

"It depends on what's at the end of it," Fitz said as they walked down the deserted alley, their footsteps echoing off the walls.

"Only entertainment," Asia said. She stopped him at a rough wooden door with her hand on his forearm. The pressure of her fingertips caused his heart to stir, and her presence swirled around him like an intoxicating mist.

He heard the sound of laughter, music, and singing through the door. *What is this place?* There was nothing on the door to answer his question.

She instructed him, "I am Miss Jones and you are Mr. Brown." He started to speak when she laid a gloved finger on his lips. "This is my city, Captain Dunaway. You are my guest. You must do as I ask." She knocked three times in rapid succession.

Fitz heard a latch click and the door swung open. An old man in a beaver-skin top hat appeared. He blinked at Fitz and then at Asia. Fitz pulled the pistol free of its holster but kept it under his coat.

"Miss Jones," the old man said in surprise. "How delighted I am to see you." Waves of music rolled over him from within and smoke boiled through the doorway as if the interior were on fire. "Do come in."

"Mr. Ford," Asia said, gliding into the darkness. "How wonderful to see you again. This is my cousin Mr. Brown, newly arrived from the country."

Fitz stepped into the building. Ropes and pulleys hung from the ceiling to the floor in a mad web. Fitz's eyes followed the ropes upward into the darkness. Some of them were tied off with sandbags, while other ropes were knotted to heavy frames. The sight of the sandbags made Fitz shiver. They reminded him of bodies. Fitz let his eyes travel beyond the network of ropes and pulleys through a narrow opening sandwiched between a moth-eaten red velour curtain and a dingy canvas backdrop, to a shallow stage that gleamed in the harsh glare of footlights. Two jugglers, their grease-painted faces distorted by the harsh light, kept a dozen red balls in the air. They added another ball and the crowd burst into cheers and applause. They were at a theater.

"Van Winkle's Concert Hall," Asia announced.

Fitz relaxed. "Your mystery."

"My entertainment. Mr. Ford, would you be kind enough to see if my box is available and let Mr. Van Winkle know that I am here?"

"Oh, absolutely. Please, please. Wait here for my return. I'll see to everything."

When the old man had gone, Asia drew close to Fitz. Her lips were just inches from his ear and he could feel her breath.

"That is Marcus Ford. He was one of the finest Shakespearean actors on the stage. My father said that he even rivaled Edwin Booth. That was before age and the bottle did him in."

A rotund man with a large mustache brushed aside the backdrop. He took Asia's hands in his and pressed each to his lips. He stood in front of her, beaming.

"Miss Jones! Miss Jones! You've returned." The words tumbled from his mouth. "How happy you make me. Is she not radiant, sir? Is she not the most splendid creature in Washington City?"

"Mr. Van Winkle," she said. "How can any woman be as beautiful as you make me out to be?"

"Ah," Van Winkle said, shaking his finger at her, "beauty is not only appearance, lovely lady. It is that indefinable nature which causes kings to war over queens, and poets to pine away because no words exist to capture the quality that makes you unique."

Asia extracted her hands from Van Winkle's. "This is my cousin Mr. Brown."

Van Winkle eyed Fitz with mild disinterest. Obviously Fitz had not proved worthy of attention. "Mr. Brown. A pleasure, sir. Indeed. Indeed. Come. Follow me. Your box is ready, Miss Jones."

Van Winkle wound his way through the backstage clutter and up a narrow stairway, leading Asia. Fitz followed.

"I'm no longer newly arrived from the country?" he whispered to Asia.

"No," Asia threw over her shoulder. "I've granted you residency."

"How kind of you," Fitz said.

From the sound of the crowd, Fitz could tell they were well above the main floor but just to one side of the stage, perhaps on a third level, although they had climbed only one flight of stairs. They proceeded down a narrow hallway to a door that bore a tarnished brass number 3. Van Winkle fumbled through a mass of keys before he found one that he inserted in the lock. With a quick turn the door was opened and Van Winkle stepped aside, sweeping them into the box with a bow. "Refreshments will be here immediately."

Fitz followed her into the box and, pushing a curtain to one side, peered over the edge, staying well back in the box. The floor below was seething with people—men and women jammed shoulder to shoulder, downing mugs of beer and shouting to one another across the crowd. When they were not drinking they showered the stage with encouragement or catcalls. The jugglers, still struggling to hold the audience's attention, lit flame-tipped batons and threw them back and forth. Smoke filled the hall, rolling up to engulf the dozen lit chandeliers that were suspended over the crowd by thick cables. The crowd exploded as two women tore into each other. The screaming women managed to clear enough room to exchange blows. One jumped on the other and they fell to the floor, and the crowd parted to create a makeshift ring. They were the entertainment now as they rolled back and forth, egged on by the shouts of the audience.

"Are you afraid of heights, Mr. Brown?" Asia asked.

"Why do you ask?" Fitz replied, without moving.

"If you grip those curtains with any more force, you'll tear them from the rods."

"I am," Fitz said. "A bit."

"Oh, dear. And I put you in a third-floor room at home."

"That is not the same, Mrs. Lossing. I have a boarding house surrounding me. Here it is simply a low box and a pair of filthy curtains."

"I suppose there is logic to such thinking. Although it escapes me at present."

"Is this a play?" he thought to ask her.

"No indeed," Asia said, taking a seat at the small table in the box. "Welcome to the Canterbury, Mr. Brown."

"The Canterbury? What the devil is a Canterbury?" he asked, joining her.

She laughed. "Oh, if only my mother could hear you. Devil, indeed. That's exactly what a Canterbury is, she would say, the work of the Devil."

Fitz watched as the orchestra leader saw that the combatants had not yet separated, and increased the tempo. The crowd's excitement grew, and Fitz saw money exchanging hands. The jugglers, disgusted at the audience, extinguished their flaming batons and stomped offstage.

A waiter arrived bearing champagne and two glasses.

"A Canterbury," she said, as the waiter filled the glasses and left, "is the roughest sort of entertainment designed to please the basest instincts of the common people."

A dozen policemen swarmed into the center of the melee and parted the two women while trying to dodge wild punches from the mob. Others in the crowd tried to shout them down for spoiling the show.

"Then what are we doing here?" Fitz asked. "What are *you* doing here?"

She raised her glass to him in a salute. "Because I love it! My father brought me here as a child. Unbeknownst to Mother, of course, or anyone else."

"That is why you are Miss Jones? For the sake of propriety."

"Oh, yes. Propriety is important in Washington. Or at least," she said, taking a healthy drink, "its pretense. Look, we have a new act."

A large man in a black frock coat and a gleaming white shirt stepped onto the stage. The conductor, spying the newcomer, tapped the orchestra to silence. By this time the roar of the crowd had subsided, with most of the audience taking time to fetch more beer. The conductor waved his baton and the orchestra broke into the opening strains of a ballad. The singer clasped his hands together over his ample chest and sang in a deep, melodic voice.

"I don't know him," Asia said. "We'll see if the audience finds him acceptable."

"If they don't, will they hang him?" Fitz asked.

"No. But they have been known to throw things. Isn't it lovely?"

"The mayhem or the ballad?"

"Captain Dunaway, after a lifetime of putting up with strutting politicians and their scatterbrained wives, I find this sort of atmosphere refreshing." She sought his opinion. "Oh, do I disappoint you? Is this unladylike?"

"No," Fitz said, leaning his chair against the wall. He could still see the stage, but his interest was drawn to the audience. They promised the best performance. It was a colorful scene below him, laborers and mechanics of all sorts, gaudy women so dressed they could only be whores, locked arm in arm with soldiers and government workers. The noise was deafening as they argued, sang, and shouted to each other at the top of their lungs. They were gripped with abandon with no thought for anything but their own enjoyment. Fitz envied them. He wondered if he could behave the same way tonight—could he throw all caution to the wind and immerse himself in the pure joy of the moment? Would it be safe to do so? He wondered about something. "Why did you bring me here?"

"This is no place for a lady alone. You seemed a likely candidate to accompany me."

"Should I be flattered?"

"If you could suspend your all-consuming irritation at life momentarily, yes, you should be. I don't make a habit of this sort of thing. Accompanying men to the theater." She traced the stem of the glass with a delicate finger. "Let alone kissing them." She leaned forward and pressed her lips against his. He could taste her, smell her, and forget everything else in his life. When she withdrew, her eyes were swimming with laughter but something else as well—desire.

Fitz took a drink of champagne. He raised his glass to her. "Thank you," he said, finding the words. "For both."

Her eyes questioned him. "But—?" she asked.

He wanted her to understand. "I have been difficult. I apologize for my behavior." It was more than that, of course. It was the secret he held and the secret he feared that existed between them.

The singer finished. The crowd cheered, demanding more.

"He looks relieved," she said, watching the entertainer take a deep bow.

The singer conferred with the conductor and began another song.

"He has a right to be," Fitz said. "He's unharmed."

"Surely an innocent kiss could not disarm you?" She wanted to know more about him. "What troubles you, Captain Dunaway?"

"Nothing that I can share with you, Mrs. Lossing."

She was not satisfied with the answer. "You think me too bold, Captain," she said.

Fitz could tell that she was hurt by his response. "I think from the moment I saw you, I was intrigued." He wanted her to know just how much she had taken his heart. It was something he had not dared admit before but now, after tasting her lips, he knew that he was her captive.

"You could dispel this dreadful awkwardness, Captain Dunaway," she said, the words gentle and hopeful, "if you were to return the kiss."

Fitz felt the need for champagne and took another sip. His thoughts were all twisted about.

"I thought you didn't drink?"

"It's a special occasion," Fitz said. *I've failed,* he thought. *No one has contacted me, and I must go back to Prescott and tell him that I have failed. I've fallen in love with a woman that I cannot trust. It is the end of the line.*

Asia leaned forward and placed her hand on his. "Is it truly, Captain Dunaway?"

Her touch startled him and he thought about withdrawing his hand. But he did not. Instead he allowed his eyes to meet hers. He could read the empathy in her eyes and the tenderness nearly overwhelmed him. Had it been that long since he had touched a woman? Or was it his own despair that caused him to fall under her spell?

He sensed someone's eyes on him. He forced himself to look over the edge of the box to the bar. He felt his heart race as he realized how far above the floor he was. He fought back the queasiness and concentrated on the scene below. The crowd was four- to six-men deep at the long bar, each struggling to get a bartender's attention. All except one man. He was the man watching Fitz. It was Whaley.

Fitz sprang to his feet.

"Captain Dunaway? What is it?"

"Stay here," Fitz ordered.

"What?"

"Stay here!"

Fitz opened the door to the box and dashed down the narrow corridor. A man and woman were blocking the hall in a drunken embrace.

"Get out of my way," Fitz said, pushing them aside. He ran down a narrow flight of stairs, stopping at a doorway to get his bearings. It was a balcony entrance. He nearly tripped over an ancient waiter struggling up the stairs with a huge platter of food. He was on the main floor now, but the crowd was so dense he could see no way to the bar. Then he saw an opening and pushed his way between two beefy men. He swung around a whore and her lover and fought his way to a pillar. He could see the bar now. He slid his hand into his coat and pushed on the pistol, seating it into its holster. He didn't want it jostled loose in the crowd. He forced his way to the end of the bar, looking for Whaley. The man was not there. Fitz cursed and searched the mob. Whaley was nowhere in sight.

He's gone. Outside.

Fitz turned and pushed his way through the crowd. He gagged at the stench of sweat and beer. He bounced off a large man. A thick arm appeared, grasping for Fitz, and he heard cursing. Fitz dashed behind another man as a fight broke out behind him. He could hear shouts and screams and the sound of fists striking flesh. Metropolitans blocked his way, a solid blue wall with nightsticks and determined faces. Fitz ducked and slid to one side, using a group of drunken clerks as a shield. He was in the lobby now and could see the street through the open doors. Another wave of Metropolitans raced past him as he fought his way through a door and out onto the sidewalk. It was dark and a lamplighter was making his way down the sidewalk, stopping to light each lamp.

Fitz looked up and down the street. The traffic was light, no more than a few wagons and carriages. The sidewalk was crowded, and Fitz stepped off the curb and onto the street to get a better view of the pedestrians. He did not see Whaley. He was about to return to the concert hall when he felt the muzzle of a pistol in his back.

"Hey, Cap'n. Don't you turn round."

It wasn't Whaley's voice, but the pistol was real enough.

"How bout a ride, Cap'n?"

Fitz watched as two Metropolitans led a bloody drunk through the doors to a waiting paddy wagon. He thought to call out but realized it would do him no good. He'd be dead before he opened his mouth. He heard a carriage pull to a stop behind him.

"Okay now, Cap'n. Just turn slow and get in. We'll go for a ride."

Fitz did as he was ordered and opened the door of the carriage. It was a closed vehicle with curtains drawn over the windows. When he got into the carriage he saw Whaley seated across from him. The man with the pistol, a small man with a pockmarked face, climbed in. The carriage started up, and Whaley produced a length of rope.

"Lean forward so I can tie your hands," he said.

Fitz felt the pistol barrel jabbed into his ribs. The pockmarked man grinned, revealing a mouthful of broken, yellow teeth. Whaley tied his hands.

"Sorry, Cap'n," Pockmark said.

"Where are you taking me?" Fitz asked as the carriage rumbled over the brick street. The merriment of the Canterbury drifted away to be replaced by the hollow sounds of the horse's hoofs.

"You got good eyes. I didn't think you'd see me," Whaley said, sliding a plug of chewing tobacco into the side of his cheek. "I been following you for some time."

"Why?" Fitz asked. "Don't you trust me?"

Whaley laughed. "I don't know that I'd waste trust on the likes of you." He spat a jet of tobacco juice out the window.

"I don't trust him," Pockmark said. "He's too fancy for me. 'Sides, he's a Yankee. How do you know he won't tell some of his friends about us?"

Whaley concentrated on the tobacco, a slow, methodical chewing, deciding if there was something to what Pockmark said. "No." Whaley reached a decision. "No, I believe we can trust the captain. Ain't that so, Captain?"

"Oh, that's not the question, Mr. Whaley," Fitz said. "It's: can I trust you?"

Chapter 15

An abandoned warehouse
The Island
Washington, DC

An hour had passed before they arrived at their destination. Fitz was certain that they had made a roundabout circuit to hide the location. *They could have driven straight to it with a brass band and a troop of clowns,* Fitz thought as he climbed out of the carriage, *and I still wouldn't know where I am.*

He stretched his legs as Whaley alighted and gave instructions to the driver.

"Take this off," Fitz said to Pockmark, holding out his hands. He'd managed to work his wrists back and forth, loosening the rope, but his hands ached. And he didn't like being bound.

"Listen to that, will ya," Pockmark said to Whaley. "Givin' orders like he's a general or somethin'."

"You heard him," Whaley said. "Take them off."

"What?"

Pockmark whipped a knife from his coat and waved it at Fitz. He sliced through the rope in one sharp motion.

Fitz jerked his hands back, rubbing the circulation back into his wrists.

"Didn't nick you there, did I, Cap'n?" Pockmark asked. "Draw a little blood?"

Whaley pushed open a rough board door leading into an abandoned warehouse. The sharp creaking of the hinges pierced the silence of the night.

"In here," he said to Fitz. Whaley threw an arm across Fitz's chest. "Listen closely," he said. "You go in there and you throw in with us. Hear me? It's all or nothin'." Whaley would not hesitate to kill if he thought he was being betrayed. It would take nothing more than his suspicion.

Fitz pushed Whaley's arm aside and entered the darkened interior of the warehouse.

Bishop was there with two men that Fitz had never seen before. Pockmark and Whaley followed. Pockmark lit an oil lamp on a small table and rummaged through a chest in one corner of the room.

"Let it be," Whaley ordered him.

"But I'm thirsty," Pockmark whined.

"Captain Dunaway," Bishop said in surprise. "I had no idea you'd be here tonight."

"Nor did I," Fitz said. As Pockmark rose with a jug in his hand, Fitz's right fist shot out, catching the man on the jaw. He straightened, staggered back, and fell over the chest.

Fitz shook the pain out of his hand and returned to Whaley. Pockmark clambered to his feet, staring at Fitz. "What'd you do that for?"

"The rope was too tight," Fitz said.

"Enough!" Whaley commanded. "You can kill each other later but now you do exactly as I say." He warned Fitz, "I won't tell you again."

Bishop placed a hand on Whaley's arm. "Mr. Whaley, please don't. He can help us. Can't you, Captain Dunaway? He'll throw in with us, Mr. Whaley, just give him a chance."

"I already have," Fitz said. "Mr. Whaley knows that. Don't you, Mr. Whaley?"

"There's too much at stake for this foolishness," Whaley said. "Everything we do is a hanging offense. This doesn't make us brothers, Dunaway, just because we're workin' together. Don't get any sentimental notions about that."

"Why should I trust a Yankee soldier?" Pockmark asked.

"Because I have nothing left to lose," Fitz said. "If I play you false, you'll kill me. If I'm found out by the government, I'll be hanged."

Bishop watched the exchange in silence.

"You are right about that," Whaley said. "If you play me false, I'll kill you. Bishop, get me the map."

The men gathered around the spindly table.

Whaley moved the lamp to one side, took a bundle from Bishop, and unfolded it.

"The Washington Navy Yard," he said, placing a grimy finger on the map. The rough drawing showed a compound with a dozen buildings. "Here's the Navy Yard Bridge. That's 11th Street. Next to the Yard are the Marine Barracks." He tapped the map. "These are the machine shops. Here is the foundry. Here is the Pyrotechnical Laboratory. This is where the ammunition is tested. Rockets, shells, torpedoes, everything."

Fitz watched Whaley's finger slide across the map, his heart racing faster. It was one thing to bluff his way through a tough situation, but here was something different. This was sabotage. What does this have to do with Lincoln?

"What are these?" Fitz asked, pointing to two shapes in the river. He had to think this out. He had to play for time and information.

"Ship houses," Whaley said. "They're moored at the Yard permanently. They're of no value. What we want is here. The laboratory. Right around here is where they store the powder. It's good-quality powder at that." He found one of the men standing across from him. "How much do you need?"

"Three hundred and fifty pounds?" Sanderson asked Dutton.

They were sickly looking, Fitz thought, both pale with deep circles around their eyes.

Dutton said, "I'd feel better with a thousand."

"A thousand," Sanderson confirmed. "We want the finest grain. Nothing coarse."

"Why does—" Pockmark began.

"Explosive power," Dutton explained. "Burns faster, hotter. It will give us the biggest explosion in a confined space. More destruction."

"You got anything to say?" Whaley asked Fitz.

"Half a ton of powder is a lot to carry off," Fitz said. "I don't care much for the navy but I suspect even they will get suspicious."

"You take this all lightly, don't you?" Whaley asked.

Fitz ignored him. "What about sentries?"

"Most of them are here," Whaley said. "On the wall. The biggest problem will be the river patrol. They swing by about every two hours."

"What about the current?" Fitz asked.

"It ain't bad here," Whaley said.

"When?" Fitz asked.

"Early morning. Say about two."

"No, I mean what day?"

"I'll let you know," Whaley said to Fitz. "Nobody does nothin' until I'm sure we all understand what's to be done. I don't aim to get got."

Fitz looked around. "How are five of us going to move that much powder without getting caught?"

"Six," Bishop reminded him. He wanted to be included.

"What's your plan?" Fitz asked.

"We'll have a boat at the end of 4th Street near the docks. The river forms a shallow bay at this point. We row over across the bay to the Yard, make our way to the Pyrotechnical Laboratory, and get what we need. We'll get out the same way we got in. If anyone sees us, we'll fire the buildings. That should keep them busy."

"Which building is the laboratory?" Fitz asked.

Whaley pointed to a building near the water's edge. "It's about a hundred yards from the river. The sentries on the wall can't see us, but those on the ship houses might. If we keep this point between them and us, we're better off. We'll move in when the boat is at the far side of the Yard changing crews."

"They'll pick us out in the fire."

"You afraid?"

"When that building goes up," Fitz said, "it'll light up everything within a quarter of a mile."

"Then we'll have to row like hell to get across the river before it goes up, won't we?"

"What about me?" Bishop asked. "What am I to do?"

"You wait with the boat," Whaley said. "Kill anybody that ain't one of us."

"I can do more than that," Bishop offered.

"I've got all the help we need," Whaley said. He sought out the man with the gray beard. "You sure a thousand pounds will do it?"

Dutton was certain. "Properly placed and backfilled, there's no doubt."

"Please, Mr. Whaley," Bishop said. "I want to help."

"With that crippled foot? You stay back. We'll use coal oil and gunpowder just in case we have to fire it," Whaley continued. "Lay a track as a fuse. That should give us time to get back to the boat and back across the river."

"How do we get into the building?" Fitz asked.

Whaley exploded. "Don't tell me what 'we' have to do. I'll tell you what to do when the time comes."

"He didn't mean anything," Bishop said. "Did you, Captain Dunaway?"

"No," Fitz said.

"There's a wagon entrance at either end," Whaley said, calming. "They leave them partially open all the time. They want to keep everythin' cool in the building."

Fitz knew the question was dangerous, but he had to ask, "Why do we need powder?"

" 'We' again," Whaley said but without malice.

"Did you hear that?" Pockmark chimed in. "It's 'we' now . . ."

"Yes," Fitz said. "But it's my neck as well. We're going to a lot of trouble for the powder. Why?"

"Bishop, take this—" Whaley began but thought better of baiting Fitz. "*Captain* Dunaway back to his lodgings."

Bishop gathered his coat.

"Remember this," Whaley said to Fitz. "You may be everythin' you say you are but like you said, our necks are involved. I may decide to tell you everythin' when the time is right. But not now, Dunaway."

Fitz looked at the map again. "I suppose you'll find that out at the Navy Yard."

"Mister," Whaley said. "You get under my skin. I don't mind tellin' you that. Keep this in mind—by the time we get done we will have ended this war. You know how to kill a snake—cut off his head. Nothin' to it. Now go on home."

Bishop tugged at Fitz's arm. "Come with me, Captain. I'll see you home. It's late, sir. Let's be on our way."

"Go on," Whaley said. "Go with the cripple."

"Please, Captain," Bishop whispered. His grip tightened on Fitz's arm.

Bishop guided Fitz through a door and out into an alley. Seedy clapboard buildings that ran along either side of the narrow dirt street surrounded them. Bishop scrambled into a waiting carriage and Fitz joined him. They traveled in silence before Bishop spoke.

"Mr. Whaley can be difficult, but he is courageous. I've never felt that I had courage. I suppose I've never had the opportunity to prove myself. I've envied men who have."

"I don't trust him," Fitz said. He thought about the man seated next to him. "I haven't found much reason to trust you, either, Mr. Bishop."

"Mr. Whaley," Bishop said, "has had a difficult life. No education, no skills. He's intelligent, I'm quite certain of that, but it's a savage intelligence, unpredictable. He skirts the edge of polite society, Captain Dunaway. I understand that. You mustn't underestimate Mr. Whaley. He can be violent but he is a courageous man."

"You said that."

"Yes, yes. I have, haven't I? I repeat myself when I'm nervous. To tell you the truth, I was surprised he showed restraint. That is unlike him. He has a quick temper. I thought you two would come to blows. Will you be all right today, do you suppose? I was very distressed when they brought you in. Mr. Whaley still isn't convinced of your loyalty. He said as much."

Fitz threw Bishop an irritated look.

"I'm sorry, sir. I talk too much, I know that. Oh, do you see that? The sun is just coming up.

'Ah, dream too bright to last!
Ah, starry Hope! that didst arise
But to be overcast.'

"That is from Mr. Poe's 'The Assignation.' "

'For, alas! alas! with me
The light of Life is o'er!
No more—no more—no more.'

"Did you like it?"

"I wasn't listening."

"Well," Bishop said, crestfallen, "most people don't. But he was a genius. How I long to have met him. He attended West Point, you know."

"He must have been another class," Fitz said, rubbing his eyes. They were on Pennsylvania Avenue. There were few vehicles this time of night, mostly delivery wagons. A familiar stench filled the air. "Are we near the canal?"

"Yes. It is over there. I should have you home in ten minutes."

"What was he talking about? Cutting off a snake's head?"

"I don't know," Bishop said. "Mr. Whaley is very closed-mouthed about many things."

"Are there more men?" Fitz asked. "Besides those that I saw tonight?"

Bishop answered, "Mr. Whaley says that there are others."

"Are there?"

"I've never known Mr. Whaley to lie."

"That's small consolation. Has this to do with Lincoln, Mr. Bishop? Is the plan to kill him?"

"I am not certain. Sometimes Mr. Whaley talks as if they will . . . as if we will. I don't know."

Fitz's mind wandered over something that Bishop had said. "You said he showed restraint. What do you mean?"

Bishop was pleased that Fitz had been listening and then a frown crossed his face. "Only that I have seen him in a much more violent temper. I am surprised he didn't strike you. He must believe in your loyalty, otherwise—"

"What?"

Bishop said in a quiet voice, "I don't think he would have let you live."

They rode in silence but Fitz's mind would not let him rest. Asia was surely involved. She took him to the Canterbury where Whaley was waiting for him. He ached at the thought of her involvement, and by her role in his abduction. She was not who she pretended to be. But then, who in Washington was?

Whaley waited until he was sure that Fitz had gone. Sanderson swept the Navy Yard map from the table while Dutton pulled several large maps from a loose board in the wall. Whaley examined a map, threw it on the floor, and concentrated on another.

When he spoke it was intended for Dutton and Sanderson. "It has to be done by December. This don't look half-done to me."

"We have to go well around the conservatory," Dutton explained.

"Did you run into rocks?" Whaley asked. "Maybe they slowed you down?"

Dutton, heartened by Whaley's willingness to find an explanation for their lack of progress, relaxed. "The soil is very coarse," he said. "There are seams of clay throughout. We dare not make too much noise when we dig."

Whaley shot him a disgusted look. "Nothin' in this city is quiet. There's enough traffic on 17th Street to drown out a bombardment and twice that on the avenue." He turned his attention to Sanderson. "You said December for sure. You said everything would be down before a hard freeze. The weather's fixin' to turn and you're only halfway there."

"It took longer than we thought. We just can't come right out and tell the men why they're digging. Can we?"

"A bomb-proof," Whaley said. "That's what we tell them. And that's all they need to know."

"Those two men that—"

"That's done," Whaley said. "I took care of them like I take care of everythin' else. This has been planned out to the last minute and if someone doesn't do what he's supposed to, the whole thing collapses like a house of cards. Well, that ain't goin' to happen. Everyone will do what they're supposed to do. Now you go ahead and keep the men diggin' until you're all dug out. Just get the charges loaded and set. You're experts at this, ain't you?"

"It'll be done," Dutton said.

Sanderson rolled up the maps and returned them to the loose board. "What about the Yankee captain?" he asked.

"I told you," Whaley said. "I take care of everythin' around here. Including him when the time's right."

Chapter 16

October 27, 1861
The 196th day of the war
The War Department

Fitz consulted his pocket watch. He had done so countless times during the day, but the hands seemed motionless on the enameled face. He willed them to jump to the next hour as he snapped the cover shut and slipped the watch in his vest pocket. He returned to his reports without enthusiasm.

When Bishop had returned him to the boarding house, he had rushed upstairs, changed into his uniform, and headed to the War Department. He had tried to see Prescott but both he and Batterman were away, no one knew when they would return. He thought of sending a note by way of a messenger but discarded that idea. If the note fell into the wrong hands it would be a disaster. He planned to wait until the workday ended, lose himself in the stream of departing workers, and make his way to Prescott's office. And perhaps the only chance to stop the attack on the Navy Yard.

But every thought of the attack was accompanied by the notion that Asia was, after all, a traitor. Fitz told himself a dozen times that she could not be, it was all coincidence, but the claims were lifeless, and eventually died away. She had taken him to the Canterbury, and Whaley was waiting for him despite his clumsy attempt to convince Fitz otherwise.

Fitz flipped back the cover of his watch but his racing thoughts took precedence. Whaley couldn't act until tonight at the earliest. Most likely the attack would be launched early the following morning. *You still have time,* Fitz told himself; don't be rash. *"Captain Dunaway displayed unwarranted rashness,"* he remembered a written reprimand. "Dash, I call it," Fitz had told his commanding officer; an uncompromising example of dash. Fitz had lost the argument. *I've lost all of the arguments,* he thought. The army wants me to move with deliberation or dash, but they are not sure when either applies.

Which applies now, Fitz?

He never had the opportunity to answer the question.

Corporal Benton brought in a stack of reports and rosters. "Here you are, Captain Dunaway," he said, removing the old.

Fitz exploded. "Take those silly things away. What time is it?"

The shocked Benton gave Fitz a confused look and glanced at the watch in his hand.

"Blast!" If Prescott wasn't in, Fitz would try to locate Lamon.

He rushed up the stairs of the War Department and made his way to Prescott's office.

Batterman greeted him with a cool indifference, telling him to wait while he informed Mr. Prescott that Fitz wished to see him.

After Prescott heard Fitz's report, he rose from his desk and circled the room.

"Remarkable! Absolutely remarkable. The Navy Yard. Did you get that, Mr. Batterman? And possibly Mr. Lincoln. Madmen, that's what they are." He walked away from his desk, hands clasped behind his back. "One ton of powder, you say?"

"Half that," Fitz corrected him.

"Not easy to move. Dangerous, in fact." Prescott turned back to Fitz as if he were on the verge of asking a question. "For one purpose or many?" He posed. "We must notify the proper authorities. Please see to it, Mr. Batterman."

"Yes, Mr. Prescott," Batterman said, finishing the line. He dipped his pen in an inkwell and waited for Fitz to continue.

"But you don't know when, Captain? When they will strike?"

"No, sir."

Prescott returned to his desk. "Well, things are moving at a pace that I had not anticipated."

"What are your orders, sir?"

"Let me think, Captain," Prescott said. Fitz saw see him laying out the events side by side. "You were first approached by Bishop at the tobacconist after having been sent there by Mrs. Lossing. Next, you accompany Mrs. Lossing to the theater and you run afoul of Whaley. It appears that Mrs. Lossing plays a role in this, wouldn't you agree, Captain?"

"Perhaps, sir," Fitz conceded.

Prescott laughed in disbelief. "Come, man, what other explanation do you have? Surely you don't think that this is coincidence, do you?"

"I don't know, Mr. Prescott."

Prescott's face took of the look of an uncle who must explain the realities of life to a favorite nephew. "Captain Dunaway, Fitz, we must be candid with one another. You cannot ignore the facts."

Fitz chose his words. "I cannot reconcile the facts with her involvement."

Prescott shot Batterman a surprised look. "You're not the chivalrous type, are you, Fitz?" he asked, surprised. "You don't strike me as such. By God, the last of the Romantics. You surprise me yet again, Captain Dunaway. You're not protecting this woman, are you?"

Fitz felt his face redden. "No, sir."

"Because if we are to bag this lot, we must bag everyone.

Whaley, Bishop, and the others. All of them. Remember what I told you, Fitz. This is your chance for a regiment. Don't let anyone get in your way."

"I will do my duty."

Prescott's manner softened and he walked around the desk. He laid a comforting hand on Fitz's shoulder. "I know you will. I never had any doubt about that. Now, we must consider how to go about this. How does one undertake trapping a bunch of vipers? Bag them all at once, I say. Not in their lair, because they will have the advantage. We must catch them in the act. Mr. Batterman, alert Mr. Lamon. He'll see to that end of it. We'll set a trap at the Navy Yard. How does that strike you, Fitz?"

"It strikes me as risky, sir."

"We catch them in the act. You've told us how they will arrive and what they will do and how they plan to escape."

"But not when. I don't know that yet."

"No," Prescott agreed. He returned to his chair and took a seat. He locked his fingers together on his desk and fell into thought. Fitz watched him search for a solution.

"Did Whaley say how or when he would contact you?" Prescott asked.

"No."

Prescott took a breath. "Well, he must. Somehow. He does not trust you, so he will give you little or no notice. We have no choice. Mr. Batterman, contact Mr. Welles as well and inform him that we have reason to believe saboteurs target the Navy Yard. Tell him that I respectfully recommend that he keep a company of marines available, but discreetly, at the Yard. Tell him that I will pass on additional information as I receive it. Does that suit you, Fitz?"

It did not. "Mr. Prescott, suppose I can't give you any notice? I would be walking into the same trap. How will the marines know me from the saboteurs?"

"You must somehow alarm the Yard during the raid."

"How?"

Prescott smiled as if the matter bore little weight. "Be

resourceful, Fitz. Surely you've learned that. We'll set the
trap, and you lead our enemies into it. When the matter is
over, you'll get your regiment. And considerably sooner than
the six months I anticipated. You must have faith. Mr. Batterman, finish Captain Dunaway's report and draft a memoran-
dum to Mr. Welles and Mr. Lamon."

"There is a man at the boarding house," Fitz said.
"Someone who could make trouble for me."

"Who?" Prescott asked, concern in his voice.

"Mr. Woodbridge. He works for the Committee on the
Conduct of the War."

Prescott looked at Batterman as if they shared a secret.
"The Joint Committee, Fitz. The House and Senate banded
together in an effort to make sure that every man is loyal,
and every battle is a victory. Congress, my dear Captain, is a
great dumb beast that goes where it should not and does
what it was never intended to do. I'll handle Woodbridge.
Mr. Lossing, Fitz? Do you see much of the erring husband?"

"Just once, sir."

"A scoundrel," Prescott conceded, glancing at Batterman.
"He raced through his family's money, gambling, they say,
and squandered his wife's. Disloyal, I am told, and a cad."

Fitz felt that Prescott was about to dismiss him without
talking about Whaley's other threat. "Sir, what about the
danger to Mr. Lincoln? Whaley's threat?"

Prescott glanced at him. "The president is more than ade-
quately guarded by the army and Mr. Lamon. Why, you see
the reports every day, don't you, Fitz?"

"Yes, sir. It's just—"

"Bombast." Prescott brushed away the idea. "Idle threats.
Gentlemen don't go around trying to murder each other."

"Whaley is no gentleman," Fitz countered, alarmed that
Prescott found the idea preposterous.

"A figure of speech, Fitz," Prescott soothed. "I appreciate
your apprehension, truly I do, but I've been at this business
for some time."

"Yes, sir," Fitz conceded.

"Rest assured there will be no attempt on President Lincoln's life. The only blood shed will be that of the conspirators."

"I only thought it best that you be aware of it, sir."

"Well done, Captain Dunaway," Prescott said. "I'm sure that you must be on your way. We'll have the garrison at the Navy Yard strengthened. Good night, sir. Godspeed."

Fitz rose, saluted, and left.

He journeyed home, lost in thought. His mind traveled back over his interview with Prescott and the incident last night. Whaley did not trust him. But if he did not trust him, why inform him of the attack on the Navy Yard? There was Bishop's surprise at Whaley's restraint—what did that mean? If they suspected me, why not just kill me? The questions spun around his brain, chasing answers that did not exist.

He heard Prescott's voice when he defended Asia—"*you cannot ignore the facts.*"

Facts! What facts? What right did Prescott have to say such a thing? What nonsense was he talking? Was he there? *Does he know Asia as I do?*

Do you indeed?

Goddamn Prescott and Goddamn this city!

And me for a fool, Fitz thought.

Chapter 17

The Royal Boarding House

When he arrived at the boarding house, he was pleased Asia was not in the gazebo, although he thought it unlikely that she would be. The weather was turning colder and the barren trees offered no protection from the chill winds of fall. He did not know what he would say to her if they encountered one another. He realized that he had to act as if nothing were troubling him, for to appear so might give away the game—if Asia Lossing was involved.

He entered the house, went to his room to freshen up, and returned downstairs to the dining room to join the others for supper. He dreaded it, and went as a man goes to his own execution.

The others were gathered around the table, intent on their meal when Fitz joined them. Asia, as usual, was seated at the head of the table. She was engaged in conversation with George Hastings, a pleasant one from the looks of it. She smiled, engrossed in what Mr. Hastings had to say. Fitz hated Hastings and hated Asia as well, simply because they behaved as if nothing was the matter. He was surprised at his own intense feelings. They sat at the table, civil and polite, chatting about unimportant things, leaving him nowhere to unleash his rage. He wanted some reason to strike out. If she would only look at him in disgust, if Hastings would make some inane observation, if Woodbridge would insult him, if someone would say or do something.

"Captain Dunaway," Hogan said, patting an empty chair next to him. "Come and tell us all you know."

Fitz sat down. Asia did not bother to look his way.

"It's pork tonight, Captain. And yams. I'm right fond of yams. Can't get my fill. How goes it with you? Well, I trust." Hogan reached across the table and set a platter of meat in front of Fitz. "Get yourself some of those rolls, too. Fresh baked, I believe."

"You look troubled, Captain," Woodbridge said, buttering a roll. "Is the war going poorly for your side?"

"Ignore him," Hogan whispered.

"Yes, Captain," Asia Lossing said. "You do look troubled. Are you unwell? Perhaps the night air did not agree with you?"

Nothing in her voice gave away that he had deserted her last night; it was completely free of malice. Yet Fitz felt her animosity as if she had slapped him.

"Not at all," he replied.

"I believe there's something going around," Pennbrook said, his delicate lips curling up at the thought. "If it weren't for the season, I'd say it was swamp sickness. I believe I have a touch of it myself."

"Perhaps it's miasma," Hastings offered.

"Whatever a man gets is always curable with a sizeable tumbler of strong whiskey," Hogan said.

"I hear McClellan's to move south any day now," Woodbridge said to Asia. "Richmond is his target, of course. The war will be over soon." He spooned some sugar into his coffee, added some cream, and stirred the steaming liquid. "Then we'll have our day of reckoning for traitors." He looked at Fitz. The others at the table could not help but read the implication.

Fitz found his target. "Mr. Woodbridge," he said, in a voice so low the others strained to hear it. "You have been baiting me since we met. If you've something to say, say it."

He stood and threw his napkin on the table, his voice trembling.

"Captain Dunaway, restrain yourself," Asia Lossing said. The words dripped with disdain as she added for good measure, "That conduct is for taverns and bullies."

Fitz turned on her, hoping that she would understand. He saw nothing but anger and disappointment in her eyes, and he knew it was not his words that enraged her but his disappearance last night. He bowed, acknowledging his punishment. "Mrs. Lossing, I apologize if my words offended you. I was simply speaking the truth."

"I have a right to my opinion and a right to express it," Woodbridge said, his conviction slipping away.

"If you continue to draw your rights," Fitz snapped, "you had better be prepared to draw a pistol. I'll see you in Hell before I accept another insult."

"Captain Dunaway!" Asia said, jumping to her feet. "I will see you in the library, sir. Now!"

Fitz watched as she left the dining room. He felt a tug on his sleeve. It was Hogan.

"Stay clear of her claws. She has a temper like a wildcat."

Fitz followed Asia out of the dining room and into the library. He closed the door.

"How dare you behave in such a manner in this house?" she demanded, biting off each word. "Do you think I condone your actions?"

"I said what I thought."

"Don't patronize me, Captain Dunaway. You can shoot that pompous boor for all I care, but not in this house. Do you understand me? I'm sick of this business. Not in my house, sir! If there is going to be one safe haven of sanity in this madness, it will be my house."

"The man is insolent."

"He is insolent! My dear Lord, don't you look in the mirror every morning?"

"My honor—"

She cut him off. "Spare me talk of honor! This war is on

account of honor. Men's honor! You arrogant, opinionated bastard!"

Fitz watched as she spun away from him. She collected herself. He had never seen such passion in a woman before and her attack startled him. He saw her shoulders rise with each breath, the curve of her waist, the way her red hair softened the gentle outline of her long neck. He wanted to hold her and rest her head on his shoulder. He wondered what it must feel like to gather her up in his arms.

She turned back to him. "Why did you leave me?"

"I saw a man," Fitz said, the ridiculous words sticking in his throat.

"A man?" she asked. "What does that mean?"

"He is a man I am working with. Someone who is helping me."

She closed the distance between them, and he read the hurt in her eyes. "Helping you to do what? Is Woodbridge right about you?"

"No."

"You did not return. What am I to make of that?"

"I'm sorry. Nothing. It meant nothing."

"It did to me, you arrogant, impolite martinet!"

"Please, Asia," Fitz said in desperation. She was twisting his words and flinging them back at him. He had no way to respond. "I am trying to explain but I can't tell you why. Will you trust me?"

"No. I will not trust you," she said. "Trust got me a spineless husband and a mountain of debts. I will not trust you."

Fitz lost his temper. "I am not your husband! The man is a damn fool." He trapped her arms in his hands, his grip biting into her flesh. "Any man who leaves your side should be shot." He drew her to him and kissed her. She tried to pull back and then to push away, but his arms encircled her. His lips traveled over hers, and then, she responded. He could feel her breathing soften as he drew her even closer. Her breasts nestled against his chest and the tip of her tongue ran over his lips. He had never been so inflamed in his life.

She drew back. Some of her anger had drifted away and in its place rested confusion. "How could you have abandoned me?"

He shook his head.

"Can you give me no explanation, Fitz? Don't I deserve that at least?"

Fitz closed his eyes and sought her lips. "I wish to God I could, yes."

He stroked her hair, letting his fingers travel down the back of her neck and around to her cheek. He kissed her again, his lips lingering over her lips, parting them enough to let his tongue slide into her mouth. She returned the kiss but pushed him back.

"What sort of man are you, Captain Dunaway?" she asked. "A hero one moment, a cipher the next."

"No sort, to speak of."

"At times I think I see you as you really are—a kind, generous soul. You are that sort, aren't you? I was right, wasn't I?"

"I never thought of myself as such," he said.

"You are," she said. "I know I am right. It is my curse to know people as they are." A frown crossed her face. "You are different. I see your qualities. I see so much hidden from view. What do you hide, sir? What is behind those kind eyes?"

His heart pounded. He could not tell her.

"You are not the iron man that you pretend, Captain Dunaway."

He said, "I am coming, slowly, to find that out."

"What? Fitz Dunaway admits that he is human?"

"No, only that I am not iron."

"It's doing you no good," she said. "I am afraid. You trouble me, Captain Dunaway, with the same degree that you interest me. You are in some difficulty, aren't you, Fitz? It is serious, I can feel it. The others talk about you. Woodbridge is convinced that you are a traitor."

"Has Woodbridge convinced you that I am?"

"No, Fitz," she said. "But I don't know about you. I don't know what you are about. You confuse me." She hesitated, as if she had found what she wanted to say, but feared the words. "I will not open myself to harm. I did that for Henry to my everlasting regret. It is a horrible thing to say but I am glad that his drinking and cards keep him away from this house. I will not burden myself with feelings again."

"I understand."

"If you understand, tell me what troubles you," she said and then added, "I see a storm raging inside of you, Captain Dunaway, and I fear it will sweep you away."

He could not bear to hurt her. He felt himself drawn to her scent, the smoothness of her skin, the deep calm of her eyes as they sought to understand him. He had never encountered these feelings before and he was intoxicated beyond all reason. "You see me as I am," he said, because he could think of nothing else to say that would convince her of his feelings. "You enchant me."

"Yes," Asia said, accepting that he would not reveal himself to her. She slipped from his arms and walked to the fireplace. "I should have firewood brought in," she said, picking up a poker and stirring the dying ashes. "If you are a traitor," she said to the fire, "I could not bear to know it. I won't ask any questions of you." She set the poker in the stand. "You must never involve me in this business. Promise me, Fitz."

He moved to her and took her in his arms again. "I will not," he said, and kissed her. She returned his kiss, throwing her arms around him. Her hand moved to the back of his neck, and he shivered with excitement. She pushed against him and the heat from her body made him hold her tighter.

"Supper is getting cold," she whispered.

"I had forgotten about supper."

She forced him away. "A good hostess cannot afford to forget about the well-being of her guests. You will return to the table and make amends with Woodbridge."

"That fool—"

"Oh, yes. If you expect to remain in this house or at my side, you will make amends."

"You don't know how much you ask of me," Fitz said. "I never learned to curb my tongue."

"Is that true?" Asia smiled. The smile disappeared. "Promise me, Fitz. You will not make me a party to your actions."

"I will not," he said, and then he wondered if just the opposite had happened—if she had involved him.

Chapter 18

Asia and Fitz had returned to the table and eaten their meals without speaking to one another. Asia was polite, talking to the men gathered around the table, sharing the latest war news. Woodbridge had spent most of his time observing Fitz, or passing whispered remarks to Hastings. Hogan had seemed quiet, intent on conquering the mound of food he had ladled onto his plate.

Too many thoughts crowded Fitz's mind as he ate, and later as he excused himself and sat in the library, alone. Thoughts about the Navy Yard, of course, and about Prescott and the whole sour mess he found himself trapped in.

It was late and the house was silent after supper. He thought about Asia as well. He thought of the taste of her lips and the warmth of her body when it was pressed against his. He wondered if she was thinking of him.

And after a time he realized his mind occupied itself with her almost to the exclusion of everything else. I am not a very successful spy, he concluded, and settled on leafing through *Harpers* and *Leslie's* weeklies, and browsing through the *National Intelligencer*. He recalled the sweet pain of longing for a war that had been denied him, and seemed to be drifting away.

He poured over the newspapers, studying the maps, reading the accounts of the war at sea, the blockade, the regiments being raised in the East and in the West. A vast ring of armies encircled Washington, somewhere at the end of the dusty roads that radiated from the Capitol. They were out of Fitz's reach, growing, training, measuring the time until they stepped off.

He helped himself to a brandy from a small cabinet against the wall and tossed a log onto the fire. The flames consumed the wood in an excited shower of sparks. The bitter taste of the brandy reminded him why he did not drink. He tossed the remains of the liquid into the fire, which reacted with an angry spit.

He saw the image of Woodbridge in the curling flames and wondered what thoughts hid behind the man's narrow eyes. Fitz had made an enemy, a cunning one, one well versed in the intrigues of this hateful city. Another politician who approached the shore with muffled oars. Fitz had found himself hating Woodbridge and at the same time hating Prescott.

He smoked his pipe and then, knocking the ashes into the fire, closed the damper in the fireplace and climbed the stairs to his room. The house was quiet except for the soft ticking of a hall clock, and the tiny flames of the wall lamps that hissed in the darkness. He felt melancholy. He wondered if this was a common thing after a man aches to hold a woman close to him. Asia had wrung emotion from him like water from a facecloth. This was not the first time he had given his heart—the major's daughter had demanded that as well as his uniform—but it was the first time he had been so overwhelmed that his senses seemed to have flown from him. Fitz thought her name and the longing increased—Asia.

He knew no more of her than she knew of him. Or did she know more than she claimed? He entered his room and struck a match to find the lamp.

Henry Lossing was sitting in the small chair against the wall. He looked seedy and ill-used in a wrinkled suit mottled by stains.

"Captain Dunaway," he said, raising clumsily a half-filled glass in greeting.

His presence startled Fitz. Lossing was not armed, or at least a weapon wasn't showing, but Fitz was certain that he was dangerous, fortified with whatever was in the glass. "What do you want?" Fitz asked.

"Just a visit with one of my lodgers," Lossing said. "You have nothing to worry about from me. I'm not so sure the same can be said of you."

Fitz edged close to the bed, putting as much distance between himself and Lossing as possible in the small room.

Lossing took a drink. "Do you mind if I ask you, sir," he began, "what your intentions are with my wife?"

"That's not fit talk for gentlemen," Fitz said, realizing how stupid he sounded. Lossing's wife had been in his arms just hours before.

"Oh, no. No," Lossing said, swaying unsteadily. "You misunderstand me. No, I'm not the jealous type. I ask only because of your well-being, don't you see?"

"I don't understand," Fitz said, very uncomfortable. Lossing was much too calm to suit Fitz.

"She is a very determined woman," Lossing said. "She never settles for less than she thinks she deserves. I myself am a poor example of a man who could not satisfy her many demands."

Fitz thought about striking Lossing, but he knew that would bring about nothing but chaos. He settled on, "You're drunk." He did not want to hear more about Asia because he feared that it might be true.

"Of course I am," Lossing confirmed. "And greedy and broke. What can I say?" He opened his arms. "I am less than the ideal husband. You, on the other hand, might be the ideal suitor. Brave, handsome, you don't drink, do you? No, I didn't think so. There is an air of mystery about you, however."

"Get out," Fitz ordered.

Lossing finished his drink and threw the glass against the wall. It shattered with a bang.

"In my own house?" Lossing asked. "You're ordering me about in my own house? I may be the cuckolded husband, Captain, but I won't be ordered about."

"Get out now," Fitz said. "Or I'll throw you out." He heard muffled voices and footsteps and knew the household had been awakened.

Lossing staggered forward, doubling his fists. "Captain Dunaway," he said, his voice trembling in rage. "Have you been familiar with my wife?" He swung a wild blow at Fitz's head, and staggered forward. Righting himself, he threw another punch. Fitz dodged both.

There was a quick knock at the door and Asia was in the room. She pulled a housecoat close around her. Clara stood just behind, holding an oil lamp.

"You're just in time, my dear," Lossing said. His fist came up, brushing Fitz's cheek. That was the last straw.

Fitz struck him on the chin and Lossing reeled back, collapsing into the chair.

"Captain Dunaway? What is the meaning of this?" Asia demanded.

"Ask him," Fitz said, massaging his knuckles.

Excited voices filled the hallway behind Clara. It seemed all the boarders were anxious to find out what had happened.

Asia drew Clara into the room and closed the door. She turned to Fitz. "I asked you a question, Captain Dunaway."

"The man was in my room," Fitz said, angered by her tone. "He swung at me. The third time demanded a response."

"He's drunk," Asia said. "Couldn't you have taken his condition into allowance?"

"I waited for the third blow." Fitz was shocked at her response. "You make it seem as if this is my fault."

Asia helped Lossing to his feet. "Clara, please take Mr. Lossing to his room." After they were gone Asia made sure that the hallway was clear. She closed the door once more.

"Captain Dunaway, I would have thought you capable of more forbearance under the circumstances."

"Circumstances being that that man invaded my quarters and assaulted me," Fitz returned.

"You know very well what I mean," Asia said.

"I don't understand you," Fitz said. "That man, husband or no, accosted me. I was defending myself. What troubles him is his business and he had no right to bring it to me."

"I asked you to be more sympathetic," Asia said, her eyes flashing. "His situation has been difficult and as I told you, I am responsible for it."

"Mrs. Lossing. You did not place the cards in his hand, nor pour the whiskey down his throat, and I am reasonably certain you did not direct him to my room."

Asia stepped back as if he had slapped her. "You bastard. I revealed myself to you and now you mock me."

"You're not listening," Fitz said, frustrated.

"Captain Dunaway," Asia said, her words ringing with finality, "you have said nothing that I care to listen to." She fled the room, the tail of her housecoat snapping after her.

Lossing pulled away from Clara, staggered down the back stairway and out into the yard, finding the path that led to the carriage house. He heard someone behind him.

"You're in no shape to talk," Whaley said, pushing Lossing into the carriage house. He closed the door and lit an oil lamp. "Where have you been?"

"Upstairs," Lossing said as he made his way to the room that housed the carriage tack and his brandy bottles. He pulled on the door, frustrated by the latch's stiffness.

Whaley leaned against the tack room door, blocking Lossing's attempts. "I need you sober."

"Go to hell," Lossing snapped.

"Sober," Whaley said, catching sight of Lossing's chin. "Someone got you good."

"I need a drink."

Whaley pulled him away from the door and threw him down on the iron step of a carriage. "First we talk." He tossed Lossing a leather purse. "For bringing them in. How are you going to get them out when the job's done?"

Lossing looked up, confused.

"The engineers that you brought up from Virginia. They'll want to go home soon."

"I didn't know they were engineers," Lossing said.

"You do now."

"I've got it all mapped out. They've got to come up to Gries Bluff and come across near the rapids. It's better that way. Better to come down from the north." He looked up at Whaley, trying to focus. "Engineers, huh? Why do you need engineers?"

"I'll contact you when I'm ready," Whaley said, ignoring the question.

"Yes," Lossing confirmed. "I'll need more money," weighing the purse in the palm of his hand. "It gets expensive, you know."

Whaley leaned on the front wheel of the carriage. "You always want more. I'll be happy when more turns into enough."

"It's an expensive business," Lossing said. The thought of more money captured his attention and he failed to see the disgust in Whaley's eyes. "When can I get it?"

"At the Haven," Whaley said. "In two days." He studied Lossing's bruised face. "You stick your nose in somebody's business?"

"It was my business," Lossing said. "My wife."

"Who did it?"

"Dunaway," Lossing said, and staggered to his feet. "In my house."

Whaley smiled. "Well. See how things happen. I told you to watch him. You've done more than that, I see." He slid a plug of tobacco into his jaw, taking care that it was properly placed. "That might serve our purpose after all."

"What?" Lossing asked.

"Rachael's Haven. Two days. You'll get your money," Whaley said. He flipped open the tack room door latch. "Help yourself," he added as he left the dim interior of the carriage house.

Chapter 19

November 8, 1861
The 235th day of the war
The War Department Building

The note was on Fitz's desk when he arrived at work. *Come to the City Market at 9:30 p.m.*, it read, and it was signed *Bishop*.

He consulted his watch. It was just before noon—time to inform Prescott that he had been contacted. His fingers had trembled when he opened the message, but after he read the words came the thought that this could be a trap. There was no way to find out if it was unless he did as he was ordered.

At noon he raced to Prescott's office, relieved to see that Will's door was closed. He had no idea what explanation he would give his friend for his visit to the assistant secretary of war.

He entered the outer office and found Batterman seated at his desk, dining on hardboiled eggs and cheese. The private secretary looked up in surprise.

"Captain Dunaway? Can I help you?"

"I need to see Mr. Prescott."

"He isn't in," Batterman said, patting his lips with a napkin. "Can I help you?"

Fitz showed Batterman the note.

Batterman read it. "Bishop? Isn't he the crippled poet?"

"Yes. When will Mr. Prescott return?"

"Not for several hours," Batterman said. "What does this mean?"

The questioning irritated Fitz. Had this man no sense of urgency? "I don't know," Fitz said. "I must speak with Mr. Prescott."

"I'll send someone to find him," Batterman said in an indifferent tone. "You will go to the meeting, of course?"

"Yes," Fitz said. "But, I would prefer to attend knowing full well I can count on assistance."

"But you don't know what they plan?" Batterman asked, examining the note as if the answer were somehow embedded in the paper.

"I don't know, sir," Fitz said. "But it must involve the Navy Yard."

"Yes," Batterman said, "or something else. I will keep the note. You will keep your rendezvous. We will provide all of the assistance that you require at the Yard and capture this lot of traitors in one fell swoop. Is that to your liking, sir?"

"Yes," Fitz said. "As long as you remember I am the one most likely to suffer the consequences if you don't."

Fitz hurried to the boarding house that evening and changed into civilian clothes. He was fortunate. He did not see Asia, and the other boarders were gathered in the parlor, reading or engaged in parlor games. He didn't want to speak to or see anyone. He was tired of people and their ideas and their opinions and their intrusion into his affairs. *They complicate my life,* he told himself as he was changing. *It's better to be who I am alone than who people want me to be.*

He took the omnibus to the City Market, a sad string of lonely, dilapidated shacks abandoned to the freezing darkness. He alighted from the vehicle, swinging easily from a rail at the rear, and stepped to the ground. He carried his pistol, and he carried a sense of purpose as well. This was for him, everything—who he was, how he behaved, how he controlled his life. It wasn't the battlefield he knew, but it was the only one that he had and he meant to fight well on it. He only hoped that Batterman had managed to arrange for assistance, but he had little faith in the man, he was too much the clerk. Clerks, he snorted. A city of clerks, a government of clerks. Clerks for every purpose—lurking in doorways, behind pillars. *Stop it!*

The chill picked at Fitz as he passed the shuttered buildings, keeping close to the dark shacks, he felt less of a target in their deep shadow. The stench of the canal hung in the air and his eyes watered. The sky was overcast, somber, foreboding, and thick with anticipation.

He stationed himself near a rough wood structure, his back against the solid wall. He thought of pulling out his pipe but realized that the smell of tobacco would give him away. Still, he longed for the warmth of it.

He heard the occasional rumble of vehicles as they passed in the distance and horses blowing as they coughed in the frigid air. He heard no human sounds. No decent man would be out on a night like this if he could help it, and certainly not this close to the canal. He rubbed his hands together, trying to drive some heat into them, and he drew his head as deeply into his overcoat as he could. The cold fingers of the night air found their way into his clothes.

Not like the frontier at all, he thought. Here a damp cold twisted a man's bones and chilled him through, pricking the flesh and digging deep into the muscles. Dry cold and damp cold are different, he remembered someone saying, and he had replied, "Cold is cold." But now he understood the difference.

He rubbed his arms. *A soldier's lot,* he told himself, *if the cold doesn't kill you, the heat will, or the enemy.*

He heard a noise, and his hand went to the pistol in his shoulder holster.

A voice came out of the darkness. "Captain Dunaway? Is that you?"

Bishop.

"Yes," Fitz said. "Show yourself." He slid the pistol from the holster and cocked the hammer.

The cripple hobbled into view, his breath coming in ragged clouds.

"It's me."

"Is anyone with you?"

"No," Bishop said. "I'm alone."

Bishop approached. Fitz could barely see him and did not want him any closer. "Hold there," he said. "What is this about?"

"Mr. Whaley sent me to fetch you," Bishop said. "We have plans for tonight. He said he has use for you." Bishop moved closer and looked around. "It's the Navy Yard tonight," he said in a quavering voice. "Pardon me, will you? I have to piss." He unbuttoned his fly. Fitz heard the delicate sound of liquid playing off wood. "I am so cold. I have never been as cold as I am now."

"Winter's not here," Fitz said. "You'll be hard-pressed when it arrives."

"I shall remain indoors," Bishop said.

"The Navy Yard," Fitz confirmed as Bishop rearranged his clothing.

"Yes."

"The Navy Yard is some distance away. You have a carriage?"

"A cab. Not fifty feet from here. We are to take it to 4th Street. We turn south and are met by Mr. Whaley and the others."

Fitz looked into the darkness. "Who awaits us in the cab?"

"Only the driver, sir, I assure you. Mr. Whaley was quite clear on this. I was to collect you and come to the point where 4th Street ends at the Eastern Branch."

Fitz thought over the situation. It had all the markings of a trap, but he had no choice. "Lead the way," he told Bishop. He followed the little man to the cab.

The driver sat atop his seat, a black man, the thin moon

casting a pale light over his dark face, bundled so that his form was barely human in appearance.

They climbed into the cab and it started out.

Bishop said, shivering, "I hate being cold."

"It's a temporary condition. Unless, of course, you're dead. Or in Hell."

"You don't believe in an afterlife, Captain Dunaway?"

"I never gave it much thought. What does Whaley tell you about his plans?"

"Very little. You know he is a reluctant talker."

"He is free enough with his threats."

Bishop nodded. "I am afraid you will come to blows. The thought distresses me."

"I can take care of myself."

Bishop pulled his coat closer. "He is a devious man, Captain Dunaway. He has a talent for this business, to be sure, but I see him taking too much pleasure in it. Oh, perhaps I make too much of it. My nerves, you know—they have never been strong. I'm not certain."

"What has he told you? About me?"

"Nothing. It is only my sense of what might happen."

"To the others?" Fitz asked. "What has he said to them?"

"I don't know," Bishop said in a low voice. "They seldom speak to me."

They left the cab several blocks above the rendezvous and made their way along deserted streets to the end of 4th Street. The riverbank was a sad collection of feeble wooden docks and wharves, misshapen structures that cluttered the edge of the calm black water. Fitz heard the gentle lap of the river against pilings and the faint creak of lines twisting against the current. He could make out the silent forms of a dozen small boats suckling the weather-beaten docks.

"Over here," Whaley called.

Fitz and Bishop found Whaley, Pockmark, Dutton, and Sanderson waiting near a cluster of barrels. Whaley held a signal lamp.

"Glad you could make it," he said, setting the lamp on the head of a barrel.

"It's to be the Navy Yard, then?" Fitz asked.

"Yes," Whaley said.

"What about the patrol boat?"

"That's the trick, isn't it?" Whaley, turning to Bishop, said, "You stay here with the lamp. Five minutes after the explosion you light it and swing it three times if it's safe to return."

"But—"

"You can't go. You're a cripple. There's more than enough of us to do the job. Ain't that right?"

"Bishop's more than a match for anything I've seen," Fitz said. Whaley was right, it was too dangerous for Bishop, but Fitz felt contrary enough to disagree with anything that Whaley said.

Whaley and the others laughed. "You think so? Not for this or anything else."

"What else is there?" Fitz asked.

"Full of questions, aren't you?" Whaley responded.

"I get damn few answers when I ask them," Fitz said.

"Ask the right questions and you'll get some answers."

Fitz said nothing. He knew that Whaley wasn't likely to share any information of consequence with him.

Whaley said, "Bishop stays here."

"That leaves five of us," Fitz said, looking at the two men, Dutton and Sanderson, standing behind Pockmark.

"More than enough," Whaley said. "Get into that whaleboat and grab an oar. I'll take the tiller."

"Maybe it would be best to leave Dutton here," Sanderson said. "His bones ache pretty bad and it's hard for him to get about."

"What a fine lot," Whaley said. "All right. Dutton, you stay here and keep the lantern handy. Bishop, get in the boat."

Fitz followed Bishop and the others down a rickety ladder and into a whaleboat. It was large enough to hold a dozen men, but Fitz wondered: could it hold as much black powder as Whaley planned to carry away from the Navy Yard? If not, how would he remove the powder? Pockmark settled next to him and gripped an oar. The oarlocks were greased with woolen rags wrapped around each oar handle at the lock.

"That Whaley thought of everything, ain't he? 'Didn't want to hear no oars squeal,' he says. All planned out. Knows what he's doin', huh, Cap'n? Smart man."

Whaley untied the rope and took his place at the tiller, facing Fitz and Pockmark. "Push off," he ordered. Pockmark jammed his oar blade into the piling and forced the boat away from the dock. It slid through the river.

"Pull," Whaley said.

Fitz let his oar blade dip and pulled back. He heard the water sucking at the blade and felt the weight of the water against it. At the end of the stroke, he brought the blade out of the water and back into position. After a few strokes, the four rowers found their rhythm and the boat glided across the black river, making headway against the current.

Fitz concentrated on his rowing, but he could feel Whaley's eyes on him. If Batterman did as he said, there would be a party waiting for them on the other side of the river. Or perhaps they would be picked up by the patrol boat. Fitz went over the options available to him should either occur. He had only two—pretend to be a member of the gang until he could safely reveal himself or attempt to escape. One was as dangerous as the other. If they were intercepted, Whaley would turn on him as an informer, Fitz was as certain of that as he was the rising of the sun. If he tried to escape Whaley, his would-be rescuers might shoot him. His eyes met Whaley's. The big man was watching him but there was nothing in his face that told Fitz what he was thinking.

"Stop," Whaley said.

The four oars hung in the air. The only sounds that broke the night were the hiss of the bow as it slid through the blackness and the water streaming from the oar blades. Fitz was sweating, but he shivered in the chilled air. He turned and looked over his shoulder.

Two tiny lights moved through the darkness some distance away, cutting across their bow. Fitz heard the faint chug of a steam engine, and he knew that he was looking at the running lights of the patrol boat. It was headed south and soon the lights grew smaller, drawing close together until they met, formed one large light, and disappeared.

"All right," Whaley whispered and the oars dropped into the water.

They continued rowing; Fitz lost track of the time, but he knew that they would soon reach the shore and, with it, some kind of reckoning. Whaley told him nothing; either because he did not trust him or because it did not matter what Fitz knew. Whaley planned to kill him. Fitz knew he could do nothing until Whaley showed his hand.

Whaley straightened on the stern seat and eased the tiller to port.

"Ship oars," Whaley said. "Sanderson? Get ready."

Fitz felt the boat rock as Sanderson stood and took hold of the bowline. Fitz felt the vibration and heard a crunch as the hull scraped the river bottom. He turned to see Sanderson jump from the bow into shallow water and run ashore, pulling on the line. Fitz joined the others as they climbed out of the boat, landing in shin-deep water. They pulled the boat onto the bank, stumbling over loose gravel. The narrow beach ended in a dense thicket of underbrush and stunted trees.

"Sanderson," Whaley said. "You and Pockmark carry pistols. I'll take the oil. Bishop, you and Dunaway stay here and watch the boat."

"It won't take both of us," Fitz said. He didn't want to lose a chance to signal the guards.

"You just do what I said," Whaley ordered. "You wanted Bishop to come along." He threw Bishop a pistol. "If any sentries happen on you, use this."

They moved into the thicket and were soon out of sight. The only sound was the thin rustle of dead branches, which soon faded away.

Bishop looked with alarm at the pistol in his hand. "I don't know how to use this."

"Give it to me," Fitz said, peering through the underbrush. He glanced at the pistol. It was a five-shot Belgian revolver. He thought he heard a noise and crouched. Bishop followed. After a full minute Fitz decided it was an animal making its way through the dry stands of weeds.

He turned the revolver to capture what light he could from the moon. What he saw sent a chill down his back. Every chamber was empty.

Fitz spun the cylinder in disgust. "It's not loaded."

"What?"

"Whaley gave us an unloaded pistol to defend ourselves."

"What are we going to do?" Bishop asked.

Fitz tossed the pistol back to him. "You're going to stay here. I'm going for help."

"What sort of help?" Bishop asked, shocked. "Don't leave me here, I beg of you."

"If someone comes, surrender. Don't point that pistol at them. You'll be safe." He knew the last part of his statement was a lie and he felt guilty abandoning Bishop, but he had to find someone to warn about the attack. Batterman must have alerted the Navy Yard, but he wasn't sure what Whaley had in mind.

An unsettling thought had followed Fitz across the Eastern Branch. The boat wasn't large enough to carry a thousand pounds of powder. Suppose Whaley intended to abandon someone? Perhaps two men? Would there be room to carry that much powder in the whaleboat? He calculated the weight of the men and the potential of the boat, but decided he had mixed his figures. It took him three attempts before the cold truth gripped him. They would not carry the powder away in the boat, not unless they counted on two men rowing the cumbersome vessel. Fitz should have thought of that before, he should have taken the time to reason it out.

He remembered the Academy. Will was right. Fitz's failure at mathematics would one day prove his undoing.

It was a trap.

Fitz pushed his way into the dry underbrush, fighting the wild tangle of dead branches as he forced his way toward the lights in the distance. He had his pistol with him, but he dared not think of drawing it on the marines. It would be like shooting one of his own, and he shuddered at the thought. As he moved forward he could see the thin sheen of bonfires off the broad sides of the refit buildings, huge, barnlike structures that filled the black sky. The sharp clatter of machinery rang as a counterpoint to the monotonous chug of steam engines. There was no night and day for the Navy Yard—every hour was filled with making weapons of war.

The mass of thickets was disorienting. He could hear the thunder of the machines at the Yard, but they created a confusing echo. The glimmer of the distant lights told him nothing more than that the Yard was immense. Whaley and his band could be anyplace.

He stopped. There was a heavy rustling in the thickets off to his right and this time he knew it was too loud to be an animal. He hoped it was a sentry. *But if it is,* he thought, *what will you say to him?*

"You oughtta relax," Pockmark said, appearing out of the darkness. Fitz saw a glint of a blade.

"I find that hard to do," Fitz said, shifting to face the man. He felt the weight of his pistol in its shoulder holster.

"You ain't scared?" Pockmark asked, advancing. He held the knife blade flat across his abdomen.

"I have a cautious nature," Fitz said, taking a step to plant his feet in the tangle of dead vines. "Lost?"

Pockmark smiled. "Not me, Cap'n. But ain't you supposed to be back at the boat with the cripple?"

"I was curious," Fitz said.

"Ain't nothin' gonna happen. Maybe some fireworks. Gonna be a lovely sight."

Fitz retreated to the husk of a formless bush, keeping his eye on Pockmark. He wanted the bush at his back in case one of the others decided to return and attack him from behind.

Pockmark's eyes followed him, gauging the distance between them. Fitz was about five feet from Pockmark—not far enough from that big knife.

So what is it to be? Fitz wondered. *Stabbed, and my body thrown into the river? Stabbed, and left to die on the beach? Maybe Prescott has a detail waiting near the Yard and this nightmare will be over. Then what? Caught in a crossfire? Perhaps Whaley does not intend to kill me and we go on to bigger and better things.* "We," Fitz thought ruefully, *now I'm one of them.*

A twig snapped behind him, and he spun around. The shining eyes of an opossum stared back at him. He saw the flash of the knife blade and he dropped, rolling to one side. He jerked his pistol from his holster but Pockmark kicked it out of his hand. Fitz cried out in pain as Pockmark dove at him. Fitz lashed out with his feet, striking the other man in the chest. Pockmark grunted and stumbled back. Fitz rose and struck him hard in the mouth. Pockmark reeled and tripped over a log, sprawling in the thicket. Before he could get, up Fitz grabbed the man's wrists, trying to pin him.

Pockmark spat in Fitz's face and then jerked his head up, striking Fitz across the bridge of the nose with his forehead.

An explosion of stars swam across Fitz's eyes. Pockmark pushed Fitz over on his back, pinning him, but Fitz still held the man's wrists. The razor-sharp edge of the blade was just inches from Fitz's eye. He looked up to see Pockmark's distorted face leering over his.

"Give up, Cap'n," Pockmark said, his breathing ragged. "You ain't got a chance. Let go and you won't feel a thing."

Fitz felt his grip fail as the knife blade grew larger. He wanted to scream, but the contest was taking his whole strength. He pushed himself up off his shoulders and sank his teeth into Pockmark's nose. Blood gushed into his mouth and he heard the crunch of cartilage. The injured man screamed. Fitz pushed him off and rolled to a standing position, searching for the revolver.

Pockmark was up, wiping his coat sleeve across his face.

He shook his head and moved to the right, trying to gain position. Fitz backed up, his body tensed for the attack. His foot became entangled, and he fell backward over a large piece of driftwood. Pockmark lunged at him, the knife headed for his chest.

Fitz's fingers brushed a thick fallen branch. He grabbed it, sprang to his feet, and swung it as hard as he could. It struck Pockmark on the wrist and the knife flew into the thicket. Fitz swung the branch again, catching Pockmark below the chin. The blow sent the man stumbling against a tree trunk. He righted himself but stumbled again as he reached for Fitz, then fell forward and lay still. Fitz tightened his grip on the limb, but Pockmark did not get up. He lay there in the darkness, groaning.

Chapter 20

Fitz searched the underbrush for the knife and his revolver. He found the pistol but not the knife. Gripping the Colt, he staggered deeper into the entanglement, gasping. His heart beat against his chest. He was soaked in sweat, his head ached, and he was worn out by the fight. Fear came to him and he trembled. He spat the iron taste of blood from his mouth and wiped the residue from his lips in disgust.

That was why Whaley wanted both of them to remain—Pockmark was to kill him and probably Bishop. Whaley had found out that Fitz was a spy, but how? He fought his way through the thicket as quietly as he could. Every noise, every rustle of dead leaves and sharp crack of dried underbrush sounded like a musket shot to him.

An explosion tore through the darkness, a brilliant flash followed by the heavy rumble of thunder. Shock knocked Fitz to his knees. The night was gone and in its place came a false sun, yellow and angry, eating the darkness as it climbed higher and higher into the sky. With it came a crash greater than a battery of artillery firing in unison.

Fitz fled through the underbrush, away from exploding ammunition. Invisible fingers, the husks of limbs and branches, plucked at his clothes, scratching his face, trying to hold him. He batted them out of the way, trading away silence for speed. Behind him more explosions ripped through the darkness, filling the air with the wild screams of red-hot cannon balls and shells hurled into the night sky. Fitz glanced over his shoulder and saw their flaming trails arcing high above the Yard—but they would land someplace, and on top of him was just as good as any.

He formed a plan as he ran, but the only thing that was clear to him was escape. If he was found here now, he would be shot before he had an opportunity to declare himself.

He stumbled along the edge of the beach, trying to keep the tangle of saplings and bushes between him and the fire. He looked over his shoulder. Men shouted in the darkness. They were close enough to be heard over the crash of exploding shells. Fitz sought his bearings. He listened. Was it Whaley's men or marines?

The fire did not diminish—for that, he was grateful. What he needed was more than a fire. If the sentries saw him they weren't likely to shoot. *They will challenge me,* Fitz thought, but deep inside he knew he was being optimistic. The sentries were frightened, and excited, and it was likely they would shoot at anything they saw.

There was a bright light and then a bloated thump, followed by a crack of a dozen explosions. Shells wobbled into the sky and exploded, beautiful blossoms of yellow and orange. He knew he was out of time.

Fitz dashed forward. The gravel gave way under his feet. He fell and regained his footing, running along the beach. Shrapnel plummeted out of the blazing sky with a shriek— fiery comets bombarding the earth. One crashed in a cloud of sparks less than ten feet away, another spun just over his head and disappeared toward the river. He ran madly, half-convinced that the next one would take off his head. His breath came in ragged gulps as he looked up. There was no sign of the sentries or of Whaley's band. He climbed over a scattering of rocks.

He heard a shout behind him. "Halt!" Fitz raised his arms and pivoted. Down the beach, nearly a hundred yards away, was a group of five or six marines.

"Gentlemen," Fitz shouted. "Be so kind as to lower your

muskets. I'm a friend." He watched the men confer and felt a sinking in his stomach. Give the average marine time to think and chances were he'd make the wrong decision.

He heard a musket shot and then another and then a ball ricocheted off a small rock by his foot. He slipped and felt his foot jam into a crevice, wedging it hard in place.

He heard more shots and shouting and knew a detail would be on him any moment. The idea of surrendering flashed through his mind, but the whine of Minié balls off the rocks convinced him these marines weren't in any mood to take prisoners.

Fitz twisted his foot, struggling to free it. He pushed himself against a boulder for protection and pointed the pistol over their heads. He thumbed the hammer back and squeezed the trigger. The revolver responded with three flat cracks. Misfire! More bullets whined around him and snapped over his head. He opened the cylinder gate and blew on the caps, closed the gate, thumbed the hammer, and squeezed the trigger again. Another misfire. The group had scattered, seeking shelter in the undergrowth, but they'd soon reemerge.

"This is going to require a strong letter of complaint to Mr. Colt," Fitz muttered.

His boot broke free of the rocks' grip, and he jerked it out of the crevice. He had no time left for anything but to get away. He ran along the beach and in the distance saw the outline of the whaleboat, and standing next to it—Bishop.

"Get it in the water," Fitz shouted. "They're right behind me." He saw Bishop turn and put his shoulder against the boat's bow. He was struggling with the weight of the boat, the uncertain footing of the beach, and his infirmity.

Fitz heard a musket discharge behind him and someone shout, but he did not hear the telltale whistle of a ball passing close by. He was safe from the gunfire, for now.

He slid next to Bishop and, clamping his hands on the boat's gunnel, pushed with all his might. He could feel it slide along the gravel until he was in cold water up to his shins. "Get in," he ordered. He threw himself over the side of the boat, landing on one of the seats. He snatched up the oars and pulled. "Row!"

Bishop rowed with all his strength as Fitz turned the boat's bow from the beach. He strained against its weight as he dug the oar blades into the dark water. They crawled away from the beach at an insanely slow pace. He heard more shouts from the shore and glanced up to see several men aiming muskets at them. They appeared to be only fifty feet away.

They cannot miss, Fitz thought, and he prepared to die.

There was a crash and a cloud of blue smoke enveloped the men. This time bullets whined around him, and he heard several strike the heavy wood planking of the boat.

"Row!" Fitz shouted, both frightened and exhilarated. He was not dead. They had missed at a ridiculous distance, and he almost felt the need to taunt them.

Fitz and Bishop rowed in unison, putting a healthy distance between themselves and the shore. Soon, the land was claimed by the darkness. The only sounds were the rush of the water under the bow and the oar blades slicing into the river, accompanied by their own labored breathing.

Fitz was aware of another noise. "Stop. Stop," he said, holding the dripping oars in the air.

"What?" Bishop asked.

"Wait," Fitz said. He lowered his heard, concentrating on the sound.

"What is it?" Bishop asked in a frightened whisper.

"I don't know." There it was again. Fitz peered into the darkness, willing himself to locate the source of the noise. He heard it again. It was mechanical. It was a steam engine. A light pierced the night. "The patrol boat."

"What?"

"Row."

"But I can't . . ."

"Row! I've been shot at too many times tonight to give someone else another chance. Row."

"But I can't," Bishop said. "I am worn out."

Fitz grabbed Bishop by his shirtfront, pulling the little man toward him. "Listen to me," he whispered. "Row, or I will chuck you out into the water."

"But I'll drown."

"Then row," Fitz said, releasing him. "And put your back into it."

They slid through the black water. Fitz kept one eye on the sweeping light and another on Bishop. The poor man was shaking, but he kept a steady pace at the oars.

"Don't fear, Mr. Bishop. We'll get clear of this yet."

"How . . . can you . . . remain . . . so calm?" Bishop asked, the words coming in short bursts between each pull at the heavy oars.

The light swung around, searching. "Stop. Stop," Fitz whispered.

Both men froze, the only sounds the rough pant of the steam engine and the water sucking at the boat's hull. Fitz heard a shout and the light swung in their direction.

Fitz grabbed Bishop's coat sleeve. "Over the side!" He jumped over the gunnel, pulling Bishop with him. The little man let out a cry but it was cut short by the crash of a dozen muskets. They hit the water as the Minié balls tore into the boat, sending chunks of wood flying in all directions.

Fitz grabbed one of the oars to stay afloat and pulled a sputtering Bishop next to him.

Bishop gasped for air. "Help!"

"Shut up," Fitz growled. "Do you want to get us killed?"

"We can surrender," Bishop sobbed. "Let us surrender."

"The minute we lift our heads they'll shoot," Fitz said. He judged that they were about three-quarters of the way across the inlet. If they struck out in the direction they had been rowing, they should reach land with no trouble. The current was minimal and it was too dark for the men in the patrol boat to see them. He glanced at Bishop.

"Mr. Bishop," Fitz said, remaining calm for his companion's sake. He spit out a mouthful of water. "Here is what we

are going to do. We are going to set out for the shore. We
don't have far to go"—actually Fitz didn't know how far
they had to travel—"but if we stay here we're going to die."

"But I can't swim," Bishop said, so innocently that Fitz almost laughed.

"Yes," he said, "I know. But you can hold on to my coattail, can't you? Keep to one side so my legs are free and keep
a tight hold on my coattail." Fitz found himself shivering and
then realized just how cold the water was.

Bishop pulled free. "I can't. I'm a cripple."

Fitz looked at him. "Well, I can't carry you on my back."

Tears welled up in Bishop's eyes. "I can't swim."

"All right," Fitz said, taking him by the shoulder. "Come
on. We'll think of something."

"No," Bishop said, shaking his head. "No. No. I can't do
it."

"You'll do it. You've got one good leg. Hold on and kick
with your good leg."

"No. I'm afraid."

"I know that!" Fitz said. "I am, too, but that's all that we
have. You said you didn't have courage. Well, now is the time
to prove that you do. I'll do the work, you just float. When
we get to the other side we'll be on the Island, right?"

Bishop nodded.

"That's where you live. That's where you have your books
and your poetry. You'll be safe there. Has Poe anything to
say about stinking rivers that need to be crossed?"

"I don't know," Bishop said, his teeth chattering.

"Well, when we get across, you can write your own poem
about it."

Bishop managed a reluctant smile and wiped the tears
from under his glasses.

"Good," Fitz said. "Let's go."

"So this is what it's like to have courage," Bishop said.

"Yes. Inconvenient, isn't it?" Fitz gasped as he threw himself forward. "Kick!"

He struggled to keep his head above water, his arms and

legs digging into the clinging blackness. He felt Bishop's feeble attempts to kick as his grip on Fitz's coat tightened. A dark shape loomed out of the darkness. Fitz, startled by its appearance, ducked. His head sank below the surface of the foul liquid, and he sucked in the horrible stuff. He fought his way back to the surface, his arms stretching out to make headway, his legs kicking. His fingers brushed something that oozed in his hand. It was a dead cow, its bloated carcass thrusting stiff legs into the night air. He turned his head and threw up but swam on.

The cold stabbed at him. He gritted his teeth and continued to swim, his body trembling as frigid hands clutched at him. His wool coat, soaked, began to freeze, encasing him so that each kick, each thrust of his arms moved them only inches. Everything was heavy—his clothing, his boots, Bishop, everything conspired to drag him beneath the water. They were not moving, they could not be moving. His arms and legs felt as if they had been pierced with swords. The muscles across his shoulders burned, a searing flame that almost made him cry out. He heard Bishop's ragged breathing, and felt his clumsy kicks. The cripple's crying increased, and his efforts stopped.

"Bishop! For God's sake, help me. I can't do it alone."

The reply was far away. "I'm tired. Cold. I'm cold."

"If you don't help me we'll both drown."

"Cold," Bishop said, the strength wrung out of his voice.

The Island hung on the horizon, taunting Fitz. With each stroke of his arms, Fitz felt his head dip a little more below the water and take longer to reemerge. He was losing. He could make it if it was not for Bishop's weight. All he needed to do was let the cripple slip into the inky water and be done with it.

"Read me—" Fitz began and then realized it wasn't right. His mind was dulled, the cold water sapping his senses as quickly as it was stealing his warmth. He kicked at the water, his arms falling listlessly into the darkness.

"Tell me," he said, straining to keep his arms and legs moving. "Recite." That was it! Reciting poetry. That was what poets do. His mind was wandering. *Bishop. What do I want him to do?*

Fitz shook his head, trying to clear his thoughts. "Bishop! Recite some poetry. As loud as you can, man!"

"Can't—"

"Poetry. Anything!"

Fitz felt Bishop struggle to lift his head.

"Recite?"

"Yes! Yes. Anything."

"Yes," Bishop said, his voice no more than a breath.

"It was many and many a year ago,"

"That's it!" Fitz said. "Kick and recite."

"In a kingdom by the sea,"

"Kick!"

Fitz felt Bishop's legs begin to pump.

"That a maiden there lived whom you may know"

He gasped, sucking in water, and threw up.

"Keep going, man."

"By the name of Annabel Lee;"

"Louder. Kick."

*"And this maiden she lived with no other thought
    Than to love and be loved by me."*

"Louder! Kick!"

"I was a child and she was a child,"

His voice gained strength.

"In this kingdom by the sea,
But we loved with a love that was more than love,
I and my Annabel Lee;"

Fitz felt Bishop hesitate.
"What is it?"
"I can't. I forgot. I'm cold."
"The hell you can't," Fitz said. His body was bound in chains. He was nearing his end. "Talk! What was her name?"
Bishop sobbed.
"Tell me!"
"Annabel Lee."
"Louder!"
"I can't."
"Louder!"
"Let me die—" the little man gasped.
I can't make it, Fitz thought. *I'm going to die.*

"With a love that the winged seraphs of heaven
Coveted her and me."

"Go on! Kick!"

"And this was the reason that, long ago,
In this kingdom by the sea,
A wind blew out of a cloud, chilling
My beautiful Annabel Lee,"

"We know about chilling," Fitz said numbly, his arms clawing into the darkness. "Don't we, Bishop?"

"So that her highborn kinsmen came
And bore her away from me,
To shut her up in a sepulchre
In this kingdom by the sea."

I can't do it, Fitz thought. *I can't do it.*

"The angels, not half so happy in heaven,
    Went envying her and me;
Yes! that was the reason (as all men know,
    In this kingdom by the sea)
That the wind came out of the cloud by night,
    Chilling and killing my Annabel Lee."

Fitz's foot struck something soft. It was the mudflats near the docks. He kicked, trying to find solid ground to support his weight. God was teasing him—first there was ground, then nothing, then muck that threatened to pull him under, and then solid ground.

They staggered onto the embankment and lay still. Fitz rolled into a sitting position and beat his arms and legs with his fists. He could not feel the blows. He struck harder, trying to hammer life back into his frozen body. He pulled at Bishop until he was sitting upright and formed his hands into fists.

"Do what I do," he ordered.

Bishop looked at him and nodded. He beat at his legs.

Fitz felt his legs and fists aching from the cold. Any kind of feeling was a victory. He stumbled to his feet.

"Get up," Fitz said. "Walk."

"I can't. My legs won't move."

Fitz jerked Bishop up and slapped the little man across the face. "Walk," he said, his voice dull with fatigue. "Lean on me."

They made their way up the embankment and struggled to the roadway. They staggered across the street and found shelter under the side porch of a dry goods store. Huddling together, they rested, each finding a modicum of heat from the other.

Fitz noticed a small window at the end of the porch. He led Bishop to the window. He could see very little in the darkness, but he knew the window would be locked from the inside. He pulled his sleeve over his fist and tapped a pane of glass. It shattered and fell away. He reached through the window until he located the latch. He unlocked it and pushed the window up but it stopped halfway. He would not fit through the opening.

"Go in and get us blankets and matches. And coats if you can find them," he ordered Bishop. "I'll stand guard."

Bishop nodded and slipped into the building. After a few minutes he returned, carrying two coats. He handed the garments to Fitz and crawled back through the window.

"I think I heard something," he said. "I think someone was in there."

"As badly as we stink, they won't come within ten miles of us." Fitz threw him a coat. "Put this on." He slipped the other over his shoulders. As they huddled together in the darkness Fitz asked, "Where are we?"

Bishop thought for a moment. "Straight across," he pointed. "There is the Island."

"I thought we were on the Island." Fitz said.

"No. You see? The canal."

"I'm not about to swim that," Fitz said. "I've done enough swimming for one night."

"There is a footbridge just a hundred yards north. We can cross on there."

"How far is it to your rooms?"

"A quarter of a mile at least."

Fitz looked at the sky. He could see light in the east. "If we don't freeze, daylight will catch us. Let's hurry."

They stumbled on, Bishop falling behind until Fitz took the cripple's arm in his. Even with help Bishop's strength was failing, and Fitz knew it. He counted cadence, each command urging one more step from his companion. But the count was for Fitz as well. He was frozen and could not remember having been this tired. He knew that he nothing left to give and he did not want to die in the gutter. That was no fitting death for a soldier. His head dropped as they walked, and he watched one muddy shoe place itself in front of the other, like some battered machine taxed beyond endurance. The cadence continued, but his voice weakened.

They crossed the footbridge, the steps drumming a hollow

march on the thick boards. When they reached the other side Fitz knew, by the dilapidated buildings and heavy stench, they were on the Island. They turned south.

"Here! We're here," Bishop cried.

Fitz looked up. Bishop broke free and hobbled toward his boarding house. Fitz followed him into the building and up the dark stairway. He waited, wanting to scream with frustration as Bishop fumbled for his key. Finally the door opened, and they fell into the room. Fitz closed and latched the door behind them and slid to the floor, as darkness enveloped him.

Chapter 21

November 17, 1861
The 244th day of the war
The Island

Fitz awakened to the thick, rich scent of food. His stomach reacted by growling. The sound of a gentle rain broke through the darkness, but he was warm and dry so that he knew that he was inside, out of the elements. His eyes fluttered open, and he forced himself up on his elbows to take in his surroundings.

He was lying on the floor in Bishop's front parlor, covered by several blankets. He saw Bishop, his back to him, standing at the stove.

"What time is it?" Fitz asked.

Bishop turned. His hair was disheveled, but he was clean and his clothes were dry. He had obviously had time to come to terms with last night's ordeal.

"Just after six," Bishop said, sliding a spoon into a bowl and handing it to Fitz. "It's beef broth. From my landlady. It's very good. It will warm you. Go on. Try it."

Fitz remembered the bloated carcass of the cow in the river. "Does it have to be beef?" he asked.

"It's all the food I have," Bishop replied.

Fitz took the hot bowl and set it on the floor next to him. He blew on his stinging fingers.

Bishop said, "Be careful it doesn't burn you."

Fitz looked out the window. The rain rolling down the glass distorted the gray sky. "Six o'clock?"

"PM," Bishop said.

"PM? Then we've been here since the morning?"

"The day before yesterday. You've been asleep for hours."

"Blast!" Fitz said, pushing himself to his feet. He looked down to find that he was wearing a nightshirt several sizes too small. "What's this?"

"I had to send your clothes to be cleaned. They're in the bedroom. There is a washroom at the end of the hall. You can clean up. It's only a quarter. I had to take some of your money for the laundering."

Fitz, angry with himself, said, "I've been here too long."

"I sent a telegram to the War Department to tell them that you were indisposed and would return to work tomorrow. I hope that was acceptable."

"Prescott will have me shot," Fitz said, finding a chair. He picked up the bowl and cradled it on his knees as he ate. He gulped the hot soup, burning his gums and tongue. Bishop handed him a thick slice of bread. Fitz tore into it.

"Have you heard from Whaley?" he asked.

"No. Nothing. There is quite a bit in the newspaper." Bishop pulled a paper from beneath an open book and handed it to Fitz. "I was reading poetry to relax."

Fitz took the paper and froze at what he saw. The head-lines read: EXPLOSION AT THE NAVY YARD and below that ACCI-DENTAL EXPLOSION OF MUNITIONS SUSPECTED. SEVERAL DEATHS. He looked at Bishop. "Accidental? Are they mad?"

"Perhaps they don't know," Bishop said.

Fitz searched the article, his revulsion increasing as he read. Six marines were known to have died and three of them were burned to death. Fitz let the paper drop from his hands.

"What do you think?" Bishop asked. "Did we do well?"

Fitz grabbed Bishop by the lapels. He wanted to break him in half. "We killed our own! Do you call that doing well?"

Bishop fought to pull Fitz's hands away. "Please, Captain!

You're hurting me. Please unhand me." Fitz could not see Bishop's pain nor hear his words—all he knew was that six men were dead, and he was the cause of it. He was angry and ashamed and he hated Prescott for making him be a part of this. He was a part of killing marines, not of spying or gathering information, but of murdering Union men. But it was Whaley who had led the attack, Whaley who had killed the men. Fitz knew he would kill Whaley—somehow he would kill him.

"Captain? Please?"

Bishop's startled face appeared through Fitz's anger. He released the little man. Bishop fell to the floor, pulling at his disheveled collar. Fitz looked at his hands. He could have killed Bishop and it wouldn't have mattered. The idea stunned him as he looked at the frightened man. Bishop crawled to a chair and pulled himself up.

"What did I say? I'm sorry. What did I do?"

Fitz shook his head and turned away. "I have got to go." He ran his fingers through his hair and found it thick with grime. He turned to Bishop. "Get me some hot water for a wash." He stank of the river and sweat. "Did you hear me? Do it now!"

Bishop stumbled to his feet. "I'm sorry for what I said. Whatever it was."

Less than an hour later, Fitz had washed, shaved, and dressed. Despite being cleaned, his clothes had a pungent smell. "Where is my pistol?"

"Here. Here," Bishop said, removing a stack of books from a shelf. He reached behind another pile of books and pulled out the pistol. "I didn't know what to do with it. It's very dirty."

Fitz pulled it from Bishop's hands and left.

He found a cab after searching for nearly half an hour, but the cabbie was reluctant to take him as far as the War Department until Fitz promised him an extra fifty cents.

Fitz fought to collect his thoughts during the ride. He felt helpless, lost in a morass of lies and trickery where everything was an illusion except falsehood; that was the one distorted certainty.

I cannot do this, he told himself. *If there is a God in heaven, please, listen to me, I cannot do this! I cannot kill my own.*

Then what will become of you?

Fitz slumped back into the seat as he struggled to come to a solution. *But you have to.*

Yes, he agreed, worn out with regret.

The cab stopped in front of the War Department and Fitz stepped out. He paid the cabbie and dashed into the building. His presence in the War Department reignited his rage. It centered on Prescott and his insufferable secretary. They don't know what it means to be a soldier. They don't know how it feels to kill a man nor have a man try to kill you. They don't know what it means to be surrounded by death and for some indescribable reason find, in the midst of the most hellish carnage on earth, a sense of calm and purpose.

Fitz threw open the door to find Batterman sitting at his desk. He cocked an eyebrow at Fitz.

"Yes?"

Fitz ignored him and made for Prescott's door. Batterman jumped to his feet to block the way.

"Mr. Prescott is not in," he said.

Fitz tried Prescott's office door. It was locked. He turned on Batterman. "Where is he?"

"At home," Batterman replied, nonplussed.

"There was no semblance of a trap at the Yard," Fitz said. "Except by the wrong side. I was almost killed by them and my own kind and my worthiness as a spy is certainly at an end."

"I don't understand," Batterman said.

"I am found out. Whaley sent one of his own to kill me.

The whole episode was a disaster from the beginning. I thought you told me that all was in readiness?"

"It was, sir," Batterman said. "I consulted with Mr. Prescott and he made all of the preparations. I witnessed his conversation with Secretary of the Navy Welles, myself."

"Where does Prescott live?"

"Really, Captain Dunaway, I can't see that troubling Mr. Prescott is necessary," Batterman said. "If you return to your room and refresh yourself, I'll notify Mr. Prescott you called."

"Mr. Batterman," Fitz said. "I will see Mr. Prescott tonight."

Batterman, at a loss for words, conceded. "Very well. He has a house on the corner of 4th and New Hampshire."

Fitz pushed past Batterman and hurried downstairs.

He found a cab at the corner of Pennsylvania Avenue. He gave the driver the address and fell back in the seat, overwhelmed. It had all fallen apart. Good, loyal men had been killed at the Navy Yard and he had been a party to their deaths. He had warned Batterman, who had supposedly warned Prescott, but it was a disaster.

The cab arrived at its destination and Fitz sprang down, paying the fare. When he turned, the view stunned him. Here, in the midst of his anguish, was a home whose windows were brilliant with candlelight. Music echoed into the street, a stirring martial air. There was a carnival in Prescott's home.

Fitz, rooted to the sidewalk by the unrestrained gaiety that welcomed him, hesitated in disbelief. A knife had been driven deep into his heart. The sight was beyond comprehension—men had died, he had failed, and a celebration was in progress.

He took the stone steps in a dream. He twisted the ringer next to the door. It opened to reveal a Negro man in tails. The man's first look warned Fitz that he knew Fitz was not a guest.

"Yes, sir?" the Negro asked, closing the door behind him to protect those inside.

"Mr. Prescott," Fitz managed. It was not his voice that spoke but that of a man who had been beaten down by circumstances. "I need to see Mr. Prescott."

"Who shall I say is calling, sir?"

"Captain—" Fitz began but felt somehow that he no longer deserved the rank. "Dunaway."

"Will you remain, Mr. Dunaway," the Negro said and disappeared inside.

Fitz was tired and thought about sitting on the stoop but decided instead to hold his ground. His head had dropped in shame and he gritted his teeth to stop the tears.

Then bright light spilled over Fitz and the Negro motioned him in. He led Fitz to a doorway off the hall and stood to one side. It was obvious that Fitz was to go in. He saw Prescott standing near a roaring fire.

"Fitz," Prescott said. "My dear man." He came forward, arms outstretched, and taking him by the hands led him to a chair near the fire. "Curtis? Please bring my guest a brandy."

Soft leather arms wrapped themselves around Fitz and the heat from the crackling fire washed over him.

"Fitz," Prescott said, settling in a chair facing his. "My dear boy, I thought you were dead. How wonderful. I can't tell you how pleased I am that you are alive."

"I did not—" Fitz said but lost track of what he wanted to say. He wanted to tell Prescott he had failed and because of his failure loyal men had died, but he could not find the words.

"Now, Fitz, everything is all right," Prescott said, easing his concern. "It's not what you think."

"I failed," Fitz said.

Curtis arrived with two brandies. "I told your guests that you were called away for a short time, sir."

"Yes, Curtis. Very good," he said and then turned to Fitz. "Fitz, are you hungry? Do you need some warm clothes?"

Fitz shook his head and took a gulp of the fiery liquid. It burned his throat.

Prescott dismissed Curtis with a nod. When the door was closed, Prescott edged closer to Fitz. "We must set some things straight, my dear boy. From the looks of you, you've had a particularly bad time of it. Now"—he sat back, offering salvation—"your mission was a success despite the unfortunate mishap at the Yard."

Fitz looked up, incredulous.

"The conspirators were killed in the explosion, Fitz. I have proof incontrovertible of that. Dead, sir. Destroyed in the cleansing fire of retribution."

"I don't understand," Fitz said. "The newspapers—"

"Will print whatever is fed to them. We must always be careful to downplay such incidents lest a gullible public assumes it is yet another example of Rebel verve."

Fitz gave him a puzzled expression. He had no idea what the word meant.

Prescott grew sincere. "Fitz, you must believe me when I tell you that you did splendidly. Things did not go as planned, this is true, but things went our way nevertheless. Is it not so on the battlefield? The best-laid schemes, so to speak?"

"Yes," Fitz said, listening.

"Those scoundrels are dead. The danger is past. And you, sir"—he rose with satisfaction—"will be rewarded."

It all fell into place. Everything that had been wrong was rendered right, and a great weight was lifted off Fitz's shoulders. Prescott's words had dispelled his guilt and vanquished his shame in a matter of minutes. He was saved.

"I thought—" Fitz said. "I thought I had failed."

"You must not think that, sir," Prescott said. He glanced at the snifter in Fitz's hand. "Would you like some more brandy? Perhaps a cigar? By God, sir, you shall have anything you want."

Fitz looked down at his coat. His skin still crawled with filth. "Some fresh clothes. A hot bath. A real bath."

Prescott laughed and waved Fitz out of his chair. "Why don't you return to the boarding house and treat yourself? Rest for two days and then return to your duties at the War Department as if nothing has happened. We need to keep up appearances, you understand. I'll have Curtis bring my carriage around." They walked into the hall. "Are you sure I can't tempt you with a bit of hot food?"

"No, sir," Fitz said. "But thank you."

Prescott smiled and called for the servant. He was giving him instructions when the pocket doors to the front parlor slid open and a maid appeared, carrying a tray of half-empty glasses. Music floated through the narrow opening and Fitz saw the light of a hundred candles sparkling off crystal chandeliers and the diamonds that clung to the necks of gowned ladies on the arms of fashionably dressed gentlemen. The doors were parted for only an instant but the scene was so full of life and beauty that Fitz was mesmerized by it. He saw couples chatting and he heard unfettered laughter, but then the lovely world that had been revealed to him drew to an end with the closing of the doors, shattered.

In the parlor, near the thick folds of red velvet drapes, he saw Colonel William Ferrell Moore listening intently to Asia Lossing.

Chapter 22

The Royal Boarding House

When he arrived, the house was silent and dark. He walked through the front door to find the hall empty, his shoes drumming on the parquet floor, the doors to the parlor, library, and dining room closed. Fitz thought how odd it was that Prescott's house was blazing with entertainment while the large Lossing house was stripped of all humanity. It was late, of course, and the only sign of life was the low light of an oil lamp near the base of the stairs. It was a courtesy for those who came in late.

Fitz trudged up the stairs, his hand on the banister, guiding him. He was tired and despite Prescott's reassurances, deeply troubled over what had happened.

Whaley and his men were dead. Well, not Bishop, but Fitz never thought of the cripple as dangerous. And not the man who had been left near the docks with the signal light. Fitz's brain was so burdened with fatigue that he could not recall the man's name. Sanderson. Dutton? Surely he had been killed or captured. Considering the predisposition of the marines at the Navy Yard to use their muskets, he must be dead.

But a thought stayed with him up the stairs and down the narrow hallway, the sound of deep snores traveling under the thick wood doors of the other bedrooms: what had gone wrong? Batterman had been forewarned and surely Prescott as well, and he in turn had advised the Secretary of the Navy. And yet the party, his party, had landed and the Pyrotechnical Laboratory had been fired and the marines had made no attempt to capture anyone. *Didn't they know that I would be there?* Fitz wondered as he peeled off his clothes and pulled his nightshirt from under the pillow. *"Best-laid schemes,"* Prescott had assured him, as if he was not concerned at all.

He slid into bed, shivering as the cold sheets enveloped him, folded his arms behind his head, and stared into the darkness.

The sight of Will Moore speaking with Asia in Prescott's house tormented him, and yet he did not know why. Was he jealous of his old friend? Did Will, for whom it seemed everything came without effort, have an interest in Asia? A romantic interest? Fitz's mind clarified. It took the time to linger on that point just to torment him.

No, Fitz decided, his eyes growing heavy. Was it social, then? One having known the other under different circumstances? But as Fitz traced his own journey he became aware of common threads. Will handed him over to Prescott, who then handed him over to Asia, who might have a connection to Bishop, and then to Whaley.

He lay still, reeling off ideas because his mind was battered and deprived of sleep. He knew that he was not thinking clearly, he ordered himself to rest as the broken fragments of his thoughts wandered clumsily about.

Before he fell asleep one last notion made itself clear—a happy consideration amidst the dark contemplations. He had done his duty and fulfilled his responsibility. Mr. Prescott should be happy and Mr. Lamon, the suspicious man with the black eyes, must be satisfied. Fitz would now get his command and everyone who played a role in this distasteful venture would be left behind in this filthy city while he went off to war at the head of his regiment.

His eyes shot open at the thought of leaving Asia behind. Fitz allowed the image only a fleeting consideration before

his eyes closed and his body relaxed, comforted by the soothing arms of the soft featherbed. He felt a sweet longing,
thinking that he might not see her again, and the feeling surprised him. It was not enough to keep him awake, however,
and, his snores joined the others.

Chapter 23

November 21, 1861
The 248th day of the war
The War Department Building

Fitz left the War Department and stepped into a frigid, soaking rain. He shivered as he walked, the cold washing over him. Rain hung from the brim of his kepi before falling away and soaking his uniform. But his discomfort did not matter. He would have his regiment.

He had rested for a day, not the two that Prescott suggested, and returned to the War Department, reviewing schedules and duty rosters, noting that under most of the entries in the category of "Presidential Guard" was written an ominous "Declined." The officers reported Lincoln had asked in a casual manner, *"Who would want to harm a fellow such as myself?"* Guards were posted around the Executive Mansion but were restricted to the gates, with none walking post on the grounds.

Fitz could do nothing but note that the president, in his pleasant manner, had decided against a cavalry escort or even an increase in guards. Meanwhile, the work on the War Department bomb-proof continued in case the Rebel troops made a run at Washington.

Where might I be posted? he asked himself as he drifted with the crowd. The huge Army of the Potomac grew stronger with new troops arriving each day. Newspapers carried reports of grand reviews and of General McClellan, charging up and down solid blue ranks as a cloud of staff officers struggled to keep up. Politicians called for an advance on Richmond and in place of the flattery they had showered on McClellan when he first arrived in Washington, now questioned why the army had not moved. When they did, Fitz resolved, he would be with them.

He decided, after traveling two blocks, that the West would suit him as well. Get as far from Washington as humanly possible, leave politics and politicians safely behind.

The rumble of a heavy carriage and then a few scattered cheers interrupted his rumination as a sleek landau, drawn by a handsome set of matched whites, glided through the traffic. At the carriage's large open window Fitz saw the bearded man he had met in the Telegraph Office—it was the gaunt face of Abraham Lincoln. The president leaned forward, acknowledging the crowd with a casual wave. Fitz thought the president was paying particular attention to him but then realized it was unlikely. Lincoln was too far away. The landau pulled away at a steady clip and President Lincoln was gone.

"That's Seward with him," a man at Fitz's side observed.

"Who?"

"Secretary of State," the man said, amazed at Fitz's ignorance. "My God, man, don't you know your own government?"

Fit did not know who Seward was and he wasn't bothered by the fact. The sight of the thin man in the carriage came back to him. He wondered if Lincoln knew how much danger he had been in. He was no fool, Fitz had known that the first time that they had spoken. He must know death is a constant companion in war.

Fitz's thought of war returned him to Will Moore. He turned, retracing his steps to the War Department. He had to know what Will was doing at Prescott's house with Asia and what the two spoke about. He would not bother dancing around the subject; he planned to ask Will straight-out. He decided as he strode back to the building that too many people in Washington did not know how to say what they thought without some elaborate preamble. Fitz congratulated himself because he never had any difficulty saying what he thought and then remembered it was exactly that trait, as Will so often reminded him, which usually led to his downfall.

Fitz climbed the broad stairs two at a time until he came to the second floor. The gas lamps shone brightly—men were working, and through the open doors he saw the array of clerks who managed the army, laboring over stacks of documents. He realized he had become one of them.

Will's office door was open, and a corporal sat at a reception desk, shaking a cloud of crushed bone from a pounce box onto a document. He glanced up.

"Can I help you, sir?"

"I'm here to see Colonel Moore," Fitz said, filled with conviction. He would have answers to his questions and make no mistake about it.

"Colonel Moore?"

"Yes," Fitz said. "Is this not his office?"

"Yes, sir, but he's just about to leave."

"I must see him," Fitz said, when Will appeared at his office door.

"Fitz? Are you all right? My God, you look terrible."

"I was just explaining, sir, that you have orders," the corporal said.

Fitz did not understand.

"Fitz. Come in," Will said, beaming. "Come in. We'll talk."

Fitz followed Will into his office. "What orders?"

"General Henry Halleck has sent for me," Will said. "Imagine Old Brains himself. I had no inkling."

"Where are you to be posted?" Fitz asked, stunned at the news.

"The Western Theater, Fitz. I'm to be assigned to his staff. But I'll tell you now I won't stop until I'm given my own command."

"You can't go, Will," Fitz said. "I need you here. I need your help."

"Oh, don't be absurd, Fitz. You'll prove yourself. You'll have your regiment in a month or two." He stuffed papers in a valise. "Right out of the blue. If there ever was an act of Providence, this is it. Imagine, Fitz," Will said, "I'm going to war."

Fitz felt his world floating just out of reach. "Will, please don't go. There is too much going on. I don't know who to trust. Prescott—"

"Now just stay out of Prescott's clutches, tell him exactly what he wants to hear, and all will be well," Will said, dismissing Fitz's concerns.

Fitz, angered, said, "I haven't anyone to trust, Will. You can't get me into this mess and then run off."

Will turned on him. "Now see here, Captain Dunaway, I have my orders and you're addressing a superior officer. I won't have any disrespect in my office."

Fitz could barely speak. "How dare you talk to me that way? This is not the first time you've gotten me in one of your messes, Will. I saved your bacon then and now it's time for you to come through for me."

"That is a debt repaid, Captain Dunaway," Will said. "And it is a mark of ingratitude for you to bring it up."

"I—"

"If it weren't for me, Fitz," Will argued, "you would still be in the guardhouse, wasting your career and the war away. I don't know what's come over you except to say you've let your emotions take sway. You must do your duty and hope for the best. I cannot, and will not, help you if you abandon your good senses."

Fitz had to make Will understand. "I need your help, Will," Fitz said. "I don't understand. I saw you—" The room tilted.

"You're ill, Fitz," Will said. "You must go home and rest. Things will be set right. I promise you. You act as if I've betrayed you somehow. For God's sake, man, I'm your friend."

"Prescott—" Fitz lost his train of thought. *Why can I not make myself understood?*

"Fitz, I cannot delay. Rest, calm yourself, and for God's sake keep your temper in check. I don't have time to talk. Now, go on," Will snapped the catch on his valise. "All will be well, you'll see."

Will's manner stunned Fitz. He was being set adrift, and by the same man who had cast him into this mess. "Such words," he said, certain Will had chosen opportunity over friendship, "coming from you, are especially painful. I have never denied you help."

Will stiffened. "You are dismissed, Captain Dunaway."

Fitz left the office. He found himself on the street, blocks along in his journey to the boarding house before the significance of his friend's departure sunk in. He was alone now— abandoned. There was no one with whom he could speak about what troubled him. He was trapped in a city awash with rumors and intrigues.

He felt sorry for himself as he walked, but even that feeling was pushed aside by a sense of betrayal. He should have told Will. What? He feared something was terribly wrong. That what he had to show for his endeavors were more suspicions. The feeling continued to prod him with a single, frightening thought: it's not over. Anger was his only companion on the long journey to the boarding house. *He has brought me to this and now has gone off.* He shivered and turned his anger toward the damp cold.

He rubbed his arms to keep warm.

Cold rain tunneled its way down the back of his neck and he pulled his shoulders up, shutting out the water with his collar. His greatcoat was at the boarding house and he wished he had it. His thoughts wandered.

He remembered standing guard as a plebe at the Point through New York winter rains. He was not allowed to stand in the guardhouse, he had to be visible to the corporal of the guard at all times. The cold Hudson wind had slipped under his wool cape and clawed at his skin, an attack supported by the perpetual dampness. Cadet Dunaway shivered through his watch, until another plebe had relieved him long enough to let him find warmth at a nearby fire and snatch a gulp of steaming coffee. Will, risking demerits, was his savior. Good old Will. He felt ashamed to have spoken to his friend harshly, but lately shame was Fitz's constant companion.

Asia. He remembered the touch of her hot skin and the taste of her lips and the passion with which she responded to his kisses. A wisp of her hair fell loose over her white shoulders and it brushed against his cheeks.

Asia.

Is it love, then, Fitz? Not the touch of a soldier's woman, but real love? Gray shapes hurried past him, anxious to be out of the rain. The city streets were somber avenues of shallow brown ponds and meandering creeks. He was alone on the deserted field. Where was everyone?

He cursed himself for not hailing a cab, but in his muddled head he knew this was punishment for his transgressions.

He coughed and wiped the rain from his face. He caught the rank stench of the river. The smell hung on him, swam over him, and reminded him that he was responsible for the death of those marines. The rain drew his strength away. He sensed he was ill, but he chastised himself for giving it any thought. *Don't give in to it,* he ordered himself, but tremors crept into his bones and a racking cough sprang from his chest. Cold and heat alternated throughout his body.

Things moved around him, ghostlike in the rain. Indistinguishable, unimportant. No matter, no matter. His thoughts were fragmented and clumsy; there was no sense to them.

What an ungodly city! A steaming jungle in the summer

and an icebox in the winter. A canal of garbage and an Island of sedition.

He chuckled as the fog enveloped his mind. There is something wrong with my eyes, he thought; they are covered with some sort of mist.

He felt someone grasp his shoulders. It was a Negro man and beside him was a Negro woman. Who were these people? They looked familiar, but Fitz was unable to recall their names. His temples throbbed, and he put his hand to his forehead. His kepi slipped off, but he knew if would be too much of an effort to pick it up.

The man spoke to him, but the words were muffled. Fitz shook his head. The woman held up an umbrella and the rain beat against it. There was a door in front of him, and steps. The man and the woman were on either side of him, guiding him forward, their arms under his. He wanted to thank them, but he could not think of what to say. He knew that if he closed his eyes, the throbbing pain in his skull would ease and that was all that he wished for. He just wanted the pain to go away.

He heard a voice, a woman's voice. She was standing at the door with a blanket. She had red hair and her arms were outstretched, and Fitz knew he wanted to slip into her embrace and into the warmth of the blanket. The woman with the red hair looked at Fitz with sadness, and he wondered what troubled her. His foot struck a step and he stumbled forward. They were talking in some foreign tongue, and all Fitz could do was shake his head.

The warmth of the house washed over him and he cast about for some indication of where he was. A blanket was flung across his shoulders and he was led toward a flight of stairs, but it was all a dream. The walls were floating and people glided rather than stepped, and all he could hear was a rushing in his ears.

The headache became worse, an augur boring into his skull, and he gritted his teeth to keep from crying out. His body was suspended above the earth and he thought: *I'm dead,* and the notion made him laugh.

He heard the Negro man say, "Out of his head," and some other words that drifted away.

Asia said, "Fitz."

Chapter 24

November 26, 1861
The 253rd day of the war
The Royal Boarding House

Asia's touch wakened Fitz. He felt her fingertips glide across his brow, followed by a warm cloth draped across his forehead. Fitz opened his eyes. Sunlight painted the window next to his bed. Asia hovered over him.

"Good morning," she said.

He tried to speak, but his mouth was as dry as dust and his throat was parched. All he managed was a tiny croak.

"Wait," she said. She brought a glass to his lips, letting a few drops of cold water coat his lips and tongue. He swallowed, his throat raw, and licked his lips.

"What happened?" he managed in a hoarse whisper.

"You've been very ill."

"How long?"

"Four days."

Fitz closed his eyes. Four days. He tried to speak but nothing came. She gave him more water. "Does anyone know?"

"You mean the army? Yes. I had the doctor inform them, which seemed to satisfy everyone. How do you feel?"

"Horrible," Fitz croaked. "My mouth tastes as if I've been chewing leather."

"That's the illness and the medicine. Do you want to sit up?"

Fitz replied with a nod. Asia helped him sit up, positioning the pillows behind him. When she bent close to him he could feel her warmth and he wanted to reach out to her, but he was too weak even to raise his arm. She gave him more water and then summoned Clara, ordering her to bring soup.

"Four days," he said.

"Yes," Asia said. "You are lucky. The doctor said the fever was quite advanced. You could have died."

Fitz wondered if it was such a poor alternative. Every bone ached and a dull pain clamped his head like a vice. He glanced at Asia, and strained to focus. He wanted to see her reaction when he asked her the question that haunted him. "I was at Mr. Prescott's the other evening. I saw you there with Will Moore. Colonel Moore." It was as much as he could muster.

Her eyes narrowed in thought and then she looked at him in surprise. "For God's sake, Fitz, why didn't you make yourself known?"

"I was indisposed," he said, his response striking him as false and ridiculous. He saw she thought so as well.

"Well, indisposed or not, would it have taxed you to pass a few words with me?" she asked, piqued. "And as far as Colonel Moore, yes, I was speaking with him, as I do with many people at Mr. Prescott's gatherings."

"He is my friend," Fitz said. "I didn't know that you knew each other." The words sounded stiff and unnatural. Worse, he felt like a petulant child.

"I didn't know him before the night of the party," she replied. "Why does it concern you that I was speaking with your friend? If it's jealousy on your part, I want you to dismiss it. I am quite familiar with that destructive emotion, having been exposed to it the entire time of my marriage."

"Prescott—" Fitz started, hoping that he could find a way to ask her why she was there, without making it seem like he did not trust her.

"Knew my father," she said. "No matter how large this wretched city gets it will always be a town where everyone knows everyone else." She fought to remain civil. "Are you satisfied?"

"I'm sorry," he said. It was stupid of him to mention it.

"Why does this matter?" she asked. "Prescott and your Colonel Moore? Why are you so distrustful?" She looked at him, her caring eyes searching for a reason. "What has happened to you?"

He shook his head in frustration—reasons, causes, explanations, were just out of arm's length. Fitz understood none of it. "I'm to leave Washington soon," he said, falling back on a subject that at least held out some hope.

"Are you?" Asia asked.

"The war," Fitz said.

"Of course," she said.

Asia removed the cloth from his forehead, refolded and replaced it. The action calmed her. He wished the cloth were ice-cold to draw the heat away from his forehead and dull the throbbing.

"It's best, I suppose," Asia said, resettling the cloth on his head. "You are eminently unprepared for life in this city. When?"

"Soon, I hope," he said and winced at his own words. It made it sound as if he was pleased to leave her, but he was not. She was his one sanctuary, her presence and the sound of her voice his only solace.

"I see." Her words were distant, edged with pain. Fitz had hurt her, and he hated himself for it. "A command, I suppose?"

"Yes."

Clara brought the soup on a small tray, and Asia stood. "Clara, please assist Captain Dunaway," she said. "I must attend to my other boarders." She stopped at the door but did not turn. "My mistake, Captain Dunaway, is that I opened myself to you. Shame on me for neglecting my own well-being."

Then she was gone.

Clara offered him the soup in silence. He sat up in bed and took the tray from her, laying it across his lap.

"You ought not to treat her that way, Captain," Clara said. "She's a good woman. She cares about you."

Fitz ate. He sensed that there was more to say.

"Mr. Lossing, he's one to watch out for. He's got a mean streak."

"I thought as much," Fitz said.

"I heard them arguing," Clara continued. She handed him a napkin as if the action would somehow mitigate her indiscretion. "Mr. Lossing, he said some terrible things to Mrs. Lossing. On account of you."

Fitz hesitated before dipping the spoon in his soup.

"None of it was true, and she told him so. But he ain't a man to listen. You oughtta know these things."

"Why?" Fitz asked. He had no reason to lose his temper with Clara, and regretted his anger.

"'Cause she don't deserve two bad men in her life," Clara said.

Her words cut into Fitz. He felt helpless and alone. "Take it away," he ordered Clara. "I'm not hungry."

Later, as he lay in bed, he listened to the house sleep and thought of Asia. He did not know about women. He knew about men and making war and the sharp excitement of battle—but he did not know about women. What complicated creatures they are, he thought, and what a fool I was to get involved with her. He resisted even thinking her name, for if he did he knew he would realize just how much she cared for him. And how much he cared for her. He felt sick at the thought of the harm that he had caused her and at the trust he had betrayed.

How was it that his arms ached to hold her and his heart was ready to burst from his chest? *What manner of man am I?* he asked. But his only answer was the sweetness of longing for her. Fatigue claimed him, and he slipped into a deep sleep.

*   *   *

Fitz judged it to be early morning, for the sky outside his window told him as much, when a voice awakened him. He thought at first he was dreaming because he had incorporated the voice and soft knock into a troubling memory of his visit to Prescott's. It took him just a moment to realize someone was calling his name. He sat up and had to steady himself as the room tilted. He was weak but he fought back the illness. "Yes?"

"Come downstairs, to the carriage house," the man's voice instructed.

It sounded like Lossing.

"Why?" Fitz asked. "What do you want?"

"I have news," Lossing said, in a low voice. "It's about Whaley."

Fitz swung his legs out of bed. Testing them on the floor, he was certain that he could walk.

Whaley? How did Lossing know about Whaley? Fitz tried to sort out what he had heard. "Ten minutes," he said.

This was bad business, but he had no idea how Lossing and Whaley were tied together, or even if they were. *This could be about Asia,* Fitz thought. Clara said the two had argued. Perhaps Lossing wanted to confront him. No, no. Fitz rejected the idea. It had to involve Whaley. But how? The man was dead. Did Lossing have information about Whaley? Fitz felt his stomach pitch, he had been certain he was no longer a spy, but now his hopes had been snatched away by a voice in the middle of the night.

He slipped his trousers on over his nightshirt, pulled on his boots, and tossed his coat over his shoulders. Fitz hesitated and then picked up his pistol. He unlocked his door and opened it, peering into the dark hallway. Seeing no one in either direction, he slipped to the servants' stairway. He knew it would lead him to the back porch, and from there to the narrow backyard and to the carriage house beyond.

The cold swam over him as he opened the back door, staring over the snow-covered ground. The moon was almost gone, but enough of its light remained to cast a blue haze over everything. The sky was clear, the stars bright, the only movement trails of gray smoke that floated out of neighboring chimneys. No sounds met him as he eased down the steps and into the yard. The whole scene was dead and foreboding. The frigid air clutched at him. He drew his coat close around his shoulders as he walked, feeling the reassuring weight of the pistol in his pocket.

A clatter echoed from the carriage house. Fitz stopped. His hand went to his pocket as the danger became obvious; he was standing in the open, while Lossing had the protection of the outbuilding. He cursed for having gotten himself in this fix.

He listened and heard the noise once more, followed by a horse snorting in the darkness. It was nothing more than a restless animal, Fitz thought as he advanced. He froze in alarm as he wondered: what made him restless?

He pulled the pistol out of his pocket and snuck to one side of the doorway. He tested the wooden handle and found it moved without a hint of noise. He swung the door open, and waited for any sound to betray a presence in the gloom. Letting his eyes adjust to the darkness of the carriage house, he stepped in. He kept his back to the wall as he crept deeper into the interior.

"Lossing?" he called.

"Here," a voice said.

"Light a lamp," Fitz said, and then stopped. Silence. "Light a lamp so I can see you," Fitz ordered. He thumbed the hammer of his revolver back to full cock but kept it pointed down. He did not like this. He crouched. He saw a movement in the shadows and tensed, ready for anything. There was a noise behind him, just a whisper of a footstep, but before he had time to turn, he heard the dull report of a gunshot.

The night exploded into a million stars.

There were people around him and then voices cut way into the mist that surrounded him and he felt himself being pulled to his feet. People were talking in excited spurts, words running over one another punctuated by shouts and a cry of alarm.

Fitz shook his head, trying to return order to his befuddled brain. He was being held.

"Here now," Hogan warned from behind him, his thick hands clasping his shoulders. "Let's have none of that."

Fitz gazed to either side. Hastings, bearing a strange, apologetic look, used his body to pin Fitz's right arm in place. Pennbrook, his nightshirt flowing in a cold breeze that passed through the carriage house, had his left. Woodbridge was stooped over a dark bundle lying on the dirt floor next to the wheel of a carriage. Fitz had seen enough dead men to know that he was staring at another. A black pool spilled across the frozen ground, creating a random pattern amid the peaks and valleys of wheel ruts.

Woodbridge, a revolver in his hand, stood. "Mr. Lossing is dead." He glanced down at the revolver, as if the weight of the weapon was evidence enough.

Fitz heard a rush of voices behind him and a woman cry out. It was Asia, and then Fitz knew what was happening. The dead man was her husband, and he was the murderer.

He saw Clara and Asia kneeling at her husband's side and heard sobbing before he was dragged outside, up the back stairs, and into the kitchen. He tried to speak, but Woodbridge stopped him with a wave of the pistol.

Hogan disappeared and returned with a chair from the dining room. The men forced Fitz to sit.

"Canfield's gone for the police," Woodbridge said, savoring his authority.

Fitz had regained his senses enough to say, "I didn't kill him." He said it but he wasn't sure. He couldn't remember what happened. It was dark, talking, and there was a tremendous flash.

"Here is your pistol," Woodbridge said, holding up the weapon. "It has been fired, I can smell as much and one chamber is empty."

Fitz focused on the pistol. His eyes still watered from the cold and his brain needed coaxing to come round, but he was sure of one thing. "That isn't mine."

"It was at your side," Woodbridge said, surveying the members of the self-appointed posse. The aroma of wood fires and frying bacon hung in the air. "I say poor Mr. Lossing confronted you and in a flush of righteous anger over your unwarranted attention to his wife, struck you. You, being the coward you are, managed to shoot him before you fell. The bullet struck him between the eyes, blowing his brains out."

"I didn't shoot him," Fitz said, fighting to rise. He was pushed back into the chair. "That isn't my pistol. That's some sort of foreign make. I carry a Colt."

Canfield entered the kitchen followed by two Metropolitan policemen. "I am here," Canfield announced.

"I observed as much," Woodbridge said, smiling at Fitz. The look said everything—now all that is left is the hanging.

Chapter 25

November 27, 1861
The 254th day of the war
Old Capitol Prison
Washington, DC

"My name is Colonel Wood," the large officer with a bushy black beard said. "I'm superintendent of Old Capitol Prison. You are Captain Dunaway?"

Fitz, his wrists and ankles manacled, sat at a wooden table across from the colonel. A captain and two soldiers stood guard behind him. He had been searched and his possessions confiscated. He had said nothing since being turned over to the provost guard.

"You are Captain Dunaway?" Wood tried again.

"Yes," Fitz said. He had never been so angry in his life and yet he knew he could not give vent to his rage. Far more was at stake than the death of one man. "I did not kill anyone."

"I think it is in your best interests, Captain," Wood said, "to be straightforward about this. You were found next to the body. Your fired pistol was at your side. Who do you think killed Mr. Lossing?"

"I didn't kill him," Fitz said.

Colonel Wood nodded to a soldier. "Put him in a cell." To the captain standing next to him Wood said, "It shouldn't take long to get to the bottom of this."

Fitz was pulled to his feet. "I want to speak with Thaddeus Prescott. I must talk to him. He'll explain everything. I was working for him. He knows the truth." The two soldiers dragged Fitz out the door. "At the War Department!" Fitz shouted at Wood. "Assistant Secretary of War Prescott. Tell him I'm here. Tell him what happened."

The guards took Fitz down a long hallway and up a flight of stone steps to another level. Cells faced each other across a narrow corridor. A cold, damp wind blew down the cellblock. The barred windows in each cell were open to the weather except for wooden shutters that hung on either side of crude windows. Prisoners called out to the guards, pleading for blankets or food, or begging to be released. Fitz heard several crying.

The guards stopped him in front of a cell and unlocked the door. He was shoved in and fell against a low bed. The door clanged shut behind him as he struggled to his feet.

"Get Prescott!" Fitz called after the guards as they left. "Tell him where I am." He slumped onto the bed and, after a minute, the cellblock became quiet. He looked up. The thin, barred window let sunlight into the cell. He shivered and curled up on the cot, trying to keep warm. The heavy manacles dragged on his hands and hate rose in him like bile. He clenched his fists until the knuckles were white. He'd find out who killed Lossing, and when he did, that man was dead. He felt a dagger plunged into his heart as he remembered Asia kneeling over the dead body of her husband, struck dumb with disbelief.

She thinks I killed him, Fitz realized, sickened by the idea. There is no telling what sort of poison Woodbridge is spreading about.

He tried to separate every element of what had happened, stripping one from the other so that he could examine the events. He *had* heard Lossing through the door, he was certain of his voice. The carriage house. Lossing mentioned

Whaley. How did the two know each other? Was Lossing one of Prescott's agents? Why didn't he make himself known?

How did Lossing know that I was involved with Whaley? Fitz asked himself, sitting up. He stood, his fatigue and the cold forgotten. Was it Asia? Was she a part of this? Fitz willed himself not to think of her. He could not stand the thought of her being involved.

His mind traveled back to his first meeting with Prescott and then, like the glass slides of the magic-lantern shows he enjoyed so much, scene after scene appeared before his eyes. This time it was not the wonders of Egypt or the majestic Alps of France, but glimpses of events that led him to Old Capitol Prison. He saw Will Moore in the carriage on the way to his first meeting with Prescott, and the dark, suspicious face of Ward Hill Lamon—Lincoln's friend "Hill." And then there was Lincoln, oddly like a toy he had owned as a child that flopped about, long arms and legs dancing. Those cool gray eyes shattered that image, intelligence shining through them like a beacon in the darkness.

Fitz pushed his cuffs under the jagged edge of the manacles to soften the burden.

Whaley. No man to underestimate. Dangerous and cunning. Lossing knew him—how? The miserable cot beckoned and he yielded.

He covered himself with the threadbare blanket and studied the cellblock.

He was in the last cell in the block—a stone wall and stairs were to his right, and an empty cell and then a stone wall to his left. There was no one in the cell across from him, and no one next to him, but he could hear people farther down the cellblock.

He pulled his arms and legs closer to his body and pulled the blanket around him. He began to think.

Who shot Lossing? It had to be Whaley. But the man was dead. Couldn't it have been one of Asia's boarders? Woodbridge? Hogan? Lossing had been searching for Hogan, hadn't he?

Why make it appear as if I had murdered Lossing? No, no, Fitz thought, *it makes no sense.* He thought of Asia, kneeling next to the still form of her husband.

It had to be Whaley. If, Fitz's weary mind countered, he was really alive.

He let his head fall back against the brick wall. All of this is senseless, he thought, closing his eyes.

Prescott will come. He will hear about this and be here in a matter of hours. It was all a dream and I will be released. Fitz drew himself into a ball to conserve body heat. He wished Will were there and then the unthinkable drifted in his mind: suppose Will was involved? Not Will. Good old Will.

He awoke with a start and realized it was nearly dark. He must have been asleep for hours.

"Guard!" he shouted. "Guard? Is anyone there? Guard?"

The other prisoners shouted as well, and Fitz heard the heavy clump of boots on the stone stairs. A rotund sergeant with a greasy beard and bulbous nose appeared. Keys jangled on his belt.

"What is it, sonny?" he growled in a sleepy voice.

"What time is it? Where is Prescott?"

"Who in the hell is Prescott? Is that all you wanted? If I were you, I'd worry about a lot more than the time. For instance, where my neck was going to be about two weeks from now."

Fitz threw off the blanket and hobbled to the cell door. "I must see Assistant Secretary of War Prescott," he said. "You must get word to Prescott that I am here. Send word to the War Department that Captain Dunaway is in Old Capitol Prison. If you can't find him, contact Mr. Ward Hill Lamon."

"I know you're here, sonny," the sergeant said. "And that's enough."

Fitz held his anger in check. "Sergeant, I work for the War Department. I work for Prescott. Get word to him."

The sergeant scratched the back of his neck in thought and yawned. "Well, I'll tell the captain, and he'll tell the colonel, and the colonel'll decide who gets what word. Until then, shut up and go to sleep."

"Sergeant—"

"Sonny, I ain't foolin'. You got them other prisoners stirred up, and I had to walk all the way up them damn stairs and me with two bad legs and piles. Now, shut up."

The sergeant disappeared down the stairs. Fitz was conscious only of his own breathing and the sickening feeling that he had been abandoned. Prescott should have been here by now. *Surely he did not believe I killed Lossing? That's not possible, he can't believe it.*

He slept fitfully that night. Even after forcing the heavy wooden shutters closed, it was frigid in the cell. He heard other prisoners moaning and wailing against the cold. He covered his ears with his arms to muffle the pathetic sounds, but he gave up. Their sobs were a constant drone that crept into his skull. Cold shook his body until all the strength was wrung from him, leaving his senses numbed. He dreamt of a fire, more blankets, and his greatcoat, anything to keep the cold from him.

During the terrible night he kept asking himself, *Where is Prescott?*

The next morning brought a tin cup of steaming coffee— little more than water—and a half loaf of dry, stale bread. Fitz took them from the jailers, grateful for the warmth that spread from the cup through his fingers and hands. He held the cup close to his face and let the steam warm the tip of his nose while he savored the aroma of the coffee. He sipped it, trying not to burn his lips. It was weak but delicious. He ate standing up, leaning against the cell door. He tore at the hunk of bread, gnawing at it until a piece broke away. His mouth was dry and it was difficult to chew, but he managed to take a drink of coffee to moisten the bread. As he ate, his teeth crushed something brittle and he knew that the bread was wormy. He didn't care, it was the finest meal he had ever eaten.

The jailers disappeared after all the prisoners had been served. Fitz nursed his bread and coffee, and took stock of his surroundings. He studied the manacles on his wrists. They were standard army issue, a loop of coarse iron, encircling his wrists, with the two ends tethered by a long chain. A key, no more than a rod, he knew, opened the barrel lock. The leg irons were the same, except of heavier construction.

The rough metal scoured the skin of his wrists, raising red welts. His trouser legs protected his ankles from the same fate.

Fitz finished his coffee and bread and was surprised at how refreshed he felt. He hopped back to his bunk, wrapped himself in his blanket, and studied the interior of his cell.

The cell door could be opened only with a key—held by the fat sergeant or another jailer. And the manacles? He examined them. *I could get out of them,* he thought, *if I had a key.* He stood and inspected the bed. It was of rough timber construction with pegs holding the frame and legs together. He lifted the straw mattress. It rested on wooden slats placed every ten inches. He let it drop and looked around. A large rusty bucket to be used as a necessary sat in one corner. It offered no help unless he planned to throw the contents at his keepers. There was his blanket. He felt a strange affection for the thin piece of cloth.

His eyes fell on the shutters. The wood was dry and shrunken, and they barely covered the window opening, but at least they kept some of the cold out. He pulled open the shutters, welcoming the sun's warmth. The wind was still, which somehow kept the chilled air at bay. Fitz was thankful.

He inspected the window and the bars. They were well cemented in the stone window frame. There was no chance of escape through the window.

He returned to his bed and wrapped the blanket around his shoulders. Where the devil was Prescott? *He doesn't really think I killed anyone, does he? He has to know what's going on.*

He thought of Asia and he could feel her gentle hands caressing him. *She cannot be involved in this,* he told himself, but too many questions remained. *I don't know,* he confessed, and with the confession came an aching in his heart so intense he felt his chest would explode.

He grew frustrated that he continually vacillated from believing her to doubting her and he condemned himself for being weak. Like her dead husband.

There was a commotion in the stairway. Several men were coming up the stairs, he could hear their voices and the sound of footsteps. He waited, watching the doorway.

Colonel Wood, the greasy sergeant, and Ward Hill Lamon appeared.

"Mr. Lamon," Fitz said, struggling to reach the bars with his legs shackled. "I've been imprisoned for murder. I did not do it."

"Henry Lossing," Lamon supplied, glancing at the manacles on his wrists.

"Yes, sir. But I did not do it. I've asked for Mr. Prescott. I lost hope that he would come."

"Well, Captain Dunaway," Lamon said, his voice booming against the brick walls. "I'm looking forward to seeing you hang. You are a damn traitor and a murderer to boot."

Fitz felt as if he had been struck. "What?"

"Prescott won't be here. He told me everything. I've read the reports. So you threw in with the Rebels. Well, serves me right trusting a man from Tennessee."

"I did nothing of the sort," Fitz flared. "Who told you this?"

Lamon's eyes narrowed to dark slits. "You did, you traitorous bastard. I read Prescott's reports. They were your words, were they not? They told me about your raid on the Navy Yard and your dalliance with Mrs. Lossing. There were other reports as well, from those at the boarding house. You and Lossing had words, he warned you away from his wife."

"I'm no traitor, and I didn't kill anyone. Talk to Prescott, if you don't believe me, he'll set this straight."

Lamon thundered, "For God's sake, man, he signed the order imprisoning you."

"What?" The word came as no more than a whisper and Fitz had to summon all his strength to utter it.

"I warned him about you from the beginning and luckily he soon came to realize you weren't the patriot that you pretended to be. You're a traitor and the best place for you is at the end of a rope. I just thank the heavens Mr. Lincoln was not endangered."

Fitz found his voice. "Prescott?" He edged forward, confused, his mind racing over what he had just heard, that perhaps he was mistaken about what the man had just said. "Prescott told you this?"

"Every bit of it," Lamon said. "Why, if it weren't for the legalities of the thing, I'd see you hung right now."

Fitz shuffled to his bunk, stunned. His legs failed him and he slumped on the mattress. Lamon was still talking but to Fitz the words droned on without substance.

It was Prescott. And Batterman. Clerks—clerks know everything. Nothing is done in Washington without them. Fitz remained silent, unfeeling, his mind incapable of grasping what was being said. Prescott sent Will to the West, far away from Washington, far from the web that he was spinning around Fitz. There was no one to help him. Prescott had turned on him, Will Moore was a thousand miles away, and Asia was burying the man that Fitz was accused of killing. What a fool I've been! Prescott used me to further his scheme. But what scheme was it?

He looked up at Lamon. "I didn't do it," he declared. "I'm no traitor. How many times do I have to say it? Prescott and Batterman are the traitors. Those were not my words you read. Batterman doctored them. Listen to me. They plan to do something."

"I ought to break your neck here and now," Lamon spat. "You Rebels twist truth around so much, it's unrecognizable. Who else is involved? Tell me!"

Fitz sprang to his feet. "Batterman, you fool! Prescott. They plan to kill the president. They plan some action—"

"Who?"

Fitz advanced on Lamon, his frustration carrying him forward. "Whaley. Bishop. The others. Batterman—"

"You are a liar. Whaley was killed in the explosion. I don't know anyone named Bishop. The president is safe, and you are a Goddamn liar."

Fitz backed away from the cell door, his eyes flashing with defiance. "You and your kind can go to Hell," he said, each word dipped in acid. "I'll do things my way from now on."

Lamon turned to Wood. "What are you feeding him?"

"Bread and water, twice a day. And a little coffee."

"Once a day," Lamon ordered. "No coffee." He stared at Fitz, a cold hatred in his eyes. "You'll tell me everything, or you'll starve to death. Let's go," he ordered.

The group left. Fitz calmed himself so he could think. Prescott was the traitor. Trust no one, Prescott had said. Start with your own house, you doddering old idiot!

Fitz spun around, looking for something to throw. He staggered forward, bound by the shackles, and struck one of the shutters with his fists. He cried out with pain as the shutter slammed against the window frame with a crash. It bounced back and flew off its fragile hinges, bouncing on the floor at Fitz's feet.

He doubled over, drawing his aching fists into his stomach in agony, cursing his situation. He was close to tears, not from pain, or fear, but out of sheer rage and frustration. He wanted to hit someone, or kick something, anything to strike out. He was bound by more than shackles. He was encased in an iron web of lies spun by the men who were supposed to give him the only thing he wanted, command of his own regiment. His regiment! To lead a few men in a desperate battle, he had dreamed of that as a boy. He had charged docile cattle scattered in a skirmish line across a broad meadow, willow sword raised, thin legs pumping, bare feet pounding through the thick, cool grass . . .

Then he saw the two nails.

One was torn from the rotten wood of the shutter and lay on the stone floor of the cell. The other, its head nearly eaten away with rust, protruded from a shattered board. He knelt, the manacles restricting his movement, fighting to keep from toppling over. The nail beckoned him—its shank coyly hidden, buried in the worm-eaten wood. He was a man dying of thirst who catches the sheen of rainwater on a broad leaf.

Fitz looked around, fearful that the noise of the falling shutter would bring someone to investigate, but there was no sound on the staircase. He picked up the loose nail, a crude iron shaft. Pinching it between his fingertips, he inserted the shank through the keyhole into the barrel of the wrist manacles. He felt no resistance, no contact with anything but the sides of the keyhole. He drew out the nail and repositioned his fingers, allowing as much of the shaft to enter the hole as possible. He tried it again.

The nail was too short.

Fitz pulled it out and threw it across the cell in disgust. He pinned the other nail between his fingertips and tried to pull it from the wood. It barely moved. His fingers were stiff from the cold, and his hands were made of stone. He placed the ends of his fingers in his mouth and breathed on them, trying to drive the numbness away. He held the board with his left hand and pushed the nail back and forth with his right, loosening the wood's grip. The sharp ridges of the stamped nail dug into his fingers, slicing through the skin. The tips of his fingers ached, and he could not tell if the nail was moving. Blood welled up around the shank.

He felt the nail shift.

He pushed at it harder, driving it against the wood, pulling it back and pushing it forward again. Back and forth, back and forth, until he could feel the nail wobble in the hole. Gripping it as tightly as he could, he pulled on the nail.

The nail gave way. He wiggled it, willing all of his strength into this action. The nail slid upward, and it was free.

Fitz fell back against the bunk, looking at the long sliver of iron trapped in his bloody fingers. For the first time in days he felt a sense of triumph.

He looked about, clutching the nail to his breast. It was his salvation, the beginning of his escape.

Chapter 26

November 29, 1861
The 256th day of the war
Old Capitol Prison

Fitz slept that night, despite the cold air that rushed in through the bars of the open window and the constant sounds of suffering drifting from the other cells. The next morning, a jailer saw the mess in Fitz's cell and reported it to an officer.

"Well," the officer announced, "I guess you'll get used to doing without shutters. You can freeze for all I care."

Fitz watched them leave and began working the nail in the keyhole. It slid into the locking mechanism. He closed his eyes and probed, trusting to his sense of touch—imagining the interior of the lock and turning the nail until he felt resistance. The tumblers. He visualized the nail in the cylinder, feeling the end of it scratch across the crude tumblers. *Patience,* he told himself, and then he opened his eyes with a hollow laugh.

If only Will could see me now, he thought.

He rested several times. His fingers cramped, and his hands and wrists ached. He stopped once when a jailer appeared with his ration of bread and water. It must be noon, he thought. He heard voices and someone coming up the stairs. It was the greasy sergeant. Fitz was accustomed to his rough voice and his heavy tread, but the other voice was too weak to make out. The step was uncertain, accompanied by a hiss. Fitz hid the nail in the mattress and covered himself with the blanket.

"The second floor," the sergeant announced with a burp.

Bishop stepped from behind him.

"This lot is as dangerous as the rest," the sergeant said. "Secesh. Smugglers. Spies. We get all kinds."

Bishop blinked as if he were just emerging into sunlight. "Who is this man?" he asked, pointing to Fitz.

"Oh! Ten times worse than the lot. A murderer and a spy to boot. First they'll hang him. Then they'll shoot him." The sergeant laughed at his own joke. "Hey, sonny. You're going to be famous. This fellow's from the *National Republican*." He turned to Bishop. "You won't forget our deal?"

Bishop smiled. "No, sir. No indeed." He slipped the sergeant a gold piece.

"Ain't you forgettin' my bottle?"

"I'll have it delivered tonight. I wonder, can I ask this man a few questions? For the article?"

The sergeant frowned and scratched his head, digging into his scalp with filth-encrusted nails. "Okay. Just don't use his name and don't use mine. It took me thirty years to get these stripes. I don't want to lose them overnight."

"Of course," Bishop said. "You can stay if you wish."

The sergeant ran his sleeve under his nose and sniffed. "I've got coffee boiling. Come back down in ten minutes, and I'll give you a cup."

Bishop watched the sergeant leave before he spoke. "How are you, Captain Dunaway?"

Fitz did not reply.

"I'm sorry to find you here. It must be a terrible experience," he said, compassion reflected in his eyes.

"Did Whaley send you? Because if he did, you can go back and tell him that he is a dead man."

"Oh, no. No, sir," Bishop said, shocked. "I came on my

own. Mr. Whaley doesn't know that I'm here. He's alive, you know."

Fitz sat up. "Why are you here?" It would take nothing to reach through the bars and snap the little bastard's neck.

Bishop moved closer to the cell door and scanned the corridor before replying. "To help you, sir."

"Do you have a gun?" Fitz asked, pushing himself out of the bunk. "A knife?" *Move slowly, don't alarm him. The chains are long enough to get your hands through the bars.*

Bishop looked crestfallen. "No, sir. I don't. I didn't know what to do. I thought you might tell me."

Fitz inched toward the cell door. His hands shot through the bars and locked around Bishop's throat. "You can go to Hell," he said in a ragged whisper.

Bishop tore at Fitz's hands. "Captain. Please," he gasped. "Please." His eyes pleaded for mercy.

"You and your kind have done enough," Fitz said. He released Bishop and the little man stumbled against the bars of the opposite cell, pulling at his collar and tie. He loosened them and sucked in air.

"I came to help, sir," he gasped. "I want to help you escape."

"So Whaley can kill me, too?"

"This has nothing to do with Mr. Whaley," Bishop said. "I came alone. This is my idea."

"Why?"

Bishop swallowed and adjusted his glasses. "Because you saved my life. Because you're the only man who has ever treated me as an equal. Not as a cripple. And you never condemned my love of poetry."

Fitz shook his head. He found Bishop's explanation hard to accept. "I've experienced nothing but treachery at the hands of you and your friends. Why should I trust you?"

Bishop hesitated. "I don't know," he said. "I've never lied to you. And I respect you. That should count, shouldn't it? Over the years, I lost sight of my own value. I am a person of substance. No matter how little. You made me remember when you helped me to swim the river. Maybe it wasn't much of an adventure to you—I mean that it didn't mean much to you. But it did to me. You gave me a chance to prove myself. Nobody's ever done that before."

Fitz considered Bishop's words. The cripple waited for him to speak.

"You can help me escape," Fitz said.

"Yes."

"It won't be easy getting free of this. Once I get out, I don't know what I'm going to do. Where I can go."

"You can stay with me as long as you want," Bishop said, and then brightened, knowing that Fitz trusted him.

"Have you a plan?"

"The sergeant thinks I am a reporter. I told him I want to write an article about the prison. I promised him two dollars and a bottle of whiskey. When I come back tonight, I will have the bottle. I'll put a sleeping draught in it. When he succumbs, I will take his keys and release you."

"There are other guards on duty."

"Three," Bishop said. "They make their rounds every four hours. At ten, two, six, and so on. They'll be in the guard-room at midnight, when I come back. The sergeant won't want to share his whiskey, so I'll suggest we come up here and drink it in one of the empty cells." He beamed, proud of his preparation.

Fitz smiled. "You've been busy," he said, impressed with the little man's thoroughness. "He has a dozen or more keys on his belt. Which one opens the cell doors?"

Bishop was ready with the answer. "The slimmest," he chirped.

Fitz grinned at the man's obvious pleasure. He reviewed every aspect of Bishop's plan, seeking flaws. He was tired and his brain stumbled. He rubbed his face. It was no good, he could not think clearly. Better to dive in and risk everything. "The other prisoners might become alarmed. They could alert the other guards. Have you thought of that?"

Bishop said, "Yes. The guardroom is at the bottom of the stairs and to the left. They keep the door closed because of the cold. We can close the door here, at the top of the stairs."

"You *have* been busy," Fitz said. "How do we get out of the building?"

Bishop pointed to the end of the hall. "We can go down those stairs. They lead down to a brick pavement and then out to the yard. The guardhouse and kitchen will be to our left. We go straight past the gallows to the alley. Once there we can easily make our way to 1st Street East." He noticed Fitz's shackles. "Oh, dear. I hadn't considered those."

Fitz looked down. "Don't worry about these. Bring a revolver and a knife. And matches."

Bishop nodded. "Tonight. Midnight."

"Yes," Fitz said. And then, just to make sure everything was clear, he said, "Bishop? At the slightest sign of treachery, I'll kill you."

"I could not betray you, Captain Dunaway," Bishop replied. "Even if it were to save my own life, I would never betray you. You are my one true friend. A friend of the South. You are, aren't you? Of course you are. Forgive me." His eyes held hope. "Tonight."

Chapter 27

Old Capitol Prison

Fitz worked throughout the afternoon to unlock the manacles, the blanket wrapped around the chains to muffle the sound. The guards made their rounds, barely looking, content to shake the cell door to make sure it was locked. He wondered if it was a way to remind him of his imprisonment. They carried muskets with fixed bayonets. A fearsome-looking weapon but cumbersome in close quarters. Get inside the sweep of the bayonet, belt buckle to belt buckle and the fight becomes even. That was the trick.

By late afternoon, his back and shoulders ached. He stopped to rest several times, let the feeling return to his fingers, and stretched to ease his stiff muscles. He began again, forcing himself to continue. He bit his lip so deeply in concentration that he could taste blood, and once he threw the nail across the cell in anger. He fell against the brick, drained, and closed his eyes. When he opened them again it was with a renewed determination. He retrieved the nail and began the process over again.

Nearly two hours later, the tumblers clicked free.

He sat, stunned, hardly daring to believe he had succeeded. He blinked and found the manacle on his left wrist hanging open. He forced himself to think back to how he had done it, but could recall nothing except the general placement of the nail in the cylinder. It took Fitz much longer to free his right wrist and by that time he was so worn out that he made himself rest before trying the leg irons.

He drew his legs close to his body so he could reach the cylinder of the shackle on his right ankle. He stopped to blow on his fingers, warming them so he could manipulate the nail. His fingers were senseless, his back burned, and his legs cramped.

Fitz was on his own save for Bishop, and Bishop was known to Prescott and Whaley, so it would be only a matter of time until the little cripple's body turned up in the Canal.

They are going to kill the president, Fitz thought. But how?

You can kill one man easily enough, one tyrant, according to some. And gain what? The destruction of the government, the end of the war, and the freedom of the South?

He freed his right ankle and rested, lingering over all he knew about the president. Kill one man, kill the right man, and you have chaos. There were guards when Lincoln chose to employee them. Sentries at the Executive Mansion, cavalry escorts when he went out, if the president accepted them. But a sharpshooter, a marksman with a good weapon was just as effective as a cannonade. Then why steal half a ton of gunpowder?

He yawned, rubbing his eyes with the heels of his hands. He worked the nail in the keyhole of the left shackle. What was going to happen? And when?

In three hours, he felt the leg iron drop. He rewarded himself with a feeling of triumph but he did not lose track of the obvious, he was still locked in a cell with no hope of escape except Bishop. It was a slim hope but it was better than nothing.

Now all he had to do was wait.

Chapter 28

November 30, 1861
The 257th day of the war
Old Capitol Prison

S now drifted in through the window, bright white flakes
tumbling in the light of a soft moon. They danced about
the cell, swirling until they fell exhausted to the floor.

Fitz, sitting on the bunk, shook with the cold and tore the
blanket into long strips. He might need them to tie up the
sergeant, he might not. But he had them just in case, and
being cold was a small price to pay for preparation.

Was his escape a trap? A way to silence him?

Was he to end with his bullet-ridden body outside of the
prison—killed while trying to escape? No, he could trust
Bishop—he had to trust Bishop—he had no other soiled card
to throw in this dirty game.

The cellblock was silent except for an occasional muffled
cry or the rhythmic snoring of the other inmates. A burst of
wind brought a cloud of snowflakes into the cell, and they
tumbled madly about Fitz, warning him he must hurry.
When he was done with the blanket, he positioned his feet
and hands so the manacles and leg irons appeared secure. It
was no more than an hour before he noticed voices.

The filthy sergeant came first, his hollow and obscene

laughter echoed off the brick walls of the stairway. Fitz lay down with his head against the bars, pretending to be asleep.

"I hope this ain't none of your fancy stuff," the sergeant said, appearing in the corridor. Bishop followed behind, visibly nervous. "It don't have a kick. Nothin' to it. Waste of money. We'll go on down a bit, find a nice, quiet cell."

Bishop glanced at Fitz in a panic.

"What about here, sir? This cell will do nicely."

"Huh? No. I don't want that traitor watchin' me. To hell with a man who kills in cold blood. We'll go on down."

"Sergeant, if you don't mind. I hate to be a bother, but it's my leg, you see. The pain is nearly unbearable. I can't walk much farther."

The sergeant stopped. He appeared drunk. "What is that? You diseased? What's wrong with your leg?"

"A childhood infirmity. It's very painful, especially when the temperature falls."

"Yeah," the sergeant said. "I've got bad knees. Swell up tighter than Dick's hatband. We can stop in here," he said, motioning to the cell across from Fitz. He swung open the cell door. "You'll have to stand. There's only one bunk, and I'm sittin' on it. Gimme the bottle." He jerked the bottle from Bishop's hands, pulled the cork out with his teeth, and entered the cell. Falling on the bunk, he tilted the bottle and drank.

Bishop looked at Fitz and then back to the sergeant.

"You know," the sergeant said, wiping his mouth with his sleeve. "I can tell you all about these people. Make a nice story. Sell a lot of papers. Oughtta make you some money. 'Course," he added, waving the bottle at Bishop, "if it makes you money, it oughtta make me some, too."

"Indeed," Bishop agreed. "How are you feeling?"

The bottle stopped. "Feelin? Hell, I'm feelin just fine. What kind of a question is that? You ain't tryin to poison me, are you?"

Bishop laughed. "No, no. Certainly not. I'm just being courteous."

"Mmm," the sergeant growled. He took several more deep swigs and complained about the prison and the inequities of the United States Army. After thirty minutes he started swaying. He set the bottle at his feet, threw his legs onto the bunk, and lay down. Heavy snores filled the cell.

Fitz waited. Bishop gave him a stricken expression, looking for direction. Fitz nodded for him to continue.

The little man carefully removed the large key chain from a hook on the thick leather belt around the sergeant's waist. The keys clinked together. Bishop froze. Holding the keys with his left hand, he eased the ring free with his right. He sorted through the keys until he found the one for Fitz's cell door.

Fitz watched the snoring sergeant for any sign of movement. Bishop crept across the corridor and inserted the key into the lock.

"You bastard," the sergeant cried behind him. He rolled out of the bunk and pulled himself upright. "I thought I smelled something," he slurred, rushing at Bishop.

He clamped his big hands around Bishop's shoulders and spun the cripple around. The key ring dropped to the floor with a clang.

"I'll choke the life out of you," the sergeant said, trapping Bishop with his broad hands. They struggled and the drunken soldier stumbled back against Fitz's cell.

Fitz heard the prisoners cry out, awakened by the scuffle. He knew the noise would bring the guards up the stairs.

He kicked the leg irons free and grasped the chain of the wrist manacles tightly. Throwing one manacle through the bar, he slipped the chain under the sergeant's chin. Catching the manacle in his hand, he jerked with all his strength, driving the chain under the soldier's chin. The sergeant dropped Bishop, a ragged gurgle escaping from his throat. His fingers dug at the chain, but Fitz leaned back, pinning the man to the cell bars. The sergeant twisted, trying to free himself.

"Knock him out," Fitz ordered Bishop.

Bishop staggered to his feet, dazed. "How?"

"Use your pistol!"

The sergeant strained to pull away from the bars and lashed out with his legs. Bishop darted out of the way and searched through his topcoat. He pulled out a revolver.

"Hit him," Fitz commanded as the sergeant thrashed about.

Bishop grabbed the pistol by the barrel and, thinking better of it, took it by the grip. The sergeant, his eyes bulging, saw what was going to happen. He swung his arms to fend off the blow. Fitz tightened the chain until his arms ached. Bishop drew back and struck the sergeant between the eyes with the barrel of the pistol. The big man went limp.

Bishop looked at Fitz in surprise. "I did it!"

"None too soon," Fitz said, shaking his arms to force the circulation back into them. "Unlock the door." Fitz gathered the strips of blanket as Bishop found the key and inserted it into the lock. The door swung open with a squeak. Fitz pulled the limp guard into his cell, snapped the manacles on his hands and feet, and gagged him with the blanket. "Three guards?"

"Yes," Bishop said. "All in the guardroom downstairs. Now what do we do?"

Prisoners in the other cells called out, begging to be released, pleading for blankets and food.

"Hurry," Fitz said. "They'll hear us."

"No, no," Bishop said. "The doors are closed."

"Give me the bottle," Fitz said. "And the matches." He nodded to the closed door at the end of the corridor. "Open it."

"They'll hear us if we open the door!"

"Yes," Fitz agreed. "Open it."

Bishop handed him the sergeant's half-empty whiskey bottle, and dug in his pocket for a box of matches. As he swung open the door, he said, "I brought everything that you asked me to."

Fitz smiled at the little man. "You've done well." He emptied the whiskey on the mattress in his cell, it was rotten canvas filled with dried straw. He took the matches and pistol from Bishop. As an afterthought he said, "It is loaded, isn't it?" He opened the guard and saw the blunt ends of caked powder.

"Yes," Bishop replied in a hurt tone. "I have a knife, too." He pulled a knife out of his belt. Its broad blade gleamed in the moonlight.

Fitz said, "You're a one-man army. Put that thing away before you cut off a leg. Go on over in that other cell." Bishop did as he was told.

Fitz struck a match and was rewarded with a flame and cloud of sulfur. He waited for it to climb the match stem, and then he threw it onto the bunk. The mattress erupted with a whoosh. He joined Bishop in the cell and shouted, "Fire! Fire!" The cries of the other prisoners filled the corridor, led by a woman's high-pitched scream.

They heard soldiers running up the stairs. More prisoners' voices filled the corridor with shouts of fear. Black smoke rolled out of the window as flames ate at the mattress.

Two soldiers appeared, muskets in their hands, and made for the fire.

Fitz pointed the pistol at them. "Hold! Put the muskets down." The soldiers froze and each placed his musket on the floor. "Where's the other guard?"

"Gone for help," one of the soldiers said.

Fitz pulled Bishop out of the cell and motioned for the two soldiers to get in. He slammed the door closed with a clang, and Bishop locked it.

"Come on," Fitz said, racing down the stairs. They raced down a hallway and reached a side door. Fitz stuck the pistol under his arm and threw the heavy latch.

"Halt!"

He turned to see a guard raise his musket. Bishop jumped in front of him as Fitz heard a sharp bang. Bishop jerked and fell against him. Fitz aimed the pistol at the startled soldier.

"Run," he ordered the soldier. "Run before I kill you!"

The soldier disappeared and Fitz grabbed Bishop's sagging body. He swung open the door and found himself in the yard.

"Oh, I'm shot," Bishop moaned. He cried out in pain as Fitz forced him to walk. He held Bishop up, struggling across the brickyard with the man's weight, passing the silent gallows. They stumbled through a low gate and entered a narrow alley.

"Come on," Fitz said. "We've got to go. Walk." Fitz realized that he had no idea where they were. "Are your rooms close by?"

"Yes," Bishop gasped. "It hurts. Please let me be."

"Where? How do we get there? Tell me!"

"Wait! Wait. Let me get my bearings."

Fitz propped Bishop against the wall and he looked up and down the alley. "There. Go to that street and turn left. It will take you across the Canal."

They were on the wrong side of the Canal. They'd never make it across a bridge without being stopped. Fitz put Bishop's arm over his shoulder. "Come on. We don't have much time."

They shuffled along the alley, Fitz supporting his wounded companion. He knew the army would have patrols out as soon as the alarm was raised. He could have shot the guard, maybe he should have shot him. No, too many innocent men had died on account of him.

They were on 1st Street when the Capitol's unfinished dome loomed out of the darkness. A heavy snow was falling.

"Come on," he urged Bishop.

Great wet flakes fell to the ground, covering everything with a white veil. Fitz forced Bishop on, taking as much of the little man's weight as he could. Reaching the Capitol was their only hope. They struggled up the hill, and Fitz searched for a hiding place.

"Where are we?" Bishop asked, his voice faint.

"The Capitol. There are some sheds around here. We'll hide in one and rest."

"Oh, yes. Please. I'm so tired. I would like to rest."

The wind picked up, throwing the flakes into Fitz's face. He blinked, trying to drive them from his eyes. He was wet and cold. He saw a lean-to, its front covered by a billowing canvas curtain.

"There we are," he said, speeding up. "You can make it. Just a few feet more." He guided the wounded man to the shed and, throwing back the curtain, helped Bishop inside. Piles of lumber filled the dark interior. Fitz pulled down the curtain and found a place for them behind a stack of timbers. He let Bishop slide to the ground. The wounded man moaned in agony. Fitz remembered the matches. He gathered bits of wood and, hands trembling, built a small fire. The spark of the match filled him with hope. He nursed the flame until it caught and burned. He found more scraps of lumber lying about and laid them on the fire, until its glow filled the shack. Then he tore open Bishop's topcoat.

His vest, already dark with blood, oozed more with each ragged breath. Fitz laid his hand near the gaping wound.

"How—how is it? Is it bad?" Bishop asked.

"No," Fitz lied. "We can get you to a surgeon and sew you up."

Bishop sucked in air, like a child whose sobbing has left him breathless. "What—" he struggled to form the words. "What—is—the truth?" His face twisted with pain, and he grabbed at Fitz's hand. "Captain Dunaway! It burns."

"I know. Rest easy. We'll move out shortly," Fitz said. And then he remembered. "What was the lady's name?"

"Lady?"

"The lady in the river. Mr. Poe's lady? The kingdom by the sea?"

"Annabel Lee," Bishop said. "In a kingdom by the sea. Why?"

"Your poem kept me going. I don't think I would have made it without your poem. Keep it in mind and you'll survive this night."

"It is Mr. Poe's poem, Captain Dunaway, not mine. Annabel Lee. She must have been very beautiful." Bishop coughed. His lips foamed with blood. "I am cold. So cold. I smell bread. It smells delicious. Might I have a drink of water?"

Fitz noticed that Bishop's glasses had slid to one side of his face. He adjusted them. "Yes." He ventured outside and gathered a handful of snow, looking around. The hillside was barren of any movement. He returned to Bishop and holding the snow above the man's lips, squeezed until ice-cold water trickled out. Fitz continued, listening to Bishop struggle for breath as his tongue searched for water.

Fitz had to know. The question had haunted him for too long and he feared it would drive him mad if it was never answered. If he didn't ask Bishop now he would never know. But he was afraid of the answer.

"Is Mrs. Lossing involved?" Fitz asked. "Is she a Rebel?"

"Mrs.—Mrs. Lossing? No. No. She is not one of us."

"How did you know to find me in the tobacconist's shop?"

Bishop lay still and his eyes remained closed. Fitz felt like a ghoul questioning him.

"Whaley sent me—follow you. The White Lot. Mr. Whaley and I."

"She isn't a part of this," Fitz said, relief flooding over him. She did not send him to the tobacconist's to be found by Bishop.

"Who is involved?" Fitz asked.

"Whaley knows. He knows everything. No one else."

Prescott was the leader, Fitz thought. Batterman was his second with Whaley and his band of foot soldiers. He felt Bishop's hand searching for his.

"What else are they planning? Bishop? What else?"

"Very soon."

"The president?" Fitz asked.

"President?"

"How?"

"I don't know. I am cold."

"The president? Bishop? Do you know how and when?"

"Captain Dunaway?"

"Yes. I'm here."

Bishop's eyes found Fitz. Tears rolled down the little man's cheeks. "Are you one of us? The truth, sir. Are you one of us?"

Fitz took Bishop's hand in his. It was cold, and his breathing was so slight it was nearly undetectable. The truth. In all of this mess the truth has been as elusive as moonbeams.

"No," he said. "I am a Union man."

A smile crossed Bishop's lips. "Ah, well. I suppose it doesn't matter." Bishop's mouth went slack, a small breath escaped him, and his head fell to one side.

Fitz laid Bishop's hand across his chest. Maybe he was right. Maybe none of it mattered.

Chapter 29

Fitz pulled the collar of Bishop's coat close to his face and turned away from the other three passengers in the omnibus. The vehicle rolled slowly up Pennsylvania Avenue, its two-horse team plodding through the thick layer of newly fallen snow. The city was asleep under the pale light of dawn, deserted and unreal, as if Fitz was wandering the streets in a dream. No one talked on the omnibus, and the deep snow muffled the vehicle's wheels. Those people who were about were nothing more than huddled dark shapes, warding off the cold, darting from one building to another.

He was so tired he could hardly keep his aching eyes open, and he could feel the thick stiffness of Bishop's blood on the topcoat. He had taken it from the dead man, as well as what little money Bishop had, headed back to the street, and caught the omnibus on its return trip up Pennsylvania Avenue. He knew there would be few passengers riding away from the Capitol building, and he hoped a man with a stained coat several sizes too small thrown over his shoulders would not be noticed. He was right. His companions, all men, were asleep, apparently trusting the driver to let them know when the vehicle reached their stop.

Fitz glanced at their sleeping forms. Something about them was odd. Fitz studied them before he saw it.

Flour covered their trouser legs and dusted their hair. Flour?

Fitz shook his head. Never mind. Keep awake. Keep your eyes open. He craned his neck and looked around. His eyelids threatened to droop, and how he longed for sleep. Just a bit, a minute or two.

"State Department!" the driver called out as the omnibus crossed New York Avenue.

Fitz rubbed the weariness from his eyes, made his way to the rear platform, and stepped from the vehicle. He plodded along Pennsylvania Avenue behind the Executive Mansion, snowbound on the broad, white lawn of the Presidential Park. The conservatory gleamed under the yawning rays of the newborn sun. He kept his head down as he passed the War Department and turned left on 17th Street. He walked up to I Street and turned right.

People were beginning to stir now, the city was awakening. Fitz paid no attention to merchants opening shops or clerks hurrying to work. It was all he could do to keep going. The deep snow pulled at his shoes, beckoning him to slow down, calling to him to rest. His calves ached, and his feet and legs were soaked, the trousers stiff with ice. He did not stop walking. I Street crossed Pennsylvania Avenue near 21st Street. Fitz proceeded to 22nd Street and turned left, coming to the Lossing house from the west.

It was a decision he had made as he sat in the freezing shed next to the body of the man who had saved his life. He needed a place to stay, to build his strength and collect his thoughts. He could not go to Bishop's; he was not even sure that he could find the street again. There was nowhere else in the city where he could hide. It left only one refuge, but one that had to be obvious to Lamon as well. There was the danger he would be captured at Asia's and his presence would implicate her. She could turn him away, the man who murdered her husband. Or, she could send for the police. What choice did he have? Where could he go? Not far, he was certain. He had little strength left.

He stood at the corner of G and 21st streets, watching the back of the boarding house. He saw no one. He studied the windows of the buildings along the street. They were covered with a thick frost, and gleamed in the early-morning sun. If someone waited for him behind one of those windows—a policeman, or a soldier, or perhaps that fool Lamon—Fitz could not see them. He tried to force his fatigued brain into action, but his thoughts were jumbled. He found himself drifting off and knew he had to act. Was it safe to go on?

Better to be shot from hiding than to be hanged, he thought. No, by God. Neither one.

He hurried to the back of the boarding house, glancing in every direction for some sign of the enemy. Now there was an irony—the enemy. His own kind, Union soldiers. *The enemy now,* he thought, set on him by the men he was asked to trust.

Fitz pushed open the wooden gate next to the carriage house and found himself in the backyard. He passed the out-buildings and climbed the stairs to the back door that led into the kitchen. He knocked, peering between the curtains. He could see shadows through the steam-covered glass. Inside, a figure approached. Fitz tensed, ready to fight.

The door opened, and Clara gasped. She glanced about and motioned him inside. Taking him by the arm, she led him into the pantry.

"Stay here. Don't move," she said.

"I can't," he conceded. "I'm all done in."

"Stay quiet, sir. Don't make a sound."

Fitz slumped to the floor in gratitude, and his eyes filled with tears. He folded his arms across his knees and bowed his head. Asia was not involved. He let his head fall back against the wall and wiped the tears from his eyes. He sighed and nearly fell into asleep.

The aroma of food washed over him and his stomach rumbled in return. From his position he could see coffee boiling on the stove and platters of fresh bread on the table. He thought of dashing out and snatching up what he could and returning to the pantry, but he dismissed the idea. He heard Asia's voice.

"I told you tradesmen are not to come before ten o'clock."

Her back was to Fitz. Clara's eyes signaled Asia to turn.

"Fitz," she whispered. She clutched Clara by the shoulders. "Go. Go. Take the coffee in," she ordered.

He felt her hands on his face, at first reassuring and then hesitating. "I thought you were imprisoned."

"Not anymore," Fitz managed in a ragged voice. "Don't turn me away. Please."

She hesitated but he understood. All she had seen was her husband dead on the carriage house floor and Fitz in the hands of his captors.

"I did not—" he began but her fingertips flew to his lips.

"Let us not speak of it. It's dangerous for you here."

"I hoped," he said, still shivering from the cold, "that you would not turn me away."

"Captain Dunaway, I cannot do that." She smiled in resignation. "You must wait here until the house is cleared. I'll close the pantry door and return for you when breakfast is over."

"Can I have some food, please? Coffee."

"Yes. Yes." Her eyes widened in alarm. "Are you injured?"

Bishop's coat, his blood. He shook his head, knowing it was real, but somehow it seemed as distant as a long-ago dream. She was gone but returned. A plate of bread and a cup of coffee were placed on the floor next to him. The bread was fresh baked, and it reminded him of what Bishop had said—*"I smell bread."* The pantry door closed and he was in darkness.

Chapter 30

December 2, 1861
The 259th day of the war
The Royal Boarding House

Fitz awoke with a start and sat up. He was in a large dimly lit room filled with boxes and trunks. A slice of light, through a single window at the far end of the room, traced edges of rafters and beams above him. He examined his bed. He was lying on a pallet of blankets and quilts. He remembered following Clara up the narrow stairs and the sight of a makeshift bed. And then, darkness. He heard the sound of a door opening. He slid off the pallet and crawled behind a pile of boxes, waiting.

"Fitz? Where are you?"

It was Asia. She was dressed in black—mourning for her husband. He stood, his body stiff and heavy.

"What are you doing there?" she asked, holding a lamp above her head. "You should be resting."

"Are you alone?"

"Of course I'm alone. I brought you milk and sand-wiches." She set the lamp next to the pallet. The sandwiches were wrapped in a napkin, which she opened and placed on the floor. As he approached, she held out a glass of milk. "Drink," she commanded.

He returned to the pallet and began to eat, stopping only

to gulp down the milk. He never stopped searching the shadows, waiting for someone to spring at him. To take him to prison. Asia waited patiently for him to finish.

"What happened?" she asked.

He told her all that he could, leaving some things out because he still did not understand them, and others, because they touched on her. His account was of Bishop, Whaley, and his imprisonment. He could not bring himself to talk about her husband's murder or Will's departure. He was convinced that if he did, it would shatter the fragile connection that remained between them.

"I am truly sorry about your friend Bishop," she said, her eyes glistening. "And for what has happened to you."

He collected himself and asked, "What time is it?"

"Nearly three. Are you certain about Mr. Batterman?"

"Yes," Fitz said. "Batterman. Prescott. Maybe others. Maybe the whole damn government."

She watched him eat before she said, "I cannot believe it about Prescott, although I had my suspicions. Father was convinced of his loyalty to the South. Henry—" She stopped.

Fitz felt sick. He knew that the subject had to come up. He knew that they would both be brought round to her husband's murder.

"Tell me," Asia said, preparing herself.

Fitz knew what she was asking: did you shoot him? He felt that at the same time she accepted the possibility he might have. She was as entangled in uncertainty, Fitz realized, as he.

"Your husband came to my room," he began. "He wanted to talk. I was to meet him in the carriage house. I suspected he was in league with Whaley. I don't know how. When I entered the carriage house, I heard a noise and then a gunshot. I was struck on the head. The shot came from behind. To one side of me. Asia, I did not kill him."

He watched her as he spoke, hoping she would see the truth of it. Large tears rolled down her cheeks. She wiped them away and Fitz knew she cried as much for her role in a marriage that had long ago evaporated, as for the death of the man she had once loved. When he finished, she remained silent and then nodded her acceptance of his account—the book was closed, never to be reopened.

Fitz let time pass, let her grieve, and then remembered. "Lincoln is in danger. I am certain of it."

"Oh, Fitz, it can't be."

"Before this mess, I would have said the same thing. Now, I expect anything to happen." He looked at Asia, cheered by her presence. "Thank you for the food and shelter."

"It is nothing. Clara made the sandwiches. Some farmer's cow gave the milk."

"I trust you," he said, wanting some way to tell her everything in a few words, especially how he felt about her. "I trust you with my life."

She turned the subject to a practical consideration. "What are you going to do?"

"I don't know."

"You'll have to leave the city when you're well enough. You can stay here until then."

"I can't stay here. I can't involve you in this."

"I already am," Asia bristled. "Did I say that you had to leave my house right this minute?"

"No," Fitz said. "I didn't say you did. I am leaving because I care about you."

"Blast it, Fitz, you are the most infuriating man I ever knew!"

"Are my belongings still here?"

"Your belongings? No. They were picked up by the provost guard. That is how I heard about your arrest. Why?"

"I would like my pipe."

"Fitz," Asia said. "I will buy you a new pipe. Now get some rest." She stood to leave.

"Asia," Fitz said. "President Lincoln. I don't know how to warn him. No one will believe me. But I'm sure of it. The man is in danger."

"Do you know the circumstances? When and where?"

"I don't know."

"Well," she said, "you've got to take care of yourself. The government can take care of its own. Do you want to bathe now? The house is empty."

Fitz tried to stand, feeling he had to force himself into action. She helped him up and held him. The pressure of her body against his felt wonderful. He pulled her closer, but she resisted him.

"When you are quite well enough, Captain Dunaway," she said.

After bathing and shaving Fitz returned to the attic, wearing clothes that belonged to Henry. He was tired, but he could not sleep. He sat on the pallet and lapsed into thought.

Batterman, Prescott, and Whaley were in league. It was all a grand design—throw Lamon off the scent by offering up a sacrificial lamb. Captain Thomas Fitzgerald Dunaway. Lamon is given false reports, told the Rebels were killed in an explosion, and Fitz's credibility is destroyed when he is accused of murder. The only other connection is Will Moore and he is sent West.

Fitz brushed the dust from his trouser leg, his mind wandering.

Assassinate the president. How and when?

Fitz looked at the trouser legs again and remembered the men on the omnibus this morning. Was it only this morning? Flour covered their trousers and shoes, and it was in their hair as well. Bishop smelled bread as they hid in the shack near the Capitol. There was a bakery nearby. These men were returning home from their work at a bakery.

What has that to do with anything? Fitz chastised himself. *Keep to the subject.*

Fitz heard the door open. He watched a light approach. It was Asia. She held a cup of coffee in one hand and a newspaper in the other.

"Hot coffee to warm you," she said and held up the newspaper, "and so you can keep up with the war news. How are you feeling?"

"Better," he said.

She sat down and handed him the cup. A stout aroma swirled from the cup and he closed his eyes in appreciation before tasting it gingerly.

Fitz felt she wanted to speak but was reluctant. He recalled what she had told him sometime ago: don't make me a party to your actions. It had gotten well past that; she was hiding him, and that was treason.

Asia pulled her knees under her chin and wrapped her arms around them, studying the floor. "I want you to leave the city. I want you to be safe."

"I—"

She shook her head. "Just be quiet," she said. "Nothing else matters now."

"I have—"

"I care for you, you ridiculous man," she said. "I should know better. If my father could see me now. Oh, how he would laugh!"

Fitz had nothing to offer. He had no plans and no idea in mind of any action he could take. Of course he wanted to leave the city, but he couldn't run away. What did she expect him to do? What did she want of him?

"Well, Captain Dunaway? Are you at a loss for words?"

"You always seem to have words enough for both of us," Fitz said. "If you would give me time, I probably would have come up with the appropriate response."

She asked, "Did you ever speak from the heart? Truly from the heart?"

Fitz leaned forward, pulling Asia into his arms. He kissed her deeply. Her arms encircled him. The presence of her body and the sweet scent of her flesh filled his world. The burning pressure of her lips against his inflamed him. He felt the fullness of her breasts against his chest, and he pushed against her, demanding more.

They parted long enough for Fitz to whisper, "Lay with me."

Asia brushed her fingertips over her lips and then pressed

them against Fitz's, tracing every feature until they came to rest on the tip of his tongue. Her eyes were glassy with desire.

"Yes," she said.

They rested on the rumpled quilts afterward, each lost in their own thoughts. Asia, her head nestled against his shoulder, spoke first.

"What will happen to you?"

Fitz knew what she meant. It was only a matter of time before he was found out.

"I don't know," he whispered, reaching to stroke her hair.

"I will help you get out of the city," she said, taking his hand and kissing his fingers.

"No. You can't help, and I can't leave Washington."

She turned and looked at him. "You can't stay in the city, Fitz. It's absolute madness."

"I won't stay in this house."

"I'm not talking about that. You can't stay in the city."

Fitz pulled her closer. She propped herself up on her elbow.

"Listen to me," she said, her voice soft but urgent. "I don't want to lose you."

"You won't."

"I will if you stay here. I can help you to get out of Washington. To Alexandria or Fairfax Courthouse. To Baltimore and then to Philadelphia."

"No," he said, and then explained. "It would do no good. The men who did this to me are here. They will murder Lincoln. I can do something to prevent that."

She sat up. "How will it help if you are dead?"

"I can't leave. I have my duty."

"Oh, well! What good is a man of duty without the sense God gave a goose?"

"I can't go."

"Listen to me," she said. "This city is full of treacherous men. My father's health was broken because of such men. His heart failed him and he withered away. I watched him die, Fitz. I stood by his bed when my mother could do nothing but weep, and watched the best man I knew take his last breath. This city killed him, you fool! These hate-filled, petty, inconsequential men did that to my father. I've seen what the city can do to good and decent souls, Fitz. Leave this hateful place."

"Asia," Fitz said, "I can't."

Asia reacted as if he had struck her. "I will not live through it again. Leave now. Tonight. You cannot go to the authorities—they think that you're a traitor. The president is well guarded. Let the army take care of him."

"It is not enough."

"You're the only man who can save him? Is that it?" she asked. "Why, you stupid bandbox soldier!"

He knew that she did not mean it. She was angry and frustrated. "Asia—"

"Shut up! This is the perfect time. I can rent a boat and have you taken across the river."

He shook his head and looked at her, trying to make her understand what he had to do. He had no choice.

"I see," she said, defeated.

"You forget, Asia, I am a soldier," he said. "If only a bandbox soldier. There is no other way to prove my innocence. I have been betrayed but it is very little compared to what might happen to Mr. Lincoln."

"Go, then." She stood. "Avenge your Mr. Bishop. Duty, honor, country? Is that what this is about? Your own guilt? Are you as shallow as I first thought, Captain Dunaway? What manner of man are you?"

"Asia—"

"Answer the question! Tell me, please, because I do not understand. Is this a game to you, Fitz? You want your regiment, you want to lead men into battle, you want to don the uniform of your country—it is everything that *you* want with a single-minded purpose I find staggering. I don't think you've given it the least bit of thought."

She was right, of course.

Asia stared at the floor in silence, sensing her argument

would not sway him. "Well, then, I am the one who is a fool to care for such a man as you."

Fitz rose and took her in his arms. "Please, Asia."

She pulled away, and he followed, reaching for her. She threw her hands up, warning him away, and he read betrayal in her eyes.

"Asia," he said. "I must go. Everything that you said about me is true. But you did not say that I have any other choice. If I do not act, I will regret it to the day I die."

"Regret? Why," she said, her tone filled with sarcasm, "Captain Dunaway is human after all. This is a cause for celebration. A day unlike any other."

She was afraid, and fought her fear by turning her anger on him.

It seemed the only thing that connected them was silence.

"I'll give you money and clothing," she said, defeated. "I'll have a horse saddled for you." She turned. "Good-bye, Captain Dunaway."

She was gone. Fitz slumped to the pallet and stared at the newspaper lying next to the tray. Its headlines stared back at him. There was news of the Western campaigns and something about the blockade. One story told of the speculation that the enemy was building an ironclad. Next to it was an insulting declaration about the Union by some member of the British royal family. Just below, on the left side of the front page, was an article with a headline that caught Fitz's attention: THE PRESIDENT'S REPORT TO CONGRESS. He read it twice before he recognized its importance. He snatched up the newspaper and unfolded it, exposing the article. The president's report was to be given to the assembled members of Congress tonight.

Fitz devoured the words, trying to understand. He recalled the workmen's shacks scattered around the Capitol, and the stacks of marble blocks, and the vast rigging of cables, cranes, and derricks used to haul workers and materials to the dome. A perfect place, Fitz realized, for an ambush.

And then he remembered the powder from the Navy Yard.

What was it? A thousand pounds? Did Whaley and his men manage to steal that much black powder? How would they transport it to the Capitol?

In crates, Fitz reasoned. In barrels secreted among legitimate materials. There must be several hundred workmen a day laboring over the Capitol dome, it would be no challenge to move a dozen or so extra barrels into the building.

Fitz forgot the newspaper and analyzed what he could put together of the plot to kill the president. Plant the powder below the Congress—in a basement area, or an alcove of some sort. It was a sturdy building, Fitz realized. He wondered if a thousand pounds of black powder would make an impact, and then he reminded himself that the purpose of the bomb was not to destroy the building—it was to kill a man.

Fitz could not go to the army with this, they would not believe him. He would have to get to Mr. Lincoln. *If I can reach him at the Capitol before he enters,* Fitz thought, *I can warn him. Perhaps he will listen.* He glanced at the newspaper again, disgusted at the idea. This was murder, killing a single man, and this was no way to make war. A cowardly action, Fitz decided, and he vowed Prescott, Batterman, and Whaley would pay for it.

He realized as well that he had as much a chance of being shot tonight as he had of reaching the president.

Chapter 31

December 3, 1861
The 260th day of the war
The Royal Boarding House

Fitz waited in the pantry. He could hear the others in the dining room and knew it must be nearly six o'clock. It was full dark and a heavy snow was falling. Clara approached bearing a topcoat and a soft felt hat. She handed him a knife and small pistol.

"These belonged to Mr. Lossing," she said, handing them to him. "There's gloves in the pockets. A scarf, too. It'll get cold out. There's a purse with eighty dollars in it, in the inside pocket. Here's a hat."

Fitz slipped into the coat and took the hat. "Did Mrs. Lossing say anything?"

"She didn't say nothin'," Clara said, helping him with the coat. "But I could tell she was scared. There's a horse out back, all saddled. It's Terry, Mrs. Lossing's favorite. He likes to pull at the bit so keep a tight rein on him."

"You tell Mrs. Lossing thanks for me. Tell her I'll be back." He pulled out the purse and handed it to Clara. "I won't need this."

"Captain Dunaway? Whatever you're doin', don't get yourself killed. I'm afraid that poor lady couldn't take much more."

Fitz touched the brim of his hat in good-bye, and left.

*   *   *

He found the horse, tied in the yard, and settled into the saddle. "It's you and me, Terry," he said, stroking the horse's muzzle. "If I'm found out we may have to run for it." The horse tossed its head as if it understood. Fitz tightened his coat against the falling snow and spurred the horse.

When he reached Pennsylvania Avenue, he was relieved to see a sea of humanity streaming toward the Capitol. It was a gay scene, the lights catching thick snowflakes in their glare, people's breath, frozen in the chill, hanging above the crowd like a fog. Union flags and colorful banners were held over the crowd and at least a dozen brass bands vied for attention. The throng cheered for the Union and victory, waving torches back and forth. The store windows along the avenue were ablaze with lights, giving the whole scene a sense of warmth and holiday despite the frigid cold. Ahead, on the Hill, the Capitol appeared to be on fire. Hundreds of torches and a dozen bonfires surrounded the building. People sang and cried out as a company of infantry, marching with gleaming bayonets and measured steps, parted the crowd on their way to the Capitol.

Fitz kept his head down and the horse at a walk. He did not want to attract attention. As he rode he thought what he had to do, and every step closer to the Capitol revealed the thinness of his plan. Get inside the Capitol—and do what? Maybe nothing, he decided. Maybe shout an alarm. Maybe nothing will happen tonight. But he knew that was a false hope.

Terry tried to back away from the noise and swirling mass of people.

"You've got more sense than me," Fitz whispered. "I ought to let you decide what to do."

The crowd surged forward, waving flags, shouting for Uncle Abe, calling for death to Jeff Davis and the Confederacy. Sparks from the fires mixed with the snowflakes. The dirty brown trail of oil lanterns suspended on poles drifted above the scene, forming a thin smudge over the crowd.

Fitz wondered if any of these people really knew what war was like. No, he told himself, these are flag-waving warriors and fast-talking soldiers who have not yet seen the carnage of battle.

Two blocks from the Capitol, he broke from the crowd and turned left, trotting up 3rd Street. As he rode on, the turmoil of celebration faded. He turned right on C Street, passing the railway station. It was quiet, with only a single puffing engine alongside the building. Everyone was going to hear the address, he thought.

Fitz was on Delaware Avenue, with the Capitol in front of him, just two blocks away. He dismounted and led Terry to a clump of bushes near a large, dark house. He patted the knife in his waistband and withdrew the pistol from his pocket. Hefting it in his hand, he decided it would be better to conceal the weapon until he needed it, if he needed it. He tied Terry's reins to a dilapidated iron fence and patted his neck.

"Don't go anywhere," Fitz said. "I may need you."

He walked forward, watching the crowd milling around the Capitol, shadowy forms silhouetted in the harsh glare of a thousand fires. He could make out soldiers, their muskets and swords at the ready, and a long line of carriages that seemed to stretch around the building. It looked like there was a guard posted every twenty feet. It would be no easy task slipping by them.

Fitz stopped, chewing on his mustache in thought. He felt the cold and slid his hands under his armpits to warm them. He was shivering. This was a different kind of battle, an enemy who could not be seen, and a field of unknown circumstances.

And then he had a plan.

He headed for the carriages. He came up from behind, taking care to keep them between himself and the line of soldiers guarding the Capitol.

He would use the vehicles as a shield and try to work his way around the building until he could find an opening of some sort. When he reached the sentries he would be asked to show a pass—there was no way around that. *I'll have to find a way,* he thought. And then what?

Well, at least I have a plan.

He was unhurried, using the shadows thrown by the blazing fires as his refuge. He sought the darkness, sliding in and out of it.

The sound of a brass band shattered the quiet, and cheers swarmed out of the night. Fitz walked on, glancing about as if his interest in the scene was not life and death, and all the time questions kept jabbing at him: What was to happen tonight? How could anyone get at the president?

Fitz thought of Asia; what if she was right? Maybe he should have fled the city. If he was recaptured, Bishop would not be there to help him. He thought of the little man.

He stopped in surprise. He smelled the warm aroma of baking bread. That's it—now he remembered. The old Senate chamber in the basement of the Capitol had been converted into a huge bakery to furnish bread for the troops. The men on the omnibus had been bakers. Surely the flour was delivered in huge barrels. Barrels large enough to conceal a thousand pounds of black powder.

"Don't move."

Fitz froze.

"Put your hands above your head and turn around."

He did as he was told.

Batterman was before him, holding a revolver. Next to him stood a fat soldier, pointing his musket at Fitz.

"Captain Dunaway," Batterman said. "Where have you been?" The secretary threw open Fitz's coat and removed the pistol and knife. He slipped them into his pocket.

Two horses reined to an empty carriage stood nearby. "Go find a driver for this carriage," Batterman ordered the fat soldier. After the soldier departed, Batterman motioned Fitz against the carriage door. "Don't be foolish, Captain. I know little enough about firearms, but I know how to pull a trigger."

"You're a traitor," Fitz said.

Batterman said, "That description depends on whose side you fight for."

"You killed Lossing."

Batterman shook his head. "No. That was Whaley."

"Why? I thought he was one of yours?"

"He was to a point. It worked out well, don't you think? You being charged with his murder? As for the rest of your troubles, I will take some credit but there's more than enough to go around."

"You or Prescott?" Fitz asked. "I was the stalking goat from the very beginning, wasn't I?"

"If you have any complaints," Batterman said, with a smile, "take them up with him when you next see him."

"What are you going to do?"

"Return you to Old Capitol Prison, of course. You have a date with the hangman."

"You know what I mean. You're going to kill the president, aren't you?"

"Oh? I underestimated you, Captain. I thought you nothing more than a hothead."

"Well?"

Batterman peered over Fitz's shoulder. More cheering broke out and fireworks sputtered into the darkness. Star shells exploded overhead, showering the Capitol building with a cascade of falling stars.

"Why are you so inquisitive now, Captain Dunaway? It would have been better for you if you had questioned Mr. Prescott's offer before you became a part of it."

"Answer my question."

"Don't give me orders, Captain. You're in no position to do so. An insolent attitude is what got you into this in the first place. We had to find a way around Mr. Lamon. Colonel Moore came to Mr. Prescott about you. Coincidence is always suspect until it's seasoned with happenstance. We were fortunate. You were not."

"I ought to kill you," Fitz said.

"I am not the enemy, Captain Dunaway. Lincoln and the Black Republicans wage an illegal war on the South. I am a Virginian, sir. I am defending my homeland. Tyranny often assumes the guise of patriotism, Captain. Mr. Lincoln and his Black Republican friends have disregarded the Constitution and the will of the people. Your Illinois ape has sullied the sacred document that gave purpose to this nation. This nation was created of revolution and is based upon the precept that when in the course of human events it becomes necessary for a people to throw off the shackles of tyranny—" Batterman stopped, and took a different approach. "Not every man in the North supports this war. There are thousands of others who feel the same way as I."

"He doesn't understand," a voice said from behind them.

Prescott, consumed by a huge topcoat, muffler, and hat, joined them.

"Captain Dunaway doesn't understand—do you, Fitz?"

"Prescott, you—"

"Yes," Prescott said. "Here is the simple truth of it: Laws bind up this nation. The strength of those laws, like barrel hoops around staves, keep it intact. Disregard those laws, supplant those laws with convoluted logic or villainous intentions, as Lincoln and his cohorts have done, and the whole thing collapses into itself. I am interested in saving the Constitution. The fate of the nation is determined within the framework of our most important document."

"Mr. Lincoln is trying to save the Union."

"A matter of perspective, my dear boy. It pains me that you've come to this end, but such is war. Your presence on the scene worked out splendidly."

"It won't end the war if you blow up the Capitol—"

"Blow up the Capitol?" Prescott asked, perplexed. "Why would we do such a thing?"

"The president's speech tonight. He's speaking to the Congress tonight and you plan to kill him by blowing up the building."

Prescott burst out in laughter. "Captain Dunaway, if there

ever was a political innocent in this great country, it is you. Why would I wish to damage such a lovely building? And, I might add, a stout one at that? You mean the president's annual address to Congress." He shook his head, chuckling. "Delivered by a clerk, Fitz. The president never sets foot in the Capitol."

"But—"

"We're making a dead tyrant, Captain Dunaway, not a martyr." He pulled his pocket watch from his vest pocket, snapped open the case, and held it up to catch the light. "They should be meeting in Mr. Lincoln's office within the hour."

"I wish I had a revolver," Fitz said.

"But you don't, Captain Dunaway." Prescott turned to Batterman. "Do what you will with him," he said, and walked off.

The fat soldier returned, dragging an old black man in livery by the arm.

"Mister," the black man said, "I keep telling you this is Mr. Hamlin's coach. I drive for him."

"Shut up, you damn darkie," the soldier said. "I got my orders."

Batterman fished a piece of paper from his pocket and showed it to the soldier and the driver.

"My name is Batterman, private secretary to Assistant Secretary of War Prescott." He nodded at Fitz. "This man is wanted for murder and treason."

The fat soldier stood a little straighter, gripping the musket in his white-gloved hands. Fitz thought of Asia's bandbox soldier.

"We are going to return him to Old Capitol Prison," Batterman continued.

"Mister," the driver said. "I drive for Vice President Hannibal Hamlin, and he'll cuss me like a Methodist if I run off and leave him."

"Get up there, you old fool," the soldier said. He opened the carriage door for Batterman.

"After you, Captain," Batterman said, waving him ahead with his pistol. "Ride with the driver," he ordered the soldier.

"Yes, sir," the soldier mumbled, then handed his musket to the driver and climbed into the seat.

Fitz sat in one corner of the carriage as Batterman entered and closed the door. "All right," he shouted. The carriage wheeled out of line and swayed into motion.

"How will you do it?" Fitz asked as the vehicle picked up speed.

Batterman placed a finger to his lips. "Mustn't give away too much," he said.

Fitz's eyes dropped to the pistol in Batterman's hand. The muzzle, pointing at Fitz's chest, never wavered. Even if the secretary were blind, he could not miss his target at this range.

There has got to be a way, Fitz told himself.

"Whatever you're thinking, Captain," Batterman said, "don't delude yourself. I would be just as happy to have you die at my hand as to hang, although your ability to survive impresses me. We certainly expected to leave your body at the Navy Yard, but Whaley lost you in the confusion. Now, however"—Batterman waved the pistol at Fitz—"it would be foolish to attempt anything."

"I'm not a fool," Fitz said.

"Some men confuse foolhardiness with bravery. It's a common malady with soldiers, I am told."

Fitz knew he had little time. The sounds of bands and cheering were falling behind. Soon it would be too late to do anything. And he would be behind bars once more.

Batterman glanced out the window. "It's all done now, Captain Dunaway. There is nothing you can do about it. We're almost at the prison. There is no one left for you to whip with a pistol now."

Do something! Fitz told himself. What? If he could just get the pistol—perhaps distract Batterman long enough. He noticed the hammer. It was on half cock. The pistol couldn't be fired.

"Mr. Batterman," Fitz said. "I haven't acquitted myself

very well during this adventure but then again I wasn't on a field of my choosing." His anger built, and he was glad that Batterman didn't notice. "But there is one thing I feel it best that you know about me."

Batterman lifted an eyebrow, interested. "What?" he asked.

Fitz grinned. "I'm a bearcat for a fight."

He lunged across the narrow space. Batterman started in surprise and pulled the trigger. Nothing happened. Fitz slapped the weapon aside with his left hand and brought his right fist into the secretary's nose. Batterman cried out as he tried to fight back, but Fitz used his body to block the other man's arms. He drove his fist into Batterman's face, again and again.

The carriage stopped with a lurch, and Fitz heard the soldier shout something. Fitz fell on his back to the carriage floor. Drawing his knees to his chin, he waited until the door started to open. Then he kicked with all of his might, driving the door into the fat soldier's face. He heard the man shout in pain. Fitz rolled out of the carriage and saw the soldier on the ground clutching his nose. He kicked the musket away and motioned for the driver to get down.

"Don't shoot, mister. I ain't done nothin' to you," the driver said.

"Get this piece of trash out of the carriage," Fitz ordered the driver. "Get up and help him," he told the soldier. "You're not dead."

The two men pulled Batterman from the carriage and laid him on the snow-covered street. Fitz picked up the musket and threw it into the carriage and slammed the door shut. He fished Batterman's pass from his coat and then he turned to the two men. The driver stood with his hands held high above his head. The soldier cupped his nose, blood streaming through his fingers.

"Put your hands down," Fitz ordered the driver. "How far are we from the prison?"

"About a block."

"Get over there and tell whoever is in charge that there's a bomb planted in the president's house. This man is part of the plot." Fitz climbed into the driver's seat. "Get to it!" he ordered the two men and then snapped the reins. The horses bolted forward.

"Look at me! Look what he did," the fat soldier said to the driver. "He busted my nose and got blood all over my brand-new uniform."

The driver fixed him with a disgusted look. "Mister, your mammy and pappy must be sorely disappointed in you." Then he headed off in the direction of the prison, the cloud of falling snow enshrouding him.

Chapter 32

The carriage sped along the snow-covered streets as Fitz whipped the horses to a gallop. He had learned enough about Washington to know if he wanted to arrive at the War Department in time he'd have to stay off Pennsylvania Avenue. At 14th Street he pulled hard on the reins, sending the top-heavy carriage careening on two wheels onto E Street. He heard a cry of alarm as he flashed by group of civilians on their way to the Capitol and then realized that the carriage was not righting itself. He threw his body to one side, hoping his weight would bring the vehicle back on four wheels. He felt the wheels hit the brick pavement with a jarring thud.

The carriage raced past the Treasury Department on 15th Street and he then found himself on the grounds of the President's Park. He glanced to his right. The Executive Mansion, picture-perfect in a setting of glistening white snow, its windows filled with glowing candles, sat unsuspecting against the night. Against a night that belonged to evil men.

Fitz suddenly knew what it was—he knew the plan. It had come at Batterman's smirk: the bomb-proof. He had thought it odd a simple bomb-proof would take so long to build, but he had dismissed it as the way things were done in Washington. Now he realized that Whaley and his men were tunneling under the Executive Mansion; they were going to mine the northwest corner of the building. Lincoln had his office on the second floor and a massive explosion would drop the building in on the president and his cabinet. "We're making a dead president," Prescott had said—kill Lincoln and the South gains yet another advantage. They had won Bull Run and sent the Union army packing. Now all they needed to do was murder Lincoln.

The carriage rumbled across the uneven ground and over frozen bridle paths hidden under the snow. Each jolt tossed Fitz into the air and nearly threw him out of the seat. Sliding onto 17th Street, Fitz tightened his grip on the reins and pulled hard to the right. The rear end of the vehicle spun to the left but straightened as Fitz urged the horses on. On his right ahead was the Navy Department Building and across 17th Street was the Winder Building. And facing that, the War Department.

He wound the reins around his wrists for a better grip and jammed his heels into the dashboard, willing the horses to a dead stop. A wide-eyed sentry at the War Department entrance watched him jump from the carriage boot into the deep snow.

"Come with me," Fitz shouted, racing into the Telegraph Office. There were four young men on duty. It had been a slow night, the armies never moved in winter, and the telegraphers were lounging around their desks, talking, when Fitz burst in. "My name is Captain Fitz Dunaway. There's to be an attempt on the president's life." The sentry rushed in behind him, not sure what to do.

One of the men shot to his feet, stunned. "What?"

"Who knows him best?" Fitz asked.

Another man, catching the urgency of the situation, rose and pointed at a flaxen-haired soldier sitting next to him. "Andrew. He and Mr. Lincoln talk poetry all the time."

Fitz jerked the surprised man out of his chair. "Andrew, get over to the Executive Mansion and inform Mr. Lincoln there's a bomb planted beneath his feet. Get everyone out. Drag him out by the scruff of his neck if you have to, but get him out."

To Fitz's relief, Andrew said, "Yes, sir," and disappeared out the door into the snow. Fitz turned to another man. "Where is the bomb-proof?"

"Downstairs," the man said, pointing out the door into the hallway.

Fitz pulled out Batterman's revolver to make sure that the caps were in place. "Do you have firearms?"

"No," one man began when another chimed in. "Yes. Yes. There's a locker out in the hall."

"You, you, and you," Fitz said, indicating two operators and the sentry, "come with me. Can you get the Capitol on that thing?"

The operator who remained seated glanced at the telegraph key on his desk. "Yes," he said.

"Good," Fitz said. "Send to whoever is in charge. Arrest Assistant Secretary of War Prescott and his private secretary, Batterman."

The man was about to key the message but stopped in midmotion. "On whose authority?" he asked.

"Lincoln's," Fitz said, then motioned to the three men to follow him.

They ran into the hallway and one of the men pointed to a wooden cabinet with a stout lock securing the door. Fitz turned to the sentry, jerked the musket out of his hands, and drove the butt through the door with a crash. He threw the weapon back to the soldier and ordered, "Help yourselves."

The men grabbed a pistol each and one of them tossed a sword to Fitz.

"Listen to me," Fitz said. "There are probably fuses leading from the basement to half a ton of black powder at the president's house. We've got to go in, disperse the powder trail, and round up the traitors. This is no time to be delicate. If anyone makes a false move, shoot him." He glimpsed a battered door at the end of the hallway. "There?" The men nodded. They had one chance only. If Whaley's bunch caught on they could fire the powder trail, and no one would be fast enough to catch it. "Be quick. Don't give them a chance."

No one answered but Fitz was certain that they understood. Fitz opened the door and eased down the stairs. He heard noises far ahead, and saw a lamp's glow in the darkness. A laugh was cut short by a harsh command. Fitz was relieved to find that someone was still there—that meant that the fuse hadn't been lit yet. But it would take no time to strike a match or lower a torch to the powder trail. It could be over in a puff of white smoke, and if Andrew hadn't convinced the president, so could Mr. Lincoln's life.

Fitz's eyes grew accustomed to the darkness as he felt solid earth below his feet. Thick support columns, along with crates, barrels, and countless other clutter, filled the basement.

It was perfect. Bomb-proofs were being built all over the city. Having one built at the War Department made perfect sense. Workmen could be hired, told to dig, and that was that. Anyone who became suspicious could be dealt with. Fitz thought of the two workmen pulled out of the canal. It would take engineers to site the tunnel and maintain its depth, or even experienced coalminers. Getting the powder in would be no problem. It was, after all, the War Department. It was probably how Whaley had gotten the explosives out of the Navy Yard, by order of Assistant Secretary of War Prescott. And everything so perfectly tied up—in a lovely noose around Fitz's neck.

Fitz held out his hand to stop the others. He saw shadows gliding along the walls in a gallery just off the main room. The voices were louder now, and he feared they were out of time. He glanced at his men.

"I'll go first," he whispered. "Don't shoot. There's powder in there and we'll go up with it. Don't let anyone strike a match."

"What should we do with them?" the soldier asked, his young voice breaking.

"Use your rifle butt," Fitz said. "Knock out a mouthful of teeth. That always gets a man's attention." He looked at the men. They were ready.

Fitz burst into the room. Pockmark was against a wall twisting a fuse together. Sanderson and Dutton had just finished laying a trail to a junction. At that point the junction split into three black trails. The men stopped, frozen in the cold light of an oil lamp.

Dutton reacted first with a shout of surprise. He lit a match and dropped it on the powder. It exploded with a soft cough, filling the room with smoke. Fitz saw the fire racing along the powder trail, but before he could get to it, Sanderson drew a knife and swung it at him.

Fitz jumped back, and the gallery turned into a melee of swinging fists and muskets. Sanderson stood between Fitz and the advancing flame, swinging the knife at his stomach. Fitz dodged the blade, trying to avoid the others as they fought in the crowded arena. Powder barrels were scattered about, and the dirt floor was covered in black granules. A single spark from a discharged pistol would send them all to Heaven.

He got close enough to Sanderson to land a blow from his pistol, but it glanced off the man's shoulder. Stunned, Sanderson backed up but still held the knife in his hand, daring Fitz to come on.

There was a soft cough as the flame reached the junction of three trails. It was just feet from the tunnel mouth.

"You're too late," Sanderson said, and charged.

Fitz stepped back and stumbled over a half-empty barrel. He then kicked at it, sending it into Sanderson's path. As the man tried to dodge the rolling barrel, Fitz stepped up and cracked him across the bridge of the nose with his pistol. Blood exploded across the man's face, spraying Fitz. As Sanderson grunted and raised his hands to his face, Fitz rushed.

He bowled Sanderson to one side and threw himself on the fire, grabbing at the trails with both hands. He heard shouts behind him, and then the hard thud of a rifle butt being driven into someone's body. Rubbing out the middle trail he rolled over to see Sanderson's knife sweeping toward him. He brought his leg up, striking the other man in the groin.

"Get him, someone!" he shouted, diving for another trail. The burning powder threw out a thick cloud of pungent smoke as the fire raced toward the tunnel opening. Sparks spat outward as Fitz scrabbled on his hands and knees, trying to overtake the flames. He dove and landed on the powder, scooping loose dirt over the trail until the flames disappeared.

One more. One more. He watched in horror as the last flame disappeared into the tunnel. He raced after it, half-crawling and half-scampering in the low tunnel. It was just ahead, a shimmering white fire, bouncing through the darkness. The stinging smoke filled his eyes and the stench burned his nostrils. He heard shouts behind him but didn't know if his men had the day. All he knew was if he did not succeed in catching the dancing flames, the president would be killed.

He threw himself forward and threw dirt on the flame. He whipped his hand back and forth, mixing dirt and powder together into an impotent mess. The burning powder sputtered, threw an arching spark at the ceiling of the tunnel, and Fitz was surrounded by darkness. The flame died with a final hiss.

He crawled out of the tunnel, dispersing the other trails. When he got to his feet he saw Dutton, Sanderson, and Pockmark lined up against the wall, held captive by his tiny army. Dutton was bent over, blood streaming from his head.

"Where is Whaley?" Fitz asked.

Pockmark said, "Dead."

Fitz snatched Sanderson's knife from the soldier, and drove it into Pockmark's thigh. The man screamed and collapsed. Blood welled between his fingertips as he writhed in pain.

Fitz stepped up to Sanderson. "Where is Whaley?"

"Gone," Sanderson answered. "Just minutes before you arrived."

"Where?"

"He didn't say," Sanderson said. "I swear to God he didn't say where. He just said he had to make his report."

Pockmark's wailing was reduced to a low moan as he

rocked back and forth on the floor. To make his report, Fitz knew exactly where Whaley was headed. He turned to the sentry. "What's your name?"

"Billy Rockwell," the soldier said.

Fitz stifled a smile. It was obvious that the man had gotten his first taste of action, and he liked it. "Billy, you and I are going after a bunch of polecats." He questioned the two telegraph operators. "Can you two handle things here?"

"Yes, sir," one of them said.

"What now, sir?" Rockwell asked, running after Fitz out of the gallery and up the stairs.

"Now, Billy," Fitz said, leading his army of one to the carriage, "we go to Congress."

Chapter 33

The carriage horses were winded and Fitz was certain another six inches of snow had fallen, making passage to the Capitol treacherous. Most of the crowd had either made their way to warmer quarters or surrounded the bonfires blazing on the Capitol grounds.

Fitz abandoned the carriage on West Street and with Rockwell beside him sprinted toward Capitol Hill. He no idea of what he was going to do, but he had a purpose: to confront Prescott, or, failing that, capture Whaley. How didn't enter in to it.

"What are we going to do, sir?" Rockwell asked. His breath burst from his lips in quick, pale clouds.

"First we have to get in," Fitz said.

"How?"

"We brass our way in," Fitz said. "Just pretend everybody but you is a damn fool."

"Maybe we ought to wait for orders," Rockwell offered.

They neared a sentry post. "I've done too much waiting, and I'm through taking orders."

A corporal of the guard snapped to attention and moved his musket to port arms. "Halt," he ordered, blocking Fitz's way.

"What's your name?" Fitz demanded.

The corporal surprised, stammered, "Cuyler, sir."

Fitz pulled Batterman's pass from his pocket and thrust it at the soldier. "I'm with the War Department and this pass permits me access."

Cuyler took the document and held it so a nearby bonfire illuminated the paper.

"I'm on urgent business, corporal. There's no time to waste. It's to do with traitors."

Cuyler looked up, alarmed.

"How many men have you at this post?"

"Three," he said, and then added, "sir."

Fitz snatched the pass from Cuyler, folded it, and slid it in his pocket. "Leave a man here and the rest of you accompany me."

"Sir, we have orders not to quit our post for any reason," Cuyler said.

"Fine," Fitz said, motioning to Rockwell. "Billy, get Cuyler's three men and follow me."

Cuyler brought his musket up to bar the way. "Sir, I can't permit you to pass."

"Corporal," Fitz snapped. "You saw my pass and you know who I am. I am here by order of the president and we are going to proceed. Rockwell"—he threw over his shoulder—"move!"

"Yes, sir," Rockwell said and pushed past Cuyler. "Stand aside."

The young soldier rounded up the guard and double-timed it up the snow-covered drive toward the Capitol. He had taken Fitz's lesson to heart.

As they ran up the hill Fitz knew he was right. Whaley would have gone to report to Prescott. After which he most likely would make his way south. If he did, Fitz knew, he would be lost forever.

Prescott would be a different matter. He was immune, he and Batterman both. No one would believe the assistant secretary of war and his private secretary were involved in a plot to kill the president. It was madness to make the accusation and Fitz was certain that without proof, no one would believe him. Even with proof, Fitz decided, his chances weren't good.

He had no choice. The president was safe, there was a victory. But the architect of his assassination could go on as if nothing had happened. The man who conspired to kill the president could remain at his post in the War Department. That, Fitz knew, would not happen.

"In for a fight," he vowed as he ran, "in for a funeral."

"Sir?" Rockwell, beside him, asked.

"Listen to me, Billy," Fitz said. "We're going to place the assistant secretary of war under arrest. You saw the bomb-proof and the powder trail, so you know about the plan to kill the president. He is the man responsible. Once you have him, do not let him go. Have someone fetch Ward Hill Lamon, but do not turn Prescott loose."

"Where will you be, sir?"

"I'm going to bring a scoundrel to ground."

They trotted around a cluster of workmen's shacks, through a patch of carriages, and up the marble steps.

"Are your weapons charged?" Fitz called as they ran up the steps.

The soldiers behind him replied that they were.

They reached the top of the stairs. Ahead of them was a set of huge wooden doors guarded by at least a squad. An officer detached himself from the group and came toward them. *Brass it out,* Fitz ordered himself. He hated to have come this far just to be stopped. He made straight to the officer and did not give the man a chance to speak.

"Stand aside," Fitz ordered. "Urgent War Department business." He had to hurry. He knew there was a chance Whaley was already gone.

"What?" the officer, a young captain, asked.

"Inside, Billy," Fitz ordered Rockwell. He turned to the captain. "No one's to leave this building. Pass it to the other posts. By order of the president, no one is to leave this building." He knew there was little hope of the order being obeyed, every senator and congressman would be certain the order applied to everyone but them.

Fitz was already past the captain when the officer reached out to stop him. "Sir—"

Fitz flew at him, his eyes flashing. "You tell the president why his orders were disobeyed. Then you tell General Scott how you failed to do your duty despite being so ordered."

The captain stepped back, shocked at the outburst. He gestured for Fitz to pass.

Fitz caught up with Rockwell in the Rotunda. It was dim inside, despite a dozen lamps hung around the perimeter, and very cold in the building. Every step seemed multiplied a hundred times as it echoed across the marble floor.

He heard voices, low and distant, and from the cadence he could tell someone was giving a speech. It was to Fitz's right. He made out two thin streams of light edged along a pair of heavy velvet drapes. The session must be in there, Fitz decided. Prescott must be in there.

Fitz noticed a huge dark shape on his left and realized it was the frame for the dome. Within its interior was a vast field of canvas walls—probably the only way to reduce the bitter winter wind that rushed in through what remained of the structure.

"Ready," Fitz whispered to Rockwell. "You're to hold Prescott by order of the president. Send for Mr. Lamon. I'm going to find another member of the conspiracy."

"How do we find them, sir?" Rockwell asked.

Fitz pointed to the wall of canvas suspended from the center of the Rotunda. Rockwell nodded his understanding, and waved the others to follow.

It was a speech—someone was reading Lincoln's address. Prescott had to be there, Fitz reasoned. He had to be visible to the others so no one suspected his implication with the assassination. If he was there, Whaley would have to find him to report. Two scoundrels at one throw.

His fingers touched a rough surface that floated away. More canvas, he realized. Canvas curtains hung to keep the night air from the audience gathered to hear the address, to protect the interior from the elements. It was a labyrinth of canvas sheets. A perfect place to hide, a wonderful place for an ambush.

He saw the light ahead blossom into a pillar, and he knew that someone was entering the Rotunda. Two men, he thought, their forms barely visible in the low glow of the lamps. He stopped, throwing his hand up for the others to halt. He was too close to be exposed now. He focused on the two, a large man and a smaller man, engaged in conversation. Their voices were nearly lost in the darkness. Fitz cursed them for taking this time in that spot to talk politics. The longer he was delayed, the greater the chance Whaley would flee.

An errant breeze, heavy with the frigid night air, brushed the curtain behind the two, spilling a patch of light into the darkness. It washed over one man's face and Fitz froze. Prescott. The other had to be Whaley.

He advanced, his heart pounding like a kettledrum, willing the two not to look, not to see retribution descending on them. It was Whaley, with his criminal sense and his nerves attuned to danger, who turned. That caught Prescott's notice and he stepped back, trying to make out what had captured Whaley's attention.

"Who is it?" Prescott called. His manner was authoritative and confident.

Whaley chose a different strategy—he inched away from Prescott, sliding deeper into the darkness. If he didn't act now, Fitz knew, Whaley would escape.

"Seize that man," Fitz ordered, pointing at Prescott. The words were hardly out of his mouth when he saw Whaley bolt into the darkness. He heard Rockwell and the others rush by him and Prescott's strangled cry. Fitz ignored everything but Whaley's dim shape blending into the surroundings.

Fitz ran across the Rotunda floor, and collided with another set of heavy canvas curtains. He batted at them, fighting the rough walls. He pushed his hand through, forcing the fabric aside. He found an opening. He entered. Snowflakes tumbled out of the night sky through the open dome. He edged along the curtain, his eyes sweeping the interior, watching for any sign of movement.

Where was Whaley?

Fitz heard a noise above him. He saw a dark shape suspended on the wooden crane that towered over him. It was Whaley.

"Blast, man," Fitz said. "Couldn't you have stayed on the ground?" He slipped the revolver into his waistcoat, gripped the crossbeam, and pulled himself up.

Ice coated the beams, and the blowing snow peppered Fitz's eyes, making it difficult to see. He grasped each timber, planting his feet, not daring to climb until he was sure of his footing. He climbed, one cross-member at a time, slowly, his breath coming rapidly. He gazed into the night sky. Whaley was nearly lost in the snow and darkness.

Fitz cleared the protection of the partially completed dome, and the wind tore at him with a vengeance. Ice crystals stung his hands and face. A gust of wind nudged him, and he gasped in terror, wrapping both arms around an upright. He was shaking with fright. Somewhere near him, a star shell went off with a crash, showering him with sparks. He ducked to keep the burning particles out of his eyes. Support cables holding the massive crane erect hummed in the darkness, the wind plucking them like a demonic harp.

Forcing himself to reach for the next timber, he looked up. Whaley aimed a pistol at him.

Fitz cried out and swung to one side. He heard a crack, and then the sound of the bullet as it whizzed passed him. His feet slipped out from under him, and he fell. His hand shot out, and he grabbed one of the cables. He hung there, swinging until he could kick his way back to the frame. He looked up, but Whaley was already on the move. Fitz did not draw his pistol—he could not bring himself to release one hand.

He climbed faster, ignoring the frigid wind that battered him, threatening to tear him off the crane, and the cascade of fireworks came at him from every direction. When he felt safe he glanced up. Whaley was gone; he'd reached the top.

Fitz remembered the heavy rope that hung from the end of the boom arm, tied off to blocks of marble at the foot of the Capitol. That was where Whaley was headed. He was going to climb down the cable and make his escape in the darkness.

Fitz's fingers were numb and his arms ached. He locked his heels into each foothold, for fear he would slip. *Don't look down,* he ordered himself.

The crane swayed, and his heart jumped to his throat. *No, no, it's not moving.* But there it was again, a fluid motion, like a sapling yielding to a gentle breeze.

His hand found the edge of the crane's boom arm. He was on top. Pulling himself up he looked over the edge. He could see Whaley ahead of him, racing for one of the cables that secured the end of the long boom to the earth. His eyes never left Whaley as he scrambled himself up and onto the narrow boom. He stood up, planting his feet as far apart as he dared, hoping to find a way to steady himself on this devilish beast. The crane wavered, the vibration running through his legs and into the pit of his stomach. A sharp wind pushed at the boom and it trembled. He swallowed and felt sick. He forced himself to walk, his legs liquid, and the boom quivered with each step. He pulled the pistol from his pocket as he crept forward and thumbed the hammer back. He was almost to Whaley. He brought the pistol up.

Whaley jerked a heavy bolt free from the cable lock, spun, and threw it. Fitz ducked to one side to dodge the bolt and lost his balance. His leg slipped between two cross-timbers and he fell, landing on the boom. The blow knocked the pistol from his grip. He fumbled for it as it danced on his fingertips, but it jumped from his hand and disappeared in the darkness.

He looked up to see Whaley draw his pistol. Fitz took hold of the boom arm and threw his weight to one side. The massive structure swayed. Whaley staggered and fell back.

Fitz edged forward, his eyes never leaving Whaley's pistol. Whaley fought to regain his foothold when Fitz threw himself against the framework again. The arm sliced through the air, breaking free of the rope tie-down Whaley had loosened by withdrawing the bolt. It swung back over the Capitol dome and ground to a stop, the thick wooden timbers screeching in protest. Fitz jumped to his feet and ran forward as Whaley regained his footing. Fitz drove his shoulder into the man's chest. Whaley staggered back and fell to his knees, the pistol falling from his hand. Fitz fought to steady himself in the wind.

Whaley got to his feet and charged Fitz. He threw his arms around Fitz's waist and tried to lift him into the air. Fitz brought his fists down on the back of Whaley's neck, beating him until he broke the man's grip. Stepping back, he pulled Whaley up by the hair.

"This is for Lincoln," he said, driving his fist into the man's face. He felt the satisfaction of bones breaking. Whaley staggered back but kept his footing.

"And this is for me," Fitz said, landing a fist against Whaley's nose. The big man fell on his back, shaking the arm, but rolled to his feet. He wiped the blood from his face, and his eyes narrowed with hate.

A gust of wind tipped the boom to the right, jarring every timber of its frame. Fitz felt his feet snatched out from under him, and he landed on the wooden beams, his breath knocked out of him by a huge fist. Whaley rushed, and Fitz rolled to one side. The wrong way, he realized, as he fell into space. His right arm shot out, and he crooked it around a brace. Gasping in fright, he flung his left hand outward, struggling to find a handhold. The wild motion of the boom swinging back and forth filled him with sickness. Without thinking, he looked down.

Far below him was the yawning black mouth of the unfinished dome and, on either side, the vast snow-covered roof of the Capitol wings. Miniature bonfires tended by a thousand tiny figures surrounded both.

Fitz jerked his head away from the scene, saw the vague outline of a cross-member in the darkness, and reached for it. His fingers were inches from it when Whaley's boot appeared above him. *He's headed back to the crane,* Fitz thought; *he's going to climb back down.*

Fitz grabbed the cross-member, the sharp edges of the wood biting into his hand, closed his eyes, and muttered an oath. Swinging his body back and forth, he felt the boom slip to one side, the timbers creaking. The boom flew through the air. Slowed by the remaining securing cables, the boom jerked to a stop with a loud bang.

Fitz heard Whaley curse—and fall. Fitz climbed onto the boom and struggled to his feet. His legs shook beneath him.

Whaley staggered upright.

"I'm going to kill you, soldier-boy," Whaley said, doubling his huge fists.

"No," Fitz said, in a voice weak with exhaustion. "You won't."

Whaley rushed at Fitz. Fitz waited until he was almost on him, and then he dropped to the boom, gripping the timbers as tightly as he could. Whaley had no time to stop. He stumbled over Fitz, and with a scream, fell headlong into space. The scream followed him into the snowy darkness.

Fitz lay still for several minutes, his head throbbing. It took all his effort before he could pry his fingers free of the timbers. He tasted copper and spat to clear blood from his mouth. He felt ill and squeezed his eyes shut, fighting to calm himself. He rolled over on his back and opened his eyes, breathing deeply. Snowflakes fell at a furious pace, and above him fireworks burst in the night sky, their bright light painting the low-lying clouds with red, yellow, blue, and orange.

He knew it was not over. He would have to explain all that

had happened to the army and the government, and he could not stand the idea of facing any more bureaucrats. He knew also that he would see Asia again. He smiled.

He remembered the climb back along the boom and down the crane. The smile disappeared.

Chapter 34

June 24, 1862
The 436th day of the war
Near Murfreesboro, Tennessee

Colonel Thomas Fitzgerald Dunaway crooked his leg around the saddle horn and watched the 104th Ohio Volunteer Infantry Regiment, his regiment, march southward; a long, slow, deliberate snake winding its way along the dusty road. Their uniforms were faded and tattered, their Enfield Rifled Muskets scarred with use. All of the things newly minted volunteers felt they needed to survive as soldiers had long since been discarded along the Tennessee countryside. There were so few of them left now, 238 out of 946 men— and this after only several months. They were lean veterans of ill-fated campaigns, and ill-planned battles, and perhaps it was true, as another officer had commented to Fitz, the 104th were like English Bulldogs—you can beat them time after time and yet they still come back at you. Perhaps.

They had the soldier's look about them, hard, defiant, skeptical, wary—disdainful of unproven officers and men and reluctant to the point of insubordinate. By God, he knew, they could fight.

Fitz rubbed his left forearm, trying to draw away the pain from the deep furrow plowed by a Minié ball at Cumberland Junction. It was still an open wound, draining into the filthy bandage he had wrapped around the arm. Now it was a nuisance, hurting more than it had when he felt his arm go numb on the battlefield.

He patted his horse's thick neck, sliding his fingers through the coarse hair of the black mane, and pulled a letter from his tunic. He flipped it open with his right hand, pulling apart the pages with his teeth, and laid it across his knee. He read for the hundredth time:

> *Dearest Fitz,*
> *I hope that this letter finds you well and in good spirits. I have read the newspapers constantly, seeking mention of you and your regiment. Looking every day for some little intelligence . . .*

Fitz looked up, his eyes traveling along the column. Look for us at Corinth, he thought, or Clarkesville, or on those murderous heights above Clinch Bend where the dead lay in long, dark windrows. Look for the wounded being burned alive at Cumberland Mountain as the gray smoke billows from the underbrush. Cover your ears to keep out the high-pitched screams as flames lick through the underbrush, and the wounded try to crawl away. It is a devil's race, a horrible game, and the losers feel the searing fingers flicker over their bodies.

He remembered another letter, Will's letter in Lincoln's hand, as the president strode on sticklike legs back and forth in his office, as intent on the cracker and bologna sandwich he had clutched in one hand as he was on the letter, extended for reading in the other.

The White House was bundled in a heavy snowfall, creating a storybook Christmas of blazing candles and ringing church bells. But that was outside. Inside, Fitz's destiny was in the hands of a few men and a distant friend. Will Moore's earlier letter to him had come on the heels of a hastily composed telegram, wired from Lexington, Kentucky.

I beg your forgiveness. I was more concerned
with securing glory than with helping a friend.

Fitz had wired in return:

Think nothing of it. We survived long division
and ciphering to the rule of three. The rest is nothing.

Fitz watched the snowfall through the tall windows of the
president's office. The only noise besides the crackling of
burning logs in the fireplace was the sound of the president's
two young boys racing up and down the hallway outside
Lincoln's office.

Fitz grew a bit impatient with Lincoln as the president labored over the letter. It was but two pages, could the man not
hurry? But then Fitz remembered how methodical Lincoln
was, taking all the time he felt he needed to understand what
was put before him.

Secretary of War Cameron had been there, in the office on
the second floor of the Executive Mansion that Whaley had
targeted. And Ward Hill Lamon, still suspicious despite both
Prescott and Batterman giving a confession of sorts. He
looked at Fitz as if this were some grand scheme to kill the
president and the powder situated in the tunnel not thirty
feet below them inconsequential.

"Dunaway, your friend writes a first-rate letter," Lincoln
said. "He vouches for everything you said." He held the letter for Lamon to see. "Our young friend here did a service
for us, Hill."

"I still think there ought to be a trial, Lincoln," Lamon
said. He shot a glance at Cameron, who declined to comment.

Fitz had heard that the secretary of war was in trouble.
Questionable contracts and bribes, it was rumored.
Somehow, Fitz thought, Hogan was involved.

"I think we'll dispense with the trial," Lincoln said, wiping some cracker crumbs from his vest. "Too much going on, anyway." He turned to Fitz. "So you were promised a regiment?"

"Yes, sir," Fitz said.

"Well, we seem to have plenty of those lyin' about," Lincoln said. "It's fighters we lack. How about that, Dunaway? Do you shy away from a good fight?"

"No, sir," Fitz answered.

Lincoln smiled his approval. "Well, that's fine. What do you say, Cameron? Can we fix this fella up? Send him off to war? It's a promise, you know. Even if the fella doin' the promisin' was a scoundrel."

"We can, Mr. President," Cameron said. "You simply need sign the commission and I will see to it that the orders are issued."

Fitz realized how gaunt the president looked, and there was no satisfaction behind Lincoln's smile.

"Would you gintlemen give me a moment with our newly minted young colonel?" the president asked.

Lamon cast a suspicious look at Fitz as he rose and strolled to the door. Cameron, looking befuddled, followed. The secretary of war appeared beaten and confused. Rumor said another man would soon take the Pennsylvanian's place in Lincoln's cabinet.

"Off to war," Lincoln remarked, putting Fitz at ease. "You know, Dunaway. I marked you as a fighter the moment I laid eyes on you." Fitz watched the president slide out a chair and sprawl. His long legs stuck straight out, and his feet flopped to either side. Lincoln caught Fitz's eye. "Big, ain't they?" He rolled his feet back and forth with appreciation. "I can wrap these boys three times around a ladder rung and stand upright in a blizzard." He grew somber, slipping his hands into his pockets. "You know, Dunaway, I do the very best I know how. The very best I can. If things come out all right in the end, what's said about me won't matter. If the end proves me wrong, ten thousand angels singing my praises won't make it right. I want the fellas who do the fightin' to know there's an honest man at the wheel. When you get out there to do your duty, I'd appreciate, if you've the time, a prayer or two on my behalf. If you git the chance."

"Yes, sir."

Lincoln stared at the carpet between his legs, lost in thought. When he spoke, his high voice was tempered with grief. "I do hate sending boys out to die. There's been too much dyin'."

The president remained silent and Fitz wondered if he should take his leave. He wanted to say something to Mr. Lincoln, find some comforting words to dispel the melancholia that surrounded the man. But he knew nothing would help.

Lincoln pulled a pocket watch from his vest, held it at a distance, and squinted. "Dunaway, duty calls. I've got to go and shake a few hands." He unfolded himself and stood, a weary smile creasing his weathered face. "Come see me agin. Never mind the formalities, just come right in." He laid his long hand over Fitz's shoulder and squeezed. "Who knows, Dunaway, we both may yet survive this terrible struggle."

Fitz was given his regiment, the 104th Ohio, with orders to proceed to the West.

Fitz glanced at Asia's letter and thought he caught her scent. It could not be. The letter had stayed in his breast pocket where his own sour sweat had washed away the gentle fragrance of lilacs that had belonged to her.

She had seen him off at the station. He had marched his regiment in from the countryside and through the streets of Washington, across Benning's Bridge and down Maryland Avenue to Massachusetts to the train station. The fife and drums kept a lively tune, and the men marched well, but Washingtonians had seen too many soldiers pass down their dusty streets to be very much affected by the sight of another long blue column. There were a few, scattered cheers, and most didn't bother to glance in the direction of yet another regiment off to war.

When they arrived at the station, Fitz halted the regiment and gave the men a few minutes to bid farewell to their loved ones. He saw Asia make her way through the crowd, straight to him. He removed his hat, feeling his heartbeat quicken.

"Captain Dunaway," she said in that detached way of hers.

"Mrs. Lossing," he replied.

She looked around. "You have your regiment and you have your war."

"I do indeed," he said. "And now the two are about to meet."

"How are you for writing letters, Captain Dunaway?"

"Poor," Fitz said. "But I am certain I will improve."

"Splendid," she said. She threw her arms around his neck and kissed him. He felt the old surge of passion return as he pulled her against him. She laid her cheek against his chest. "You know the address, of course. I expect letters to follow. I plan to read every one, armed with a cigar and a good bottle of whiskey."

"I shall write each with that image in my mind."

She stood back, and their eyes met. "I know this is what you want, Fitz. I only pray God keeps you well."

Fitz kissed her and then lifted her chin in his hand. "While you're at it, ask God to protect all pedestrians should you venture out in your carriage."

A wicked smile crossed Asia's lips. "Why, Captain Dunaway, how good of you to remember."

"A warm day," he noted, squinting in the sunlight. A company of cavalry in fours, a dark cloud on the bright hillside in the distance, galloped across the ground.

Mighty as an army with banners, Fitz thought. Was that what Will said?

An orderly raced by, but the men of the 104th did not bother to turn their heads. They were worn out, and galloping youngsters held no interest for them. *How close I have come to these men,* Fitz thought, wondering what Asia would make of the sentiment.

Her voice, strong and vibrant, came back to him. *"Have you no friends, Captain Dunaway?"*

Why yes, Mrs. Lossing, 238, in fact. And with each day I will have fewer. He turned to the letter again.

> *I fear for you, Fitz. You are too innocent for your own good. You see things clearly but only as far as you can see them. You will have your regiment and fight your battles. In the end I suppose you will receive everything you desire. But, dear Fitz, you must promise to be safe, for without that, nothing matters.*

"Colonel?"

Fitz saw Captain Ridenour standing in the shade of his mount, his bushy mustache glistening with sweat.

"Yes, Francis?" Fitz asked, folding the letter with one hand and stuffing it into his tunic.

"They have just sent orders down the column that we are to stop and fall out for thirty minutes," Ridenour said. He was from a prominent family of Philadelphians, but Fitz never asked him how he came to be in Ohio.

Fitz chuckled. He knew the reason for the order. "This army has stragglers, eh?"

Ridenour nodded down the column. "They must have men stretched from here across the Tennessee." He beamed at Fitz. "But not Ohio men."

"No," Fitz said. "Not Ohio men. Very well, acknowledge the orders."

Ridenour saluted but Fitz stopped him.

"Francis? How are the men?" Fitz asked.

"Why, the men are fine, sir," Ridenour said. "Mouthy as can be, but it's to be expected."

Fitz said nothing. *What you mean to ask,* he told himself,

is how am I doing for the men? But he could not ask. He could not wash away his doubts with a few kind words from a good man.

"I'll tell you, Colonel," Ridenour said. "It's been tough. These boys have been through hell, and come back through Hades. But you know what, sir? They went because you led them. Not because you ordered them to go but because you went first. I think it says something, Colonel. I surely do."

Fitz said nothing but nodded, and watched Ridenour make his way back along the column. He was passed by another staff officer galloping down the road.

The man reined up hard in front of Fitz and tossed a salute. Fitz didn't bother to reply. He was too tired, and he didn't care for staff officers.

"Colonel Dunaway," the man said. "Colonel Beveridge's compliments and the brigade has been ordered to take the lead when the march continues. He instructed me to relay to you the 104th has the honor of leading the brigade, sir." It was a mouthful to be delivered in one breath, and the officer seemed relieved to have completed it.

"My compliments to Colonel Beveridge," Fitz said. "Please inform him the 104th is honored."

The officer saluted and disappeared down the road in a cloud of dust.

What is it you wish, Fitz? he heard a voice ask. *To lead a regiment,* he replied.

	DATE DUE	
AUG – 5 2008		
NOV – 5 2008		
MAR 3 0 2009